the Wife's Tale

CHRISTINE WELLS

MICHAEL JOSEPH
an imprint of
PENGUIN BOOKS

MICHAEL JOSEPH

UK | USA | Canada | Ireland | Australia
India | New Zealand | South Africa | China

Penguin Books is part of the Penguin Random House group of companies
whose addresses can be found at global.penguinrandomhouse.com.

Penguin
Random House
Australia

First published by Penguin Random House Australia Pty Ltd, 2016

1 3 5 7 9 10 8 6 4 2

Text copyright © Christine Wells 2016

The moral right of the author has been asserted.

Cover design by Alex Ross © Penguin Random House Australia Pty Ltd
Text design by Samantha Jayaweera © Penguin Random House Australia Pty Ltd
Cover images: woman by Getty Images/Peter Zelei, castle on coast by
Getty Images/Alphotographic, all other images from Shutterstock.com
Typeset in Sabon by Samantha Jayaweera, Penguin Random House Australia Pty Ltd
Colour separation by Splitting Image Colour Studio, Clayton, Victoria
Printed and bound in Australia by Griffin Press, an accredited ISO AS/NZS 14001
Environmental Management Systems printer.

National Library of Australia
Cataloguing-in-Publication data:

Wells, Christine J., author.
The wife's tale / Christine Wells.
9780143799894 (paperback)
Detective and mystery stories.
Family secrets–Fiction.

A823.4

penguin.com.au

MIX
Paper from
responsible sources
FSC® C009448

To my darling, most beloved mother, Cheryl

Saltwater Cottage, Isle of Wight, England, 1811

My dear son,

I commend these memoirs to you, so that you have the full account of your history as far as I am concerned in it.

As a Lady Novelist, I have been criticised for revealing too much of my past, while distorting the facts and displaying a blatant disregard for the truth. I have not deigned to answer my critics in public.

What did they expect? By its nature, fiction is a pack of authentic lies designed to mislead and beguile. If people who claim to know the fabric of my life wish to pick over my tales for loose threads and wrong stitches, that is their business.

And what is truth, after all? Histories are written by the victors and the oppressors; memoirs shine a happy light on men's achievements while brushing less savoury doings 'neath the carpet. Scandal sheets add a pinch of veracity and a spoonful of surmise to a crock of lies and peddle it to the public at sixpence a dram. Husband and wife maintain the polite fiction of fidelity, while enacting very different dramas elsewhere.

For truth is a matter of perspective. And what is real may be evoked by the wildest flights of fancy.

The legal action that disgraced me is a case in point. What lies were spun about me by both sides! Despite oaths and rules of evidence and penalties for perjury, in that court room the grossest fabrications and sentimental play-acting were stamped FACT. And there was I, forced to fold my hands and lower my eyes and never speak a word in my defence. Silenced, impotent, and condemned to remain so until every last shred of hope was gone.

I offer you this tale so that you may know the events that led to my downfall. And yes, my dear son, I cast myself as heroine, little though I might be thought to deserve the role.

I shall endeavour to be as prejudiced, thick-skinned and self-serving as others who have presumed to tell my story. It is only a fair balance of the scales, after all.

So. You have been told how your father died. You have been told that his murderer, an African manservant, fled the country and was never brought to justice. That is their story. Now hear mine.

The question on that bright summer's day was not who wanted your father dead, but who in the world did not . . .

CHAPTER ONE

Liz

Brisbane, Australia, present day

Liz Jones dived for the phone on the nightstand as her 'Eye of the Tiger' ring tone shattered the pre-dawn stillness. Cursing under her breath, she juggled the mobile and stabbed at the 'off' button. The phone stopped ringing. A heavy silence descended.

She peered through the gloom at the other side of the bed. Tony lay still, one arm flung across the covers, the other wedged under the pillow beneath his head. Her shenanigans with the phone hadn't woken him.

She blew out a breath. Thank God for that. Only one person would call her at this hour of the morning. Tony would be furious if he found out.

It was 4.35 a.m. Liz had dressed in the dark with ninja-like stealth, a skill honed from routinely leaving for work before any sane person would be out of bed – even her exercise junky husband. But this morning it was crucial that Tony didn't catch her in the act. If he woke up, she'd have to account for why, on the day they were about to fly to Phuket for a luxury vacation, she was creeping around the bedroom in her business suit, a pair of black Ferragamo pumps in hand.

She listened to the steady, slow inhale and exhale of Tony's breath as he slept. A sudden, goofy feeling of tenderness washed over her at the sound.

Liz took a moment to study his dark features in the dim light: the odd vulnerability of closed eyelids fringed with short, spiky lashes, the single caramel freckle high on his cheekbone that she teasingly called his beauty spot. His lips, softened in sleep, not pressed together in a disapproving line as they so often were these days.

An impulse to trace his stubbled jaw with her fingertip made her reach out her hand.

She stopped and let it fall. Either he'd be annoyed she'd woken him, or her gesture would lead to more. Either way, he'd make her late. When they were lazing on pool lounges, sipping cocktails with paper umbrellas in them, there'd be time for appreciating her husband. Then, after a month of travel, she and Tony would take the remaining two months of her sabbatical to begin renovating their house.

Dating from the early 1900s, the Queenslander was a charming old lady, but over the years she'd grown saggy and tired. The 1970s bathroom tiles, the ratty beige living-room carpet, rusting gutters, rotting stumps and wonky steps cried out for attention.

Liz sighed. The house wasn't the only thing that needed structural work. Her marriage had turned into a fixer-upper too. She wasn't kidding herself that this holiday would solve all their problems, but time alone together without constant interruptions from her demanding boss would be a jolly good start.

She flicked her phone to silent, intending to call Nick back. Then she saw he'd sent her a text, moving their meeting to ten and asking her to come to his house, instead of the office as planned.

She glanced at the clock. As long as they kept it brief, she could squeeze Nick in before she had to leave for the airport at eleven. In the meantime, she'd dash into work to cross a few last-minute items off her list.

Right. She was dressed. Ticket, money, passport. Her carry-on was packed and ready in the kitchen. Tony would deal with their checked luggage.

She slipped into the ensuite bathroom to dab on some makeup. With her dark colouring and olive skin, if she went without she'd look jaundiced. Bit of foundation, a quick tidy of her eyebrows, slick of lipstick and she was done. She ran a brush through her long hair, making it crackle with static. Damn, she hated winter.

Snatching up her handbag, she padded to the door and eased it open.

'Liz?'

She froze, her hand tightening around the door knob.

Tony sucked in a long draught of air and released it in an irritated sigh. The bedsheets rustled. 'What time is it?'

'Go back to sleep,' she said in a soothing whisper. 'Nothing to worry about. I just have to . . . um . . .'

He switched on the bedside lamp and shoved a hand through his military-cut black hair. Tony was lean and tanned, a poster boy for physical-education teachers. Extreme sports like running up mountains were his favourite pastimes, but when he wasn't punishing his body with exercise or lecturing her on the virtues of kale, Tony was a pretty easygoing guy.

But he didn't look easygoing now, with his eyes narrowed to slits against the light. He took in the full, business-suited glory of Liz and his expression hardened.

She opened her mouth to explain – not that it would help. Without a word, Tony switched off the light and rolled to his stomach, yanking the covers over his head.

'Hey, gorgeous. Thanks for coming.' As always, Nick went in for the cheek-kiss. Liz had never thought much about it until her secretary had remarked enviously on the unprofessional custom. Ever since, the brush of Nick's lips on her skin had made her feel self-conscious.

To combat this, she quipped, 'I risked imminent divorce to get here this morning. Better be good.'

'It is,' he said, and showed her into the house.

Anticipation hummed inside her as she followed Nick through a spacious entry hall. The ceilings soared high above, and a light fixture that looked like an enormous ball of spun toffee was suspended over the staircase.

A property developer with various other commercial interests, Nick always had something new and exciting on the go when it came to business. This time there seemed to be an even more heightened energy about him, edging almost into anxiety.

From the little he'd divulged about the proposition he wanted to lay before her today, she'd gathered it was something significant. At first, hope had flowered within her, but her native hard-headedness reminded her that Nick would scarcely behave this way if his proposition was a promotion for her.

No, this was something vital, perhaps even personal, for Nick.

In the years Liz had worked as head of Nick's in-house legal team, she'd met with him in all kinds of places, from his office to his yacht, from tiny outback towns to mud-churned construction sites. But she'd never been to his house before.

A modern mixture of polished concrete, glass and chrome, the sprawling multi-level structure was scattered with Danish 1960s furniture and bold flares of colour. The back of the house opened onto a long, sparkling pool, landscaped tropical gardens and an uninterrupted view of the central business district.

Nick's home was a show-piece, perfect for entertaining. Yet the only feature in which she saw his personal taste reflected was the modern art on the walls. At least, a high percentage of them were naked women, so she assumed that was down to Nick.

No sign of Yolande this morning. Were they fighting again? Nick was a terrible husband. After his first marriage ended in disaster, Liz wondered why he'd been so quick to saunter down the aisle again.

'Come in, come in,' said Nick, shepherding her through. 'Let me get you a drink.'

'Water will be fine, thanks.' It wasn't as if this was a social call. She'd worn a suit to stress the business nature of the meeting, but when Nick had strolled out to greet her in a polo shirt, a cream wool pullover and a pair of drill shorts, she'd felt silly.

His bare feet were a little hairy, she noticed. Not hobbit-hairy. Perhaps no hairier than any other bloke's. But she liked to think of him as having at least one physical flaw, minuscule though it might be.

The rest of him belonged in a Ralph Lauren ad, but she'd had a lot of practice at ignoring Nick's tall, dark handsomeness. They'd been friends at university. Or, to be more accurate, they'd shared a few business classes and he'd criticised her boyfriends and cribbed off her notes.

Even in those days, when her girlish heart had pined for him, she'd known Nick McCann was out of her league. And that was before he'd made his zillions. Now, with so much water – and so very many blondes – under the bridge, Liz felt no more than a distant, exasperated fondness for the man, much the same as she'd feel for a younger brother.

Ignoring her request, Nick carried two Bloody Marys, complete with celery swizzle sticks, out to a table by the pool.

It was a perfect winter's day, warm in the sunshine but with a fresh, cool breeze brushing the pandanus leaves. The lap pool reflected a vast blue sky.

The pool cabana and outdoor furniture displayed the same streamlined cool as the rest of the house. Her chair, with its sleek lines and sunken bottom, was designed for someone in a bikini, not someone wearing a pencil skirt. She shifted to the edge of it, trying to get comfortable.

Nick settled down to chat about nothing, a frustrating habit that had taught her patience. He didn't ask about her vacation. On the one hand, she was grateful; on the other, she was irritated at his self-centredness. All that mattered to him was that she was there to serve.

Liz took out a notebook and pen, slapped them on the table, then slid out her phone in case Tony called. She switched the phone to silent, then took a healthy swig of the Bloody Mary. Wow, it was strong.

She eyed Nick. 'Are you trying to get me drunk so I'll say yes to this proposal of yours?'

'Oh, you'll say yes,' said Nick.

I'll be the judge of that, thought Liz. Aloud, she said, 'See, this is why I'm your lawyer. I'm not a pushover and I don't believe everything people with straight white teeth and a lap pool tell me. Come on, spill.'

'Okay.' Nick lounged back in his chair and clasped his hands behind his head.

'I want to buy an estate called Seagrove on the Isle of Wight, but the owners don't want to sell to me. I need to make them an offer they can't refuse, but these are tricky people. I've already tried throwing money at them, but the English upper class would rather drown in their tea cups than admit they can be swayed by money alone.'

Liz raised her eyebrows. 'They must have been tempted, surely.' How many people held on to their principles these days when offered filthy lucre?

He shook his head. 'The place is an absolute disaster, financially. I've told them I'm trying to preserve the house, that I care about their traditions. But I get the feeling they'd rather have the place fall down around their ears than see it leave the family.' He paused. 'And they especially do not want to sell to me.'

Liz poked around in her Bloody Mary with the celery stick, watching the tomato sediment lift in a dark red cloud. 'What, because you're not British? Or because they think you'll turn their heritage into a housing development?'

She hadn't meant to be rude, but Nick looked wounded.

'Sorry. I know you wouldn't do that,' she said, making a wry face. 'But why this place? Surely there'd be better investments. Plenty of owners of other stately homes would jump at the opportunity to sell.'

He transferred his gaze to the spectacular view, but his mind's eye went beyond it, across oceans. 'No. I want Seagrove.'

She knew that tone. When Nick made up his mind about something, he pursued it with singular drive and focus.

He went on. 'I need someone to go there and do some digging, a little secret due diligence, if you will. Delve into the history. Get to know the people, the area, come up with a novel proposal for buying the place that will be acceptable to the family. But don't let them know what you're doing. If they find out you're associated with me, they won't help you.'

'They weren't won over by your powers of persuasion? They must be tough nuts to crack.' She sipped her drink. 'Why ask me to do this?'

He fixed her with his keen gaze. 'Liz, it's important to me. It's not for the company, it's just me this time. You're the only one I can trust.'

Liz mentally threw cold water over the warm glow that spread through her chest. Nick was as charismatic as a cult leader, and equally facile. He couldn't help it. He instinctively said what people wanted to hear.

Reading between the lines, he meant she'd have to do this work on her own time without pay. Now she began to understand the urgency. Her sabbatical. He wanted her to work through her time off.

Not a chance.

And yet, she couldn't resist. 'So, what's in it for me?'

He smiled. 'How about an all-expenses-paid trip to Paris when you're done?'

She fished the celery out of her drink and crunched on it. 'If you're going to insult me . . .'

He laughed. 'Okay, how about this: if you get me what I want and we do the deal . . .' He paused. 'I'll move you into an executive role. It would mean more responsibility, higher pay. Further down the line, there might be a seat on the board. And not just because you're doing me a favour, either. You deserve it. You're almost ready.' He shrugged.

'I'll just push my plans for you forward a little. If you think you can handle it, that is.'

Liz met his eyes – blue eyes as bright and limpid as the Australian sky – and swallowed hard. 'Right. That's . . . tempting.'

Her mobile vibrated, but she let it go to voicemail, trying to take in the implications of what Nick wanted from her, what he was offering in return.

This had always been her goal, to use her position as in-house counsel to gain enough commercial experience to move into the business side of the corporate world. She didn't want to be company secretary. She wanted operational experience, a seat on the board. This was the opportunity she'd been waiting for.

And all she had to do was negotiate a deal to buy a house from some English aristocrats.

'What do you think?' said Nick.

His voice jerked her out of her dream, back to cold reality. She couldn't go to the Isle of Wight. Not now. Not when she had three months of marriage restoration to do.

With her index finger, she traced the wet ring her glass had made on the table top. 'Could this possibly wait until I get back from sabbatical?'

'Three months?' Nick shook his head. 'I want to move on it now, before they find another solution to their problems.'

She'd been right. He was taking advantage of her time off. She narrowed her eyes at him. If she hadn't known better, she'd think he deliberately set up these choices. Work or Tony. Work or Tony.

But no, Nick was neither so devious nor so attuned to the tug-of-war that went on inside her almost every working day.

Her choice was clear. If she'd learned anything from her parents' split, it was that a career should never take precedence over the people you loved. If she reneged on her promise to spend her sabbatical with Tony, she'd damage their relationship beyond repair.

Her chest felt tight, that same feeling of panicked suffocation that came over her whenever Tony talked about wanting children.

Not now. Not yet. I haven't done everything I need to do.

'Come on,' said Nick, getting up and reaching for her empty glass. 'I want to show you something.'

Liz checked her watch. There was still a bit of time before she had to leave for the airport. She followed him into the house and up the floating staircase.

'Let me guess,' said Liz as they turned down a hallway. 'You have etchings up here?'

He grinned. 'Something a little better than an etching. Or at least, I think so.'

He opened a pair of double doors into a darkened room that turned out to be a study, furnished with an enormous antique desk. Three out of four walls were lined with bookshelves. The fourth . . .

Nick switched on the light and Liz gasped. What had, at first glance, appeared to be a woman's ghostly form looming out of the darkness was in fact a life-sized portrait of a lady in late eighteenth-century dress.

She was a dark-haired beauty, dressed for riding in a habit of rich, deep red. Her face was vivid in a way women's features in most portraits of that era were not – blue eyes, high cheekbones, cherry lips and black, slashing brows. Her beauty must surely have been improved upon by the artist, for it seemed too vibrant to be real. She might have been the model for a porcelain doll, but for her purposeful stance and the intelligence in her eyes.

'Stunning, isn't she?' said Nick.

Liz glanced at him. 'Who is she?'

'This is Delany, Lady Nash.' He half sat on his desk as if settling in to recount a story, his gaze switching back and forth between Liz and the portrait.

'And she lived at Seagrove,' Liz guessed.

'Yes. She has something of a chequered past, but you can read all about it in the materials I'll be sending you. She was the sister-in-law of an ancestor of mine, if that's not too convoluted to follow.'

'I see.' Liz tilted her head, ignoring Nick's sideways glance. 'You're family, then. You're related to the people who own the house now.'

He nodded. 'Delany's husband was Lord Nash, the owner of Seagrove. My many-greats grandfather was the younger son of the house, the brother of Lord Nash.'

'So your direct ancestor, the younger son . . . what was his name?' said Liz.

'Julian. Some said he was Delany's lover.'

'Now I'm totally confused,' said Liz.

Nick scratched the back of his neck. 'It's complicated. Look, Liz, I meant what I said. I need you to help me. You're the only one I trust.'

Liz felt her resistance melting. Nick was a very difficult man to refuse. That was probably one reason he was so successful in business.

'*Nick!*' The front door slammed. Liz heard the crash of keys being tossed onto a hard surface, footsteps on the ground floor, the squeak of running shoes as the footsteps quickened.

Liz started guiltily, even though she had nothing to feel guilty about.

'Up here, sweetheart,' Nick called. In an undertone to Liz, he said, 'Whatever you do, don't leave me alone with her.'

'What? Why?' Oh, no. She did not want to be in the middle of this, whatever 'this' was.

When Yolande came in, Liz experienced a familiar twinge of pea-green envy. Nick's wife wore her blonde hair in a simple pony tail. Her body was sheathed in lycra and her face devoid of makeup, but she still managed to look a million dollars.

Liz tugged at her pencil skirt.

'Hello, Liz.' With a nod in her direction, Yolande stalked over and smacked the magazine she carried into Nick's chest.

'Ah,' he said, one hand curling reflexively around the glossy rag. 'Morning, darling. Been to the gym already?'

His wife ignored the question. Her eyes flashed but her voice remained calm as she snatched back the magazine and waved it in Nick's face. 'Do you mind explaining this?'

Frowning, Nick took the copy of Stars Weekly and turned it the right way up.

A glimpse of the magazine cover made Liz's stomach turn over. It showed Nick at a Sydney beach canoodling with a buxom, bikini-clad blonde who looked oddly familiar. Needless to say, the blonde wasn't Yolande.

The headline screamed: 'LEILA'S LATEST SQUEEZE'.

Leila Martin. Australia's newest contribution to the Victoria's Secret franchise.

With a slight break in her husky voice, Yolande said, 'Frankly, Nick, I don't care what you do or with whom, but I *do* draw the line at public humiliation.'

'Sweetheart, I'm so sorry,' said Nick, who didn't look at all sorry to Liz. Honestly, when he'd married Yolande over all the bimbo gold-diggers who were after him, Liz had held high hopes. Clearly, she'd been wrong to think Nick could change, even for someone like Yolande.

'What can I do to make it up to you, darling?' said Nick, spreading his hands. 'Diamonds? A new car?'

'Not this time.' Yolande's expression was determined, but Liz saw that there were tears in her eyes. Liz's heart went out to her, but this was one aspect of Nick's life she could not be involved in.

'Speaking of time,' Liz said, attempting to sidle toward the door, 'I'd better go or I'll miss my plane.' She glanced at her watch and realised that in fact, she was already fifteen minutes late. 'Honestly, I have to go.'

'No, Liz. Stay,' said Nick and there was a calm note of command in his voice that she knew well.

Still, she would have argued, but Nick's mobile rang. He took it out of his pocket and read the display. To Yolande he murmured, 'I'm so sorry but I have to take this.'

He answered and asked the other person on the line to hold.

'Darling. Yolande.' He slid his hands down her arms and bent to look into her face. 'We'll sort this out, okay?'

Shaking her head, she broke away from him and ran out of the room, joggers pounding on the polished wood floor.

Nick caught Liz's eye. 'Go after her, will you? Make sure she's all right.' Then he turned and picked up his phone again, clearly without a doubt that Liz would obey.

The skunk! It wasn't enough that he had her running around after him like a dogsbody at work. Now she had to console his poor, wronged wife.

She heard a crash and a tinkle of glass from below. 'Oh, hell.' She flew down the stairs as fast as her pencil skirt would let her, to find Yolande in the kitchen, cradling one hand in the other.

There was blood all over Yolande's hands, and Liz couldn't immediately pinpoint the source. The thought of suicide flashed through her mind, but then she saw the deep gash in the meaty part of Yolande's hand, below her thumb.

'It was an accident,' said Yolande miserably. 'I only wanted a glass of something to settle my nerves and I . . .' She swallowed a sob, tears leaking from her eyes. 'Oh, God, Liz. What am I going to do?'

Liz shot through the automatic doors to the airport, her carry-on case juddering along in her wake. She stopped short when she saw the queue at the baggage counter. The electronic board behind the desk showed a different flight number from the one on her ticket.

Every polite cell in her body told her to line up with the rest of those poor schmucks, but she'd never have a hope of catching her flight if she did that. She didn't have much of a hope no matter what she did.

She looked around for Tony, but of course it was useless. Wherever he was, he was unlikely to be in this part of the airport. Suddenly she felt panicked and very alone.

She'd managed to make Nick understand that his wife needed his immediate attention and seen them both off to the hospital before she raced to the airport. Traffic had been horrendous and she'd experienced another delay in the long-term car park while she waited for the courtesy bus to take her to the airport terminal.

She must have rung Tony twenty times but he wasn't answering. If only she'd taken his call instead of ignoring it during her meeting with Nick!

Tony was mad at her. He had every reason to be mad. But didn't he owe her a chance to explain? If she hadn't been caught up with Nick and Yolande, she would have made it here on time.

Digging in her handbag for her passport and ticket, Liz went up to the first official-looking person she saw.

Please let the flight be delayed, or even cancelled.

'Excuse me . . .' But as Liz began to speak, the walkie-talkie at the attendant's hip crackled to life. Ignoring Liz, the attendant answered it and began an involved conversation with someone at the other end about re-routing baggage.

Liz couldn't find anyone else who might be able to wave her to the front of the queue, so she ducked and threaded her way through the crowd until she came within sight of the departures board.

For a few seconds, the flight numbers and destinations jumbled into alphabet soup. Forcing herself to calm down, she scanned the board, line by line. The flight to Phuket wasn't listed.

She made her way to the shorter line for the baggage drop and queued there, trying Tony's mobile again. Once again, she heard his voicemail message.

'Damn it, Tony! I'm at the airport. Ring me back, will you? Please?' She ended the call, half wishing she could erase the message and start again with less of a whimper in her voice. She hated sounding needy.

Trying not to inhale the cloying mix of perfume and perspiration that wafted from the woman in front of her, Liz swapped her handbag over to the other shoulder. What if Tony had been delayed somehow?

What if he hadn't arrived at the airport? She'd assumed his lack of response was some sort of passive-aggressive punishment, but maybe it wasn't. Tony could have lost his phone, or forgotten to turn it on.

Maybe he'd crashed his car. But wouldn't he have called her? Unless he was injured . . .

Something tightened around Liz's throat.

Don't be ridiculous, she told herself when she arrived at the head of the queue. Far more likely that Tony was too livid to talk to her. After all, what if they couldn't change the tickets? That was thousands of dollars down the drain and who knew how many days of their holiday lost.

But the issue went deeper than that, didn't it?

Behind her, a boy of about ten with a white skull on his black t-shirt kicked Liz's carry-on case in a desultory rhythm. Resisting the urge to turn around and snarl, she picked up the case and put it in front of her, out of the kid's reach.

He started kicking the heel of her shoe.

'Next, please!'

A smiling, well-groomed clerk listened to her explanation, took her ticket and tapped a few keys.

'I'm sorry, Ms Jones.' The clerk's serene smile was undimmed. 'Your flight closed half an hour ago.'

Though she'd expected that response, a heavy weight dropped into Liz's stomach. She licked her lips. 'Can you tell me if Anthony Wilkins was on the flight?'

The clerk's smile faded. 'I'm sorry, we can't give out that information.'

'But he's my husband. If you check, you'll see we were sitting together. I paid for both our tickets.'

The woman's thin eyebrows lifted a fraction, and Liz felt herself redden. After a few more seconds' hesitation, the clerk tapped some keys.

'Yes, I see that you were travelling together, so I can tell you whether Mr Wilkins boarded. Just one moment, please.'

The key-tapping seemed to go on forever this time. What was the woman doing, writing a novel?

Liz cleared her throat and lied. 'Uh, my husband has an appointment he needs to keep. He's, uh, he's giving a seminar at a conference in Phuket and he has to be there on time, so . . .'

Shut up, Liz. What did this woman care why her husband was flying to Phuket without her? Why should Liz care if she cared? And what did it say about Liz that her primary emotion was humiliation because she had to ask a total stranger whether her own husband had left her behind?

The clerk's smile reappeared. 'Then you'll be happy to know your husband did make the flight, Ms Jones.'

CHAPTER TWO

Three hours after the disaster at the airport, Liz was heading to the Sunshine Coast hinterland, vintage Bon Jovi blaring out of the car stereo. Her ears blocked as her little red Mazda flashed around hairpin bends, climbing higher into the Blackall Range.

Gone. The word echoed through her with the cold, hollow resonance of the public-address system at the airport. Tony, so laid back and undramatic, had actually boarded that plane without her. It was a gesture so flamboyant, so final, so un-Tony-like, she'd had to ask the desk clerk to repeat the information.

Even then, wild scenarios flitted through Liz's brain. Identity theft. Accident. Some body-snatching alien from a Stephen King novel had replaced the real Tony with a Tony clone.

But as the silence of her mobile phone rang in her ears – he was in the air, wasn't he? He couldn't call now, even if he wanted to – denials faded away.

Winding higher into the mist that rolled off the mountain top, she turned on her headlights and slowed. Twenty minutes and she'd be home. Not that she'd ever lived in her mother's Montville cottage, but Janine's warm, welcoming presence made it feel like home to Liz.

Just before the bustle of the main street, the one with the German clock shop and the cute cafés and craft stores, Liz turned off.

'Darling!' said her mother, enveloping Liz in a warm, fleshy hug. 'What are you doing here? I thought you'd have left by now.'

The first thing you noticed about Janine Jones was her hair: thick and blonde and woolly. She kept it long, often wound in a bun at the nape of her neck. Today, she'd tied it back loosely with a purple velvet ribbon.

Liz had always loved Janine's hair. She herself had inherited her father's dark looks. Right along with the workaholic gene.

'It's a long story.' Liz hauled her overnight bag from the boot and lugged it up the shallow flight of steps to the wide front verandah. She kicked off shoes newly encrusted with rich red volcanic soil and followed her mother into the house.

Janine lived on her own in a tiny worker's cottage overlooking Baroon Pocket Dam. Painted in soft blue and custard cream with gingerbread eaves, and surrounded by a white picket fence, it was almost too charming to be real. There was a magnolia tree in the side yard and a cottage garden out the front, a mass of soft green, white, yellow, pink and purple – seaside daisies, pentas, pansies and hydrangeas in the summer. An old pink rose climbed a trellis that arched over the path. Wind chimes tinkled in the breeze.

Ordinarily, wind chimes irritated the heck out of Liz, but here they seemed right.

'Something smells good.' She brushed past the question in Janine's raised brows.

'Banana bread,' said her mother, moving through the dark, narrow hall to the sunlit kitchen. She baked tasty treats for the bed and breakfast down the road. No doubt the banana bread was off limits to family. Liz stifled a sigh. She'd missed breakfast and lunch, too, only stopping home long enough to re-pack and take off again for her mother's place.

She held up the bottle she'd brought. 'Wine for later.'

'I'm about to start on some jam tarts,' said her mother. She put on the kettle and took the tea pot down from the dresser shelf with swift, competent hands. 'Grab an apron and you can help me. Wash your hands first.'

Trust her mother to know exactly how to ease the story out. As they rolled pastry, pressed cutters and coaxed scallop-edged discs into the waiting trays, Liz told Janine about her morning.

True to form, Janine made no comment about Tony's behaviour. Which was lucky, because Liz didn't know how she felt about it yet. If Janine had criticised Tony, Liz would have leaped to his defence. If she'd sympathised with the frustration that had led Tony to make such an unequivocal gesture, Liz would have bridled.

'So, what now?' said Janine, always practical. She held her willow-pattern tea cup close to her lips and fixed her grey eyes on Liz as she sipped.

'I don't know,' said Liz, breaking off a piece of raw pastry and popping it into her mouth. Tasted terrible, of course, but that never stopped her doing it. Maybe that was her problem. She kept doing the same dumb things, hoping this time would be different.

'It depends on what he says when I talk to him next. I'm not going to rush over to Phuket only for him to say he won't see me. If he wants to flounce off like a sulky teenager, let him.'

Her mother's steady gaze told her she was the one who sounded petulant. Liz gathered the scraps of pastry dough and mushed them together, kneaded them lightly, then picked up the rolling pin and tossed some flour over it.

Something inside her had shifted while she told Janine about Tony. The thin layer of numbed disbelief cracked; a vein of anger snaked through her guilt.

She knew she'd pushed Tony too far this morning. But he'd over-reacted in a major way.

'Banana bread's ready,' said Janine, tossing her the oven gloves and turning back to the glistening, sticky mess of strawberry that sat on the stove.

Liz nearly swooned as the sweet, cinnamon-scented steam came at her in a rush. She rescued the banana bread, shut the oven door and set the temperature dial for the tarts.

Her stomach growled, reminding her that she hadn't eaten anything but a celery stick all day and it was almost four in the afternoon. She sipped her tea to stave off the hunger, then busied herself with the rolling pin and pastry cutter again, this time pressing out heart shapes to go on top of the filling.

'How's your father?' Janine spoke with a determined evenness that told Liz the wound her mother suffered all those years ago still ached.

He'd left them when Liz was a senior at high school. Not for a younger, blonder version of her mother, but for a severe-looking law professor a year or two older than Janine. For some reason, knowing they couldn't blame his desertion on that old chestnut, the mid-life crisis, made it worse.

'Oh, you know how he is,' said Liz. 'Same as ever. I don't see him much.'

'You're as bad as each other, working all the time,' said Janine.

'You know what annoys me?' said Liz, setting down the pastry cutter. 'I earn three times what Tony does and yet he expects me to keep the same hours.' Not to mention she did almost all the housework, but that was another issue. 'If Dad had missed a flight to Phuket because of work, you would have sighed and accepted it. You wouldn't have gone off without him.'

'And look how well our marriage turned out,' said Janine with a wry smile.

'You know how I got where I am?' said Liz. 'I ask myself, what would a man do? Any of my male colleagues would have gone to work this morning. So I went to work. The only difference is that unlike most of my male colleagues, I don't have a wife.'

'That's just how men are, darling,' said Janine. 'You can all go on with your feminism and your politically correct mumbo jumbo, but deep down, they still want the little woman safe at home raising babies while they win the bread and sow their wild oats elsewhere.'

Liz said nothing. What could she say? Janine's experience had taught her to be cynical.

Janine must have read something of this in Liz's expression. She shrugged. 'Why do you think I'm still on my own after all these years? Because I can do what I want, when I want. There's no man telling me how to live. I'm not sitting around waiting for him to come home, either.'

Liz thought about that. She'd never seen Janine's solo state as a matter of choice. 'You don't get lonely?'

'Goodness, no. I have my neighbours and my work, my books and my garden. As for male companionship . . .' Janine gave a surprisingly earthy laugh. 'Let's say I don't suffer from any lack in that department. And the best thing? I don't have to iron their shirts or wash their socks. I don't have to surrender the TV remote or cook a proper dinner for them every night, or even fight with them over the correct division of house-hold labour, like all you young couples do nowadays. And I don't feel possessive enough of any of them to be hurt if they see other women.'

'Sounds perfect,' said Liz.

But she wondered. She couldn't help thinking of her grandparents, Janine's mum and dad, who'd been devoted to each other for more than sixty years. Wasn't it better to share your life with someone, even if it meant compromise here and there? Besides, Liz did want children some time in the misty future, and she wanted to share that joy with Tony. Once the renovation was done, they'd have room.

She'd planned to make room for kids in other ways as well, at some stage in the misty future. She was only thirty, after all. Plenty of time for all that.

The opportunity for promotion Nick dangled in front of her was tempting enough to put those plans on hold indefinitely. But if she had any hope of rescuing her marriage, she couldn't simply take off for the Isle of Wight.

'Well, now, let's see how these turned out.' Janine upended the loaves of banana bread onto cooling racks. Liz tried not to look like the stray dog at a butcher-shop window.

The corners of Janine's eyes crinkled. 'I'm sure I can spare a slice or two for my daughter. I'll make another loaf in the morning.'

They ate piping-hot banana bread slathered with real butter from a local dairy and drank strong, black tea at the old wicker table on the back verandah.

Bees droned among the roses. Liz lifted her face to meet the gentle winter sun.

She'd been right to come here, to the quiet welcome of home. So soothing after the stress and frantic pace of city life. After Tony's abrupt desertion. She'd go mental if she had to live up here, but the cottage certainly held its charms.

Desperate to fill her time until she could expect a call from Tony, Liz went for a long hike in the bush that afternoon. Later, she sat down with her mother to a simple dinner of steak and three veg and a bottle of good Margaret River red. She drank more wine than she should have, but at least it meant she slept like a rock.

So when her phone jangled at some ungodly hour, she woke in a groggy haze. At first she couldn't remember where she was. Then realisation dropped like a stone to the pit of her stomach.

With a jolt of panic, she groped for the phone and held it to her ear. 'Tony?'

Music thumped in the background. Was he in a nightclub? Anger erupted. 'Tony, what the hell —'

'Liz!' That wasn't Tony's voice. 'Liz, my darling. I need to know. Have you thought about it? Will you say yes?'

She sat up. 'Nick, is that you?'

'Of course it's me.'

Adrenaline drained from her body. She glanced at the radio clock beside her bed. 'It's four in the morning.'

'Not in Phuket,' said Nick cheerfully. 'Come on, you need to be up and at 'em if you want to beat the jet lag.'

'I'm not *in* Phuket,' said Liz. Thanks to you.

'What? Why not? Oh, so you did reconsider. Liz, that's great! I've emailed a bunch of information through to get you started. Let's meet tomorrow and work out the details. I'll have MJ call you to set up a time.'

Liz dragged a hand over her face. 'Nick, can we not do this now? I'm tired. I need to go back to sleep.'

'What? Oh, right. Not in Phuket. I forgot. Talk to MJ when you get up.'

He ended the call and Liz, now wide awake, remembered Phuket was three or four hours behind Brisbane. She growled.

Now she'd woken up, her brain went back to buzzing. Tony's plane would have landed hours ago but he hadn't called her or texted or even emailed. She rang him, grimacing when his message bank answered yet again.

'Tony, call me back. Please. I can still get on a plane and join you. We can sort this out.'

But what if they couldn't? What if he said it was over?

For the first time, Liz faced the possibility that this was the end of the road for them.

If Tony didn't forgive her, if he asked for a divorce . . . Oh, God, she couldn't even think about it. But now the idea had occurred to her, she couldn't get it out of her head.

The worry and second-guessing that had tormented her all day rushed back. She lay there for what seemed like hours, arguing with herself and with Tony in her head.

How could he make her suffer like this? If he'd only talk to her, at least she'd know where she stood. She hated this horrible limbo state.

A new wave of fury drove her to leave another message. 'Look, this is childish. What's more, it's cruel.' She took a deep breath. 'I want to know one way or the other. If I don't hear from you tomorrow, I'll make my own arrangements.'

Common sense told her that giving Tony an ultimatum was not

the best way to resolve matters. But it was hard to act rationally when your life was falling apart.

Liz knew from experience she'd never get back to sleep now, so she switched on the bedside lamp and dug out her laptop. She hopped back into bed, powered up, and frowned as a raft of emails, each with a forest of attachments, flowed into her inbox.

'Pretty confident, weren't you, Nick?' she murmured. But then, of course, his confidence had been well placed. She was reading the emails, wasn't she? She wasn't in Phuket, too busy soaking up the sunshine to bother with Nick's mad schemes.

She scanned the various document titles until she came across one that stood out. 'Criminal Conversation Trial'.

'Criminal conversation,' she murmured. She'd never heard of any cause of action like that before. Intriguing. With a slight frown, she clicked on the attachment and read.

The Gentleman's Magazine, Vol. 12

CRIM. CON. COURT OF KING'S BENCH, 14 NOVEMBER, 1789

—

SITTINGS BEFORE LORD KENYON AND A SPECIAL JURY IN WESTMINSTER HALL

—

THE RIGHT HONOURABLE LORD NASH V. NASH, ESQ.

—

The Declaration stated, for the Defendant, on the 15th day of
April, 1789, and on divers other days and times, between that
day and the 20th day of May that same year, at Westminster, in the
County of Middlesex, and with force and arms, made an assault on
Delany, the Wife of the Plaintiff, and then and there debauched,
deflowered, lay with, and carnally knew her, the said Delany,
to the Plaintiff's damage of £20 000.

To this Declaration the Defendant pleaded not guilty,
and thereupon issue was joined . . .

Lord Kenyon

The Court of King's Bench, Westminster Hall, seethed and roiled with
a mass of bodies. Those spectators who had failed to bribe their way

to a seat close to the fray surged and flowed and spilled out into the
greater hall.

The booksellers' and drapers' stalls that once lined the walls outside
the court were long gone, but some enterprising hawkers plied their
wares to the teeming throng. Nearby pie-vendors and taverns expected
a brisk trade today. Voyeurism was hungry work. Thirsty work, too.

In fact, the Lord Chief Justice would not wager a groat on half the
audience's sobriety, though it was well before noon. The beery, sweaty
reek of humanity offended his nostrils even from his elevated position
on the bench.

He called the court to order, but at first he could not make himself
heard over the din. Gathering all the considerable power of his lungs,
Lord Kenyon issued a thunderous command to the crowd to be silent
or he would clear the room.

He gave the quieted assembly a long, baleful stare. Before him ranged
a sea of bewigged and hatted heads – here a pair of fashionable types
all powdered and patched; there a bulbous-nosed merchant with a nut-
brown wig and snuff-dusted lapels. Even a handful of women . . . One
would not like to call them ladies, whatever their pedigree, for no
true lady would deign to appear at such a notorious prosecution.

Sundry reporters littered the court room, scribbling their impres-
sions earnestly, which they would later print as scandal sheets and sell
to titillate the jaded public palate. The infamous caricaturist Gillray
was also present. Lord Kenyon scowled. Even he was not safe from the
sharp end of Gillray's wit.

With an irritated twitch at the sleeve of his robes, Kenyon turned
his attention to the jury. A group of right-thinking, affluent men, men
of sufficient means and experience to return a verdict both sensible
and prompt. Given a *soupçon* of judicial guidance, these upstanding
citizens would make the plaintiff considerably richer when he went
to bed tonight than when he'd awoken this morning. Assuming the
defendant was in a position to pay.

A ripple of murmurs ran through the throng, marking the late appearance of the principals in today's drama. Heads craned to see as both parties took their places at the back, on either side of the court room. The plaintiff, Lord Nash, was a well-looking man in a pale, ascetic way, his dress characterised by propriety rather than flair. He had an air of ineffable boredom, as if to him the proceedings were a matter of indifference.

Lord Nash's brother, Mr Julian Nash, that radical rogue and reckless libertine, was the defendant in this case. His frame was larger than his brother's, cast from a rougher mould. He was not generally held to be handsome. Yet his dark features held a potency that drew ladies to his side.

One doubted Mr Nash knew the meaning of the word *ennui*.

The crowd was permitted only the briefest glimpse of the two brothers, however. Being gentlemen, and therefore entitled to a modicum of privacy, the parties were seated behind curtains that hid them from prying eyes.

Cain and Abel, come to court to settle their differences. Kenyon approved the propriety of taste and judgement that had led Lord Nash to wield the law as his weapon, rather than a sword.

Duelling was still the prevailing manner of deciding disputes between gentlemen over offences against their honour. If one were cynical, one might say that an award of damages for £20 000 would be far preferable to finding oneself with a hole through one's heart, or spitted on one's younger brother's blade. A handy fellow in a fight was Mr Julian Nash – or so the gossip went. He'd honed his skills on many an irate husband, after all.

If Kenyon had anything to say about it – and in his court he had almost everything to say – Julian Nash would pay for his transgressions with his person if he could not pay with his purse.

Prison was the proper place for such a blackguard as would stoop to seduce his own brother's virtuous young wife. The Lord Chief Justice had presided over many a trial for criminal conversation in the past decade or so. Never had he seen an instance of such calculated depravity, of such fraternal betrayal, as this. So grave an injury demanded the highest possible damages in reparation.

Twenty thousand pounds. It was enough to ruin a man. Yet ten times that sum would be insufficient to assuage the distress and suffering Julian Nash had caused his brother.

After another call for silence, Lord Kenyon was about to invite the plaintiff's counsel to open the case when a new and flamboyant arrival caught his eye.

A dark-haired lady sailed into the court room. Like a proud little yacht carving the sea, she slipped through the gathering of gaping fools, the curling ostrich plume in her hat fluttering like an ensign in her wake. She stopped at a particular chair in the front row a short distance beyond the bar table.

The lady addressed the chair's burly occupant without a hint of hesitancy. 'My good man, I paid for that seat.' She did not seem to raise her voice, yet her words carried throughout the stilled court room.

The brawny fellow scrambled up, full of apologies, bowing low and palming the coin she held out in compensation for the loss of his vantage point.

With a brisk nod, the lady took his place. Clasping her hands in her lap, she lowered her gaze demurely. As if she had not, by her mere presence, added fuel to a scandal that would keep the Grub Street presses running hot for weeks to come.

Lord Kenyon, his shock giving way to incredulity, found his voice. 'My lady! Lady Nash, what can you mean by this?'

Her broad hat brim dipped and curled rakishly, cavalier-style, to shade her features. When she rose in her place and lifted her chin to address him, a shaft of light from the window high above struck her face, and her beauty burst upon him.

He'd seen likenesses of her in sketches, in the Romney portrait at the Royal Academy, and most recently in lewd cartoons in print-shop windows. They had not done her justice. There was an aura about her that could not be captured even by the finest artist. Whether it lay in the decided elegance of her movements, the candid clarity of her expression or the vitality of her presence, he knew not.

Beneath that hat, lush ringlets of deepest ebony rioted in ordered profusion. A heart-shaped face, flawless skin, eyes so intensely blue they seemed to glow beneath those dramatic black brows. Lips that brought to mind every sonnet about lips ever written. *Cherry-ripe* . . .

Before he could recover from his stupefaction, she answered him. 'My lord, is it not permitted for any citizen to watch these proceedings?'

Dragging his mind back to the matter at hand, Kenyon leaned forward and pressed his palms down on the blotter before him. 'That is quite beside the point, my lady. The wife concerned in a prosecution for criminal conversation never appears at the trial. It is unheard of.'

He glanced toward the back of the court, where her husband Lord Nash sat silent. Whatever reaction he might have to his wife's unwelcome intrusion was concealed by muslin hangings.

'The damage to your reputation, ma'am . . .'

Her voice silvered with gentle mockery. 'My lord, the damage was done when my husband barred me from my house and my children, and served his odious writ on his brother. He has already ruined me, despite my innocence, and regardless of the outcome of this case. To add insult to injury, I may not even defend my reputation by joining as party to the action. The least I deserve is to confront my accusers by my presence, if not through my attorney.'

Mr Garrow, counsel for the plaintiff, was on his feet. 'My lord, I object. This is wholly improper. My client's lady wife has no standing in this matter and cannot be called as witness. She may not sneak in her testimony by the back door.'

Ignoring the interjection, Lady Nash addressed the Chief Justice. 'I would not have spoken at all had not your lordship desired me to explain my presence.'

'My lord, this is most irregular.' Garrow sent a furious glance sideways at his colleague, who lounged at the other end of the bar table. Mr Erskine, for the defendant, rubbed the side of his large nose and read his brief, affecting deafness. Had the wily advocate planned this? Or was Lady Nash off on some mad frolic of her own?

It wasn't merely irregular, as Garrow said. It was an outrage to decency. The lady would be obliged to watch, and be watched in turn, as every sordid detail of her affair with her brother-in-law was extracted from witnesses, picked over, highlighted and debated by counsel. From love letters and trysts to overheard moans of passion and stained linens, all would be laid bare.

And yet there was that proud set to her shoulders, the fine, determined line of her jaw . . .

'Be seated, ma'am,' Lord Kenyon told her heavily. 'And hold your tongue. As Mr Garrow pointed out, this is not a forum for you to argue your case, nor to air whatever grievances you might have.'

She raised her hand as if taking the oath. 'I shall be as silent as the grave, my lord.'

'Be sure that you are,' he said. 'If your presence further disrupts the proceedings, I shall order you to leave forthwith.'

'Yes, my lord.'

He stared at her with a suspicious ferocity that had made many a perjuring witness shake in his shoes. The lady bowed her head, but the gesture did not fool him into believing her cowed. He felt a petty urge to eject her from the court on the grounds of sheer effrontery.

With a sour taste in his mouth, Lord Kenyon addressed counsel. 'Mr Garrow, you may proceed . . .'

Liz

Tony didn't call. He didn't text. There wasn't enough banana bread in the world.

Liz pushed a slowly congealing breakfast fry-up around her plate while her mother read the paper. Ordinarily, it was a treat to wander down to the Pepper Mill for eggs and bacon. The only times she gave herself a free pass to indulge in what Tony termed 'heart-attack food' were on her infrequent trips to Montville.

The churning in her stomach was only partly due to the wine she'd drunk last night. Even the coffee she'd ordered seemed too rich to keep down.

'Do you want some of this?' Her mother indicated her own breakfast, a concoction of raw grains, acai berries and chia seeds topped with a snowy dollop of organic natural yoghurt.

'No thanks, Mum.' Just looking at that virtuous mess of healthy goodness made her crave chocolate. With a side of chocolate.

As her mother became absorbed again in her newspaper, Liz put down her fork and took out her phone.

The account of the Nash trial had taken up only two slender columns of space in the document Nick had sent her. She needed to see if there was a more detailed description of the proceedings somewhere online.

In no time at all, she found a print copy of the trial transcript for sale on a rare used book website, but there was no corresponding electronic version that she could download.

From studying legal precedent, not to mention Dickens's *Bleak House*, Liz had always had the impression that court cases in Georgian and Victorian times were protracted and deathly dull, full of arcane procedural niceties and mountains of paperwork.

While that might have been the case in matters such as *Jarndyce v. Jarndyce*, it seemed proceedings for criminal conversation were more like a spectator sport. Basically, criminal conversation was an action available to a husband against his wife's lover for sleeping with her. Imagine the chaos if that still existed!

Her research had taken her to Blackstone's *Commentaries on the Laws of England*, a kind of bible in legal circles in the late eighteenth century. According to Sir William Blackstone, the action originated in the tort of trespass.

What Blackstone didn't say, and what Liz subsequently discovered from further reading, was that the action for criminal conversation was akin to suing someone for damaging your car. A woman was a chattel, the possession of her husband. Therefore, if another man sleeps with her, he's damaging the goods, so to speak. The amount of damages a husband could win from his wife's lover was astronomical in the late eighteenth century. No wonder it had been such a popular cause of action, despite the scandal it caused.

Nick had told Liz that Julian Nash was rumoured to have been Delany's lover. But she certainly hadn't expected that the affair would have been the subject of a court case. The circumstances of the trial were so juicy she was dying to know the full story.

Liz clicked on the other attachments Nick's assistant had sent through. Some were copies of letters, but the scans weren't great quality. She couldn't possibly read them on her phone. There was also a nice, meaty article about the history of the Seagrove estate and the Nash family, which she'd print and read for background later.

Then she came across some cartoons, drawn in the style of Rowlandson or Gillray. It was so typical of that ebullient, rollicking, rude Georgian era that Liz immediately smiled as she enlarged the image.

The caption read: 'Lady N— undresses for the populace'.

A dark-haired, pretty woman in a bedroom simpered in the direction of the closed door. On the other side of that door, a queue of gentlemen in powdered wigs lined up behind one man, who crouched with his eye to the keyhole.

Another man stood near the queue with his hand raised, as if directing traffic. A speech bubble floated up from his mouth: 'I should charge admission, by Jove. My wife must earn her keep.'

The distinctive steep eyebrows of the beauty in the picture told Liz this must be Delany, Lady Nash, the woman in Nick's portrait.

Nor was this the only caricature of the scandalous Nashes. Liz flicked through the attachments. It seemed the criminal conversation trial had created a furore in the media of the day. Nothing told her what had happened to Lady Nash once the case was decided, though.

She thought of Delany's portrait, and the determination in that striking face. This was a woman who had been made notorious by her own husband making her affair with his brother public. And he had done so in the hope of a rich return.

Had she shrugged off the gossip and held her head high? Had she resumed life with her husband as if nothing had happened? Had she sought refuge with her lover, perhaps? Or had she been shunned, shamed, and fallen into elegant prostitution, as many spurned wives did in that era?

The answers to these questions might be at Seagrove.

Janine flicked a page of her newspaper and made a sarcastic remark about the current political situation. Liz started, slamming into reality. She'd been so absorbed in the Nash affair, she'd forgotten for an all too brief period about her own marital troubles. She wasn't sure whether she should be comforted or appalled by that.

Automatically, her mind resumed its tug-of-war. Tony hadn't called or emailed. He wasn't in transit or asleep. He was ignoring her. What was she going to do?

What if he was finished with her? What if he continued to reject her attempts to get in touch? Potentially, she had three months to fill without work, without vacation, without Tony. That was dangerous.

Liz gazed out over the ridge to the cow-dotted farmland beyond. She couldn't stay here. She couldn't start the wallowing process in earnest or she might never climb out of it.

Looking to the future, what would she do when he came back? She couldn't see them carrying on with the house renovations as if nothing had happened. How could they return to normal after this? How could a marriage survive such a seemingly final gesture as Tony had made?

Hurt and anger flared up inside her. Hardly stopping to consider that by this one action she might change the course of her life, Liz picked up her phone and called Nick.

CHAPTER THREE

Liz washed up on the shore of the Isle of Wight like flotsam, bedraggled in body and spirit. The exhaustion of flying across the world after the emotional upheaval of Tony's desertion seemed to have knocked the stuffing out of her. She wished she could crawl into a nice warm bed and stay there for a century.

Having learned from experience that her style of driving was incompatible with narrow English country lanes, Liz hadn't hired a car, which would have been the most sensible mode of transport to use on the island during her stay. When she'd told Seagrove's manager her plans to take a train and a bus to Seagrove, the woman had insisted on sending someone to collect her from the ferry terminal at Ryde. What a relief.

Only during a conversation on the ferry did she learn that buses no longer stopped near Seagrove, because part of the closest roadway had recently fallen off the cliff. She tried not to be daunted by that.

On arriving at Ryde, Liz could have wept with gratitude when she saw a tall individual holding a sign with her name on it. His attention wasn't on Liz, or on the crowd disembarking from the ferry, but on a paperback novel in his hand.

'Boy, am I glad to see you . . .' Her driver looked up and her words trailed away as she saw his face.

No man had a right to be that handsome outside a Hollywood movie. He was tall and lean, with that rumpled elegance that seemed coded into the DNA of a certain type of Englishman, and there was a healthy, outdoors look to him, all tousled hair and golden tan. The laughter lines at the corners of his eyes and the deep furrows on either side of his mouth gave his face character, and a little age, too. She guessed he must be older than she was, but not by much. And those eyes . . . sea-green and changeable, like the waters that lapped against the nearby shore. He wore faded jeans and a t-shirt that had a tiny rip at the shoulder seam.

His gaze flicked over her without interest. 'Is that all you have?'

She looked down at herself. Then she realised he was referring to her lack of luggage. Most of her summer wardrobe was in Phuket with Tony, so she'd decided to pack a carry-on suitcase and buy the rest here.

'Yes, that's it.' Her mouth twisted a little at the thought of Tony. 'Long story.'

He didn't seem the least bit curious to hear it but reached for her carry-on and headed with it toward the car park. Stopping at an ancient Range Rover, he unlocked it and stowed her case on the back seat.

Could this be the lord of the manor?

'I'm Liz, by the way,' she said, hoisting herself into the car.

He looked down at the sign he'd been holding with her name on it, then tossed it to the back seat. 'Morning.'

Without taking her lead and introducing himself in return, he climbed in beside her. His physical presence seemed to fill the cabin. What was he, six-four? Liz was no midget. She'd once heard herself called a 'strapping wench' by the senior partner at her old law firm, but she felt tiny next to this man.

He glanced at her as he backed out of the parking space, eyes glittering in the golden tan of his face. Was it her imagination or did his gaze linger with slight puzzlement on her hair? Nothing she'd done to it that morning could get the strange kink out of it.

She supposed he had a right to judge. While it was as uncontrived as the rest of him, this man's hair was a work of art. It was brown, streaked with every shade of highlight, from caramel to tawny to gold, and shaggy as a surfer's. She'd no doubt the colour was natural. He didn't seem the type to sit in a salon with little strips of foil sprouting from his head.

'So . . . what's your name?' she prompted, because it didn't look like he was ever going to volunteer the information. A wave of tiredness hit her. What time was it in Australia? She didn't have the energy to work it out.

'Theo Nash,' he said.

She'd been right, then. What was the lord of the manor doing playing chauffeur? Didn't he have minions to do that for him?

Liz stifled a yawn. 'Nice to meet you, Theo.' She rested her head against the window and tried not to fall asleep.

She still hadn't managed to corner Nick on the real reason he'd sent her here. When questioned further about their conversation in his study, he'd turned annoyingly vague.

That was uncharacteristic of him, come to think of it. Once she'd agreed to go to Seagrove, he'd sent a package of printed information she hadn't yet had time to read. He'd restated her mission to negotiate to buy the estate, but that wasn't all he wanted.

What had he been about to say when Yolande had interrupted them that day? When Liz had pressed for more on the phone, he'd told her that once she'd settled in and read the material he'd sent, he'd be in touch to discuss strategy.

He'd thanked her for her care of Yolande, and reading between the lines, Liz took it that Nick had managed to smooth things over with his wife. Maybe Yolande's accident had given him the jolt he'd needed. Liz hoped so, for Yolande's sake.

The landscape rattled by in a blur of deep green hills, fields, and meadows spotted with sheep. She knew enough of the island's geography to predict they would head inland to get to Seagrove, so she wouldn't see much of the coastline. The chalk stumps of the Needles, the island's most famous landmark, were situated well to the west. Her destination was on the island's south coast, maybe half an hour's drive away.

If she'd hoped for a tour-guide-style commentary on their journey, she was disappointed. Theo kept his eyes on the road, muttering now and then when the actions of another motorist displeased him, or raising an index finger from the wheel in acknowledgement when some obliging person pulled onto the shoulder of a narrow lane to let him pass.

On the whole, she was glad Theo wasn't too interested in talking. While she knew she ought to pay attention to the countryside, the motion of the car soon lulled her into a doze.

A sharp bump woke her. She opened her eyes. They'd left the smooth asphalt and were rattling and bouncing along a lane that was little more than a goat track. Liz looked out Theo's window and saw water on the horizon.

Beyond the track, the cliff fell away steeply, giving her a jolt of vertigo. Her brain told her the edge was some distance away, but her hand gripped the armrest on the door beside her. As if that could keep them from tumbling over.

A structure came into view, but it wasn't the grand Georgian edifice she'd expected. The Range Rover puttered to a stop outside a large, gabled two-storey house with dormer windows and a thatched roof. It squatted amid an overgrown garden, as if hunkering down, bracing itself against the elements.

She blinked. 'This isn't Seagrove.'

'No,' said Theo. 'The Big House is about a mile or so that way.' He pointed in a direction she assumed was north. 'This is Saltwater Cottage, where you're staying. All booked and paid for.'

Before she could get it herself, he grabbed her case and headed up the path.

The garden gate hung loosely on its hinges, flapping rhythmically with the stiff sea breeze. Liz caught it on the backward swing, pushed it open and followed him.

'Cleaned it up a bit,' said Theo, looking around. 'Needs a deal more work, though.'

While clearly old and as scruffy as her driver, the cottage was clean. That was a relief.

'As long as there's a bed and a bath, I don't care,' said Liz. Would decent plumbing be too much to hope for?

Nick's assistant had made the booking in Liz's name. What was MJ thinking, placing her so far away from the real action? If Liz was supposed to be digging for information, didn't it make a lot more sense for her to stay at the house? Well, she'd see what could be done about her accommodation when she got her wits together.

Liz squinted up at the bare light bulb that hung on a long cord over the stairwell. 'I'm guessing you don't have wi-fi here.'

'Not even mobile reception,' said Theo, in a tone that bordered on the self-congratulatory. Liz checked her phone. He was right.

The cottage had an uncanny atmosphere, as if ghosts whispered through cracks in the walls. She often felt like that in old buildings. You didn't get too many houses of this vintage back home in Brisbane.

She followed Theo into the low-beamed living room that adjoined the small entry hall. He yanked open the curtains on the front window and sunlight flooded the room.

He'd called the place a cottage, but it was a large house by Liz's standards, made of stone and covered in a thick blanket of ivy. It was draughty and musty, and she didn't doubt the chimney was blocked with birds' nests or the carcasses of sundry climbing animals.

Luckily, it was summer. She wouldn't need to make use of the fireplace. Besides, if she had anything to do with it, she'd be staying up at the 'Big House' in no time.

'Hold on,' Theo said, opening a cupboard under the stairs, 'I'll turn the power on.'

'Are you the caretaker, then?' asked Liz. She managed to keep her voice deadpan. Something about this man – perhaps his unwillingness to exchange more than monosyllables by way of conversation – made her want to needle him.

When he didn't answer her, she peered around at him, to see that he was watching her with a slightly bemused expression.

'Actually, "caretaker" is a good way of describing it.' He held up her carry-on. 'Put this in the bedroom, shall I?' He headed up the stairs.

Liz followed him. He hadn't sounded offended by her cheek, which was just as well. She was supposed to be getting to know these people, after all. 'Are you Lord Nash? The owner? Sorry. It's just that you're not dressed like a peer of the realm.'

'My Order of the Garter is at the dry-cleaner's,' he said over his shoulder, but she caught the glimmer of a smile as he opened one of the doors off the landing.

'Well, you can't blame me,' said Liz, encouraged by the spark of humour. 'I expected a bluff squire type in tweeds and a waxed jacket, at the very least.' Not a sun-drenched god in jeans and a ripped t-shirt. Not quite your average Mr Darcy.

He grimaced and set down her luggage. 'I do not, thank God, own any tweed.'

'Ah, but you do have a Barbour. Am I right?'

He looked a bit defensive at that. 'It's a very practical piece of outerwear.'

She grinned. 'Now it's your turn to ask me if I rode over here on a kangaroo. Or if I'd like a cold beer. You can even call me "mate" if you like. I don't mind.'

Theo shook his head and turned to leave.

'I don't happen to like beer,' she called, jogging downstairs after him. 'But a good South Australian shiraz, on the other hand . . .'

She caught up with him, suddenly desperate for company, any company. Even taciturn, shaggy, slightly bemused male company. 'Actually, I'd love to see Seagrove. The house, I mean. Is it an easy walk?'

He dug his hands into his pockets. 'You could walk. Or there's a bike in the shed you can use.'

One corner of his mouth quirked up as if something about the latter suggestion amused him.

She narrowed her eyes. 'Thank you. I might go with the second option.' She hadn't ridden a bike for years, but how hard could it be? 'Could you tell me how to get there?'

He gave her directions, and when she became utterly confused – orienteering had never been her strong suit – he sighed and drew her a map on the back of a receipt from Arty's Bait and Tackle Shop that he found in his pocket.

'Got it?'

'I think so,' said Liz, smoothing out the creases in the docket. 'I'm good with landmarks and left and right, but when you start talking compass points, you've lost me.'

He turned to go. As he reached the gate, she called after him, 'A pleasure to meet you, *my lord*.'

He didn't answer, just dipped his head and raised his hand in a resigned wave.

Forget the wine, Liz would have sold her granny for a long, uninterrupted sleep, but if she lay down now she'd probably wake in darkness and then she'd never find her way.

After a long, hot shower, she felt just this side of marvellous, quite equal to the task of a cycle to Seagrove. She was drying her hair when an old Jeep pulled up in the drive outside and a slight, middle-aged man in a flat hat and tweeds got out. From the back seat of the Jeep, he collected an enormous basket.

Liz ran down to meet him.

'Hello!' she said, a little breathless as she opened the gate for him. 'Let me help you.'

'No, no, I have it, thank you.' The gentleman smiled at her. Grey eyes beneath tufty white brows contained wisdom and a gentle humour that made Liz warm to him instantly.

He raised his burden to show her, saying, 'A welcome basket from the Big House, as requested. I do apologise. It should have been here when you arrived.'

She invited him in and he moved past her to the kitchen, hefting the basket onto the counter. It contained all sorts of home-made goods in addition to a few staples and – wonder of wonders – a bottle of wine. Silently, she blessed the ever-efficient MJ for arranging it.

'You're a lifesaver!' Liz thanked him, adding, 'Would you like a cup of tea, Mr —?'

'— Jackson. No, I mustn't stay. At least, I've been sent to fetch you up to the house for afternoon tea.' He gave a self-deprecating cough, his gaze flickering to her wet hair. 'If that's convenient?'

This was unexpected. Clearly the invitation hadn't come from Theo.

'Of course,' said Liz. 'That's so kind.' An opportunity to visit the house seemed too good to refuse, particularly if it came with afternoon tea. Maybe there'd be wi-fi.

Liz tied her hair back in a pony tail, grabbed her laptop and a notepad and headed out to the car.

There was no hurry, Mr Jackson told her, so he took a circuitous route to the house and showed her some of the sights along the way. The coastline was postcard-perfect, with fields so green they seemed almost iridescent, flowing down to chalk cliff faces that in turn gave way to small coves and bays. He showed her Steephill Cove with its jumble of huts and eateries. She loved the sleepy Victorian town of Ventnor, with its steep, winding street that ran down to the boardwalk. Along the front ranged a strip of restaurants and tea rooms, an ice-cream parlour, a fish and chip shop and the pirate-themed Spyglass Inn at the end.

As the Jeep laboured up the incline to the town centre then headed back toward the house, Liz thought she might now have the answer to Theo's ill-concealed scepticism about her riding the bike to Ventnor. She'd forgotten she was staying on the edge of a cliff.

She learned that Mr Jackson's wife was the cook at Seagrove and that the couple lived together at the Lodge, a comfortable house nestled beside what used to be the main entrance to the Seagrove grounds. It had traditionally belonged to the gate keeper, but the gates themselves were no more.

'I appreciate the lift.' Liz watched Mr Jackson's liver-spotted hand change gears as they climbed another hill. 'You must have better things to do than ferry me about.'

'Not at all,' said Mr Jackson, his eyes crinkling at the corners. 'I've been put out to grass, as the saying goes.'

His tone was so determinedly cheerful that Liz suspected Mr Jackson was anything but reconciled to retirement. He couldn't have been much more than sixty and appeared in the prime of health.

'Did you work at the house?' said Liz.

'Used to be head guide when they still did tours,' he answered, shrugging. 'But times change.'

Jackson, with his dapper dress and lovely, quiet ways, was a more believable lord of the manor than Theo, in Liz's opinion. She'd have laid money on the fact Jackson had been excellent at his job, too. The indignation she felt at what sounded like an enforced retirement was hardly a rational reaction when she didn't know the ins and outs of his situation. But Mr Jackson seemed to her to be precisely the sort of employee a house like Seagrove needed.

'How many years of service have you given them?' she asked.

'Oh, I've been here in one capacity or another since I left school. I managed the estate until they sold off all the land.' He sighed. 'That's when I became head guide at the house. But they stopped admitting the public a few years before Theo's father died, so . . .'

'So the family dismissed you after all those years?'

None of her business, of course, but she liked Jackson already; she hated to think of how his loyalty had been rewarded.

Jackson's lips pressed together, then relaxed. 'Actually, I resigned. Still, I have a generous pension and my wife and I have a tenancy at the Lodge for life. I can't complain.'

Liz sensed it wasn't about the money. She would have liked to find out more, but just then, the Jeep turned off the road and into a driveway lined by trees.

Jackson explained that the few acres surrounding the house were called the Park. Hundreds of years ago, deer had wandered at will over the grounds. While the setting looked natural, in fact the landscape had been shaped to within an inch of its life, to show not only the house but each glimpse of the estate to best advantage.

The famous Lancelot 'Capability' Brown was responsible for this idyllic beauty. Woods had been cut down and new ones planted. Hills and dells built up or dug out where none had been before. And of course, there was the obligatory serpentine lake with its small island and grotto, not to mention a folly in the form of a ruined tower built on the northern Down. Jackson said it had not happened here at Seagrove, but elsewhere, entire villages had been moved out of sight so that nothing marred the rural tranquillity of the scene.

In its heyday the Seagrove estate had comprised not just a house but a village and tenant farms and several other houses and cottages as well. Saltwater Cottage, where Liz was now staying, had been the Dower House where the mother of the incumbent baron would live once her son was married. Another house on the Undercliff, Marine Cottage, had been an informal seaside retreat centuries before, its gardens devoted to cultivating subtropical plants due to the unusual microclimate there.

As he spoke of the estate's history, pride lit Mr Jackson's face. He might have been put out to grass by its present owners but his love for this place was undimmed.

'And here we are,' said Jackson softly, as they rounded a bend in the drive.

Liz wasn't often at a loss for words, but she fell into awed silence as they puttered up the avenue. Chestnut trees arced over their heads, shading the drive and providing a frame for the magnificent mansion ahead.

'Built in the Palladian style, you know,' said Mr Jackson, as they emerged from the avenue into the open. 'They liked the classical lines of ancient Greece and Rome in those days.'

And yes, Seagrove might have been modelled on the Parthenon or some other Grecian temple. It was a squared-off U shape that embraced a fountain now lying dormant in the centre of the circular drive. Each protruding wing was surmounted by a triangular pediment, ornately carved, and the walls were fluted with the suggestion of columns. A rose window above the front door seemed just right. It drew and pleased the eye, breaking up all those straight lines without being gaudy or overly ornate. Elegant restraint seemed to be the watchword of this particular architect.

Tall cedars and ancient oaks flanked the house, while a sweep of lawn expanded on either side of the drive in front of it. Despite the classical influence, this house seemed perfect for its setting. The quiet, grave beauty of Seagrove made something inside Liz ache with want.

She had never considered herself covetous or materialistic. This hunger – no, *craving* would be the better word – was new to her. As someone from suburban Brisbane, she could only imagine how it must feel to own a place like this. Not only own it, but be part of it, of a family that had lived here for centuries. To feel as if you belonged to the house even more than it belonged to you.

Guiltily, she pulled herself up. She ought, rather, to think about the labour that had gone into building edifices like this, the poor downtrodden souls who had doubtless been exploited by this family over those same centuries.

Faced with the breathtaking sight of Seagrove, it was hard to keep that in mind.

Had Nick felt a similar longing? Was that why he was so determined to buy the place? More to the point, how would she ever persuade Theo to give it up?

With something of a flourish, Jackson steered the Jeep around the fountain and pulled up on the drive outside the house.

'We're going through the front door?' said Liz. 'Fancy!'

Jackson chuckled. 'You needn't feel too honoured. They don't send the hoi polloi to the servants' entrance these days.'

'Not even colonials like me?' said Liz.

Jackson tilted his head toward her and spoke out of the side of his mouth. 'Try not to mention the colonies.'

Liz gave a dramatic sigh. 'My poor dear great-great-great-grandmother. Transported for stealing a loaf of bread.'

'Really?' said Jackson.

'No, not really.' She grinned. 'I'm afraid my family history is much less interesting. They came out after the First World War.'

The first thing she noticed when she jumped out of the car was the blanketing quiet, as if the woods surrounding the house swallowed all sound. She couldn't resist glancing over her shoulder. 'Is the house haunted?'

'Oh, yes,' he replied, as if paranormal activity were a matter of course. 'Not as haunted as some other places on the island, however, and all of the ghosts are perfectly benign.'

She wondered if he was teasing, but then decided he wasn't. Never mind. She wasn't staying here, was she? She wouldn't ask about the cottage. Better not to know.

'Well, here we are.' They walked up the shallow flight of steps and through the open door.

The entrance hall was lofty and cool, its floor tiled like a chessboard in black and white marble. A staircase with a beautifully wrought balustrade curled upward, an enormous window on the landing allowing light to flood the space.

Around the semi-circular hall ranged a series of alcoves housing marble busts of what Liz took to be Roman emperors. Interested, she moved closer to read the small brass plaque at the base of one of them, but the sudden click of heels on the marble tiles made her turn around.

The woman was a cool blonde, very beautiful and very thin. Older than Liz, but not by much. She wore a twin-set and what Janine would have called 'slacks', an ensemble that was surely too matronly for a thirty-something woman. This must be the manager, then.

'Ms Jones? How nice. I'm Valerie Drake.'

Valerie's smile was as thin as the rest of her. Liz could tell she meant to be hospitable but it was clearly an effort.

'Of course. Lovely to meet you in person, Valerie. Please, call me Liz.'

As a matter of habit, Liz held out her hand, but Valerie ignored it. Wondering if she'd committed some sort of *faux pas*, Liz used the disdained hand to gesture about her. 'What a magnificent house. Thank you for inviting me.'

'Won't you come through?' Valerie said. 'We'll take tea in the drawing room.' She gave Jackson a curt nod in dismissal. 'Thank you, Jackson.' As if he were a servant and she the lady of the manor.

When Valerie turned to lead the way, Liz made a face at Jackson that was half apologetic, half comical. He winked in acknowledgement, but his smile was almost as forced as Valerie's.

The drawing room was dark and formal, crammed with highly polished mahogany furniture. Thick velvet curtains, swagged and braided to an alarming degree, smothered every skerrick of light that might have ventured through the windows.

'We keep it dark in here because of the paintings,' Valerie explained, switching on the electric light. 'Not to my taste, of course,' she added with a dismissive flick of the fingers at what Liz suspected might be a set of Canalettos and probably a couple of Turners, too. 'But they are valuable.'

Though cool, the room was stuffy. Not the most inviting place to take a guest on first arrival, Liz thought. If it were up to her, she'd open the curtains, paint the walls robin's-egg blue, ditch the Victorian furniture and replace it with slender Regency antiques. If the paintings were so precious, they should be kept in a gallery or another part of the house that wasn't used. Besides, it was a beautiful day. Surely tea on the terrace would show the place to best advantage?

And here she was, taking possession of a house she'd seen for the first time ten minutes ago.

Liz wished she could excuse herself from this meeting. The rudeness her hostess had shown Jackson told her everything she needed to know about Valerie. You could always judge someone's character by the way they treated people they believed to be their inferiors.

Still, she shouldn't let her dislike get in the way of pumping Valerie for information.

'Have you been working here long?' she asked, sitting down on the green velvet sofa Valerie indicated.

Valerie poured them both tea. 'I don't *work* here, as such. I'm more . . . part of the family.'

'Oh,' said Liz. *Eek*. She'd put her foot in it there.

She waited for Valerie to expand on that statement but she remained silent, handing the cup to Liz.

The sumptuous spread laid out before them on Spode china made Liz realise she hadn't eaten since she'd left her London hotel that morning. Valerie didn't partake of the feast, she noticed – no surprise there – but Liz wasn't going to let that stop her. She took a scone and plopped generous globs of strawberry jam and clotted cream on top.

'Are you Theo's sister, then?' she asked.

'His fiancée.' Valerie's tone was frigid.

'Oh.' Liz blinked. She couldn't picture it. Her gaze flickered to Valerie's left hand. Sure enough, Valerie wore the Rock of Gibraltar on her third finger.

'When Theo's father died two years ago and his mother moved away, Theo needed help with the house.' Valerie crossed her legs. 'I gave up my work in London and moved here.'

'So you're responsible for that gorgeous display of flowers in the foyer.' Liz grinned. 'I thought that probably wasn't down to the man of the house.'

Valerie shrugged. 'I get a woman in.'

The conversation was so stilted Liz wondered why Valerie bothered. Surely she didn't invite every guest to afternoon tea. Perhaps she was making these overtures because Liz had booked the cottage for two months?

Every now and then, the other woman seemed to recall that she was in the hospitality business and pasted on a smile. 'I hope you enjoy your stay at the cottage.'

Again, Liz tried to picture Valerie and Theo together and failed. But then, people had always called her and Tony an oddly matched pair —

No. She would not think about Tony. Keep your mind on the job, Liz.

She reached for a ribbon-thin cucumber sandwich. What was it about the shape of these things that made them taste so good? If someone had handed her a cucumber sandwich cut into triangles with the crusts on she'd reject it without hesitation.

She made another attempt at conversation. 'It must have been quite a change, coming down here to live and work after London. Looking after a house this size is a huge responsibility, I imagine.'

Valerie raised her almost non-existent eyebrows. 'On the contrary. It's a privilege.'

'Do you have a large staff to help you?' Liz asked, undaunted by the frigidity in Valerie's tone. She wanted to know about Jackson and whether Valerie had been the one to get rid of him. She'd believe it.

'We have a small staff. A cook, some daily cleaners, a couple of part-time groundsmen. None of them lives in, though.' Valerie gestured toward the top of the cake stand, where an array of sweet morsels were arranged. 'Do try one of these.'

'Only if you join me,' said Liz. When Valerie's face froze, Liz added, 'Oh, come on, Valerie. I bet Mrs Jackson's pastries are to die for.'

Gingerly, Valerie plucked a minuscule lemon-curd tart from the tiered stand and put it on her plate. She didn't eat it at first. Then, as if conscious of Liz's eyes upon her, she cut a piece from the tartlet with her silver fork and put some in her mouth.

A fleeting expression of mixed pleasure and surprise crossed Valerie's face. Quickly, she replaced the fork on her plate and touched her napkin to her lips.

Clearly, this was a woman who needed to be corrupted. In the nicest possible way, of course. What did she normally live on? Air?

'And what brings you here to Seagrove, Liz?' said Valerie, recovering herself. 'We don't get an awful lot of international guests, being a little off the beaten track, as you might say.'

Liz licked jam from the corner of her lips. The words tripped off her tongue before she knew it. 'I'm writing a book.'

She blinked. Where had that come from?

'Oh?' said Valerie. 'What sort of book?'

'I'm not sure yet,' said Liz with perfect truth. She wished she'd taken the opportunity to read more about the house before she'd arrived.

'So you're an author,' said Valerie. 'Have you written anything I might have read?'

How on earth would Liz know what Valerie was likely to read? She shook her head. 'Writing is just a hobby. It probably won't be published or anything.'

Valerie's expression soured. Or maybe that was her resting face. 'I see. Are you writing a novel or is it non-fiction?'

'A novel.' Liz decided that gave her a lot more scope for asking intrusive questions, and she wouldn't have to display any expertise of her own.

'What a coincidence,' said Valerie, setting the plate with her pastry, minus one bite, on the pie-crust table at her elbow. 'One of Theo's ancestors was a novelist. In fact, she lived in Saltwater Cottage, where you're staying now.'

'Really?' said Liz. 'Would I have heard of her?'

Valerie shook her head, and Liz noticed her ears were as small and neat as one of Mrs Jackson's tart shells. 'I doubt it. She wrote those dreadful gothic novels that were popular at the time. They've been out of print for centuries. But there are copies in the library if you'd like to have a look. Her name was Delany, Lady Nash.'

The lady in Nick's portrait. Now that was a coincidence. Maybe that explained why MJ had booked the Saltwater Cottage accommodation. Before Liz could say more, the clock chimed discreetly. Valerie stood up as if to end their *tête à tête* and Liz quickly wiped the look of recognition from her face. This woman was the last person she should confide in about her interest in Seagrove's past.

'I'd love to see the library,' said Liz, with only a twinge of regret for the choice tidbits she was forced to leave behind. 'Do you have internet access here, by any chance?'

'The library has wi-fi, so you can take your laptop in there, if you like,' said Valerie, leading the way down the corridor. 'I'll write down the password for you.'

'Thanks, I —' Liz broke off, staring around her. 'Wow.'

This was the kind of library they had in heaven. Or in Olympus, rather. The impossibly high ceiling featured Apollo in his gilded chariot dragging the sun across an azure sky.

'Impressive, isn't it?' said Valerie.

'When I die, I want my ashes to be scattered here,' breathed Liz.

Part of the reason she'd studied law was that she loved reading. She loved the English language, its nuance and variety. 'I wonder how many words there are in here,' she murmured. The volumes, all bound in tooled leather, seemed to whisper secrets to her through the stillness.

Valerie blinked. 'I can't say I've ever thought about it. Theo might know how many volumes there are.'

'Does anyone actually read the books?' Liz imagined the shelves would be jam-packed with valuable first editions. Locked behind glass, they didn't seem very accessible.

She'd never understood some people's obsession with the physical book. The stories, the words, were all that mattered to her. As long as she could read *them*, it made no difference whether a novel was a first edition or a dog-eared paperback someone had blow-dried after drop-ping it into the bath. But she had to admit, bound in leather and tooled in gold, this collection of volumes was a magnificent sight.

'Theo is about the only one who does read them,' said Valerie. 'I only wish I had the time! Anyway, I'm sure he wouldn't mind lend-ing you Delany's gothics. I can't imagine they're of much value and there are multiple copies, after all.'

'Thanks, I'll ask him,' said Liz, fishing her laptop out of her bag. 'Do you mind if I go ahead and check my email?'

'Of course not. I must get back to work. You can set up here.' Valerie indicated a small writing desk that seemed too elegant to pol-lute with anything as vulgar as a laptop. 'I'll tell Jackson you'll stop in at the kitchens when you're finished and he can take you home.' She looked at her watch. 'It's half past three now. Say, five o'clock?'

When Valerie was certain Liz had all she needed, she left her in the library to work.

Unable to help herself, Liz scanned her inbox. Not one of those three hundred and twenty-five emails was from Tony. Clearly, the purveyors of cheap Viagra loved her more than her husband did. She pulled out her phone to check that she had reception. No calls from him since she'd arrived at Seagrove either.

Well, she'd given him every opportunity to stop her, but now she was on the Isle of Wight, and she was committed to helping Nick buy this house. She tried to put Tony out of her head and focus on the task at hand.

She went through her emails, replying to some questions from her team that couldn't wait. She avoided answering the more personal inquiries from friends.

Then she came to a message from Nick. He wanted to organise a video conference with her as soon as possible.

She calculated the time difference. Middle of the night in Australia, but to him that probably didn't matter. He spent a lot of time doing business with people on the other side of the world. She wasn't sure that he slept at all. Maybe Nick was a vampire. Come to think of it, that would explain a lot.

She emailed back, saying she could talk now, but they'd have to schedule a meeting if he wasn't available immediately. She explained that she didn't have mobile reception or internet at the cottage, so she had to use the library at the house. She added the number of the cottage land line in case there was anything urgent.

Within seconds of the whoosh that told her the message had gone, Nick called on her video conferencing program.

With a quick look around her, Liz turned down the volume on her laptop and pressed 'accept'.

'Hey, gorgeous.' Nick's head and shoulders almost filled the screen, but Liz scanned the background to see what clues she could pick up as to his whereabouts.

It had the slightly generic, luxury feel of a hotel room. Travelling for work? Or had Yolande thrown him out?

None of her business. She should concentrate on the matter at hand.

'Sorry,' she said. 'I haven't had a chance to read the printed stuff you sent yet.'

'Fine, fine,' said Nick. 'Once you're across it you'll have ideas about where to look.'

'You're ahead of me there,' said Liz. 'I still don't know exactly what I'm looking for.'

'Well, my dear Liz, that is where things get interesting.' Nick was holding something he'd picked up from his desk. She saw a flash of primary colours and realised it was a Rubik's Cube. Either he'd solved the puzzle or it was brand-new, because the squares were uniform on each face.

'My granny told me a story once about Seagrove.' He turned the cube in his hands and frowned down at it, as if deciding how to phrase his next words. 'That's my paternal grandmother. She's gone now, but she had a mind like a steel trap. You see, we believe Theo Nash isn't the true heir. The estate should have been handed down to me.'

Liz frowned. Even she knew the rules of primogeniture. 'How can that be right? Your name isn't Nash.'

'Nash was my father's name. My mother remarried when I was two.' He shrugged. 'She took my stepfather's name, so it was easier to change mine as well.'

Nick turned the top row of the Rubik's Cube around, so that a stripe of orange showed above two rows of green. 'Good bloke, my stepfather. Ever met him?'

'Once, I think.' Liz couldn't remember him very well, but she did recall thinking the unassuming fellow Nick introduced as his father was nothing at all like his son. Now she knew why.

'Well. The thing is,' said Nick, 'that it all sounds crazy.'

You've got that right, Liz thought.

'But there are references to this place in our family papers going back generations,' said Nick. 'In fact, there was a claim in the mid-1800s by one of my ancestors against the estate.'

'The 1800s?' I said. 'When exactly did the claim arise?'

'About 1790, something like that,' said Nick.

'Nick, I hate to tell you this, but I don't think there's anything we can do about such an old claim now.' Liz didn't know much about this area of law, but she guessed that after all this time, any interest Nick's branch of the family might have had would have been defeated by intervening circumstances.

'I don't need you to prove it legally,' he said. 'I just want to know the truth. And I want *them* to acknowledge it.'

By *them*, he must mean Theo and his family.

Liz frowned. 'You think that if you convince them you're truly entitled to Seagrove, they'll be more likely to sell it to you?'

'Perhaps. But it's more than that,' said Nick. 'Liz, I need to know. It's —' He flung out a hand. 'Well, you're there. You must see for yourself. From the moment I set foot in the place, I felt like I belonged there.'

There was definitely something about this house, Liz thought. It exerted a pull over the senses. Even she, who had no claims on Seagrove whatsoever, felt that strange compulsion.

Maybe it was her natural pessimism, but this didn't seem likely to end well. 'I'd rate our chances pretty low, but I'll do my best. Give me a quick rundown of what you do know.'

'Hang on a minute.' He reached past the computer monitor for a file and flipped through it. 'Here. Okay. In 1790, Richard – that's Lord Nash – was murdered by one of his servants, leaving two sons. The elder son, Henry, died at the age of seventeen. Thrown from his horse on the hunting field.'

'So young,' Liz murmured. 'Tragic.'

'Isn't it?' said Nick. 'Never understood the appeal of hunting. Now, the younger son, whose name was Stephen, succeeded to the title and became Lord Nash, the owner of Seagrove. When Stephen turned twenty-one, a woman who claimed to have been nursemaid to the two boys came to see him. She told him that he could not be the true heir of Seagrove, because the real Stephen Nash died when he was a baby. A member of the Seagrove household took the child's remains away with her. What she did with them, no one knows. But another child was substituted for Stephen.'

'Wow.' Liz said. It sounded fanciful in the extreme. 'So what happened after that?'

'Nothing. Stephen ignored the woman's accusations. Perhaps he paid her off. Nothing came of it until half a century later, when Stephen's cousin, the man who would have inherited the title and lands but for Stephen, took up the cause. He had got hold of the nursemaid's sworn testimony, but he had no other evidence. Letters were exchanged, but the matter never went further. Then the cousin died and the matter seemed to die with him.'

'Can you send me all this correspondence?' said Liz. 'A copy of the nursemaid's statement?'

'There's no sign of the affidavit itself, just a note that there was one.'

'Right.' That was disappointing. 'And you're descended from this cousin who, according to the nursemaid's testimony, should have inherited,' said Liz, tapping her pen on her notepad.

'That's right.'

She tried to wrap her head around what it all meant. 'So you think there was some kind of changeling thing going on? I thought that only happened in books.'

Nick's gaze was avid. 'If you read what the nursemaid is supposed to have said, you'll see how it could have happened. The two boys lived on their own, with only the nursemaid and a manservant, in a country house in Hampshire. No one from Seagrove had set eyes on Stephen since he was a newborn. Stephen died. The nursemaid was dismissed. Two children arrived back at Seagrove and were brought up there as Henry and Stephen Nash.'

Liz doodled a face on her notepad. 'I have to say, it seems very far-fetched. And where was Delany while all this was going on? You can't tell me a mother wouldn't recognise her own baby.'

'By that time, Delany was no longer at Seagrove. Read her memoirs. Read the rest of the materials. You'll see what happened.' Nick tossed the Rubik's Cube from one hand to the other, making the colours spin and blur. 'I keep coming back to the same question. Why would the nursemaid lie?'

'Blackmail?' suggested Liz. 'Maybe she bore a grudge. Maybe she was mentally disturbed.'

Nick closed the file. 'The nursemaid's story wouldn't be enough even if we did have that affidavit. I need you to get me more.'

'How do you propose I do that?'

He shrugged. 'You're good at getting on with people, getting them to trust you. Chat to the family, question the locals. See what they know. Maybe talk to the historical society. But the most important thing is to get inside their archives. Great families like these always kept letters, diaries, documents. Theo Nash will have them tucked away somewhere.'

'How well do you know Theo?' Liz asked, thinking her social skills would be stretched to breaking point if she had to persuade the taciturn lord of the manor to do anything, let alone allow her to see inside his precious vault of historical records.

'I don't,' said Nick. 'All I know is he won't sell the house to me.' He tilted his head. 'Given the state of his finances, I wouldn't be surprised if he's trying to get finance from elsewhere. The Heritage Lottery Fund, something like that.'

In fact, Jackson had mentioned an upcoming fundraising event at the house. Liz squirmed. Things were getting a little murky here. 'I'm not going to spy for you, Nick.'

'Did I ask you to?' He seemed injured, and she regretted her bluntness. 'I want you to do some research, that's all.'

She sighed. 'Okay, I'll try. At least now I know what I'm writing a book about,' she muttered.

'Pardon?'

'I told them I'm writing a book so I have an excuse to be nosey. I'll tell them I've decided to write about Delany.'

'Great idea.' Nick winked. 'Didn't I say you'd be good at this? Anyway, read those bits and pieces I sent you, do some digging. Call me when you have something, okay?'

Before she could respond, he ended the conference and his picture zapped out.

More slowly, Liz turned off her side of the call and sat back in her chair, drumming her fingertips on the green leather inset of the desk.

Whatever she might have expected from this assignment, it certainly hadn't been a fairytale. Who could have guessed Nick had that much romance in his soul?

The Lost Heir. Wasn't that the name of some gothic novel or other?

As she threw down her pen, a wave of tiredness hit her. Outside, the light was still bright but a glance at her computer told her it was nearly five o'clock.

She refreshed her inbox one last time. Nothing new.

Then she hesitated. Don't do it, she told herself. Quickly, she pulled up Tony's Facebook page.

She felt an indigestion-style pain that was becoming all too familiar when she saw his profile picture. Tony in his orange and white triathlon gear, grinning at the camera after a race.

She scrolled down. He hadn't updated his status since leaving Australia. There was, however, one recent post on his timeline.

Someone called Jessica Ridley had shared a photo of a twenty-something brunette, cheek-to-cheek with a laughing, shiny-faced Tony. They both held up cocktails festooned with tiny paper umbrellas, as if toasting the camera. The status read: 'Partying Koh Samui style with Tony Wilkins!'

Fortunately, before she could do something stupid like comment on the picture or internet-stalk this Jessica Ridley person, the clock chimed and she realised it was time to go.

Forcing down the hurt and anger she felt, Liz hurried back to the entrance hall. She guessed the kitchens would be on the basement level, so she took the stairs that led down – much plainer and narrower than the ones that went up, that was for sure. Then all she needed to do was to follow her nose.

Liz found Mrs Jackson at the Aga, busy whisking what looked like a bechamel sauce, while Mr Jackson sat at the scrubbed wooden table peeling potatoes.

The cook was a round woman of middle height and middle age, with fair hair, apple-bright cheeks and a twinkle in her blue eyes. She greeted Liz warmly, saying, 'Sorry I can't stop to chat, dear. Come and see me again when you get the chance, and I'll give you some tomatoes and lovely fresh herbs from the garden.'

'I don't want to disturb you,' said Liz. 'Just let me thank you for that glorious afternoon tea. It was sublime.'

Mrs Jackson beamed. 'I'm so glad you enjoyed it.' She gave her husband a meaningful look. 'At least *some* people appreciate my cooking.'

Liz took that to be a dig at Valerie, and Liz couldn't blame her. It must be dispiriting, cooking for someone who didn't eat.

'My dear, there are many here who *do* appreciate you. Not least of all me.' Mr Jackson set the final potato on the pile and sifted the peelings into a bright green pail labelled 'Chicken Feed'. Then he kissed his wife's cheek and showed Liz out to the car.

By the time Mr Jackson dropped her back at the cottage, Liz was too tired to do anything but fall into bed. In fact, it was an effort to wash and brush her teeth and put her pyjamas on.

Once she lay down, however, her mind switched gears, racing around an endless loop of self-recrimination and blame. Every time she closed her eyes, the image of Tony and Jessica flickered to life, as if projected onto the back of her eyelids.

After an hour of stewing, she finally gave up trying to sleep and switched on the bedside lamp.

Her bedroom was old-fashioned and a little shabby, decorated in pastels and white, with an ancient Persian rug on the floor. A neat stack of brochures about the island's attractions sat on the bedside table but she didn't feel like reading those.

She needed something engrossing. Something to take her mind off Tony. She rummaged through her bag for the printed material Nick had sent her, recalling the spiral-bound photocopies of Delany's memoirs that had looked promising. She dug them out and opened the first one.

Deciphering the antique cursive was slow work. The ink had faded considerably even before the copy had been made, and the closely written hand used unconventional and inconsistent spellings. She also wrote an 'f'-like symbol for 's', which made Liz hear the text in her head with an odd lisp. Not to mention that the author was fond of emphatic flourishes, which obscured the text above and below at some points.

Regardless, Delany's story made such astonishing reading that Liz was compelled to continue deep into the night.

Delany, Lady Nash

I surrendered my virginity at the age of sixteen and three-quarters to the second footman at Selby Park. His name was Tom – at least, that's what he was called in our house. I expect he'd replaced another foot-man of that name and it was easier for Papa if this footman became Tom too. Certainly, I never thought to call him anything else.

At sixteen I was an innocent as far as experience went, but my love for the footman was not pure. Indeed, I suspect my affection had more to do with his handsome physique than his noble soul. Tom was an impressive specimen of manhood, even if one discounted the allure of the uniform he wore – a sapphire-blue livery with a confection of silver facings like icing on a cake.

Late at night when the household was asleep, I'd await him in my bedchamber in a fever of anticipation. If we'd been caught, there would have been hell to pay. Heaven knows what I would have done if these muffled couplings had brought me a child. Papa might well have killed me.

But I was so full of restless longings at that age, a powder keg of suppressed feeling. Oh, to be a man, with all the freedom and agency that entailed! All of that pent-up energy chafed at the enforced still-ness of the genteel female, of sitting and sitting and sitting for hours on end. The sitting never changed, merely the location. First in the school-room, then at Miss Lemming's seminary in Bath, then in my aunt's drawing room and the drawing rooms of other ladies in the county.

The only times I felt free were when I rode out with the hunt and when I flew in the arms of my lusty footman: hot-blooded antidotes to the slow-acting poison of life as a young lady in my aunt's care.

Our mother had died of a fever when I was twelve. Papa, having little interest in his daughters, yielded to the blandishments of our mother's widowed sister and allowed her to take over the management of my younger sister Lavinia and me.

To give Aunt Boddington credit, she meant to do her best by us. And if I had not been such a difficult female, I would have felt fortunate to have such an attentive and well-intentioned preceptress.

Aunt schooled us in every accomplishment that might be thought to attract an eligible husband. With no inheritance to recommend us, we had to rely on our family name (middling important), our looks (I was striking, my sister pretty) and our suitability for the role of Wife.

My sister was an altogether softer version of me. Her eyes were a paler blue, her hair rich mahogany rather than raven's-wing black. Her chin was more rounded, her figure attractively plump where I was deep-bosomed and narrow-waisted. The dimple in her cheek quivered beside her cupid's bow mouth when she laughed and her smile was pure, sweet delight – whereas mine was a brilliant show of teeth, often edged with mockery.

At fifteen, Lavinia was too young to marry and far too silly to deploy the cunning and strategy needed to snare a wealthy man when she had no dowry to recommend her. True, my sister was exceedingly pretty and many men would find her particular brand of innocent folly irresistible, but her prospects would improve tenfold if I might first establish myself so that I could sponsor her into good society.

In any case, as the elder sister I must be married first. Aunt was adamant about that. Lately, she had been cataloguing the various young gentlemen – and not-so-young gentlemen – who might be persuaded to take me on. Marrying me off was a task that required every ounce of her ingenuity. I had no expectations, you see, and one could not depend upon a man of means to fall so deep in love with me as to overlook my abysmal lack of fortune. That sort of thing happens rarely, much as the popular romances would have one believe otherwise.

Most young ladies in my position longed to be married, to set up their own households and enjoy the infinitesimal amount of freedom generally accorded to wives, as opposed to the utter lack thereof mere daughters possess. Neither state of being suited me. I might have been born a woman, but I did not mean to end my days singing for my supper like a canary in a cage.

Long ago, I had concluded that if one were female, one needed a fortune of one's own to achieve any genuine measure of independence. I must have known this instinctively from a very young age. For, while my sister squandered her pin money on ribbons and comfits and my brother frittered away his substantial allowance on whoring and gaming, I hoarded every penny.

A keen entrepreneur, I sold all manner of wares in secret to a pedlar who visited Selby Park from time to time – from trinkets, embroidered handkerchiefs and locks of my ebony hair, to lengths of jewel-coloured silk and Brussels lace salvaged from the trunk of finery my mother had left me. Anything and everything that I could make or to which I might lay claim was converted to lovely, lovely money.

I sold stories, too, and poems and songs, to a publisher in London. These I penned while pretending to write letters to friends and family. Thus, my relations thought me an uncommon keen correspondent, never suspecting my true purpose.

As I grew older, I lent funds to my brother and charged him interest, demanding his gold watch as surety against the debt. To his rage, I once pawned his prized timepiece because he did not repay me. He boxed my ears, but he redeemed the watch himself with his winnings from Newmarket, and he never defaulted again.

When I fell in love with Tom, I thought I'd found a man who valued my opinions and trusted my judgement. Which goes to show that one should never mistake deference for respect.

As with most things, I did not do this loving business by halves. Indeed, I blush to confess my headlong folly. This history ought to be published as a cautionary tale for silly young girls.

By the time I was seventeen, I'd saved quite a lot of money – enough, I decided, with which to run away.

Confident of my invincibility in all things, I expected to make my living from writing once my savings ran out. In the past six months or so, my songs had become popular and my publisher had commissioned several more. Aside from that, I'd heard of the kind of sum an authoress of novels might command and it seemed a fortune to me. I had submitted a manuscript to my publisher and was awaiting his verdict, doubting not at all that his affirmative would be enthusiastic, as it had been in the past.

Anticipating that happy outcome, I grew unforgivably bold. The effort of being submissive and dutiful toward an irrational and difficult parent had always grated on me, but never so harshly as when I could all but taste my freedom.

Papa had beaten me that week for some insubordination or other. I forget the nature of my transgression, but I do recall it was not only my rosy arse that smarted from that encounter. Such a blow to my pride could not be borne. At last I could leave Selby Park without a backward glance.

'Mark me, Tom,' I said as we lay together after a quick and careful tumble – for the welts on my tender parts had not yet healed – 'he'll be sorry when I'm gone.'

'Hmm?' he replied intelligently from the depths of his post-coital haze.

Impatient, I said, 'It's what I've been talking about forever. Leaving here, setting up house together.'

He opened his eyes, roused by my sharp tone. 'Not likely. What would we live on, for a start? No man would hire me if I ran off with you.' He yawned and scratched his shorn scalp. 'I'm taking the deuce of a chance with you as it is.'

'I have funds,' I said, placing a coaxing hand on his chest. 'We won't want for coin, I promise you.'

'Oh, and I suppose you think a few shillings from your pin money will keep us in fine style,' scoffed Tom.

'Rather more than that, thank you very much.' Disentangling myself from his heavy limbs, I went to a bureau on which stood prized possessions from my childhood: a wooden puzzle, a doll with real

Titian hair and sky-blue eyes, my favourite story books, a picture
Lavinia had painted of a kitten I had reared when it was abandoned by
its mother.

And finally, a mahogany box in the shape of our house.

But this was no mere replica, nor a doll's house, nor an ordinary
wooden box. My mother had once used it as a tea caddy, but she'd
given it to me for a plaything when the mixing bowl inside it broke,
thus ruining the set.

Hauling it over to the bed, I set it on the mattress, where it sank
deep into the ticking. At the base of the roof was an ivory escutcheon.
I unlocked it with the small brass key that hung on a fine gold chain
around my neck.

'See?' I tilted the box so he could look inside.

Instead of canisters of tea, the interior of the caddy contained a
mess of golden guineas, pounds, shillings and pence.

Encouraged by Tom's shocked expression, I rushed on. 'We shall
take a little cottage somewhere. I shall write novels, and you . . . Well,
you need not work as a footman any more. You could open your shop.
I know you've dreamed of it, Tom. Just think!'

Slowly, he shook his head, his eyes glittering in the candlelight.
'You never cease to amaze me, Delany Rothwell.'

I took that as a compliment. 'Then you will?'

'Lord love you, no,' he said with a chuckle. 'You'd be ruined, and
for that matter, so would I.'

He didn't take me seriously. No one ever took me seriously.

Hurt and frustration brought me, swift and sudden, to the brink of
tears. To hide my emotion, I scrambled up, turning away to thump the
box down on my dressing table. I snapped the lid shut.

With my back to him, I traced the satinwood stringing on the edges
of my treasure chest and fought to press down a rising sob. Weeping
would only make him less inclined to give my arguments credence.
I loathed the weakness – a typical female one – that overtook me at
such times.

When I had composed myself, I turned back to him and essayed a careless shrug. 'I'll go without you.'

He smiled, held out his hand. 'Come here, love. Let me show you why you don't want to do that.'

The smile that had always charmed me thrilled me no longer. Stubbornness and pride were ever my besetting sins. 'You don't think I could do it.'

He shrugged. 'Young lady like you don't know the first thing about surviving out there in the world.'

'I'll learn. We could do it together, Tom.'

'That's enough of that now,' said he, with an edge to his voice. His handsome face settled into stern lines. 'You're talking fairytales.'

'It's not as if it's the first time I've told you of my plans for us,' I retorted. 'I thought you agreed with me. You always said we'd run away together. You said we'd fly to Gretna Green.'

'Well, I didn't mean it, did I?'

When I stared at him, he put his hands behind his head and heaved a put-upon sigh. 'You fine ladies, you're all the same. If it made you feel better to think we had a future, who was I to gainsay it?'

'So it was all a lie.' My legs started to tremble. 'You've listened to me prattle on about this time after time but you never had the least intention of marrying me.'

'How was I to know you'd go through with such a harebrained scheme?'

Strange the way life can change in an instant. The kaleidoscope shifts and the person you knew and loved shatters, re-forming into someone quite different. I'd trusted Tom enough to let him into my bed: an enormous chance for me to take, and for him, too. I had been fully alive to the consequences if we were caught – or worse, if he got me with child.

My commitment to him had been whole-hearted, if misguided, but he'd only been in it for a bit of fun. What a risk he'd taken for those fleeting pleasures!

'Get out.' I tried to hold my head up, struggling beneath the weight of my utter, irreparable folly.

He stayed put, a glint of resentment beneath the insolent stare. 'Is that an order, Mistress Rothwell?'

I raised my eyebrows. I might have been seventeen and clad only in my shift, but I could achieve an expression of hauteur with the best of them. I said nothing. I didn't need to. I waited, hard-eyed and unblinking, until my lover slunk from the room.

Of course, any fool might guess what happened next.

So much money. Too much temptation. And as we have seen, Tom was not a man given to resisting temptation. The very next day, I discovered both my lover and my savings gone. Only the tea caddy remained, with the key I had so trustingly shown Tom still in the lock.

To have been duped by such a poltroon infuriated me. Instead of a pure, unfettered expression of love, our affair became sordid and low. His betrayal and theft were a fitting punishment for my idiocy. All my plans for the future crumbled to dust. Disconsolate, I no longer had either the wherewithal or the will to escape my looming fate. For a time, even my passion for writing vanished.

My publisher's prompt and robust rejection of my novel set the seal on my misery. Wry observations of county life were too dull, too ordinary, said Mr Gibbs. Gothic romances were the thing these days. He wanted hoary tales of ruined castles and ravished maidens. I burned his letter and damned its writer to hotter fires down below.

Soon after that, in the summer of 1786, Papa died of apoplexy, which was hardly a shock to those who knew the choleric Lord Selby. I was sorry in the way that one is sorry the mad old bull who has gored half the village boys has finally met his end. One rather missed the reliability of his belligerence.

I hardly knew my father. I certainly did not love him. Whether he felt a spark of affection for any of his family is doubtful. He made no provision for his female relations in his will.

In fact, after much listening at keyholes and accidental-on-purpose forays into the midst of adult discussions, Lavinia and I discovered Papa had been indiscriminate in his improvidence. He'd left his heirs not the expected wealth but crushing obligation: an Augean stable-worth of debt that could not be shifted by the labours of Hercules, much less my feckless, pleasure-loving brother.

Montagu Rothwell, now Lord Selby, stormed through the house in a towering fury. He had debts of his own that must take precedence over those left by his thrice-accursed sire. He could not be expected to support his sisters and aunt when his own gaming debts numbered in the thousands.

His few unentailed assets were sold and creditors held in abeyance by the expert advisers my father had the sense to employ. However, it became clear to me that even had I the means to escape, I could not leave my aunt and sister to sink or swim in this mess. I must look after them. As a mere female, I could never hope to earn enough money to support the three of us and help my brother into the bargain. Therefore, I must marry it.

The victim – or rather, the successful candidate – must be some-one with influence as well as wealth, someone who might award my brother a well-paid sinecure, or at least pay him an allowance sufficient to keep the bailiffs at bay. Ideally, he would be a man strong enough to take my brother in hand and shake some sense of his responsibilities into him. However, that last seemed too much to hope for.

I could not abide merely moderate success in anything to which I applied myself. Thus, I resolved to become a husband-hunter extraordinaire.

Also, I began writing again. Mostly, it was a solace and a distrac-tion from impending doom, a way to release my gathering frustration at this latest turn of events.

At least my father's passing allowed me to put my mistake with Tom into perspective. As my rancour towards him faded, I remembered some of the reasons I'd liked him in the first place. All had not been artifice on his part. Perhaps my error had been to expect too much of him. At all events, Tom had taught me a valuable lesson. The only person upon whom I could rely was myself.

My father's imprudence was harder to forgive. It seemed to me that if men insisted on running things, the least they could do was to run them well. Had my late, beloved mama been in charge of our finances, I believe she would have secured the futures of her children before she purchased a large stable of racing horses, for example, or lost £5000 in one sitting at the Cocoa Tree.

Had I been afforded my brother's advantages . . . But why dwell on impossibilities? I could only work with the advantages I, as a young lady of gentle birth and good looks, possessed.

This husband-hunting business was not for the faint of heart.

The devil of it was that we were forced into mourning for my father's passing. Upon finally emerging from our period of quiet and seclusion, however, we had no more idea of how to go about the matter than before. When it came to scaring up eligible men, we could not afford to beat the bushes in the richest coverts.

London and the fashionable resort of Bath were well beyond our means. Papa had offended the entirety of his acquaintance before his demise; aside from the odd local assembly and county matron's ball, we were not invited anywhere we would care to go.

Too proud to batten on our wealthier relations, Aunt Boddington castigated herself for not keeping in touch with influential school chums who might have sponsored me into a higher sphere of society. She castigated me for similar neglect.

Thus, we were restricted to gentlemen from neighbouring estates, and slim pickings there were. Moreover, having disdained the company of these callow sprigs all my life, even I could not achieve a credible *volte face* now that my esteemed sire had cocked up his toes. Unsurprisingly, not one of these gentlemen could stomach taking me to wife. They knew me too well!

'There's no help for it,' I said to Selby. 'You, dear brother, will have to find an heiress for yourself. A plump nabob's fortune should do nicely.'

My brother, in a fit of large-minded generosity (or perhaps to divert attention from his own matrimonial prospects), offered to bring home a selection of his Town cronies for my inspection.

'Lord help me,' I said. 'Has it come to this?'

Aunt Boddington offered me a resigned look. Undoubtedly, it had.

'Very well, dear boy,' she said to Selby. 'Let us see what you can do.'

One finger raised, I admonished, 'Let it be a man who's rich as Croesus, mind, and not clutch-fisted, neither.'

He slanted a scornful glance at me. 'Don't you think I know it?'

'If you were acquainted with someone that full of juice you'd have squeezed him dry already,' I said.

Selby reddened. 'I don't borrow money from my friends.'

No, only from your sister, I thought but did not say. Even I knew better than to provoke my brother when he'd formed a rare good intention. Perforce, I'd summarily denied all applications for monetary assistance since Tom made off with my savings.

I never breathed a word of the theft to my brother, however. Selby might be amazingly selfish, not to mention a cloth-head at managing the estate, but he had a genius for ferreting out dirty little secrets. And unlike my aunt, he held no great faith in my virtue. Had I told him of Tom's actions, he would have surmised at once how Tom came to know the existence and location of my trove.

Had Selby guessed the truth, he would have hunted Tom down and killed him – undoubtedly more incensed by the theft than by the debauch and abandonment of his sister.

I was not fool enough to harbour any great hopes of Selby's fulfilling his promise to net a collection of eligible bachelors and haul his catch home with him. However, beggars could not be choosers and I'd no better plan.

Meanwhile, I had taken up my pen once more in earnest. If Mr Gibbs wanted gothic novels, gothic novels he would have. I could not whip up a husband from thin air, but with nothing more than paper, ink and pen, I *could* create a story that might make my fortune. As a dowry, a few hundred pounds were better than nothing.

With a healthy dose of sceptical disdain, I began a wild, improbable tale, full of ruined castles, spectres, and evil villains who preyed on innocent maids.

As I fell deeper into the story, my prejudice melted away. I discovered a perverse delight in writing such rigmarole, an exhilarating glee that was wholly different from the sober pleasure I derived from my more earnest work.

I despised my heroine, Priscilla, who was both pious and feeble. Priscilla often broke off during a scene of potential ravishment to lecture the villain on morality, when anyone but a fool could see she'd do much better to club him over the head with the nearest heavy object. The hero of the piece, Percy, was unrelentingly good. So good, in fact, that if I had been Priscilla I'd have clubbed him over the head and run away with the villain.

The only character in the entire tale I could bear was the dastardly Jumeaux. I'd formed an unreasonable passion for the wicked, irredeemable blackguard. He had all the best lines of dialogue, and I resolved that when he finally met his grisly end, I would bring him back in my next romance as a ghost.

Lavinia was my first reader, and gratifyingly appreciative. Without the least sense of irony, she felt keenly every passion and fear that blossomed in Priscilla's angelic breast. Lavinia loathed the villain with a white-hot fury and her devotion to poor Percy was deep and true. When she ran out of pages to read, she begged and badgered me for more. She wept for an entire afternoon when the book wound to its mawkish close. All of which augured well for the novel's reception among London society ladies.

After five months, during which my brother still had not returned from London, *The Romance of the Moor* was ready. Now, if only I might convince Mr Gibbs to publish it. For that, I needed to pay the esteemed publisher a visit. Only a meeting in person would do.

Owing to a nature I called persistent but my aunt labeled pigheaded, I had perhaps worn out my welcome with Mr Gibbs on the subject of novels. Upon rising from the malaise occasioned by Tom's desertion, I'd bestirred myself to write to Mr Gibbs, pointing out how wrong he had been to reject my earlier effort. Convinced that my quiet, measured tale would achieve an audience, I had attempted – *ad nauseam* – to convince Mr Gibbs of the same. At length, the publisher wrote me a blunt refusal, telling me he wished to hear not one word more about my infernal novel. I ought to stick to the songs, he said, for they were popular.

When I capitulated, as I thought, and sent him a proposal for a gothic novel, he returned it without even the courtesy of a covering letter. I doubted he'd read so much as the title page.

Clearly, Mr Gibbs needed persuading that I had come around to his point of view, that my latest novel contained every element that would make it a runaway bestseller to rival even Mr Walpole's success. I would go to London with the precious manuscript and put my case to him in person. The burning question: how in Creation was I to get to the metropolis?

The answer came from an unexpected quarter. I received word that Selby had been arrested for unpaid debts and tossed into the Fleet. Would I kindly put up the funds to spring him from the sponging house?

CHAPTER FOUR

The journey to London was accomplished expeditiously. Deaf to my aunt's protests, I insisted upon going in person to secure Selby's freedom.

Despite Tom's depredations on my savings, I still had my mother's pearls – a long, lustrous rope of them – with which I was loath to part. However, I would not be without them for long. I pawned the jewels for a generous sum, comfortable in the knowledge that the trusty broker would keep my necklace by him until quarter-day, when I would bring my brother – at pistol-point, if need be – to redeem it.

I had my own business to transact in Town, or I might have demurred at lending my brother this assistance. As far as I was concerned, Selby could rot in debtors' prison; it might teach him a lesson.

However, my aunt was most insistent he be rescued – not for any sentimental reason, mark you. No, my aunt vowed that anyone held for a prolonged period in such a den of iniquity would come out more hardened in vice than when he'd entered. The Fleet was a free-and-easy establishment. Almost anything could be had in return for coin or a favour in kind. In debtors' prison, one must turn to connivance and double-dealing to thrive. My aunt feared my brother would learn that lesson all too well.

I saw the force of this argument. Our fortunes were, after all, wholly dependent upon Selby's until such time as I married.

I had my own reasons for going to London. I overcame my aunt's objections to this proposal by steadfastly refusing to hand over the requisite funds so that Mr Mathieson, my brother's land agent, might travel to Town and repay the debt.

My aunt, disapproving but defeated, said it was as well my maid, Jane, was a sensible woman – and indeed, Jane had cared for me since birth, first as nurse and later as my personal attendant. If we met with accident or trouble, Aunt instructed us to apply to her brother in Albermarle Street for assistance. Without further argument, Jane and I boarded the mail coach for London.

I discovered Selby more or less comfortably ensconced in rooms outside the prison itself. If one had the means to pay, all manner of things might be secured for the comfort of a young gentleman in my brother's predicament. For a fee, one could live under the prison's regulations, in lodgings within a designated radius of the prison. Living 'Under the Rules' was a luxury Selby could ill afford, however – hence his appeal to his family.

Selby was dicing with his manservant when I presented myself at his door. He sprang up, his expression lightening at the sight of me. I marvelled at this unwonted show of enthusiasm; he must be suffering from his incarceration more than I'd supposed.

Selby's athletic frame was not visibly the worse for his imprisonment. He wore no wig, but his dark hair was curled and tied back in a queue, his jaw close-shaven and his linen well laundered, if recklessly arranged.

'How gratifying to see you well and in spirits, brother,' I said.

Selby's welcoming expression turned to a scowl as the implications of my presence must have dawned. 'What are you doing here? My instructions were to send Mathieson.'

I nodded to our servants to leave us. When the door had closed behind them, I said, 'You should know me better than that. I do not trust anyone with my money but me.'

'Unseemly wench,' my brother muttered.

He held out his hand in a peremptory gesture but I forestalled him. 'What? Did you think I'd bring my savings here and risk being robbed?'

I lied. In my satchel was a bank draft representing the proceeds from pawning my mother's pearls, but if Selby had known that, he'd have wrested the draft from me by force. 'My assistance,' said I, 'comes with two conditions.'

Selby's face twisted and his hand clenched into a fist. 'You little —'

I raised my voice to speak over him. 'First, I wish to know who could have had the temerity to lock you up like this? Surely no ordinary tradesman would have done such a thing.'

His mouth bunched with reluctance, but he bit out the words. 'Not that it is any of your business, but it was Leveson, the coach maker.'

I blinked. 'He must be a very brave soul to risk offending you in such a manner.'

Selby rubbed the side of his nose. Was it actually possible that he looked abashed? 'Boot's on the other foot, actually. I seduced his wife.'

'*Selby!*' Now I understood. Mr Leveson was of the respectable merchant class, and as such, it was a heinous thing indeed for Selby to trifle with his wife. All the more reprehensible because in the ordinary course of things, a coach maker would not dare challenge a lord. Well done, Mr Leveson, I thought, but I kept that sentiment to myself.

'Don't moralise.' Selby paced about the room, bristling with impatience. 'I can't abide moralising females. What's the other condition, damn you?'

I put my satchel on the table and opened it. 'There is a document I require you to sign.'

In the past, I'd refused to lend Selby money without surety. He'd already pawned everything he owned of any value, so this time, his written word must suffice. There was some shame in him, after all. I didn't think his character was so black that he would repudiate the debt if it was all laid out in writing. It was just that Selby tended to remember things as they suited him, and convince himself that disagreeable obligations didn't exist.

Upon reading the document, which charged the commercial rate of interest plus expenses, my brother exploded into an angry tirade that put me in mind of Papa. I stood my ground and stared up at him, a small bulwark against his abusive onslaught, yet my stomach clenched in expectation of violence.

He wound to the end of his fury before too long, however. Possibly, he realised he would not get his money if he harmed me. Possibly, his character was not quite as bad as our father's.

When I was certain his spleen was vented, I pointed to the foot of the document. 'Sign here.'

Another protest rose to his lips but he crushed it between them. With an oath, he sat down at the table, swept the dice box from it and growled at me to bring him his writing desk.

When I had Selby's promise to repay safely tucked in my pocket, I brought out the bank draft. The urge to admonish him not to game it away rose automatically to my tongue, but I suppressed it. Even Selby must take the only sensible course in this case.

His eyes lit up. He took the draft, read it over and slapped it into his palm. 'You're a dashed termagant and a pain in my arse,' he growled. 'Be off with you, now.'

It was all the thanks I would get. I kissed his lean cheek and left.

Energised by the success of that mission, I knocked up our hackney driver and ordered him to make a slight detour on the way back to our accommodation. As I've mentioned, I had my own reasons for coming to Town.

'What will you be at now, Mistress Delany?' Jane huffed and puffed beside me, struggling to keep up with my purposeful pace. 'Your aunt will have my guts for garters, she will.'

'Then don't tell her,' I advised. 'It's hardly the rookeries. Certainly no worse than the Fleet.'

I glanced up at the dome of St. Paul's, ballooning reassuringly above. Indeed, it was but a step from my brother's temporary lodgings to Paternoster Row.

My publisher occupied nondescript premises in this precinct of literary geniuses and newspaper hacks. As I entered the establishment, leaving Jane at the front door, the pungent fumes of ink from the presses filled my head. Discomfited by the stares and curiosity to which the staff subjected me, I took the chair proffered by a young man in shirtsleeves with buck teeth and a pencil tucked behind his ear.

The offices of the publisher reminded me of a counting house, with clerks working on the ground floor. On the mezzanine above was a single enclosed chamber. That, I assumed, was Mr Gibbs's domain.

From that office came the sound of a masculine voice raised in anger, capturing my notice. I could not tell what was said, though trying to make out the words helped to occupy my time.

After a prolonged argument, the door was wrenched open and a large, handsome man in a caped greatcoat and hat erupted from the office, slamming the door behind him. His long stride took him swiftly along the landing and down the steps.

Without knowing what I did, I rose to my feet at his approach. Up close, the fellow was even larger than I had supposed. I caught an impression of dark eyes snapping with anger and impatience. As he moved towards me I saw he was not as conventionally handsome as I'd first thought. His skin was a touch too swarthy, his mouth and nose too large, his eyebrows too emphatic. The deep grooves bracketing his mouth seemed to speak of dissipation.

Yet I had never been so struck by a gentleman's physical presence in my life. There was a scarce-contained energy about him – one might almost say an animal magnetism, but for the fierce intelligence in his gaze. I felt at once that I *must* know this man. That if I did not grasp this opportunity now something vital would be forever lost.

All this passed through my mind in an instant. The man brushed past me on his stormy progression, jostling my arm. He checked, perhaps belatedly registering my sex, then turned back to tip his hat. 'Your pardon, mistress, I'm a clumsy brute.'

The apology was brusque, perfunctory. Ordinarily I would demand he do a better job of it. Yet I was unaccountably tongue-tied. This had never happened to me before.

I managed, 'It's of no consequence, sir.' What a banal thing to say! But at that moment, overhwelmed as I was, I could not summon a better response.

I have the unfortunate habit, according to my aunt, of staring boldly into a gentleman's face when I converse with him instead of modestly lowering my gaze. Thus, I caught the moment the man's air of impatience altered to something both interested and electric.

'A beauty, by God,' he murmured. 'A lady, too. What business have you here?'

The way he spoke was so frank, so direct and without the flowery compliments other men used, that I could not but believe he spoke the simple truth as he saw it.

Before I could answer, the buck-toothed clerk approached and bade me follow him upstairs. With a murmured 'Good afternoon' that did not convey the deep regret I felt at having my encounter with this gentleman cut short, I turned to follow the clerk.

I fancied the large man watched me walk away, mount the stairs and travel along the gallery to Mr Gibbs's door. Though tempted to lean over the balustrade to make sure, I resisted the urge. As I entered at the publisher's behest, I heard the slam of the street door. The man in the greatcoat was gone.

Mr Gibbs's office was a ramshackle place, in need of a good dusting. There was paper everywhere, in mountainous stacks and drifts several feet high. Framed cartoons covered the walls – some political, some positively lewd. In the usual course, I should have liked to inspect them more closely, but today I had other things on my mind.

There was nowhere for me to sit, so I stood, refusing Mr Gibbs's perfunctory offer of his own chair. Still full of my earlier encounter, I gestured behind me. 'Who was that gentleman?'

'Who? Oh. Ah . . .' said Mr Gibbs, removing his spectacles and using one of his shirt-tails to rub at the lenses, before popping them back on his nose again. 'Bit of a hot-head, that young man. But good with words. Very good indeed. Make a fine politician, if only he'd temper his views.'

'Indeed?' I raised my eyebrows, determined not to betray how eager I was to hear more. *His name. Tell me his name.*

But it seemed Mr Gibbs was not in the mood to oblige. Tucking his shirt-tail into his breeches again was a prolonged business. I waited, without prompting him or showing my impatience.

The publisher set aside one stack of papers and drew forth another, scanning the top page. 'I hope you have more songs for me, Miss Rothwell. "The Milk Maid" sold very well indeed. The score was particularly charming.'

'No songs today, Mr Gibbs.' I repressed the urge to drag the conversation back to the greatcoated gentleman. After all, I was no more likely to lay eyes on the man again than I was to fly to the moon: a conclusion that caused me a pang of regret.

I drew a bundle of pages tied with string from my satchel and thumped it onto the desk, causing a cloud of dust to puff up around it.

The publisher was already shaking his head. 'My dear girl —'

'Do but *listen*, Mr Gibbs.' My tone was crisp, as if I addressed a recalcitrant stable boy. 'I have done precisely as you asked. I have written a romance, full of kidnappings and derring-do —'

Uncowed by my admonishment, Mr Gibbs interrupted. 'But I never commissioned you to write a romance, Miss Rothwell.'

I blinked at him. 'You told me that romances are popular. So I wrote this.'

I gestured to the manuscript, wishing I might find a place to stow it among this shambles where it wouldn't be mislaid. I was half afraid that the rest of the piles and piles of paper surrounding it would turn sentient in the night and gobble it up. How did Mr Gibbs find anything in this pigsty?

'I *am* sorry.' Adopting a suave, avuncular manner, the publisher said, 'I don't have room for more novels on my list at the moment, Mistress Rothwell. Always happy to take those charming songs and your little stories. But no more novels, *if* you please.'

He levered himself out of his chair, handed me my manuscript and made a vaguely shepherding motion with his arm. 'Mind your step on the stairs now, won't you? Perkins will see you out.'

Routed by a superior tactician, I discovered myself, in short order, standing on the pavement outside the publishing house. With considerable astonishment, I turned to stare at the door that had closed firmly behind me.

Jane said, 'That didn't go well, I take it.' Her tone was as dry as dust.

Biting the thumb tip of my glove, I thought hard. There must be another way. If only I could persuade Mr Gibbs to read my novel, I was sure he would publish it . . .

Should I approach another publisher? Young as I was, I'd gained considerable experience in submitting to London presses and guessed that I would have far less chance of interesting another house than of persuading Mr Gibbs to accept my point of view.

There did not seem to be any more I could do that afternoon, however. Deflated, I stowed the manuscript back in my satchel. 'Come, Jane.'

Further along Ave Maria Lane, we approached the Chapter Coffee House, a well-known haunt of literary figures of all descriptions.

The rich smell of coffee wafted to my nostrils. Being unsure whether respectable females might freely enter the establishment, I had not intended to go in, but my stomach gave a twinge of longing. We had not eaten since breakfast. A sharp wind was blowing, and a hot cup of the stimulating beverage would be most welcome.

As I paused outside, continuing to debate with myself, I saw a distinctive figure standing in the bow window of the coffee house. As impassioned as he had been in the publisher's office, the dark hot-head who had brushed past me earlier now entertained a group of his peers with some sort of oratory, accompanied by dramatic gestures and much laughter from his companions.

I stopped short. My clutch tightening on my manuscript, I watched the gentleman intently.

Ignoring Jane's tugging on my arm, I said, 'A cup of coffee to warm us, Jane. We'll not be above a few minutes.'

Ensconced at a booth in view of my quarry, I waited for Jane to order our drinks. The strong, rich scent of brewing coffee, the odours of tobacco and dung and damp woollen coats mixed in a satisfying fug. I loved London. The bustle and excitement of it, the variety, the people. If only I could find some rich gentleman to wed, I might make my home here.

The man from the publishing house didn't notice me immediately, wrapped up as he was in whatever tale he recounted to his cronies. But I did not mind. I was happily occupied in watching his decisive gestures, the play of emotion on his emphatic, dark features. This was no enervated aristocrat. This gentleman was so bold, so alive, he held me as entranced as his colleagues. Smiting the table with his fist, he capped off his tale, drawing shouts of laughter from his friends.

With a grin that showed all his teeth, a bright contrast to his swarthy face, he drained his tankard and looked beyond his merry cohort – and saw me. Thrusting his tankard into a friend's hand, he clapped him on the shoulder and strode in my direction.

Without preamble or even a by-your-leave, the man slid into the seat opposite me. 'This cannot be a coincidence. I'd been calling myself a fool for letting you escape, and now Fate has brought you to me.'

Since our encounter in the publishing house I had recovered my composure, but I admit it was an effort to hold onto it when he smiled at me like that.

'Do sit down,' I said, a withering note of irony in my voice. Despite my determination to speak with the fellow, I saw no reason to encourage his lack of deference.

His good humour didn't dim at the implied rebuke. He held my gaze, and lights of brandy danced in those dark eyes. 'Julian Nash.' Without rising, he sketched a bow. 'At your service.'

My sister or aunt would have come over haughty and cold at such behaviour. Secretly, I was pleased by his boldness, for I'd no notion how else I would have contrived speech between us. Even I was not so forward as to approach the fellow in the midst of a rowdy group of men.

In good conscience, I ought not to have been entertaining this stranger, but the manuscript in my satchel burned too brightly in my mind and its recent rejection smarted too much to turn away the opportunity. Or so I told myself at the time. In truth I would not have turned Mr Nash away had he no connection at all to Mr Gibbs. I burned to become better acquainted with him and cursed that my time in London would be so short.

Someone above us cleared her throat with loud portent, startling me. For a moment I'd forgotten about Jane.

'Here you are, Mistress Rothwell.' She set down my coffee with a snap and sidled onto the bench next to me, all bristles and pride.

'I wish to speak with Mr Nash, here, about my novel,' I said. 'We won't be above a moment.'

'Your novel?' Mr Nash's heavy brows lifted a fraction. 'Ah, so *that's* why you were haunting Gibbs's office. I did wonder.' He tilted his head, as if considering me from a new angle. 'A Lady Novelist. Well, well. What did you say your name was?'

I opened my mouth but Jane cut in. 'You, sir, have the honour of addressing Mistress Delany Rothwell.'

'Have I, by Jove?' His brows drew together. 'Selby's daughter?'

'His sister, rather,' I said, impatient of the detour the conversation was taking. 'My father died over a year ago, sir.'

'Ah,' said Nash. 'My condolences, Mistress Rothwell.'

'Thank you. But never mind all that.' I tapped my index finger on the table, calling to order a conversation that was running away from me. 'Mr Gibbs refuses to publish my manuscript.' I managed to control my voice but I expect a hint of my indignation peeped through.

Mr Nash sat back, glowering. 'Nasty habit of his, that.'

I was intrigued. Had Mr Nash's work suffered a similar fate?

'He told me you were a fine writer,' I said. I mimicked Gibbs's staccato speech. 'Good with words. Make a fine politician, if only —'

'If only I wasn't such a firebrand. Yes, I've heard that before,' said Nash.

'He admires you, I think,' I said.

'He has an odd way of showing it.' Nash nodded to a serving maid and ordered another tankard of ale. Then he turned back to me. 'What is it you think I can do for you, exactly?'

'Ask Mr Gibbs to consider my novel.' I clutched my satchel tightly to my chest. 'He refused even to look at it when I visited his office just now.'

Nash seemed about to deny me, but then a gleam I did not quite trust came into his eye. He held out his hand in his abrupt way. 'Give it to me. I'll see what I can do. Can't promise anything, you understand. I'm in Mr Gibbs's black books myself, despite what he might have said to you. But I'll try.'

I thanked him, grateful for his help as much as for the connection the manuscript forged between us, and came away from the interview exhilarated. In that one short meeting I had secured a sponsor for my manuscript and ensured that I would encounter Mr Nash once more.

Yet after that, I did not hear from Mr Nash for over a month. Bitterly, I assumed he'd mocked me in the Chapter Coffee House that day, or that his memory was as volatile as his temper.

However, in this I'd wronged him. Julian did write, eventually, and kept writing long after the question of his helping me with Mr Gibbs became moot. Later, he repudiated our friendship and returned my letters, but I always regarded the summer that followed as the happiest of my life, full of challenge and possibility.

You may see for yourself that there was nothing lover-like in our exchanges. Indeed, the only mawkish note I ever wrote to Julian was the one I did not send. But more of that anon.

Dear Miss Rothwell,

The writer begs leave to inform you that your novel, while complete drivel from start to finish, is well-constructed and highly entertaining drivel. Moreover, it is precisely the sort of drivel that is sure to sell an overabundance of copies sufficient to delight even the stone-cold heart of our mutual friend.

As I explained to you at Chapter's, my standing with Mr Gibbs is in all likelihood considerably lower than yours. I have, however – and in accordance with your most impassioned and able advocacy on your own behalf – entreated the publisher to give said drivel due and proper consideration. What he will do now is anyone's guess. Throw it on the fire, probably, which would be rather a pity.

Nevertheless, I must urge you to consider exercising your singular talents on more serious and vital subjects than mere novels. It would be a pity for a woman of your parts to expend her efforts on drivel alone.

Yours, &c. &c.
Julian Nash

Dear Mr Nash,

I do not recall asking you to read my novel, much less express your opinion on same. I know not on what authority you judge it 'drivel' – I must suppose you know as much about novels as I do about political tracts.

However, I do not seek to quarrel with you on this point. The story is but a means to an end for me. If it sells an overabundance of copies, I shall have all the success I require. Not all of us can afford to be dilettantes!

As for 'serious and vital subjects', how can women form their own opinions on matters of great moment when they are barred from attending the House of Commons to see the debates for themselves? It is the most outrageous thing I ever heard. If you men are serious about encouraging women to take an interest in these matters, why do you then take such pains to exclude us?

No, I shall stick to my 'drivel', as you call it. A packet of nonsense by a woman has far more chance of being read than a parcel of opinions. Yet in all the nonsense, might there not be the essence of truth as the Authoress sees it? You observe how I become cleverly subtle and subversive – at least, I shall become so if my work is ever published.

To that end, I am indeed grateful for your kind offices and remain your most obedient,

Delany Rothwell

Forgive me the indulgence of including these missives between Julian Nash and me. There were many more in this vein. I must suppose they are innocent enough. At the time, I certainly thought them so.

Is it possible to fall in love at first sight? If the poets and playwrights are to be believed, so it must be. But in those days, pragmatic and single-minded as I was, it never occurred to me to be in love with Julian Nash. Similarly, the suspicion he might have formed an attachment to me never entered my head.

This might sound disingenuous in the light of subsequent events. But while I was clever and determined, I did not possess that particular wisdom that comes to a woman of experience.

You will recall that I was accustomed to an uncomplicated sort of male. My father and brothers were strangers to subtlety, and my romance with Tom had scarcely been a meeting of minds. Thus, I had no context for what developed between Julian and me. I thought of him as a colleague of sorts, a rival in wit, a confidant, a particular friend.

Far from losing sight of the need for a wealthy husband, I threw myself with gusto into the business.

From out of the blue, cards began to arrive inviting my aunt and me to this country ball, to that house party. We could not afford Bath or London, but visiting other people's houses and living off their largesse for weeks at a time throughout the summer months suited our budget to perfection. Only Lavinia gained little satisfaction from our sudden burst of popularity. She was not yet 'out' in society, as the saying goes, so she was left behind.

It was with a heady sense of hope and a feeling of undeserved good fortune that I embarked on each pilgrimage. I made a sustained effort to curb my caustic tongue and exert a modicum of charm – enough to cultivate several marriage prospects. The effort of pretence left me drained and disheartened by the end of each sojourn, but where my family's welfare was concerned, it was a small price to pay.

As I discovered much later, no chance was involved in this sudden heightening of our social activity. Of course I had Julian to thank. He was circumspect, however, and never mentioned to me that he'd used his influence to my benefit in this regard.

He and I met often at one party or another. Though I tried not to spend too much time with him – the attentions of such a rake could not add to my desirability as a wife – any event at which he was present could not be dull. The relief and stimulation of his company became like an opiate to me. Only to Julian could I speak my mind. I grew addicted to that small slice of freedom his presence afforded me.

One day, at a picnic in Richmond, I sat alone, temporarily abandoned by my current swain. We'd partaken of hampers of cold chicken and champagne. Now the other members of the party strolled along the river bank or picked wild strawberries on the hillside.

I pretended not to notice the belated arrival of one guest, but I waited for him, blood tingling with anticipation. A large, dark gentleman, carelessly dressed, climbed the hill purposefully towards me. Shading my eyes against the afternoon sun, I watched his approach. The tingle in my blood turned to a pound in my chest, for his dark eyes held a stormy intent.

Why was the mere sight of Julian so exhilarating to me? I knew prettier men with far better claims to gentility. Julian's features were rough-hewn, his nose too large and imposing, his eyebrows too thick and black, his complexion too tanned; in all, he was too much of everything to be called handsome.

And yet . . . And yet, his physical presence commanded my senses, even as his conversation engaged every ounce of my wit.

Julian greeted me abruptly. With his customary lack of patience for niceties, he dropped down beside me on the blanket, stretching his long legs before him.

'I see you are hard at work, Rothwell,' he said, with a sardonic lift of his eyebrow. Unerring, as ever, Julian's hawkish gaze found my latest conquest, a man some ten years my senior, whose pink and white skin had reddened after prolonged exposure to the afternoon sunshine.

Mr Tilton was highly eligible but his mama was likely to prove an insurmountable obstacle to my matrimonial designs. This afternoon, she'd coerced him into helping the docile Miss Colby catch butterflies among the long grasses on the river bank. However, Julian's arrival was not lost on Mr Tilton, who shot a glance spiked with jealousy back at me and my companion. So that was something.

The gentleman need not have concerned himself. I liked Julian Nash better than any other man of my acquaintance, but being a penniless younger son with few prospects, and a womaniser besides, he was no candidate for marriage. By contrast, if I succeeded in weaning Mr Tilton from his mama's teat, he would suit my purposes to perfection.

I shrugged. 'I do what I must.'

'So I've observed,' he said.

His comment rankled. I resented that Julian, of all people, felt at liberty to criticise my husband-hunting when his own existence was largely funded by his elder brother, Lord Nash.

'You're wasting your time with Tilton,' he added, plucking a long stem of grass and twiddling it between forefinger and thumb. 'You'd be better employed writing another novel.'

I did not answer straight away. Despite Julian's efforts, Mr Gibbs had rejected *The Romance of the Moor*, and the terms in which he had given me to understand that I had no talent whatsoever for writing novels were emblazoned on my brain. I might be thick-skinned in other respects, but criticism of my writing seemed to bypass my epidermis altogether and lodge like a poisoned arrow in my flesh. What had begun as a cynical attempt to make money from the latest craze for gothic novels had become an earnest endeavour. While I would never lay claim to genius or literary merit, I was proud of my novel and thought it a good example of its kind.

There was a sudden burn behind my eyes. 'Mr Gibbs has made it clear he wants no novels from me.'

Julian shrugged. 'Why would you let his opinion stop you? There are other publishing houses in London.'

'Yes, I know. I've tried them. They rejected me too.' Once it had become abundantly clear Mr Gibbs would not be moved, I'd written to every other publisher I could find.

In the excitement of having netted a pretty specimen, Mr Tilton appeared to have forgotten me. He was happily engaged in instructing the deliciously helpless Miss Colby in how to decant the butterfly from the net to a bottle. They made quite a picture, their fair heads bent together over their task. Mrs Tilton shot me a look bright with triumph.

Julian was right, blast him. I'd have to set my sights on someone else.

I sighed. 'Do you think you'll ever marry, Mr Nash?'

His gaze was fixed straight ahead. 'Why? Are you offering?' he said lightly.

'Good God, no,' I replied, with more force than tact. 'I merely wondered if you saw marriage in your future. For my part, I cannot imagine it.'

'The truth is, no woman in her right mind would have me,' he said. 'And it has never been my ambition to wed a Bedlamite.'

I laughed, as he'd meant me to, and he changed the subject.

Thus, I freely admit I had no excuse for what came later that afternoon. In a large party *al fresco*, it is a simple thing to escape one's chaperone for a time. Aunt Boddington was gossiping with her cronies and complaining of the heat. Younger members of the party were variously occupied in boating, strawberry picking and exploring the surrounding gardens.

Julian Nash proposed a walk. I ought to have refused.

Yet, drawn by the unaccustomed seriousness in his demeanour, I laid my hand in his outstretched one and let him pull me to my feet. Soon we found ourselves in the cool of a stand of willow trees by the veriest trickle of a stream, out of sight of the rest of the company.

As we strolled, silence hung heavy upon us. Light and shade flitted across Julian's face and shoulders as we moved deeper into the wood. I had tucked my hand into the crook of his arm in a companionable way, but the several rallying, friendly things I thought to utter to break the tension dissolved on my tongue. The feelings that raced through my chest now were anything but companionable.

Unable to bear it, I blurted out, 'Julian?'

He stopped, turning to face me with the most curious expression on his face. Those dark eyes, always so full of humour and wickedness, had softened to a rich warmth that seemed to envelop me.

I'd thought myself safe, walking alone with him. Now, I saw the danger – not because he was a practised and skilful lover, but because my vaunted self-control seemed to have deserted me.

With one fingertip beneath my chin, he tilted my face upward, and I did not resist. His lips, so gentle, brushed my cheekbone, the place behind my ear, my throat where the pulse quickened under his touch.

My hat lifted from my head and went spinning to the ground. A light-headed madness overtook me. The heat of his breath on my skin sent thrills coursing my body like ripples of wind through a field of wheat.

I turned my head and his lips found mine. Ah, but I could have stayed forever in that quiet glade, and damned the world outside. Had Julian laid me down among the mosses then and there, I would not have made a peep of protest.

As if compelled by some higher power, he gave a strangled oath and gripped my shoulders, wrenching us apart. In my turn, I stared up at him, longing for him to take me in his arms again, too proud to beg.

With a heavy frown, he said, 'I love you, Delany Rothwell. God help me, but I do.'

I crashed down to earth and stumbled back apace. 'Julian, you must not!' It came out as an order.

He gave a crack of laughter and shook his head.

Panic seized my wits. This was not supposed to happen. He couldn't love me. I could not love him. How could I be so *stupid* as to fall in love with a man so inconstant, so lacking in every part that made up a respectable husband? Julian Nash was no better than my father, my brother. No better than Tom.

But I could not find the strength to resist when his arms closed about me again. This time, he did not make passionate love to me. He kissed the crown of my head, then rested his chin upon it.

I felt the strong race of his heart and the rumble in his chest when he spoke. 'You are a very managing female, Rothwell, did you know that? But I'm afraid you cannot manage this. What the hell are we going to do?'

I would not confess my feelings for him. In truth, I did not know what they were. Even if I had believed myself in love, I would have refused to countenance such an inconvenient emotion.

No more than I could marry him could Julian Nash afford to take me as a bride. He needed a rich heiress, preferably one with political connections, who would help him rise in Parliament.

It behoved me to nip this in the bud, but I was too full of over-whelming emotion to react with any modicum of intelligence. When one has struggled alone for so long, to be held fast in the embrace of strong masculine arms comes as a blessed relief. One wants with all one's soul to trust in a safe haven – despite all experience and evidence to the contrary.

'Julian, you know I cannot.' I made myself step away from him. 'Take me back to the others.'

'Coward,' he said without heat.

Was I? Perhaps. I believed in male fidelity no more than I believed in fairytales. I'd be a brave fool to trade my family's security for the heady heights and dismal lows that would be my lot if I married Julian.

Besides, he had not asked me to be his wife, had he?

There was a knowing derision in his expression that spurred my pride. 'Good God, Mr Nash, do you think you are the first handsome gentleman I've kissed?'

'No, I think you are uncommonly practised at kissing,' he said with an amused gleam. 'Nevertheless, you kissed me as if your heart was in the business.'

'Then I must be an uncommonly good actress as well.'

He laughed. What an egotist! And yet, as ever, his laughter made me smile ruefully too, and I was obliged to turn away to hide it.

Oh, this was all wrong. Utter madness. Perversely, I wanted him to declare his intentions. I didn't know whether it was a matter of pride or simple yearning, but I longed to hear him ask me to be his wife.

'Run away with me.' He moved to face me, taking my hands in a firm grasp. 'Forget your family. Forget your duty. Be mine.'

I searched his face, so intense, so raw with unconcealed passion that I closed my eyes to block it out.

The crucial words remained unsaid. It came to me now that they never would be spoken. A line of poetry ran through my head: 'Come live with me and be my love . . .'

Shock strangled my breath. I choked out, 'You want me to be your *mistress*?'

His grip tightened. 'Not my mistress, and I would not be your master. We would be lovers. We would be free.'

Had any other man proposed such a thing to me I would have boxed his ears. I knew, however, that Julian meant no disrespect. His mind was on some loftier, more Utopian plane – a paradise where one ignored every basic human need but love.

To a man, such an existence meant freedom. To a woman, it meant nothing more than drudgery and dependence on a man's whims: precisely the life I'd sworn to avoid. No more than I could wrap my imagination around such a concept could I countenance such madness.

I must provide for my family because Selby certainly would not. The only way I could do that was by marrying into a fortune. To run away with a penniless younger son, ruining myself and my sister in the process . . . it was not to be thought of.

'You would write novels all day and we would make love all night,' said Julian, still with that husky note to his voice, still building a dream-house for two.

The timbre of his voice was infinitely alluring, but his words left me cold. When he tired of me, he would leave, free of encumbrances. And I – I would be left with nothing *but* encumbrances. No reputation, no fortune, no family save a gaggle of children I had little means to support. The very notion of it made fear cramp my stomach.

'Well, now that you've had your little fantasy, let me share mine, Julian. A wedding in a church to a rich man, a man wealthy enough to tow my brother out of River Tick and pay my aunt a comfortable pension. A gentleman with sufficient standing to sponsor my sister to an advantageous marriage. *That* is what I want. That is what I must have.

And it happens to be the precise opposite of what you would give me.'
I threw up my hands. 'Good God, you're not even offering marriage!'

'Marriage is only slavery by another name,' said Julian.

I gave a derisive snort, though I knew that in his mind he paid me
a high compliment. He'd spent years debating reason and rights, but I
could not turn my mind upside down in an instant. And even if I could,
the rest of the world would never accommodate such a philosophy.
There was also the niggling, ever-present suspicion that he simply did
not love me enough to make the commitment to marriage. I doubted
that suspicion would ever leave me, no matter how fluently he argued
otherwise.

Drained and disheartened, already mourning our ruined friendship, I said, 'It is impossible, Julian. You must see that.'

His face drained of colour, then hardened to anger. 'You lack the
courage to *live*, Delany Rothwell. That's all I see.' He threw out a hand
in dismissal and I felt it like a blow. 'Go. Sacrifice yourself to your family. See if any of them thanks you for it.'

We were friends no more after that. I tried to be glad.

Now that even the pleasure of Julian's company was denied me, there
was nothing to do but redouble my efforts to find a good husband.

If I did not succeed in putting Julian out of my mind, he, it seemed,
had forgotten me. Not a week passed but my aunt or some other busy-
body regaled me with tales of Mr Nash's wickedness. One would think
he had a mistress for every day of the week, to hear report.

Well, good luck to him. If that was how he chose to behave, I was
well rid of the man.

Moreover, soon enough my continued sociability brought a suitor
most unexpected: Julian Nash's brother. He was a fair man, tall
enough and pleasant to look at – more handsome than his brother if
one made a study of the matter. Yet Richard, with his smooth, quiet

manner, paled in comparison with Julian, who strode through life aflame with passion and purpose.

'My brother has sung your praises high and low, Mistress Rothwell,' Richard murmured, bowing elegantly over my hand. 'I confess my sole purpose in attending the *soirée* this evening was to make your acquaintance.'

He seemed to watch me intently as he spoke. I was well practised at masking my feelings, yet it was an effort to accept the compliment with a smile. 'Indeed, sir? Then I am flattered.'

I'd not seen hide nor hair of Julian for weeks. How odd that he should speak of me to his brother. I'd gathered they weren't on terms of great affection, though I didn't know the particulars. Perhaps Richard thought Julian's intentions were serious and he'd come to inspect me. But his manner held a flirtatious undercurrent that seemed at odds with this premise.

We conversed at length about nothing, the way one does at society events. After half an hour or so, Richard said, 'I wonder, would you and your aunt do me the honour of joining a small dinner party on Thursday next?'

Instinct urged me to refuse, but there was no rational cause to do so. Whatever Richard's motives, I was finished with his brother. Should Julian and I meet at this dinner, it would be as distant acquaintances.

'We should be most happy to accept,' I said.

And so it began: a most correct and assiduous courtship with no display of true feeling on either side. Lord Nash was loverlike in his expressions and gestures but these were executed in a rehearsed manner, almost as if he played a role. I found his attitude inexplicable, yet it suited me. Had he behaved more like a man deep in love, that would have given me pause, for I felt nothing but cordial gratitude toward him. Indeed the pain of parting from Julian occupied the better part of my soul. Civility and duty were all I had left to offer Richard.

Some women might have been pleased by Lord Nash's interest and used one brother to make the other jealous. I had no such aim. In fact, my reluctance to rub salt into Julian's wounds seemed to lend me an unwonted maidenly reserve that proved most attractive to my new beau.

As my aunt was so fond of saying, beggars could not be choosers. I would be a fool indeed to discourage Lord Nash on the basis of his connection with Julian.

Richard – as he begged me to call him – had recently been made something rather important in His Majesty's Government. Precisely what the position was, I'm afraid I could not tell you. It was a sinecure, one of those appointments that commands a large stipend for doing very little, and most coveted by a certain stamp of gentleman. Julian would have disdained to accept such a post, of course.

Richard was quiet and unassuming, except when roused to enthusiasm over any subject to do with classical antiquity. Like many gentlemen, he had completed the Grand Tour in his youth, but he had also lived abroad with a tutor for many of his formative years. He was infatuated with ancient Rome and had recently returned there once more to plunder its treasures for his galleries and gardens. Such a cosmopolitan figure had not often come my way. I thought Lord Nash the epitome of sophistication and good taste.

If Richard did not have the dry wit of his brother, his was by no means a dour personality; if he had not Julian's overabundance of passion for his fellow man nor his zest for life, well, he seemed to have none of his brother's volatility, either. And most importantly, of course, Lord Nash was rich. Among other holdings, there was an estate on the Isle of Wight that had been in the family for generations. The house was a Palladian masterpiece, if the talk was to be believed. Richard had undertaken extensive alterations upon succeeding his father. With the building works complete, it was time for Lord Nash to look about him for a wife. He had settled on me as his choice.

This sudden alteration in my prospects disoriented me. It was as if I'd spent an eternity pushing with all my might against a barred door, only to have it wrenched open from the other side. I did not fall on my face, but I did experience a curious, swooping sensation – and not the pleasant kind – when I read the letter of proposal Lord Nash had addressed to my brother.

'Paltry fellow,' remarked Selby, who despised any man not addicted to gaming and riding to hounds. 'But there's no denying he's a plump little pigeon.' My brother clapped me on the back so hard I staggered. 'Well played, Delany, my girl. Well played.'

He then betook himself to Boodle's to gamble the anticipated bridal settlements away.

'Oh, Delany, how romantic!' exclaimed Lavinia, whose particular talent was to paint life with a rosy glow. 'May I help pick out your bride clothes?'

'Of course. I depend on your opinion.'

I was sincere in this sentiment, for Lavinia had exquisite taste. If I did not enter into her transports over my prospective marriage, at least we might be at one on such vital decisions as how many pairs of clocked stockings would be indispensable to a married woman, and whether the violet silk or the cornflower-blue set off my eyes to better advantage.

For my part, having achieved my ambition, I could not understand the pall my impending marriage cast over me. The growing sense of doom that prevailed upon my spirits seemed to have neither cause nor cure. I did not possess a romantic disposition. I wanted to do my duty by my family. My lot could have been far worse. Lord Nash was neither in his dotage, nor even unattractive; quite the opposite. He seemed mild-mannered, more opaque than his expressive brother; perhaps a little distant. But that was all to the good, wasn't it? I could mould him in whatever way I chose.

'The settlements!' exclaimed Aunt, kissing me warmly. 'My dear, you did it! Lord Nash is bound to be generous, don't you think?'

I puzzled over how much his lordship might pay for the privilege of taking me to wife. I had no dowry to speak of, so only his feelings for me and perhaps our family name weighed in the balance.

But what, indeed, *were* his feelings for me? The common belief was that he'd fallen in love with my beauty, but his manner toward me skated the surface of regard. With such men it is difficult to tell whether they tamp down rampant passions . . . or whether ice lies where those smouldering passions ought to be.

CHAPTER FIVE

Liz

The morning after her arrival, Liz wobbled on her borrowed bike down the path towards the back of the Big House, laptop secured in her backpack. She'd found the ancient pushbike in the shed, as Theo had mentioned. She'd brushed off most of the cobwebs and inflated the tyres a bit with a pump she'd found nearby.

Other than the stationary variety at the gym, she hadn't ridden a bike since she was twelve years old. Tony, with his multi-geared mountain bikes, would have rolled on the floor laughing at the sight of her.

Good thing he wasn't here, then.

'Oh, come on,' she muttered to herself as she veered left when she wanted to go right.

'Look out!'

She nearly collided with Theo, who had emerged from a small outbuilding to her left. He stepped sideways, holding a couple of plants aloft to save them from damage. A shower of potting mix fell on her hair.

'Sorry.' Liz braked and wobbled to a stop, her foot skidding on the gravel path. 'I thought I had the hang of this.'

A glint of amusement sprang into his eyes as he took in the spectacle of her on the bike. 'You're a danger to yourself. You okay?'

With a breathless laugh, she said, 'I'm fine.' But on climbing off she sucked a breath between her teeth and winced, feeling tender in places she'd never felt before.

'What are you doing?' she asked Theo. 'Can I help?'

She leaned her bike against the shed wall. Its bell glinted in the sun. She smelled the earthy scent of things growing – sun-warmed fertiliser, floral and grassy notes, even the faintest sweet whiff of honey.

He shook his head. 'If you're looking for Mrs Jackson, she's gone to the markets.'

He moved past her to dump the pots he was holding into the tray of a small tractor-trailer, alongside a dozen or so others.

'I was looking for you, actually,' said Liz. 'I need to see a man about a library.'

She followed him into the shed, where large bags were stacked on pallets. The pungent, not wholly unpleasant stench of manure filled her nostrils.

With a grunt that might have been an affirmative or a negative, or merely the product of effort, Theo hefted a bag, sidestepped her and walked back out to the trailer.

She tried again. 'Valerie told me the cottage was once owned by a novelist, and that you have a collection of her books. I wondered if I might read them?'

'Don't see why not,' said Theo, walking past her again.

She unslung her backpack and put it down. 'Let me give you a hand with those.'

He shook his head. 'They're too heavy for —'

Liz had already grabbed a bag. Yes, it was heavy, but she could manage without too much strain. She'd loaded it onto the trailer and gone back for another before she saw Theo watching her with an odd expression.

As if embarrassed to be caught looking, he said a quick 'Cheers' before he lifted another couple of bags himself and moved past her.

Liz blew a strand of hair out of her eyes. A woman who could heft horse poo with the best of them was hardly in the same league as someone like Valerie. Probably, Theo had never seen a woman do something that might cause her to break a nail.

They made quick work of the job between them. Cutting off his thanks and the dismissal she knew would follow, Liz said, 'What now?'

He tossed some tools into the trailer. 'Know anything about gardening?'

'Not much, but I can learn.' She jumped into the passenger seat beside him and they set off. 'This is cool,' she said, as they bounced along in the mini tractor-trailer thingy. 'Can I drive?'

He looked at her.

'Maybe another time, then,' she said, suppressing a grin. She was starting to enjoy teasing him. He was a man of few words, but his expressions spoke volumes.

They came to a walled garden – about half an acre in size, she judged – planted with rows and rows of lettuces, cucumbers and garlic, even what looked to be pumpkins and a pear tree into the bargain. In another section, colourful ranks of flowers – dahlias, marigolds, daisies and nasturtiums – grew in bright profusion. Tomato plants heavy with fruit were planted around the perimeter.

The scent of ripening tomato, mingled with the fragrance of herbs that edged the borders, filled Liz with a sense of well-being. For someone who slaved for long hours each day in an office, the idea of working in this paradise held a lot of appeal.

'What can I do?' she said, mentally rolling up her sleeves. Gardening was not her strong point but she was willing to work hard at any menial task Theo assigned her.

Theo didn't explain anything to her, just handed her a small gardening fork and an old pair of gloves that were far too big for her. When he kneeled to weed the beds, she followed suit, getting down to business without asking questions. As they worked, Theo seemed to mellow inch by inch. He even chuckled a couple of times at her jokes.

He glanced at her as he added another weed to the pile. 'You said you're doing some research. What for?'

'I'm . . . writing a novel.' She quashed the nasty sensation that squirmed inside her whenever she lied about her reasons for being there. All she wanted to do was find out the truth; why should she feel guilty about that?

He answered her questions with more enthusiasm than he'd shown her so far, and it wasn't long before she forgot her motives and became interested in the estate's history for its own sake.

'That was Delany, Lady Nash,' said Theo, when she described the court case she'd read about. 'She was the novelist. But the books came later, I think. The scandal you're talking about was hot gossip at the time. It's still a well-known story around these parts.'

The sun climbed high overhead. Liz was sweating – another thing she guessed Valerie would never do. She wiped her forehead with the back of her hand, no doubt smearing her face with dirt in the process.

'Hang on a minute.' Theo went off to the trailer and rummaged around. She returned to her work on the lettuce patch until she felt something plop onto her head.

A slightly mangled straw hat. She squinted up at Theo, and thought once again how tall and broad he was, looming there above her, blotting out the sun. 'Thanks.'

'It's not high fashion, I'm afraid. One of my mother's dogs got to it.'

'As long as it works,' Liz said. 'I know it's silly, but coming from Australia, I didn't think the sun here would bother me. Didn't even consider a hat. Hot today, though.'

They passed a productive morning, and while the work was more physical than she was used to, she took unexpected pleasure in it. She loved being out in the fresh air, with no urgent legal problems to solve, no abusive property developers or builders to soothe, no disputes or complicated negotiations. Just good, honest work, dirt and sweat. The weeding was endless and monotonous, but it was calming too. It allowed her mind to wander, when she wasn't chatting to Theo.

He seemed to expect her to quit at any moment, and would ask her every now and then if she'd had enough. 'You didn't come all the way to the Isle of Wight to lug fertiliser around.'

'Honestly, I'm enjoying it.' She sat back and pulled off her hat to fan herself a little. 'You're helping me with my research. The least I can do is to help you out, too.' She was almost sorry that she had any other purpose in being there.

'Speaking of my research,' she added, 'do you have any pictures of Delany in the house?' She thought of Nick's painting of Delany and wondered how he'd come by it.

'There's quite a famous portrait by George Romney, but my father sold it, along with much of the house's contents, some years ago,' said Theo. 'We have others of her, painted by lesser-known artists, friends and amateurs for the most part. The Romney portrait of her husband Richard is here, though.' He glanced at Liz with a grin. 'He's not half as pretty.'

'I can imagine.' The caricatures and scandal sheets she'd read had not painted Delany's husband in a good light, even if Romney had. 'Tell me about the house itself. Do you love it?'

He shrugged. 'It's a house.'

'Oh, come on,' said Liz, laughing. 'It's a monument. Don't you feel privileged to own it?'

His brows knitted. 'It's not the house or the things in it that interest me as much as the land. Now my father's gone . . .'

She waited for him to go on, but he didn't. Gently she murmured, 'I was sorry to hear about your father. Valerie told me he died only a couple of years ago.'

Theo kept working, his face expressionless. 'We weren't close. I built up a landscaping business in Surrey and he managed Seagrove the way his father and grandfather did before him, right up until the money ran out. We . . . didn't see eye to eye on much. He let me have free rein with the gardens here, though.'

'What about your mother?'

When he didn't immediately respond Liz wondered if she'd over-done it with the questions, but after a pause, he answered. 'She struggled a long time to keep things going. She was tired. Once my father died she was happy to be shot of the place. She lives in St. Tropez.'

'Sounds very chic,' said Liz. 'What about you? Do you still design gardens for other people?'

He dug into the earth to attack a particularly stubborn weed. 'Too much to do around this place. Now I just grow and sell the plants.' He cocked his head. 'Come and I'll show you something.'

She got to her feet, feeling pleasurable aches in seldom-used mus-cles. They climbed back into what she started to think of as the Green Machine, and rattled off in the direction of the sea.

'What's over that way?' She pointed to where she could see a roof of some sort beyond the trees.

'That was the butterfly house, but it's empty now.'

'What a pity.' Another tradition let go?

He shrugged. 'I don't like keeping things in cages.' He waved a vague hand in the direction of the house. 'Beyond the park, we have a butterfly meadow. You can see hundreds of varieties of moths and but-terflies there.'

The idea delighted her. 'Can we go there now?'

From the expression on his face, she saw that she'd overstepped some invisible boundary.

'Sorry, forget it,' she said awkwardly. 'Another time, perhaps.'

They puttered past more outbuildings, greenhouses, and even-tually, a large field inhabited by a flock of uninterested sheep. Real English hedgerows studded with garnet-red clusters of young black-berries recalled beloved story books of Liz's childhood. She wished she'd be here long enough to go berry-picking, but by the time those berries were ripe, she'd be long gone.

Eventually they crossed a public road, then swung sharply right, into a sort of driveway that cut into the cliff. 'Here we are,' said Theo.

He parked the Green Machine and they strolled down a path that led along the terraced cliffside. In contrast to the lush, rolling downs they'd just navigated, the terrain here felt dryer, more like the Queensland outback, or even Greece.

Liz smelled them before she realised what she saw. 'Gum trees?'

Theo squinted up at the tree tops, then smiled at her. 'Welcome home.'

When Theo smiled like that, something made Liz catch her breath. And it wasn't the eucalyptus fumes.

She forced herself to focus as he showed her fluffy banksias and wattle trees covered with clusters of the tiny gold powder puffs, native grasses, acacias, tea trees and red bottlebrush, all planted with an eye for form and colour. They were arranged in a more ordered way than she'd ever seen at home, and the overall effect was stunning, almost sculptural.

She didn't know why the garden gave her such a warm rush of pleasure beyond the aesthetic effect. To her, the plants weren't exotic, but in the rolling green of England they were delightfully unexpected. It was like a little slice of home.

'I'd never imagined you could grow gum trees here.' She wandered about, feathering the velvety tips of the bottlebrush with her fingertips. She picked a eucalyptus leaf, crushed it in her fingers and breathed in the sinus-clearing scent of Australia.

'This is one of the only regions in Britain where you can grow sub-tropical plants outside a greenhouse,' said Theo.

Liz remembered what she'd read about the unique microclimate of the Undercliff. She smiled at him. 'It's amazing, Theo. Brilliant. When did you start this?'

He shoved his hands in his pockets. 'When I came back from my first trip to Australia . . . I must have been about eighteen? Nineteen?'

'You've been to Australia, then?' said Liz. 'Can you say "G'day"?'

'Not even going to attempt it.'

She chuckled.

'We have plants from several places here, with a garden room from each country.' He shrugged. 'It's a hobby but it keeps me interested. We're cultivating different varietals all the time.'

He showed her 'South America', a riot of colour so bright it nearly burned the retinas. A young jacaranda tree had begun to spread its purple canopy overhead. At this point during summer back home, the jacarandas would be over, but this one was only now coming into bloom. Bright pink and orange bougainvilleas rioted upon an enormous trellis that arched over a path bordering a quadrangle of lawn. It was like a cloister made of flowers.

Then they came to the most spectacular potting shed she'd ever seen. 'Oh, this is magic,' Liz said, as she stepped inside.

The tiny glass house had a pitched roof, framed in white. Row upon row of shelves around the walls held orchids in a sunset spectrum of colours, from deepest purple to red, orange, apricot and palest pink. One wall was banked with exotic flowers in every shade of white, from the palest, most translucent alabaster through to cream and gold.

'I try to grow as many as I can out of doors,' said Theo. He pointed out varieties that clung to trees, and some even growing in the ground. 'And of course, there are a few orchids native to the island dotted around the place.'

But Liz's attention was on the specimens inside the glass house. She gazed around her in wonder. 'Which is your favourite? Do you have one?'

Without hesitation, he went over to the white section and his large, dirt-encrusted hand cradled one of the blooms in a feather-light caress. 'This is the dove orchid. See?'

Liz leaned close. 'Oh, yes!' From the heart of the rounded petals emerged a shape that looked like the head and breast of a dove. On the head was the tiniest yellow protrusion, like a beak, and on each side of the breast flared a wing, mottled with a light sprinkle of magenta.

By the end of the 'South America' tour, Liz felt saturated with beauty. It seemed impossible to believe there was more.

She wanted to explore the 'Mediterranean' and 'South Africa' too, but Theo said, 'You must be thirsty. I know I am. Let's go and see if we can rustle up some of Mrs Jackson's lemonade.' He checked his watch. 'Maybe some lunch, too.'

They arrived back at the house grimy, sweat-stained and smelling of manure, but Liz felt sun-kissed and refreshed, and in charity with the world . . . she'd even managed to stop thinking about Tony for a few hours. After dusting off her hands and wiping her feet, she followed Theo inside.

It took her eyes a few moments to adjust to the comparative dimness of the cavernous kitchen. She made out the outlines of a couple of people but at first she couldn't see the details.

'Morning, Maddie.' Theo slung an arm around a dark-haired young girl who looked about ten or eleven years old.

She wrinkled her nose and held him off. 'Dad, you're stinkin'.'

'Cheers, thanks a lot,' he said with a grin. 'Come back here and say that.'

Snorting with laughter, Maddie held up her hands and moved backwards. 'Not gonna happen.'

Dad? That was a surprise. Liz took in the shoulder-length tangle of brown hair, the long spindly legs topped with denim cut-offs and a t-shirt with the Rolling Stones' lolling tongue logo picked out in hot-pink sequins.

Jeez, you think you know someone and they turn out to have a tweenage daughter.

Theo growled and held out his arms like Frankenstein's monster. Maddie ducked back. Her hand flew out and she clipped a pitcher full of sweet peas that sat on the kitchen bench, making it totter and tip.

Liz was closest. Automatically, her hand shot out to steady the pitcher. No harm done.

'Madeline! How many times?' Valerie put down her cup of what looked and smelled like peppermint tea. 'You live in a house full of precious things. You need to stop galumphing about like a baby elephant.'

At the stricken look on Maddie's face, Liz had a sudden urge to dump the pitcher over Valerie's head. Instead, she ignored her and spoke to Maddie, who was turning red and mutinous. 'Hi, there. I'm Liz.'

'Hey.' Green eyes looked up at Liz through a tangle of dark, curly hair. 'I'm Maddie.'

Valerie said, 'Madeline, don't say "Hey". You sound like someone from an American sitcom.'

Mentally, Liz rolled her eyes. Maddie rolled her eyes for real. Liz began to like the kid.

'Val,' said Theo. His tone was quiet but there was a finality about it that shut Valerie's mouth like a trap.

Hmm. Awkward.

From that exchange, Liz guessed that Valerie was not Maddie's mother. That fitted. Liz couldn't imagine a woman like Valerie having a child out of wedlock. Besides, picking on the girl for her clumsiness and her speech in front of a stranger showed lack of experience, if not downright nastiness.

Liz followed Theo's example and went to wash her hands in the butler's pantry. Drying them with the towel he tossed to her, she came back out to the table.

'So, Valerie,' said Liz, 'Theo has been telling me the history of the house. I was wondering if you'd mind if I looked around today.'

'I'm afraid I'm too busy to show you the house this afternoon,' said Valerie, with a meaningful glance at Theo. 'There's a mountain of work to be done for the Open Day.'

Liz tried not to stare pointedly at the copy of *Vogue* that lay open on the kitchen table next to Valerie's tea cup. After all, Valerie was entitled to a break, wasn't she? It was one o'clock. That peppermint tea was probably her lunch.

Valerie remembered to put on her hostess smile. 'Maybe another time.'

Mrs Jackson had come in and caught the tail end of the conversation. 'Why don't you ask Jackson to do it? He used to work here as a guide, after all.'

Tension filled the kitchen, thick as soup. Only the clinking of plates and platters as Mrs Jackson set lunch on the table could be heard.

Maddie said, 'I'll do it.' She snatched up an apple from the fruit bowl on the table. 'Come on.'

'Lunch first,' said Mrs Jackson, wiping her hands on her apron. 'Put the apple back. You can take it with you later.'

Valerie opened her mouth, possibly to object to the tour, or to the apple in case Maddie put sticky fingers on something precious, but she seemed to think better of it.

'Excuse me. I have work to do.' Valerie picked up her tea and her magazine and left.

The kitchen seemed to breathe more easily when she was gone. 'I don't think I'm ever going to get the dirt out from under my fingernails,' Liz said, inspecting them with narrowed eyes. 'I was wearing gloves and everything.'

'Occupational hazard,' said Theo. 'Bit of dirt won't kill you. Come and eat.'

He poured her a tall glass of the home-made lemonade. It was sharp and sweet and cold, the best she'd ever tasted. Their lunch was sandwiches of garden-fresh lettuce and tomato with locally cured ham on freshly baked bread. When you were truly hungry, most food tasted better, but these sandwiches were in a class of their own.

'God, these are good.' She reached over to the platter for a second round and dumped it on her plate. 'Valerie mentioned an open day,' she said to Theo. 'What's that about?'

Another eye roll from Maddie. 'Some dumb idea of Valerie's.'

'No, it's a good idea,' said Theo. 'We're always looking for ways for the house to pay for its upkeep and we've got a few investment prospects in the pipeline. It was Valerie's idea to put on a show of what Seagrove has to offer.'

'Sounds fun,' said Liz. 'What sorts of things is Valerie planning?'

'Flower show, cocktail evening. Some sort of art display. I'm in charge of getting the grounds up to scratch and Fergus, my sister Gemma's bloke, is going to help me with the heavy work.'

Maddie nodded. 'Valerie told Dad they had to play to their strengths.'

'No argument here,' said Theo. 'I just do what I'm told and thank God that in a few weeks it will be over.'

Liz sat back with a sense of repletion that came as much from the morning she'd spent with Theo as from the meal. Maddie, who had waited with visible impatience for Liz to finish, said, 'Ready for the tour?'

Theo glanced from one to the other of them, then collected their plates. 'Hold up. I'll come too. Lead the way, Miss Maddie.'

Liz was a little sorry that Mr Jackson wouldn't be the one to take them through the house; he had a wealth of knowledge he'd taken a lifetime to acquire. However, Maddie proved an informative guide. She showed Liz around the State Rooms with their faded tapestries and antique furniture. Liz's favourite room was the Chinese Parlour, which contained delicate gilt faux bamboo furniture and the most exquisite hand-painted wallpaper she had ever seen: a pale green with pink peonies and golden birds of paradise.

As they toured the house, Liz could see it would need a substantial amount of restoration to return it to the glamour of its eighteenth-century heyday. An entire wing had been sealed off and allowed to fall into ruin. 'But we don't talk about that,' said Maddie in a stage whisper to Liz.

Theo made no comment and Liz avoided meeting his eye. She assumed the rot had set in when the money had run out during his father's stewardship. He must feel the weight of obligation keenly. To arrest the decline and bring the house back to its former glory seemed an immense task to undertake.

At least the Queen's Bedchamber, with its ornate, canopied bed, was still in decent repair. 'Queen Victoria visited Seagrove several times, you know,' said Maddie.

'Yes, Victoria and Albert stayed often on the Isle of Wight at Osborne House,' said Theo. 'You should see it if you get the chance.'

From the mantel, Maddie picked up a small box, exquisitely enameled in vibrant blues and greens, and handed it to Liz. 'She gave this to our ancestor as a thank-you present.'

There were several such artefacts dotted carelessly about the place. The poet Tennyson, another Isle of Wight resident, had been acquainted with a Nash ancestor and given him a book of poetry, thoughtfully inscribed. Various leading lights of earlier times had stayed at Seagrove, for the Isle of Wight had long been a fashionable resort. When the Royal Yacht Squadron was formed, keen sailing enthusiasts flocked to the island to compete in various races.

'Do you sail?' Liz asked Maddie.

The girl shook her head. 'Dad wants to teach me but I get sick.' She made a face. 'I'm glad Cowes Week is over for the year. Dad can't think of anything else until that's done with.'

'So you're the sailor,' Liz said to Theo. That explained the hair, the weathered skin, the salt tang of him.

'Not so much these days,' he said. 'Haven't got the time to race myself, but I crew for a friend when I can.'

Maddie was going to take her up another flight to the bedrooms, but Liz said, 'No, let's not. I wouldn't want to intrude on the family.'

'It's all right,' said Maddie. 'We don't mind, do we, Dad?' She bit her lip. 'As long as you don't care about the mess. I'm afraid I didn't tidy my room this morning.'

When Theo didn't endorse the invitation, Liz said, 'You know what? Rather than the bedrooms, I'd like to see the Gallery. Is that where all the portraits of your ancestors are?'

Maddie snorted. 'What ancestors? You make them sound like they were important.' She led the way. 'We didn't have any war heroes or great statesmen or anything like that, you know. Nothing except a huge *sex* scandal. That's what we're famous for.' She said the word 'sex' as if it had inverted commas around it, and with some relish.

Theo muttered something under his breath.

'I'm sure there's more to your family history than that,' said Liz, trying not to laugh.

They came to a long room that was shrouded in darkness. Maddie ran over to yank open the heavy curtains and sneezed as showers of dust came down.

Bare floorboards creaked beneath their feet as they strolled along, with Maddie providing a running commentary on the different personalities, her soft voice echoing in the cavernous space.

'This one looks like a pirate, don't you think?' she said, pointing to a man in cavalier-style seventeenth-century dress. 'No such luck. He's supposed to have dined with Charles I when the king was incarcerated on the island. That's his only claim to fame.'

She dismissed this early Nash baron with a flick of her hand. 'There has always been a lot of smuggling on the island, you know, but as far as I can tell, our family always kept our noses clean.'

She stopped before a portrait of a mother, father and two sons. It was set against a pastoral backdrop, but quite incongruously, the scene was more reminiscent of the countryside of Italy than of England. The smaller of the two sons rested his hand on the head of a liver and white hound.

'This isn't a Gainsborough,' said Maddie, 'but usually I let people think it is. These are the brothers who fought over that one's wife.' Maddie indicated the taller boy. 'Her name was Delany.'

'Fascinating.' Liz stepped closer. The elder son, whom she took to be Richard, was fair-haired and fine of feature. She suspected it would take the younger, dark little fellow a long time to grow into his nose. Still, there was a directness and fire to the younger boy's gaze that was instantly appealing.

'And here they are again, fully grown,' said Maddie, moving down the Gallery.

Individual portraits this time, just head and shoulders. Ah, yes, the younger boy *had* grown into that nose. A striking fellow, not model-handsome by any means, but virile, capable and strong. Or was she prejudiced by Delany's clear preference?

'Julian Nash,' she murmured, wanting to touch the painting, to trace the bold lines of his face.

She turned to the other portrait. By anyone's standards, Richard was the more handsome of the two. The fair hair of childhood had deepened to dark gold. His features were regular, his eyes a clear, guileless blue.

The artist, George Romney, was a good one – not that she was any judge, but she found both portraits thoroughly arresting. It was not so much the quality of the brushwork as the emotion she sensed in each of the subjects.

Barely suppressed energy, impatience – perhaps at having to sit for the portrait – radiated from Julian. His brother, on the other hand, looked slightly peevish.

'What do you think?' said Theo.

'I don't like him,' she said, pointing to Richard.

'It seems few people did,' said Theo. 'He was practically a hermit by the time he died.'

'He was *murdered*,' said Maddie, with relish.

'See? You do have interesting ancestors,' said Liz. She knew about the murder from Nick. 'And what about Delany, his wife?' she said to Maddie. 'She wrote novels. That's something.'

'No one's ever heard of her books,' said Maddie. 'And no wonder, if you ask me. I've tried reading them. They're boring.'

'Remind me to get them for you,' said Theo. 'But you won't be able to manage them on that bike of yours. I'll run you home when you're finished here.'

They were about to move on when Valerie came in at a brisk clip. With an exasperated sigh, she switched on the electric light and stalked over to yank the heavy curtains closed. 'Honestly!'

Theo said, 'Maddie's been showing Liz our wicked ancestors. Liz is going to put the Nash scandal in her book.'

'God, I'd have thought there'd been enough written about that over the years,' said Valerie in a bored tone. 'It's so tawdry! I'm sure there must be less mucky events in your family history.'

'I find it all fascinating,' said Liz. 'But I suppose you'd be tired of hearing about it if you lived here.'

She'd thought her comment generous, given Valerie's rudeness, but the woman ignored her, saying to Theo, 'I'm having trouble with Mrs Jackson about the catering. You'd better deal with her. She won't hear a word from me.'

She power-walked away, and Liz noticed that the closed look had returned to Theo's face.

Maddie said, '*Dad* —'

'Not now, Mads.' He dug his hands into his pockets and followed in the wake of his fiancée.

Liz watched him go. 'Not one for the social graces, your dad.' She tried not to feel slighted that he hadn't even looked at her before leaving, much less apologised or made excuses. She'd only met him yesterday, for Pete's sake.

'He's got a lot on his mind,' Maddie said. While her explanation was philosophical, the girl looked downcast. She probably didn't get to spend much time with her father unless she helped him garden.

'Liz?' said Maddie.

'Mm?'

'Can I tell you something private?'

Liz tried not to show the utter terror that came over her when Maddie said this. She wasn't going to ask for help with something icky like puberty stuff, was she? Liz had heard that girls were extremely precocious in the sex department these days.

She cleared her throat. 'Sure.'

Maddie beckoned to her to move closer, until she could whisper in her ear. 'I *hate* Valerie.'

Right. What the blazes did Liz say to that?

But Maddie didn't seem to expect her to say anything. She grabbed

Liz's hand and said, 'Come on. Dad might need our help.'

'No, I don't want to interfere,' said Liz, almost tripping on the stairs as Maddie dragged her down them.

She grabbed the bannister, trying to slow their progress. 'Hey, would you like to do something fun? We could play outside.'

'I'm not a little kid,' said Maddie, towing her down another flight.

'You think fun is only for kids?' tried Liz, but she knew she wasn't going to win this one.

Maddie took her through the baize door that led to the butler's pantry, where a phalanx of silver urns and candlesticks and goodness knew what else was laid out.

'Really, Maddie, I don't — Oh, hi.' Liz stopped short, seeing Theo and Mrs Jackson. Her reluctance to get involved fled when she realised the cook's eyes were puffy and wet, and that she was holding a balled-up handkerchief tightly in her fist. 'Hey, what's wrong?'

'Nothing!' Mrs Jackson said unconvincingly. 'Maddie, run away now and take Liz with you, there's a good girl.' She glanced at Liz with an effort at a smile. 'What you must be thinking of us with all this carry-on.'

'Yes, why don't you show Liz the terrace, Maddie?' said Theo.

'Dad, what did you do?' demanded Maddie, ignoring these interventions. The girl rushed over and put her arms around Mrs Jackson. 'Or what did *she* do, I should say.'

'It's all right, lovey.' Mrs Jackson patted her wrist and smiled. 'I'm a silly old woman, that's all.'

'Dad?' said Maddie. She seemed older than her years, and so dignified and disapproving it was almost comical, but not quite.

'Everyone's a bit tense about the Open Day,' said Theo, apparently abandoning any attempt to keep the matter private. 'Mrs Jackson's finding it a strain.'

'I'm not afraid of hard work,' said the woman, firing up. 'I've catered for far bigger affairs than this in the past. It's that —' She clapped her mouth shut.

'The Witch Queen rides again,' said Maddie.

'Maddie.' The weary note in Theo's voice told Liz this wasn't the first time he'd had to referee between the women in his life.

Maddie stuck out her chin. 'She's always the one causing trouble here. What's she done now?'

Liz wanted to know that too. She ought to leave but she hated seeing the cook upset.

Mrs Jackson stared down at her hands, smoothing and pleating her handkerchief. 'It's nothing. I'm just old-fashioned, that's all.'

'In the best possible way,' Liz said, her heart melting along with her intentions to mind her own business. She sat down next to Mrs Jackson and ducked her head to catch the cook's eye. 'Maybe if you tell us what's wrong we can work something out.'

Theo said, 'I don't think —'

He stopped when Liz held up a hand. 'Yes, yes, I know. It's none of my business. But forget all that. Think of me as a trained professional – like a medical doctor, only I'm the doctor of dispute resolution. What's the problem?'

Mrs Jackson blinked rapidly, took a deep breath and let it out in a shaky sigh. 'Valerie says she's going to bring in someone from London to do the cocktail party for the opening day. He specialises in that newfangled diet food. What's it called?'

Liz looked at Theo, whose face had turned to stone.

Maddie answered. 'The tri-colour diet. You can only have foods that are green, red or orange and occur naturally in the wild.'

'Does red include meat?' said Liz. It might not be so bad.

'It does, but Valerie's a vegetarian,' said Maddie.

'Crikey!' said Liz.

The three of them stared at her.

She blinked. 'What?'

'She said it, Dad!' Maddie looked delighted and pointed at Liz. 'She said crikey!'

Liz felt the need to defend herself. 'Yes, but only in an ironic way.'

'Dad said Aussies only say crikey in movies and nature programs. ' Liz raised her eyebrows at Theo.

Theo frowned. 'We're straying from the point. What's this about the catering? I thought you were getting in local staff to help you.'

Mrs Jackson smoothed back her hair and pocketed her handkerchief. 'You've got enough to think about, Theo. Don't mind me. I'll be glad to have the time free for other things.'

'There must be some misunderstanding here,' said Theo. 'I'll speak to Valerie.' With a stern look at Maddie, he left the room.

'Good luck with that,' muttered Maddie.

Mrs Jackson picked up her cloth and rubbed vigorously at a silver butter dish. 'Don't you go badgering your father about it any more, miss. He's got enough on his plate.'

'Hand me the polish, will you?' said Liz, helping herself to a gravy boat and another cloth. 'Can Maddie help too?'

They set to work, and after a pause, Liz said, 'I take it you don't think Theo will talk her out of it.'

Mrs Jackson sent her a cynical look. To her credit, the cook wanted to maintain her stiff upper lip out of loyalty to the family, but Liz could see she was deeply hurt. Most of all, Mrs Jackson clearly feared this was the thin end of the wedge, that she'd be inched out of her job, just as her husband had been.

With Maddie's help, Liz teased out the entire story. By the end, Liz had formed the clear impression that Valerie was the source of most of the troubles at Seagrove.

That made up Liz's mind. Valerie must be dealt with, one way or another.

None of your business, Jones, Liz reminded herself. She wasn't at Seagrove to resolve these people's differences. Objectively, it would be better for Nick if Valerie ruined everything and their Open Day fell in a heap. The worse the event, the less impressed the potential investors, the more likely that Theo would be forced to sell to Nick.

She tried to imagine a cocktail party that was not only vegetarian but also excluded dairy, potato, rice, pastry and bread from the ingredients list. A very drunken one, that was for sure, with only rabbit food to soak up the booze. Or wouldn't wine be allowed either?

Liz still hadn't managed to print all the documents Nick had emailed her, so she decided to tackle Valerie in her office. If she happened to mention the catering while she was there . . .

She knocked on the door, put her head around it and explained her needs.

'Come in.' Valerie pasted on a smile when she saw Liz.

Liz glanced around the office. She didn't know what she'd expected. A bunch of fluffy kitten plates on the walls?

Instead, the office was almost futuristic in design, with an abundance of chrome and glass. Along the windowsill, where she might have expected knick-knacks or a small vase of sweet peas from Theo's marvellous garden, were black slate pots of miniature cacti. The effect was fashionable but far from friendly.

'I, uh, like what you've done with the place,' said Liz.

Valerie followed Liz's gaze. 'Thank you.' She rolled her eyes. 'You should have seen it when I took it over from Theo's mother. Chock-full of Chippendale and chintz. Hardly practical for an office.'

'I hear Theo's mother is in the south of France now,' said Liz. 'Half her luck.'

'I'll say,' said Valerie, reaching behind her desktop computer to unplug the printer cable. 'She couldn't wait to get out of here once Theo's father was gone. Can't say I blame her.'

'Oh?' said Liz. Theo had said something similar. 'She didn't like it here?'

Valerie hooked Liz's laptop up to the printer. 'The upkeep became too much for her. She spent her life struggling to make ends meet while Theo's father refused to change with the times. One can't blame her for wanting to live her own life now that Theo has taken over.'

'No, I suppose not.' Seagrove was not Lady Nash's family home, after all. Still, it must not have made it any easier for Theo to take over without his mother there.

Valerie filled the printer tray with paper while Liz bent over the laptop.

'Sorry, there are a lot of pages,' said Liz, as she cued up her documents. 'Of course, I'll pay.'

'I'll add the cost to your account,' said Valerie without the slightest demurral. She watched as Liz pressed 'print' and the machine purred. 'I hear you worked in the gardens this morning.'

Her tone was less than cordial. Was Valerie jealous? Liz looked down at herself, large-boned, a little overweight, liberally smudged with dirt. She was hardly a threat to Theo's exquisite fiancée.

She shrugged. 'I enjoyed it. It must be great having a job that gets you out into the fresh air all day like that.'

'Frankly, I couldn't imagine anything worse,' said Valerie, inspecting her manicure.

Liz hid her own hands behind her back.

Her nose wrinkling in distaste, Valerie added, 'There's always so much mud in the country. I slip away to London every chance I get.'

That didn't surprise Liz. She wondered why Theo didn't seem to see how badly suited Valerie was to life at Seagrove. She wondered also whether Valerie had a long-term plan that did not involve living here permanently. Perhaps she'd be glad to see the estate sold to Nick, although it was difficult to predict these things. Owning a country estate, no matter how badly in need of capital, added prestige to a noble title.

For the good of the family and of the house, Liz hoped Theo realised how wrong Valerie was for him. She made nothing but trouble as far as Liz could see.

Which brought her back to the original reason for seeking Valerie out: catering for the Open Day. She shrugged. 'I don't mind mud.

Besides, I need the exercise. Things have been hectic lately and I'm out of condition.'

The other woman looked her up and down critically. 'Yes, I can see that.'

Well, she'd asked for that little rabbit-punch to the guts, hadn't she? 'I've been meaning to ask you what your secret is,' Liz added, arranging her features into a guileless expression. 'You look amazing. Is it exercise? Diet? What?'

For the first time, the woman seemed to warm up a little. She smoothed her skirt over her hips. 'It's this brilliant diet. I've been on it three months now and I feel like a new woman.'

No wonder she'd been so aghast when Liz had urged her to try one of Mrs Jackson's cakes. The bliss on Valerie's face at the moment of sugar impact came back to Liz in a flash of memory. Maybe the reason the woman was so uptight was a lack of carbs. And probably a lot of other, more essential nutrients too.

Liz sighed. 'I've tried every diet out there but I can never stick to them. I have zero willpower. What's this one you're on now?'

Valerie needed no further encouragement. Liz had yet to see the woman wax so enthusiastic about anything. If she'd ever looked at Theo with a glow of adoration on her face half as potent as when she rhapsodised about the tri-colour diet, it was no wonder he'd fallen for her.

Valerie spread her hands. 'It's so simple. All you have to remember is you can only eat foods that are green, red, and orange.'

'I'd call that the M&M diet,' said Liz.

Valerie's pencilled eyebrows twitched together. 'Oh, no! You can't have sweets. Nothing processed or refined. It's eating the way nature intended.'

'Sounds fantastic,' Liz lied. 'Pity I don't have your willpower.'

The printer trilled a warning and Valerie set aside the printed pages, then fed in more blank paper. 'When you taste Raoul's cuisine you will not need willpower,' said Valerie. 'That's why I want him to cook for everyone at the Open Day. He has his own restaurant in Soho but he's agreed to come down especially for us. Once they experience how tasty such healthy food can be, they'll be converted.'

Now Liz got it. This Raoul guy was the messiah and Valerie his most ardent disciple. She wondered if Raoul looked as hunky as his romance-hero name suggested. Could Valerie have fallen for the man as well as his meals?

Would an appeal to Valerie's compassion be a waste of breath? 'Seems like Mrs Jackson might need some convincing,'

'Well, I'm sorry to be blunt, but Mrs Jackson has no say in it.' Valerie leaned back against her desk, tapping her beige acrylic fingernail on its gleaming surface, and Liz sensed her time was almost up.

She changed tack. 'You should bring Raoul down here for a trial. Do a tasting. Convince everyone it'll work.' If Theo saw for himself how truly awful the real thing was going to be, he would have no choice but to tell Valerie to let Mrs Jackson handle the catering.

Valerie tilted her head and frowned. 'I'd love to, but I don't think he'd agree —'

'I bet you're paying him a motza for this function,' said Liz. 'London chefs don't come cheap, I'm guessing. Make him earn his keep.' She shrugged. 'Could you tempt him with the local produce, maybe? Set up a tour of the best eateries the Isle of Wight has to offer? Isn't there at least one restaurant with a Michelin star? And I hear the Beach Shack does a mean crab pastie.'

That last was going too far, perhaps, because Valerie looked as if she smelled something unpleasant at the mention of such commonplace cuisine. Well, she'd leave Valerie to mull it over and hope the woman followed her natural inclination to see more of Raoul. By having a trial beforehand, Liz hoped they could nip Valerie's catering plans for the Open Day in the bud. When Theo had to suffer through Raoul's rabbit food he'd soon see they couldn't inflict it on their guests.

The printer finally whirred to a stop.

'Thanks for this,' said Liz, hefting her huge stack of pages. 'I owe you.' She hesitated. 'Listen, I can't diet but I like to run. Do you have a good circuit you could suggest? Maybe . . . six kilometres or thereabouts? Nothing too steep. I'm not up to scaling cliffs or anything.'

'There are plenty of lovely walking trails around here you could try.' Valerie went over to her desk and slid one of the drawers open. 'Here.'

She gave Liz a brochure full of maps and took some time to help orient her, given that Liz was directionally challenged and all. Valerie went to a fair bit of trouble over the business. Then she insisted on getting Liz a couple of document wallets to put her stacks of printing in.

Maybe the woman wasn't so bad. She was blinkered about this diet and had a little crush on Raoul the chef, that was all. In Liz's experience, infatuations with diets were like infatuations with men – both died quick deaths after the novelty wore off.

They should all give Theo some credit. He wasn't stupid. He'd seen enough in Valerie to ask her to marry him, hadn't he? Maybe there was a great woman underneath that uptight façade.

As Liz thanked Valerie and turned to go, Valerie's mobile phone played a classical tune. She slid it out of her jacket pocket, read the screen and blushed.

Liz accelerated out the door, but not before she heard the register of Valerie's voice go down an octave and turn husky.

The burst of charity Liz had felt toward the woman vanished. Whoever that was on the other end of the line, Liz would bet it wasn't Theo.

CHAPTER SIX

Liz was so glad to see her bed that evening she could have wept. She wasted no time in showering and changing into her pyjamas, but the long, luxurious wash invigorated her, rather than the reverse. It was still early, so she decided to do some reading until she dropped off to sleep.

She sat cross-legged on her bed with the stack of pages Valerie had printed for her, categorising them and arranging them into smaller piles.

There was a lot to go through. Pages and pages on the history of the estate since before it came into the Nash family, newspaper clippings, biographies, articles, maps, Nick's genealogical chart.

She trawled through them, skimming the first few paragraphs of each one, waiting for something in particular to catch her eye.

She decided to begin with the potted history of the house, a few pages in an old guide book that Nick – or rather MJ – had scanned in.

Seagrove had begun life as a priory, and was later awarded to Percy Nash along with the title of baron upon the dissolution of the monasteries under Henry VIII. Percy had proceeded to knock down the unpretentious building on the site and replace it with a larger dwelling that presumably better befitted his station.

Two centuries later, during the time of Richard and Julian Nash's father, that monument to Percy's pride had been considered inadequate in its turn, and a sandstone house in the Palladian style had replaced the former Tudor mansion.

When the estate came into Richard's hands, he continued his father's work, adding two more wings to the house and employing Capability Brown to create a carefully naturalised landscape surrounding it. As Delany mentioned in her memoirs, Richard had visited the Continent at about that time, returning with many exotic plants, artefacts and treasures.

In addition to the improvements at Seagrove, Richard had set to work on Marine Cottage, which was located on the Undercliff at the edge of his estate. He filled the surrounding land with fake temples, pavilions, and statuary from ancient Rome, not to mention gardens bursting with exotic plants. Liz was sorry that the only pictures of this extraordinary sounding place were black and white sketches from a guide book of the period.

As Theo had explained to Liz that morning, the Undercliff was warmed by the Gulf Stream, so it had a microclimate more akin to the Mediterranean than frigid old England. This emboldened Richard to plant a vineyard next to Marine Cottage, though by all accounts the vines had failed to produce good grapes and had been dug up soon after his death.

Liz consulted a couple of different maps and tried to pinpoint exactly where the vineyard would have been. Pretty much where Theo's exotic gardens were now, she decided. Apparently, little remained of the rest of the former baron's retreat and the land had been sold off long ago. That was a shame. It sounded like an extraordinary place.

Well, enough of Lord Nash. Liz decided to dive into Delany's memoirs again.

Absorbed in deciphering a particularly obscure phrase, she jumped when she heard a key rattle in the lock and the front door creak open.

'Hello?' A female voice, light and unthreatening, called from downstairs.

Liz blew out a relieved breath and waited for her heart to stop pounding. She scrambled out of bed and hurried to the landing. A slim, dark-haired young woman with an expensive leather holdall slung over her shoulder was coming up the stairs.

'Hello,' said Liz. 'Uh, sorry, what . . .'

The woman looked up, her gamine features breaking into a grin. 'You look like you've seen a ghost. Sorry! I ought to have rung first or something. Valerie did mention someone was staying here. I'm Gemma Nash.'

Liz took the hand the woman offered and shook it, still bemused. 'So you're Theo's sister?'

Gemma made a pistol with her finger and thumb and winked. 'Got it in one. This is my cottage.'

She moved past Liz and dumped her bags on the landing at the top of the stairs.

Liz followed Gemma back down to the living room. 'If this is your cottage, should I be here?' She said it with a sinking heart. She was so tired that she couldn't even contemplate moving all her stuff.

Gemma said, 'Don't worry, I'm not here to throw you out. Valerie likes to think the cottage is part of her domain. She also likes to keep me under her thumb, so she usually tries to make me stay at the house.'

Theo's sister looked more French than English, with that glossy cap of black hair and the effortless style that came so naturally to Parisians. For the first time, Liz became conscious of her pyjamas. Hot pink with cartoon dachshunds on them. Cute, but hardly the pinnacle of sophistication.

Damn it, she needed wine.

As Liz found the Spanish red that Mrs Jackson had included in the welcome basket, Gemma sat down on the overstuffed chintz sofa, curling her feet under her. 'What made you choose this place? We're a bit out of the way here . . . Is that syrah? I'd love some.'

Liz poured two glasses and said something vague about solitude. Lying to Valerie was one thing, but she didn't like being untruthful with Gemma. However, she supposed she ought to keep her story straight. 'I'm, uh, writing a book.'

'Really?' said Gemma, taking the glass Liz handed her. 'How thrilling.'

'Not so much. There's tons of research,' she said vaguely. 'What about you?' she asked, trying to change the subject. 'I take it you don't live here all the time?'

Liz sat down opposite Gemma and sipped her wine. That was better. She steadfastly refused to drink alone, so Gemma's arrival was a godsend. There were some people you relaxed with immediately. Theo's sister was one of them.

'I'm based in London. Interior design,' said Gemma. 'I come down for holidays and for weekends when I can. The Witch Queen wants me to teach design classes at Seagrove.' Gemma rolled her eyes. 'She'd like to turn the house into a bloody finishing school.'

'I take it you're not a fan of your future sister-in-law?' said Liz, thinking Maddie must have borrowed Valerie's nickname from her aunt.

Gemma shrugged. 'She gets up my nose, but I'd put up with her gladly if I thought she was good for Theo, poor darling. Theo, I mean, not the WQ.'

Another sip of wine and a sudden wave of tiredness swept over Liz. 'You and your brother are close, then?' she said, smothering a yawn.

'Oh, yes,' said Gemma. 'Well, we've never lived in each other's pockets, but when Dad died, I thought . . .' Her gaze seemed to lose focus and her expression darkened. She shook herself. 'Anyway, I've saved some money and I'm planning to do something with this cottage. Tart it up a bit so I can charge decent rent. And it will be somewhere nice for my man Fergus and me to stay in the off-season.'

Liz hadn't given much thought to how much Nick must be paying for her to stay here. 'That sounds like a great idea.'

As she listened to Gemma's plans to knock down walls and open up the downstairs rooms, Liz thought of her own house – hers and Tony's – and the renovation they would not be doing now. She must call the builders and the other contractors, see if she could put everything on hold. Whatever happened, she was going to lose a lot of money unless they went through with it.

'Do you need any help?' Liz asked, shaking off her gloom. 'I have a bit of experience with planning renovations myself.'

Gemma stretched out her slim legs. 'That's brilliant of you to offer but I couldn't ask you to do that.'

'Honestly, I'd enjoy it,' Liz said. She hesitated. 'You know I'm staying here for the next month at least, don't you?'

'No, I didn't.' Gemma bit her thumb. 'Fergus was going to do the work on weekends. He was supposed to be coming down next Friday to get started. Ugh, I could *murder* Valerie.' Then she caught sight of Liz and said, 'Sorry. You do know I don't blame you, don't you?'

'Don't apologise. I understand,' said Liz, thinking that in Gemma's shoes, she would have murdered Valerie long ago. 'If you can get me a room at the Big House, I'll gladly get out of your hair. But seriously, I'd love to help with the renovation and I don't mind living with the building work. It'll give me something to do while I'm here.' She added quickly, 'Other than research, that is.'

It would be a blessing to be so tired at the end of the day that she could sleep through the night without waking up to worries over the future, not to mention torturous self-recriminations about Tony. And she couldn't work on Nick's problem all the time.

Gemma considered her, seeming to weigh up how genuine her offer was. 'Okay,' she said, 'Thanks. God knows we could use another pair of hands. You can stay in the cottage as long as you don't mind a bit of noise on the weekends, and then when it comes time for us to move out I'll *make* Valerie give you a room.'

Liz yawned so widely her jaw gave a loud crack.

Gemma chuckled. 'Are you terrifically jet lagged? How long was the flight from Australia?'

'Too long,' said Liz, finishing her wine. 'I hate to be rude, but I think I'll have to crash. Which bedroom do you usually sleep in? I can move my stuff.'

'Don't be silly,' said Gemma. 'It's not like there aren't more than enough rooms to choose from, and you are paying for the cottage, after all.' She made a face. 'I'm the one who ought to go.'

There was something vulnerable about Gemma that tugged at Liz. 'No, I'm glad you're here.' And not only because she wanted someone to drink with. 'It's a bit lonely here on your own, isn't it?'

She dragged herself to a standing position and swayed a little. Whoa. One glass of wine on top of jet lag. She'd sleep well tonight.

She waved a hand. 'There are supplies in the kitchen. Help yourself.'

'Thanks,' Gemma said. 'I will.'

Lord Kenyon

When the Lord Chief Justice invited Mr Garrow to open the case for the plaintiff, the barrister did not immediately rise to his feet. In fact, he stayed seated so long that Lord Kenyon began to fear the young barrister was suffering from a nervous affliction.

Ten minutes earlier, counsel for the plaintiff had possessed all the vitality and healthful complexion of youth. Now, he sat stricken and pale, staring down at his papers as if in defeat. His hands gathered his materials, sorted them, then let them fall.

The pause lengthened. The spectators, at first curious, now shifted restlessly in their seats. The court room began to hum with low conversation. With a deep sigh, Mr Garrow drew his handkerchief from his pocket and mopped his brow.

'Mr Garrow?' prompted Kenyon. 'Are you well, sir?'

A small shake of the head seemed to bring the advocate to his senses. With slow, effortful deliberation, he placed his hands upon the baize-covered table before him and rose to his feet.

'Your lordship, I apologise. I . . .' He paused here to pinch the bridge of his nose, then he flung out his free hand in an elegant gesture of helplessness. 'The circumstances of this case are such that I find myself wholly overpowered. And yet, it behoves me to . . . Indeed, I absolutely must . . .'

The ordinarily fluent counsel was at a loss for words.

At once, Lord Kenyon understood. A gentleman such as Mr Garrow found it difficult in the extreme to lay out the salacious facts of a case such as this at any time. But to be obliged to do so in the presence of the lady who was intimately concerned in the prosecution . . . why, his every sensibility must be offended.

In a soothing tone, Kenyon said, 'Mr Garrow, your scruples do you credit. But I would remind you that your duty is to the plaintiff and to this court. Pray, proceed.'

The barrister cleared his throat. 'Yes, my lord.'

Again Mr Garrow mopped his brow. Pocketing his handkerchief, he put up both hands to make a minute adjustment to his wig. Finally, he set his shoulders, as if to steel himself to carry out this most unpalatable task. The room had grown quiet with anticipation.

When Garrow spoke, it was with a gentle resonance, almost a diffidence, quite at odds with his earlier forceful objections to Lady Nash's attendance.

'In the course of my career – nay, in the entire course of my existence,' said Mr Garrow, 'I have never encountered circumstances that have filled me with such embarrassment and distress as those I must relate to you today. That I am wholly undone by the anguish the plaintiff has suffered as a consequence of these events must be evident to all. That I must lay these facts before the court completely and faithfully, omitting not the smallest detail, fills me with repugnance. Nevertheless, as his lordship so rightly pointed out, my disgust must not prevent me from carrying out my duty to the plaintiff and to the good gentlemen of the jury.'

As Garrow regarded these good gentlemen, something of the usual spark of animation returned to his heavy-lidded eyes.

'First, I must relate who the parties are, both individually and as members of the community. Most regrettably, I must also inform you who these parties are *as related to one another*.'

Lord Kenyon glanced at the jury, who were all attention. All apart from one dandified-looking fellow who was busy picking at his finger-nails with a pen knife.

It took some moments for the judge to catch the man's eye. Under Kenyon's glower, the juror nearly stabbed himself in his hurry to put the knife away.

Smoothing down his robes, Garrow continued, and the more he spoke, the greater power and vigour his speech attained. 'The plaintiff is a nobleman of ancient pedigree in the southern part of His Majesty's dominions, the owner of a considerable estate called Seagrove, on the Isle of Wight.'

Mr Garrow laid his hand on his breast. 'Not having the inestimable honour of close acquaintance with the plaintiff, I must rely on his friend the Earl of Marston's encomia. Lord Marston said of the plaintiff: "He is such a gentleman as any father, having a daughter, might welcome with open arms as a husband for her. Once wed, he may never again concern himself for his daughter's happiness, for no more tender, affectionate and indulgent husband could be found."'

Kenyon could not help it. His gaze sought Lady Nash.

She no longer bowed her head in compliance. Her expression was one of polite and slightly pitying attentiveness, as if she were a guest in a drawing room after dinner, suffering through a young lady's inept performance on the harp.

It struck Kenyon that, due to the way she was positioned at the front of the room and to the angle of her hat, only he and the jury had the privilege of seeing Lady Nash's face.

Was this by design?

But, having forbidden her to draw attention to herself, Kenyon decided he must not allow the lady to distract *him*. He returned his gaze to Garrow.

'The plaintiff and Lady Nash married in 1787.' Here Mr Garrow tendered the marriage certificate into evidence, and continued. 'The plaintiff's devotion to his wife was such that he took the most extraordinary pains to please her, providing every ease, comfort and, one must say, luxury any young wife might desire.

'Indeed, it is no wonder at the plaintiff's captivation. He married Lady Nash when she was eighteen and possessed of every charm to enchant, every ornament and accomplishment that could contribute to the happiness of her husband. She is the daughter of Lord Selby, late of Derbyshire.'

Kenyon remembered some talk at the time of the marriage. The match had been far beyond what a young lady in Delany Rothwell's circumstances could have expected. True, she was a beauty and descended from a family of more ancient lineage than her husband's, but she had no portion to speak of. Lord Nash could have looked for a much richer bride.

Clearly the man had fallen deep in love with his wife.

Margaret

Bath, 1787

Margaret Smith prided herself on being a model lady's companion. She was good-tempered, quiet and helpful, anticipating her employer's needs without fuss or fanfare. She never lost her calm demeanour, even when Lady Verena was at her most caustic and difficult.

This morning, Margaret could have wrung her employer's neck.

They sat at the breakfast table in a rented house in Great Pulteney Street, Lady Verena perusing a letter and Margaret pretending to eat a buttered roll. Having recognised the handwriting on that letter, Margaret was agog to know what it contained. Lady Verena was in no hurry to tell her.

Her employer was an ageing beauty of some fifty years, with iron-grey hair and dark, dramatic eyes. Lady Verena's youth had been rife with intrigue, her middle years scarcely less so. The result had been an illness from which she would never recover.

For the moment, the disease was in abeyance, but with syphilis, it was only a matter of time. Margaret considered it a judgement upon Lady Verena for her licentiousness.

She could wait no longer. 'What news from London, ma'am?'

'Hmph!' came the reply. Lady Verena stowed the letter in the pocket of her cherry and white striped gown and drank her coffee. Pug sat on the chair next to his mistress, perched on a stack of cushions. He gobbled down all the bacon in his silver dish, smacked his chops and whined for more.

Lady Verena spoke nonsense to him in her harsh, deep voice, while she fed him slivers of ham from her plate. Pug's little pink tongue slobbered all over the dowager's fingers, licking up every last morsel.

Dirty, ugly creature. Margaret could never understand why her fellow countrymen were so mad for dogs. Nor how anyone who called herself a lady could feed such an overgrown rat tidbits at her table.

She tried again. 'My lady —'

'Fetch my shawl, Margaret. There's a draft in here.'

Pressing her lips together, Margaret rose.

'Never mind. Help me upstairs to change. We'll go to the Pump Room.'

'Yes, my lady.'

In the Pump Room, glasses of evil-smelling water from the spring beneath were dispensed to the populace as a cure for all manner of aches and ills. The epicentre of fashionable life in Bath, it was where

Margaret had first insinuated herself into Lady Verena's good graces, abandoning her former, less exalted mistress without a qualm.

Lady Verena might be rude and peremptory, and shockingly loose in her morals, but she was rich and she was noble. More to the point, she had a son. Two of them, in fact.

The Pump Room teemed with invalids, their attendants, and other persons who came for the gossip rather than the cure. Lady Verena held her lorgnette up to her eyes, scrutinising the assembly. 'Ah. There is Miss Lang.'

They moved to a set of chairs by one of the tall, arched windows, where a plump, bright-eyed lady sat twittering to her friends. Leaning heavily on her ebony walking stick, Lady Verena lowered herself to the vacant seat on Miss Lang's left and proceeded to monopolise her friend. The other ladies of the group drifted away, perhaps thankful to be spared the lashing of Lady Verena's sharp tongue.

Margaret perched on a chair on Lady Verena's other side. Ordinarily, she might take a turn about the room to greet other acquaintances, but today, she was on tenterhooks to hear the contents of that letter. She trusted Lady Verena would confide in her friend.

After covering a wide range of topics, from last night's concert to Miss Lang's bunions, finally Lady Verena said, 'I had a letter from Richard this morning.' She dug into the pocket of her skirts.

Margaret's chest tightened in anticipation.

'Fetch me a glass of that putrid stuff, Margaret,' Lady Verena said to her, waving the letter in the direction of the pump.

Margaret could have screamed. 'But my lady,' she said, 'you swore off drinking the waters on our last visit, don't you recall?'

The dowager's eyes glinted. 'Don't contradict me, girl. Just do it.'

Reluctant, but unable to think of a reason to remain, Margaret hurried over to the booth from which glasses of Bath's famous mineral waters were dispensed.

First she was obliged to queue behind several other patrons. Then, who must accost her but Mr Wallader, a gentleman she had once cultivated with matrimonial intent. Now she had her eye on a much bigger prize.

She got rid of him then joined the queue again, and took a glass from the smiling maid at the pump. The water was warm and slightly cloudy, and gave off a faint smell of sulphur. She was glad she did not have to drink it.

Margaret sped back to her employer, her shoes clip-clipping over the wooden floorboards. What if she missed talk of him? What if she must wait until the next time he wrote? She couldn't bear it.

But no. The two ladies still pored over the letter, grey heads together, the edges of their bonnets touching.

'I do trust he will choose wisely,' Miss Lang was saying. 'Will he not take your advice, ma'am?'

'He?' Lady Verena snorted. 'Good God, no! If I recommended a girl for Richard, he would be sure to spurn her. No, he'll find a bride on his own.'

Margaret almost dropped the glass.

'Such a handsome, well-set-up young man,' said Miss Lang. 'So eligible! To be sure, the young ladies will be on the scramble for him, will they not?'

'I daresay,' said Lady Verena, very dry.

She turned her piercing glance to Margaret. 'What think you, miss? Is my son a good catch?'

'Lord Nash is everything that is amiable,' said Margaret, through cold lips. Her hand shook as she gave the glass of pump water to Lady Verena.

'Take care, you'll spill it,' snapped Lady Verena. 'What ails you, girl?'

Margaret blushed with mortification.

'May we expect to see Lord Nash while you are in Bath, Verena?' said Miss Lang.

Lady Verena sipped her water and grimaced. 'I doubt I'll set eyes on him for months.' A gleam of malevolence sparked in her thin smile. 'It will be interesting to see whom he brings home with him. Won't it, Miss Smith?'

Delany, Lady Nash

Richard and I were married quietly, without fuss or fanfare, in the drawing room at my uncle's house. Julian did not attend our wedding, making his excuses to Richard and leaving London for the country. Unreasonably, I felt his absence as a desertion.

I had broken the news of my marriage to Julian in person. I'd believed I owed him that. Now, how I wished I had not, for the pain in his white-lipped face still haunted me. His very silence on the subject had reproached me more than rantings and ravings could have done.

I played my part in the marriage ceremony and the breakfast afterward in a state of numbness. My wedding night was upon me before I comprehended what I'd done. On that night, the irrevocable endlessness of marriage, the inescapable, awful subjugation of my role as wife, fell upon my spirit with the weight of a dead man.

My husband had a friend staying with him in London, a Mr Carver, one of those fawning creatures who batten upon wealthy men. Far from making a tactful exit so that we might enjoy our honeymoon in private, Mr Carver was to remain in the house until our departure for the family estate on the Isle of Wight.

I did not like this man. He was a renowned womaniser and gamester with a slack mouth and a habit of staring fixedly at ladies' bosoms through his quizzing glass. Even my brother had warned me to discourage my husband's acquaintance with the fellow. If Selby disapproved of the man, he must be very bad indeed.

'Can we not dispense with Mr Carver's company tonight, my dear?' I said to Richard with what I hoped was an enchanting smile, as we awaited supper in our private sitting room. 'Indeed, I should think he'd find other accommodation altogether. We are newlyweds, after all.'

I'd not intended to speak upon the subject so bluntly, nor so soon, but circumstances forced my hand. When I entered the sitting room that evening, I found three places laid at table. Our intimate supper for two was to become something quite different, it seemed. I was not yet alarmed, merely exasperated at this evidence of Richard's gaucheness. Such a total lack of sensibility puzzled me. He'd behaved with perfect gallantry throughout our courtship.

Richard took my hand and held it, tracing the palm with his thumb. Frowning a little, he stared down at our hands for a moment, then his blue gaze flicked up to fix on mine. 'I trust you will not forever be questioning my judgement, Delany.'

It was a mild reproof, but a reproof nonetheless. 'I do not question your judgement,' I said, easing my hand free. 'I express my wish that we sup together alone on our wedding night. A reasonable one, I'm sure.'

When he made no immediate reply, I added, 'Are my wishes of no importance, then?'

He tilted his head with a smile. 'Oh, not of *no* importance. But I am your husband, Delany. You must rid yourself of the notion that your wishes will ever override mine.'

The pleasant tone belied the words, momentarily confusing me. Before I could gather my wits to reply, Mr Carver came in with a bottle of champagne in a sweating silver bucket. He wore a knowing grin and addressed many off-colour remarks to my bosom that he seemed to think were compliments. But what could one expect from such a lout? To endure ribaldry about the evening ahead is the lot of a newly married couple, after all.

As that interminable supper wore on, the gentlemen conversed with growing animation and lessening restraint. They ignored me completely.

How lightning-quick was this change from suitor to husband! At least I knew where I stood now, I supposed. There would be no more intimate suppers for two. If my husband wished to enjoy a life separate from mine, I would be happy to oblige, but I'd not tolerate this brand of boorishness.

Whatever Richard's feelings for me might be, for my part, I'd hoped for a union of friendly civility. Watching Richard drinking and laughing with his friend when he ought to be gently initiating his wife into the mysteries of the bedchamber made me suspect he had set out deliberately to humiliate me. For what reason, I couldn't guess.

As it did not appear that Carver would ever take himself off, I bade them goodnight and retired for the evening. The gentlemen rose when I did, but my husband made it clear that he did not mean to join me.

As Jane removed my jewels and locked them away, I heard the gentlemen stomp into Richard's dressing room next door. Jane pressed her lips together in disapproval but said nothing. I couldn't imagine what they were doing in there. Was Carver playing valet?

When Jane laid out an exquisite night rail of the finest embroidered lawn, I hesitated, thinking Richard scarcely deserved the reward of seeing me in it after his behaviour tonight. I was tempted to order an unprepossessing flannel garment that would cover me from ankle to chin. However, Richard's boorishness was no excuse for lowering my standards. I nodded and allowed Jane to help me out of my gown. Sniggers from next door, no doubt over some rude schoolboy joke about our forthcoming coupling, made me stiffen my spine.

Once Jane had removed layer upon layer of clothing and I stood in nothing more than my shift, Richard burst in, dismissing my maid with a snarl. 'Out.'

I turned to stare at him in reproof. His appearance was sloppier than I'd ever seen it, his eyes red-rimmed, his fair hair dishevelled. He'd stripped off everything but his shirtsleeves and breeches. His cravat was gone, leaving his shirt open to reveal a pale, hairless expanse of chest. He was drunk, and in a high state of excitement.

'Ahh,' he drawled, as the door closed behind Jane with a crisp, disapproving click. 'My beautiful wife.'

I did not consider myself prudish, nor particularly shy. I even had some experience in the bedchamber, though I'd never admit that to

Richard. Yet, something insolent in his manner disturbed me deeply. I tried not to show it.

'Take off your shift.' Richard propped himself against the wall, arms crossed, as if to watch a show. His upper lip curled derisively as if he did not expect to enjoy the entertainment.

'My lord?' I had hoped the necessary consummation would be achieved under the covers, with the lights extinguished, and in a practical, no-nonsense manner. What was this?

'Your shift,' he said, over-enunciating each consonant as if speaking to an idiot. 'Take it off.'

Briefly, I considered refusing. But there was something not quite safe in the atmosphere, and I thought better of rebellion.

I obeyed my husband. With fingers that trembled slightly, I gathered the skirt of my shift and pulled the garment over my head, baring myself to his gaze.

The unremarkable coupling that followed cemented my earlier resolution. I would fulfil my part of the bargain and act as Richard's dutiful wife, but he would get no more than that from me.

CHAPTER SEVEN

The day blustered like a member of Parliament, with squalling winds and intermittent icy rain that swept through the house's portico at an impossible angle. It drenched the footman who held an umbrella over me as I crossed the courtyard to enter my new abode.

Seagrove. I had never been to the Isle of Wight before. Despite the weather and the rough crossing, my impression of the island was favourable. The house, magnificent in its proportions, elegant in its appointment, impressed me to no end.

Upon handing me out of the carriage, my new husband had promptly forgotten about me. Instead of presenting the army of staff lined up to greet us, Richard became fully engaged in seeing that his other, more precious possessions were carried safely indoors – a set of cameos and some sculptures and I know not what else. Already I found myself indifferent to Roman antiquities.

With a fatalistic shrug, I picked up my skirts and stepped over the threshold, then moved through to the great hall. One week of marriage had taught me I must shift for myself.

The maids curtsied and a set of startlingly handsome footmen in powdered wigs and green livery puffed out their chests as if on military

---

parade. The thought of Tom flitted through my brain. I exchanged a word or two with the upper servants, summing up each one. I liked the merry twinkle in the cook's eye, though observing her high colour, I made a mental note to keep an eye on the sherry. Mrs Ludd, the housekeeper, looked neat and efficient, and the butler exuded the desirable mixture of gravitas and despotism.

Handing my hat and gloves to a footman, I allowed Jane to help me shed my damp pelisse. The housekeeper was offering to take me to my chamber to make my toilette when another member of the household appeared.

Mrs Ludd seemed to know as well as I did that no introductions would be forthcoming from Lord Nash. Flustered, for it was not her place to perform this office, the housekeeper nevertheless rose to the occasion. 'My lady, may I present Miss Margaret Smith, companion to the dowager, Lady Verena.'

Richard had mentioned that his mama, the daughter of a duke, had kept her original title throughout both her marriages. Her first marriage had been to Richard and Julian's father; the second, to a wealthy nabob named Grant who had left her his fortune.

I held out my hand to the dowager's companion. 'How do you do, Miss Smith?'

Margaret Smith greeted me with a pleasing, low voice. At first glance, she appeared serene as a Madonna. Her soft brown hair and grey eyes were unremarkable but her features were finely wrought and her skin was cream and roses. She might have done more to emphasise her attractiveness but she dressed with a Quakerish severity that befitted a lady's companion. Something in her expression – in the set of her full lips, perhaps – told me my presence was not welcome.

'Will you take me to the dowager?' I smiled at her, for I hoped we might be friends. 'I wish to lose no time in making Lady Verena's acquaintance. I'm afraid my lord is quite wrapped up in his antiquities at the moment.'

Margaret Smith did not return my rueful smile. Indeed, she seemed to stiffen at the request. After a significant pause, she gestured to the stairs. 'If you would be pleased to step this way.'

'Shall I guess?' I picked up my skirts and followed Margaret up the grand staircase. 'Lord Nash did not write in advance to warn of our arrival.'

'He did not,' returned the other woman.

'Oh, that is too bad of him,' said I. 'I daresay you did not look for us to come for another month. I shall take him to task over it, I promise you.'

The companion turned back, and for an instant, it seemed that she loomed above me in a menacing way. But that was a trick of the light. The house was dim and long shadows played over the walls, making Miss Smith seem taller than she was.

'The household is kept in constant readiness for his lordship,' she said. 'There was no need for advance warning.' She turned to continue the climb.

Such a practice as Margaret Smith described must lead to much inconvenience for the staff, not to mention wastage in the kitchens. I must put a stop to that.

Had Miss Smith been less quelling, I would have questioned her about Richard's mama and her reaction to the wedding; it must have come as something of a surprise to the household. Lord Nash's mama had been absent from the nuptial celebrations, apparently due to her failing health. I'd wondered if this was the truth, or if the dowager disapproved of her son's choice. Well, I'd find out soon enough.

The dowager's domain was a sitting room on the second floor that presumably led to her bedchamber. Candlelight blazed throughout the chamber, lending the delicate gilding on the furniture a rich gleam. Amid this elegant opulence sat the dowager, regal in a modish gown of bronze silk. The room was silent, but for the snuffles and snores of a sleeping pug dog, which was curled on a plump pink satin cushion on the sofa opposite her chair. The dowager closed the slim volume of poetry she had been reading and tossed it aside. The pug gave a yip, opened one goggling eye, then closed it again.

'Well,' said Lady Verena. 'Here you are at last.' Her voice was strident, a little harsh. It seemed to strike a discordant note amid the fragile beauty of the room, the exquisite, expensive lines of her dress.

My first proper glimpse of the dowager's face was a shock. She looked like . . . My heart gave one hard thump.

'So you've met my other son,' said the dowager with a knowing arch of one heavy eyebrow. My expression must have betrayed me. 'Yes, we are alike. And not just in looks, neither. Come here, girl.' She beckoned with one heavily jewelled hand. 'Let me see you.'

I curtsied and moved forward without hurrying or displaying any reaction to the dowager's mention of her other son. Coolly, I said, 'What a pleasure it is to meet you, ma'am.'

'I must suppose you had a foul journey.' The older woman's hands gripped the chair arms. She shifted in her seat, wincing, as if trying to find a measure of comfort. Perhaps it was true that her ill-health had prevented her from attending the wedding.

'Not at all,' I said, watching as Margaret moved forward to assist the lady, only to be snapped at for her pains. 'Your son has a well-sprung chaise.'

The dowager grunted. 'I daresay. And where is he now, I should like to know? Playing with his toys, I suppose.'

I laughed at that. A less child-like man would be difficult to imagine, and yet the description was apt. 'Yes, ma'am, I fear so.'

Dark eyes favoured me with a speculative glance. 'Margaret, leave us. I wish to have a private conversation with Lady Nash. And tell Nash he may present himself to me before the dinner gong.'

Margaret's face was bland as milk. She curtsied and withdrew, her back ramrod-straight.

At the dowager's invitation, I sat down opposite her, next to the pug. 'Will you not call me Delany, ma'am?'

'Delany,' said the dowager. 'What sort of name is that for a girl?'

'The bane of my existence,' I admitted. 'My mama named me for a dear friend.'

The dowager quizzed me about my connections, examining every branch of my family tree with the attention of an arborist searching for disease. Amused rather than offended, I answered as best I might. In my connections, at least, I had nothing of which to be ashamed.

Despite her earlier show of energy, as the conversation wore on the dowager grew fatigued. Grey shaded her face and her eyelids drooped. I wondered what ailed her. Unusually for an older lady, she made not the smallest reference to her illness. I concluded that Lady Verena was proud: a failing her younger son possessed in spades.

I knew I must learn to forget Julian. I could not go back and undo what I had done, so there was no point in repining. I'd make the best of this marriage. For the sake of my family, I must.

'You will want to go over the household accounts and so forth with the housekeeper,' the dowager was saying. 'Mrs Ludd is efficient, but it's Margaret who'll show you what's what.' The dowager's incapacity had meant her companion had assumed many of her duties. I wondered how readily Margaret would surrender management of the household to me.

I nodded. 'Thank you, ma'am. I shall leave you now, if I may. I must see to the unpacking.'

'Before you run off,' said the dowager, fixing her piercing eyes upon me, 'I need to speak to you about my son.'

My shoulders tensed.

'How shall I put this?' The dowager sighed with, it seemed to me, equal parts regret and frustration. 'The way girls are brought up these days to be so mealy-mouthed and prim makes me despair sometimes. But you look to me as if you don't have any of that nonsense about you.'

I smiled. 'I don't think anyone has ever called me prim, though I hope I behave with propriety.'

'I daresay.' The older lady plucked at her skirts. 'So you won't blush or bridle when I tell you that Richard doesn't have the same, ah, animal spirits that most young bucks have. Lacks proper spunk, as my lord used to say.'

I nearly choked. 'M-ma'am?'

'No need to look so startled. All I'm saying is, it's your duty to make babies and get heirs and you won't do that with a man whose pole ain't straight, if you take my meaning.'

By now, my cheeks were burning. Our wedding night had indeed seen the marriage consummated, despite the evening's unsettling beginning. There had not seemed anything amiss with my husband's procreative equipment, or not that I could tell, at any rate.

Of course, there had been the evening before our departure from London, after Mr Carver left us . . . but I had put that down to Richard's excessive consumption of some fine French cognac and thought nothing of it. He still required me to undress while he watched me, but surely that was not so odd. Ought I to worry? I wondered how on earth the dowager knew anything of her son's proclivities in the bedchamber.

A thought occurred. In a lowered tone I said, 'You don't mean that he . . . prefers men?'

'No, no! Nothing like that.' The dowager's fingers curled over the arm of her chair and gripped it tight, as if to endure severe pain. Breathing heavily, she said, 'Remember, once you are with child, you can do whatever you wish with whomever you wish. You need never indulge in any practices you find abhorrent. But providing a male child to carry on the family line is your chief role in life. Achieve that, and then you may do as you please. As long as you are discreet.'

Margaret

He'd done it. He'd actually gone through with the wedding. The enormity of it, the simple corrosive horror, ate at Margaret's insides. She didn't know what to do with herself. Her first instinct had been to hide, but the dowager soon put a stop to that.

'Fetch her to me,' she'd said in that peremptory way of hers. As if Margaret were a servant, not a companion. One day, Margaret's pent-up spleen would erupt like a volcano; she'd spew vitriol everywhere.

Yet she'd done her mistress's bidding, gone down to greet the new Lady Nash as if she had not coveted that position ever since the day she had first heard of Lord Nash and his ailing mother on a visit to Bath. As if she had not waited and plotted and planned and insinuated and angled until she made the acquaintance of the despicable woman. As if she had not flattered and petted and tended her with dogged diligence for years.

As if she had not suffered.

And he'd brought home that woman. Delany Rothwell. Spoiled, beautiful, more self-assured than any young woman who called herself a lady had a right to be. The way Delany had patronised and tried to put Margaret at ease – in her own home, no less – made her want to scratch out the girl's blue, blue eyes.

The dowager had liked Delany on sight, that much was plain. Lady Verena had sent Margaret away while she spoke confidences to Delany that Margaret could only guess at. What had she said to her? Surely not . . . No . . .

Margaret cringed anew at her gaffe over dinner. She'd gravitated without thinking toward her usual chair, so busy resenting Delany Rothwell, she'd forgotten that as well as supplanting Margaret meta-phorically, Delany had literally taken her place at table.

Never more could Margaret happily lose herself in the daydream that she was mistress of this house. She dreaded the morrow, having to relinquish her position to this upstart.

She squeezed her eyes shut, remembering with searing clarity the look of pity in Delany's eyes, swiftly veiled.

Well, they would see which of them was more to be pitied. Margaret would not leave. She would stand and fight. There was nowhere else for her to go.

'I've been thinking,' said the dowager, running her fingers through Pug's fur. The horrid little thing sat on the dowager's lap, snuffling and slobbering and shedding hair all over her, but she never seemed to regard it.

'Yes, ma'am?' said Margaret. What now?

Lady Verena gripped the edges of her shawl and pulled them closer about her. 'There's a draught in here. Do you feel it? Pug feels it, don't you, Pug?'

There was no draught. The room was stuffy and hot, but Lady Verena would feel a draught in the Congo.

'I'll draw the curtains, shall I?' said Margaret, crossing the sitting room to do so. She waited, but the dowager seemed lost in thought. After a few moments, Margaret prompted, 'You said you were thinking, my lady?'

'What? Oh, yes. I was thinking we should decamp.' Her eyes narrowed. 'Better for the newlyweds if we ain't here peering over their shoulders.'

'I'll tell Polly to see to the packing,' said Margaret after only the slightest pause.

The last thing she wanted was to leave Richard when he'd just returned after a three-month absence. However, she couldn't afford to show opposition to her employer. She'd work on Richard instead.

Margaret picked up a paisley shawl that lay discarded on the floor. 'May I ask where . . .?'

'Bath.'

Margaret bowed her head, busying herself with folding the shawl. The dowager enjoyed the society of Bath. While her health never seemed to alter one jot as a result of all the physick she undertook there, her spirits certainly improved. She said it did her heart good to hobnob with people who were far more cankered and feeble than she.

Bravado, of course. There was no recovery from the disease that plagued Lady Verena. To Margaret's way of thinking, syphilis was an affliction sent by God to punish the wicked.

Not that the woman was repentant. Shocking, the stories she told when she'd had a deal too much 'medicinal' brandy. One of the great indignities of Margaret's position was being forced to listen to the lurid details of Lady Verena's discreet yet colourful amours.

'You disapprove of me,' the dowager said once, years ago, when Margaret had slipped and let an inkling of her disgust appear.

A companion's position was always precarious, subject to the whims and caprices of her mistress. Alarmed, Margaret had hastened to reassure. 'My dear ma'am, indeed, I do not.'

The dowager waved a thin hand. 'It's a matter of supreme indifference to me, you know. There are very few persons whose opinions I value, and you, my dear sweet hypocrite, are not one of them.'

The only person my lady seemed to care for was her younger son. Julian was the apple of her eye – being, as Richard often said, so very much like his mama.

Rumour had it that Julian was a by-blow, and that his father was in truth the Earl of Eldon. The earl was dead now, having blown his brains out over a woman – not Lady Verena, one presumed.

That the wild Julian Nash was related to Richard even through one parent was almost inconceivable. The two of them were total opposites.

Julian never had money. He was forever applying to his brother to fund this or that scheme – mostly to do with alleviating the plight of the poor. As if that could ever be done. Hadn't Jesus himself remarked that the poor would always be with us?

Richard would refuse his aid, and then Lady Verena would enter the fray.

In the end, Richard would give in. Not because he was persuaded of the merits of whatever mad scheme Julian was undertaking, but because he did not wish to offend his mama.

Everyone knew the dowager was not long for this world. Lady Verena was that rare woman – an independently wealthy widow – and therefore she did and said what she pleased. She could have afforded to make her home anywhere, but she'd insisted on moving back to Seagrove when her second husband died.

The better to plague her elder son, Richard said.

Well aware that Richard had his eye on a second inheritance, Lady Verena made life as difficult for him as she could. Margaret was forever trying to make peace between them but she'd only succeeded in negotiating an uneasy truce.

'I wish the old bitch would die,' Richard said to Margaret once when they were alone in his library. He had embarked on an ambitious history of the Isle of Wight and she was acting as his amanuensis.

Like a child, Richard made the least mischief when he was kept busy, so Margaret had encouraged him to continue work on the tome. It was to be published privately and expensively, bound in tooled Morocco leather. Everything of the highest quality, a masterpiece, a collector's item.

The quiet hours she spent with Richard in his library were the happiest of her existence. She directed and shaped his research, organised his notes, rewrote his awkwardly phrased passages as flowing periods. He was unaware of how she steered him, as if he were a boat and she the gentle hand at the tiller.

She prided herself on her exquisite tact and diplomacy. She'd managed to allay Richard's feelings of inferiority and suspicion until she was able to make suggestions and corrections whenever she deemed them necessary. She wished she might assist him as well in the matter of his overbearing mother.

Margaret knew how to get rid of an unwanted woman. Particularly a sick, old, unwanted woman. One need only bribe a doctor to certify her insane and lock her up, either in Bedlam or in a private attic somewhere with a nurse and a guard. It was then a simple matter to apply for control of her fortune. When the dowager was at her most difficult, Margaret entertained herself with the thought of assigning her that fate.

Fortunately for the dowager, she still had powerful friends. Not to mention one son who loved her. The remedy so many had successfully employed against their wives and mothers could not answer here.

Margaret and Richard must wait until the dread disease that presently lay dormant in the old lady rose up to claim her. Margaret was rather looking forward to those final helpless days, the revenge she would wreak for every slight.

'Are you at liberty, Miss Smith?' Richard put his head around the door of his mother's sitting room.

A clench of her stomach. A breathless pause. He still needed her.

'Already?' said the dowager with a bland smile. 'Run along, Margaret. Don't keep my son waiting.'

With a respectful curtsy, Margaret obeyed.

In the library the following morning, Margaret concealed a whirlwind of emotion and conjecture while she waited for Richard to check some reference or other he had misplaced.

He returned to his desk, fingertip marking the place in a slim periodical, and settled himself back in his chair. When he resumed dictation, only a small part of her mind was engaged in the task her hand carried out.

It pleased her beyond measure that he had sought her out almost immediately upon his return. He had not relegated her to the background, even if his marriage to Delany had dashed her fondest dreams to dust.

She would never forgive him. She would never forget. But a woman with no prospects and no place in the world must develop an uncanny ability to set aside deep hurt. And besides, she did not despair. While there was life, there was hope. So many women died in childbirth these days, after all. Any number of things might happen.

Margaret had observed Richard and Delany closely the previous evening and discovered no sign of love or attraction or even compatibility between them. That was far better than she'd dared to hope.

When she'd first set eyes on Delany, Margaret's heart had sunk to her boots. This flamboyantly beautiful woman could not fail to enslave any man.

But then Delany had opened her mouth and Margaret's relief nearly bowled her over. Too self-possessed, too commanding, prideful to the brink of arrogance. This girl would never do for Richard.

What on earth had possessed him? Margaret couldn't fathom it. Of course, he would not discuss his choice of wife with her. Not unless driven to do so by anger . . . or some other emotion. Margaret was adept at inspiring confidences. She would bide her time.

Now, as she patiently reworded Richard's history of the nearby village of Bonchurch, she considered ways to introduce the topic closest to her heart.

'Ah, there you are, Richard.' Dressed in a deep russet habit, Delany stood in the doorway, pulling on a pair of leather gloves. She offered Margaret a nod and a smile and said to her husband, 'I'm riding out. Will you join me?'

Margaret watched Richard closely, saw the faint frown of annoyance before he bowed. 'As you see, my dear, I am much occupied. Perhaps some other time.'

'Occupied? With what?' said Delany, coming further into the room.

Margaret's hand moved involuntarily in a protective gesture. She didn't go so far as to cover her work, but she resented Delany's assumption that she might simply waltz in and scan Margaret's pages of neat cursive.

Richard said, 'You may read it when it's finished, my love. Not before.'

'But what is it? Are you writing a book?' Delany tilted her head, as if adjusting her opinion of her husband. 'Why did you never tell me?'

Richard cleared his throat. 'It is nothing. A mere trifle. I am compiling a history of the island.'

'Oh.' Delany's face brightened with what Margaret judged to be false interest. 'It sounds fascinating.' Her gaze flicked to Margaret.

'And Miss Smith is your secretary, I see.'

Her expression held cynical amusement and a hint of that omni-present pity. Margaret lifted her chin.

Richard said, 'If you don't mind, Delany, we have much to do, as I've been so long from home.'

Margaret experienced a rush of smugness at his dismissal. The sensation was so pleasurable that she was obliged to bite back a smile.

'Ah, then you must not let me keep you from your labours,' said Delany, turning to go. At the door, she turned back with a swing of heavy skirts. 'Let me know when it is finished, won't you? I might be able to put in a good word for you with my publisher.'

On an airy wave, she departed.

Richard, who had risen to his feet when she came in, stood staring at the empty doorway. His face held that curious blankness Margaret often observed when he dealt with his mama.

She wondered what had happened between Richard and Delany after he'd left her last night.

She traced the skin at her wrist, where the sleeve of her spencer covered a bracelet of purpling bruises.

Delany, Lady Nash

The rain had lightened to a drizzle when I rode out on the morning following my arrival at Seagrove. I was eager to see my new home and to shake off the concerns that plagued me. After that unsettling talk with Lady Verena the evening before, I'd waited with a twinge of apprehension for Richard to come to my bed. Nothing untoward occurred, however, and I hoped that our nocturnal activities might produce the desired result.

Yet my mood was far from sanguine and I decided a good gallop in the fresh air would clear my head. The stable block at Seagrove was palatial in size and appointment. My own father had lavished more on the upkeep of his horses than he had on his daughters, but even he had not aspired to quarters such as this.

I declined my groom's offer to accompany me with a flippant comment that drew a shy smile from the lad, and set off on Artemis, my gentle mare. Papa had been an excellent judge of horseflesh and it was a matter of pride with him to see his children mounted well. I trusted Artemis to carry me safely anywhere I wished to go.

Inclement the weather might be, but it did not disguise the gentle, rolling welcome of the downs, nor mask the fresh, salt tang of the sea air. A few straggling sheep dotted the green slopes, and at various points along my ride a vista burst upon me of breathtaking beauty – vivid green turf cutting away to white cliffs and teal-grey sea.

I meandered along the coastal path that hugged the cliff edge, gazing down to the small coves and rocky beaches below. It was as if a giant sea monster had taken great bites out of the island, leaving the white chalk cliffs, sheer and imposing, behind him.

There was no danger of becoming lost with the crumbling tower of the folly, a landmark one could see for miles around from its perch on the highest hill to the north of the house. At length I reined in at the edge of a cliff and gazed out to sea.

Aye, there was beauty here at Seagrove. In the scenery, in the house. But what lay beneath?

Had it been Lady Verena's intention to disgust and frighten me with her frank discussion? I did not think so. I believed her to be as she appeared: a woman of experience, who wished to ensure the succession by sharing that experience with me.

She had not been specific about the supposed nature of Richard's . . . proclivities. She had been positive on one point, however. His bent did not run to men. That was a consolation, though I wondered if Richard had a mistress. Of course, no one would tell me if he had, but it would be a good thing to know. I had asked Selby but he'd refused to discuss the matter. For an out-and-out scoundrel, Selby could be downright prudish when it came to his sisters.

I had not expected to enjoy bed-sport with Richard overmuch and therefore had not been disappointed. My husband might have been a well-looking man, but he did not cause those sensations in me that a mere glance from Julian provoked.

Richard wanted a mother for his sons and a well-bred chatelaine for his newly reconstructed home. I had every intention of living up to my side of the bargain I'd implicitly struck with him. My greatest ambition was to look after my family the way my father and my brother had failed to do. I would be a good wife, a competent householder and a charming hostess. If I did all this and managed the business of begetting an heir, I would have repaid my debt.

I tried to console myself with the knowledge that whatever my husband had in store for me, I must only endure it until I became pregnant. After that, I counted on a nine-month reprieve. I wanted to get with child immediately, the better to soften Richard toward my plans for my sister and aunt. Lavinia should want for no opportunity to secure a kind, generous husband who adored her. Aunt Boddington, too, required a pension, which necessity Selby had conveniently overlooked when negotiating with Richard's lawyers.

These were things I intended to accomplish. When one considered the vast sums Richard lavished upon his house and his stables and his scraps of Roman marble, it did not seem to me that I would be asking too much. Still, I needed to tread warily.

I urged Artemis into a canter then broke into a gallop. The muted thunder of my horse's hooves pounding the sodden turf, and the feel of the wind buffeting my face and whipping at my hair soothed me in some measure. The powerful animal moving beneath me, sensitive to the lightest direction from my hands on the rein, restored my equilibrium.

Whatever the future held in store for me, I would face it squarely. There were many worse fates than being mistress of a place like Seagrove, after all.

CHAPTER EIGHT

I discovered I was with child within a few months of arriving at Seagrove. I was never so glad of anything in my life – not only because it meant the cessation of attentions that were repugnant to me, but because I looked forward to all of the joys motherhood brings.

Breaking the news to Richard was a happy event. His delight was genuine, I believe. I don't think anything I did before or afterward pleased him half so well.

Never backward in seizing the advantage when I found him in a genial mood, I outlined my plans to invite my sister and aunt to Town with us in a few weeks' time. We would be in London early this year for the impeachment of Warren Hastings, former Governor of Bengal – a matter that Mr Fox and his friends (including Julian, I am sorry to say) had gone to great lengths to bring about.

Richard assured me he would insist on bearing every expense of my sister's debut and pronounced himself happy that I would have company to amuse me while he was occupied elsewhere. He would be much exercised with the trial and with political business while my sister and I made our curtsies to society.

As if a thought struck him, Richard frowned. 'But will it not fatigue you to do the social round, my dear? Might it be better to bide here at Seagrove until the child is born?'

Aghast at the notion, I reassured him. 'My lord, I'm as healthy as a horse.' Besides, the doctor told me I must not ride any longer and life at Seagrove would be deadly dull without riding. My little yacht, the *Betsy-Ann*, would have to lie idle also; already I was finding the rocking of the boat and the pungent, fishy smells at the seaside too much for my constitution to bear.

'You must not be anxious on my account,' I went on. 'Aunt Boddington will chaperone my sister, so I shall be spared any entertainments I don't care to attend.'

My hand sought my belly. 'Nothing shall harm this precious life, I promise you.'

He looked at me curiously. 'The prospect of motherhood pleases you?'

'Yes, of course.' Did he think me unnatural? Like any woman I knew, I longed for a child to love.

Without too much further argument, Richard gave way and reiterated his pleasure at having my sister and aunt stay with us in Town. Thrilled to have succeeded in persuading him to my point of view – not least that he had agreed to defray the expense involved in Lavinia's debut – I scribbled letters to my relations.

We must make haste, I wrote, for all three of us would need to purchase new wardrobes in the latest mode before we set foot in the elegant salons of the metropolis. Not to mention the necessity of acquiring hideously expensive and elaborate court dresses.

Such giddy excitement as I felt on reaching London cannot readily be described. We three ladies had never spent so much money in our lives. We made ourselves drunk on silk and lace.

It gave me such pleasure to see my dear, pretty sister dressed so becomingly. My aunt, too, grew positively regal in both stature and mien.

Before long, we were in the thick of the social whirl. Despite her earlier reticence, my aunt's schoolfriends had not forgotten her. And there were any number of people ready to make the acquaintance of the rich Lord Nash's new wife and her pretty sister.

It was not the fashionable practice for husbands and wives to go about together to social events. We took a box at the opera, of course, and attended the inimitable Mr Sheridan's plays at Drury Lane. But other than those few outings, I went one way and my husband quite another. That suited me very well, for Richard had developed an irritating habit of correcting and admonishing me in front of others. I was too well bred (and too conscious of the likelihood of reprisals) to voice the retorts that sprang to my lips on such occasions. If we had spent much more time in society together, my tongue would have been raw from biting it.

With my aunt keeping a close eye on my sister, I experienced a newfound freedom. I attended salons crammed to bursting with intellectual giants of the age. I was drunk on ideas, and only wished Julian was with me to share my intoxication.

Whenever we met, which was unavoidable, he acknowledged me with a distant greeting and walked away. Whispers of his latest feminine conquests forever rippled in his wake. I told myself I was glad. I wished I had the courage to demand he return my letters. I wished I could bring myself to burn the letter to him I'd never sent.

Still, if these encounters disturbed me, it was a small price to pay. My dear Lavinia was having the time of her life. I had not been so absorbed in my own affairs that I had failed to notice and do my utmost to encourage a blossoming romance between my sister and a most eligible gentleman.

'Oh, Delany!' In the wee hours after the Grandsdens' ball, Lavinia fell back against the coverlet on her bed. 'My head is in a whirl. It is too good to be true!'

She clasped her hands to her bosom, eyes shining. 'Is not Mr Burton the handsomest, kindest man you ever set eyes on?'

I laughed. 'Indeed he is. And what is more, I believe he is equally taken with *you*, darling.'

How clever of my sister to fall in love with someone so eminently suitable. Mr Burton was a wealthy gentleman with extensive property in Gloucestershire. Moreover, his disposition was delightful; he was generous and kind to a fault. Lavinia could not have chosen better.

The day Mr Burton asked Lavinia to be his wife was one of the most satisfying of my life. Her fate had been a constant concern to me. I'd so wanted her to be rich and happy. How gratifying to have my fondest wishes granted.

'Richard, I have wonderful news.' I burst into my husband's book room, eager to share my delight.

I halted, however, when I saw Margaret Smith. She sat opposite him at his desk, with a pile of bills before her and some sort of ledger full of figures written in her tight, neat script.

Without even asking me the cause of my exclamations, Richard said in mild reproof, 'You interrupt, my dear.'

'Forgive me,' said I, largely unrepentant. I had never much patience for formality, and it was only Margaret, after all. I smiled at her. 'Miss Smith, I count you as one of the family and do not stand upon ceremony with you.'

When they both stared at me blankly, I sighed, my good humour deflated. 'I should come back later, I suppose.'

'No, stay,' said my husband. He gestured to the work in which he and Margaret were engaged. 'For all this concerns you.'

That sounded grim. I pasted a serious expression on my face and tilted my head in inquiry.

'I have here a pile of bills,' said Richard, gesturing to the papers at Miss Smith's elbow.

'Oh, dear.' Stricken with remorse, I put a hand to my cheek. 'Have I been criminally extravagant? I needed an entirely new wardrobe, you know —'

'These are not your bills, ma'am,' said Richard. 'They belong to your sister and aunt.' He tapped the desk with his index finger. 'They should be sent to your brother, should they not? I cannot conceive how they came to be directed to me.'

Of a sudden, I felt as if the floor had been whipped out from under me. My heart plummeted to the cellars below. That Selby would agree to defray the expense associated with what he dismissed as 'petticoat business' was inconceivable. It had never occurred to me to ask. Despite the sums he'd squeezed out of Richard upon our marriage, Selby was always on the brink of financial disaster, living hand-to-mouth until each quarter day.

Conscious that Margaret regarded me steadily through those tranquil eyes of hers, I licked my lips. 'When you consented to my sister's being presented under my aegis, my lord, you agreed to defray the expense.'

I distinctly recalled it. The conversation had been a difficult one for me. My pride did not bend easily and I'd been obliged to all but grovel to Richard on the subject. As I'd expected, once his initial exuberance about the baby calmed, he grew less and less enthusiastic about the idea that my aunt and sister would come to us in London. However, by dint of flattery and tact and outright supplication, I had managed to persuade him to remain true to his promise. It must have occasioned him no small degree of satisfaction to have me beg.

Richard straightened the ledger before him so that it lined up with the papers on his desk. 'I recall no such agreement.'

My jaw dropped. A most inelegant expression, I've no doubt, yet I was shocked and appalled that he should disavow knowledge of the last of these exchanges. Richard's acquiescence to the scheme was emblazoned upon my memory.

The knowledge that Margaret remained an interested witness to this discussion brought heat to my cheeks, but I did my best to ignore her.

I said, 'Do you want me to quote your very words, Richard? For I assure you, I never should have invited my aunt and sister to Town if you had not explicitly agreed to defray the expense.'

Truly, the world seemed to revolve in reverse. Would I be obliged to have such agreements written in blood from now on?

I'd never seen the least indication that Richard was parsimonious. He spent fortunes on his Roman marbles and such. He took an inordinate amount of pride in his own clothes, and was not above buying himself an extravagant jewelled stick pin or an elaborately embroidered silk waistcoat whenever the fancy took him. He owned one hundred and fifty pairs of shoes, for heaven's sake!

Richard paid his servants wages that were fair, if not generous, and Selby had been well satisfied with the marriage settlements, even if I had not. Richard had no sisters, so perhaps he was unaware how vital it was to introduce Lavinia to eligible gentlemen. The gowns we'd purchased for her were no mere frivolity. They were an investment in my sister's future. An investment that had paid dividends.

Perhaps he needed all this explained to him. My gaze flickered to Margaret and back to Richard. 'If we could discuss this in private . . .'

'There's nothing to discuss,' said Richard. He gestured to the bills. 'I shall redirect these and your brother may deal with them as he chooses.'

'Selby won't pay,' I said tightly. 'You know he won't.'

Richard had seen how it was with my family when he'd paid his addresses to me. How could he believe Selby would begin to honour his obligations now? Besides, I doubted the various mantua-makers and modistes in London would have extended us credit had they known Selby would be responsible for footing the expense. They would think I'd duped them, leading them to believe my sister and aunt were well provided for by my husband.

I snatched up the top bill. It was from Madame Duchamps, for a striped spencer of twilled silk.

'How do you know these are not *my* bills?' I demanded of my husband.

Margaret spoke. 'I required your maid to make an inventory of your garments.' She smiled pleasantly. 'Perhaps you would like to look over the list and make sure I have it right.'

I stared at her in disbelief. Having failed to make a friend of Margaret Smith, I had largely ignored her, thinking her nothing at all to do with me. By now, I was accustomed to Margaret's being privy to every intimate detail of our lives. I could have resented her for the way she interfered, but she led such a narrow life that I could hardly begrudge her the petty pleasure of thinking she'd bested me on occasion. When all was said and done, I was the mistress of this house and she little more than a servant, subject to my mother-in-law's whims. I would not lower myself to squabble with her.

I decided that if Margaret would not absent herself from this discussion, I would pretend she didn't exist. Moreover, I refused to be embarrassed by a circumstance that should rather embarrass my husband. After all, he was the one intent on pinching pennies when he could well afford to fund my sister's debut.

Indicating the bills with a wave of the hand, I addressed my remarks to my husband. 'This cannot be such a great sum. Perhaps an advance on my pin money . . .'

'Margaret?' Richard raised his eyebrows at her in inquiry.

After all, I thought, what use had I for pin money next quarter? Following a period of confinement, I'd be wholly occupied with the new baby and have no need of the frills and furbelows required for gadding about in Town.

I had no idea how much my female relations had spent on their accoutrements, but it could not amount to an entire quarter's allowance, could it?

Apparently, it could. With a pulse of anger beating in my throat,

I waited while Margaret diligently totted up the figures in her ledger. Finally, she read out a staggering sum.

'I believe you are overdrawn on your next quarter's pin money already,' she added.

Despite my noble intentions, at that moment, I dearly wished to pull Margaret Smith's nose for her.

I shrugged and said to Richard, 'Do as you wish, my lord. But you might as well throw them on the fire as to send those bills to Lord Selby. I hope Mr Burton does not get wind of it, for he proposed marriage to Lavinia only this morning, you know.' I paused. 'Shall I be obliged to send my sister to the altar in rags?'

That shot across the bow made Richard sit up straight. He would not for the world offend the Burtons, who were a well-connected and powerful family.

Disdaining to curtsy, I turned on my heel and walked out.

For myself, I did not care about my husband's wealth. I would never have sacrificed my freedom if personal luxury had been my only reward. While I took as much pleasure in pretty things as the next woman, jewels and silks were not vital to my happiness. All I needed was security for my family. I'd depended on Richard to provide it.

Would I never learn? The only thing for which a woman can depend on a man is disappointment.

There was nothing else for it: I must order more gowns immediately, to stave off the duns until such time as I had contrived to persuade Richard to my point of view. If my credit with the mantua-makers remained good, surely they'd overlook the debts of my aunt and sister.

The sooner Lavinia was married to Mr Burton, the easier I would be.

Richard's recalcitrance over those bills afforded me grave disquiet. Far from the malleable husband I'd expected, he had proven untrustworthy, manipulative and dishonourable. He had enjoyed humiliating me in front of Margaret, that was certain.

I never told my female relations about the way he'd denied his obligations. How it irked me to see them fawn over him, flattering him and expressing their gratitude for his generosity. And all the while, he accepted their accolades as his due.

Denied the outlet of a good, refreshing gallop at the risk of endangering the child I carried, I threw myself headlong into a series of songs and poems to vent my spleen. I even began a novel. Some of it was rather good, if I do say so myself, but of course I could not send them to Mr Gibbs. Richard had forbidden me to court notoriety by continuing to sell my compositions to the public.

Finally emerging, at my aunt's demand, from the chrysalis of artistic endeavour, I spread my wings at balls and routs and masquerades.

London's fashionable life was predicated on pretence. A lady might have a piebald litter of children from six different fathers as long as she never admitted to an affair, or made a fool of her husband by pining openly after her lovers. One might do anything, within reason, as long as one was discreet.

Such practices did not sit well with my forthright nature. I despised hypocrisy, so it was fortunate that I did not fall in love with any of the gallants who flitted around me.

Far from showing jealousy, Richard seemed to revel in the admiration I excited among the members of his sex. He displayed me as he displayed his other acquisitions, encouraging me to be as extravagant as I liked when it came to my own adornment. Something about his evident pride in me as his possession rather than his helpmeet soured my pleasure in pretty things.

He invited my most assiduous *cicisbei* down to Seagrove with us when we returned there for a brief respite from the metropolis. He never seemed so pleased with me as when he basked in the envy of other men. Just how avidly he courted that envy, and what he was prepared to do to secure it, I did not know at that time.

I had persuaded Lavinia to accompany me to the masquerade one evening, escorted by Mr Burton and a charmingly diffident crony of his, Lord Fingley. At the last minute, Richard announced his intention of accompanying us.

I did my best to appear pleased. My intention was to give Lavinia and her amiable fiancé time alone together before the wedding while I amused myself dancing and quarrelling with my friends over politics. I was never a part of the Devonshire House set, but I was fully in sympathy with the principles Mr Fox – and Julian Nash – so eloquently espoused.

I kept my opinions secret from my husband, who was a firm supporter of Pitt, and whose hatred for Mr Fox ran deep and vicious. With Richard present tonight, I would be obliged to curtail my activities and curb my tongue.

The Pantheon roared with the noise of conversation and laughter and music. My sister wore a Harlequin costume, matching her fiancé's, so they were easy to pick out in the crowd. By contrast, I had donned a nondescript blue silk domino and a simple black mask in the Venetian style.

Seeing my sister safely occupied and that my husband had discovered a circle of his own friends, I slipped away.

I was seated with one of my admirers on a couch against the wall of the ballroom. I had been endeavouring to extract from Mr Green the latest political gossip but he was more interested in inveigling me into the shadows for a kiss.

So much for stimulating conversation, thought I. But I did wish to know how the debate had gone in the House that day and he wished very much to kiss me. I offered him an exchange.

'Tell me every detail of what Mr Burke said today and you shall have your kiss, sir,' I said.

His eyes glittered beneath the mask. 'And what part of you may I kiss, my lady?'

'My . . . foot!' I said, laughing, lifting my skirts a little and pointing my toe for his inspection. The shoes I wore that night were exceeding pretty, embroidered with silver thread and studded with sapphires.

Swiftly, more swiftly than I'd anticipated, Green encircled my ankle with his hand and possessed himself of my appendage.

In my surprise, I reacted without thinking. As I made haste to scramble for balance and wrench my foot from his grasp, my toe clipped Green in the eye. He reeled back, screaming in pain.

Serve him right for trying to steal what he had not yet earned. As he bawled in agony, I smoothed down my petticoats and scanned the crowd for more amusing company.

'Still making grown men cry, Delany?'

I turned my head and looked up.

A man in a black domino loomed over me like Mephistopheles, so large and menacing that he made my rakish companion appear effeminate and silly.

'Julian,' I whispered, rising as if drawn by some invisible force.

'My lady. My lady, help me!' bleated Green, feeling about for me blindly on the empty couch with one hand, while the other was pressed to his eye.

Julian regarded Green in silence for a moment. Then he offered me his arm. 'Shall we?'

I'm afraid I abandoned my injured friend without a second thought.

My hand trembled as I laid it on Julian's sleeve. Despite my past and the intrigues of recent months, truly, I felt as if I'd never touched a man before.

He drew me into the dance: a minuet, stately and slow. Each measured step, each touch of his hand, was like exquisite torture. Neither of us spoke, but the set of Julian's shoulders, the hardness about his mouth and jaw, betrayed anger.

In what cause, I wasn't certain. Jealousy? Disgust? Perhaps, the old fury of a man forced to stand by while the woman he loved married another.

The overwhelming effect of Julian's presence on my nerves made it seem as if we two were the only ones in that crowded ballroom. Struggling for composure, I concentrated on my steps, on my posture, on the proud tilt of my chin.

Even through my guilt, a low hum of conjecture buzzed in my brain. Julian had kept his distance from me since I'd arrived in London. Why was he here now? Indeed, why accost me thus at a public masquerade rather than presenting himself at his brother's house? I wanted to speak frankly to him, but even more than the movements of the dance, his stony expression forbade the attempt.

What else could I have done? I wanted to shout at him, pound on his chest with my fists. If I'd run away with him, what would have become of my sister and aunt? Of my brother?

When the dance ended and we had bowed to each other, I clutched his hand when he would have drawn away. 'Might we go somewhere quiet?'

He raised a black brow. 'How would that look?'

'It is a masquerade. No one would remark upon it.'

'One infers you have some experience in the matter,' he murmured.

'Indeed,' I said coolly, releasing him. 'As, I'm sure, do you.'

He regarded me for some moments. Then he said, 'I think not, madam.'

He bowed once more and strode away, making me wonder why in heaven's name he had asked me to dance in the first place. On balance, I wished he had not. I swallowed down the hurt and disappointment, for of course I had no right to either of those emotions.

'Delany? There you are,' said my sister, catching my hand as I turned away. 'I wanted to tell you: Richard is looking for you. He says it's time to leave.' When the carriage came to take me home and deliver Richard to his club, my husband said, 'Did I see you with my brother tonight?'

I knew Richard disapproved of Julian. In the months I'd lived at Seagrove he'd scarcely mentioned him but to abuse his character. He hated his mother for foisting her 'bastard' on his father and despised his late father for acknowledging the boy as his own. It was an insult to have shared bed and board, not to mention parental affection, with such a base-born creature.

From this, I suspected Richard would not tolerate it if I sought to renew my friendship with Julian.

Something large and sharp seemed to lodge in my throat, but I managed to respond without emotion. 'Yes. We danced the minuet.'

'Did you, indeed?' said Richard. Inexplicably, his lips curved into a satisfied smile.

Late that evening, when I had retired for the night, Richard brought two gentlemen up to his Curiosity Cabinet. Originally the chamber had been his dressing room, but he'd lately fitted it out with glass-fronted cabinets to display his most precious possessions – Chinese lacquer, ivory carvings and porcelain, cameos and other trinkets from Pompeii.

Often, there would be one or two particular, trusted friends in a gathering whom he would invite to view his more unusual finds. On this occasion, though, he'd chosen poorly, for a scuffle broke out between the other two young bucks. The subject of their argument became all too apparent to me as I undressed in the chamber next door.

As I discovered that night, Richard's most unique possession, the one he displayed to select friends through a spy-hole drilled in my dressing-room wall, was me.

I do not propose to go into detail on this subject. Suffice to say that the practice had begun on our wedding night with Mr Carver, and it continued until my belly became heavy with child.

In the meantime, I developed a talent for shutting off my humiliation. We never discussed the matter, but it became clear to me that without the stimulation of such voyeurism, Richard could not perform his husbandly function.

That night, the full import of Lady Verena's lecture on my wifely role slammed home. The shame I felt at this degradation, never

knowing which of the men I might meet in society had already
watched me in private moments, must either be swallowed or ignored.
To ensure the succession, I must endure whatever treatment Richard
dealt me.

Such was my lot as a good and dutiful wife.

When one first enters the fashionable world it seems bewilderingly
overpopulated. On closer acquaintance, however, it becomes clear that
everyone is related to everyone else and one meets the same set of people wherever one goes.

Bored with empty wit, adulation, snubs and condescension, I
resolved that once I saw my sister married I would retire from London,
claiming fatigue.

Richard, who desired to impress Mr Burton's family with his
munificence, offered to defray the cost of a lavish wedding breakfast.
I manoeuvred him into making the suggestion directly to Mr Burton so
he could not renege later, and Richard remained true to his word.

This time, I made sure my aunt was provided for, interfering in the
most brazen way in the marriage settlements, much to my brother's
ire. Poor Mr Burton was obliged to carry the burden of my aunt's and
sister's dressmakers' bills into the bargain. However, he was so delirious at winning such a pretty, sweet wife that I believe he did not mind
paying through the nose for her. On the day of her wedding, Lavinia,
buoyant and happy, folded me in a crushing hug and whispered her
happiness into my ear. I believe my joy nearly matched her own.

I had given up on Selby's reform as a lost cause, so with Lavinia
married and my aunt comfortably situated in a house in St Alban's,
I had achieved everything I'd set out to do. With a sense of satisfaction
in a job well done, I looked forward to greeting the new life it would
be my duty and privilege to protect.

I thought often of Julian, who remained in Bath far longer than I'd expected. Rather than come to Town with us, the dowager had gone to stay with her niece in the famous spa town. She'd rejected Margaret's company on that particular sojourn, and both Richard and Margaret were glad. They had much work yet to do on Richard's history.

The dowager was a faithful correspondent. Since that first rather daunting meeting, she decided in her capricious way that she liked me. She and I dealt together very well; her wry pronouncements and frequent jocularity made me laugh, and loosened the sometimes restrictive atmosphere of the household. I missed her and felt bereft of an almost-ally.

Lady Verena's most recent letter was full of Julian. He had devoted himself solely to her entertainment while there. I should have laughed to have seen it! The passionate, impatient and erudite Julian, taking the dowager's arm on a promenade about the Pump Room and curbing his stride to match his mother's deliberate pace; procuring glasses of the foul-smelling waters for her to drink; listening patiently to the various descriptions of ailments Lady Verena's friends poured into his ears.

I read the account of Julian's attentiveness aloud to Margaret and Richard at the breakfast table, but the missive won a sour look from my husband.

'Very likely,' he said in that dry, almost querulous tone he used when speaking of his mother. 'One week of false smiles from my brother and she's in transports.'

Margaret's hand reached out. For a moment, I thought she would set her fingers on Richard's sleeve. Instead, she smoothed an infinitesimal crease in the table cloth by his hand. 'I should go to her.'

'No,' said Richard, pausing in buttering a roll. 'I need you here.'

Margaret lowered her gaze. 'Yes, my lord.'

His tone admitted no argument and her submission seemed complete. I was surprised, then, to hear a muted bustle the following morning, and to see Margaret's traps loaded into the family travelling coach, which stood on the drive outside.

'You are going to Bath after all?' I asked. Far be it from anyone to tell me what was afoot.

'Yes.' She drew the strings of her reticule tighter and fixed me with her unsettling, wide-eyed stare. 'I am persuaded that my lady's niece, while a good sort of woman in her way, is wholly unacquainted with Lady Verena's constitution. She ought not to permit such gallivanting as has been conducted under Mr Julian's aegis.'

I did not believe Julian needed anyone's permission to do as he wished. Nor, in fact, did Lady Verena. I did not say so, however. Marking the resolution that lay behind the eternal serene smile on Margaret's lips, I thought that I should like to be a fly on the wall during that tripartite encounter.

In the event, there was no such encounter, for Julian had left Bath before Margaret arrived. During his stay, he'd disrupted Lady Verena's treatments, surrounded her with gaiety and assisted her in perpetrating all kinds of mischief, from disobeying her doctor's orders as to regular leeching, to gaming at a discreet house in Laura Place. He'd no sooner upset every careful arrangement Margaret had made for the dowager's welfare than he'd gone again – much to Margaret's indignation, as she wrote to us later that month.

'Still, I'll wager your mama enjoyed herself,' I said to Richard with a rueful smile, setting Margaret's letter aside. I rather liked the idea of Julian and his mother setting Bath by its ears.

Richard gripped my wrist in a hard, tight hold that made me gasp in pain. 'Oh, you do, do you? Admire my brother, do you, Delany? Cuts a fine figure, does he not? With his whoring and gaming and his turning our mother up sweet to see what he can get from her. It's all of a piece!'

I forced myself to keep my gaze lowered as he ranted. His grip tightened until I wondered if my bones might break.

Once, I would have argued and challenged. Now, with the growing life in my belly to consider, I could only seek to appease. 'I'm sorry, Richard,' I said, trying to keep my voice steady. He could not hurt me here, surely. A servant might come in at any moment. Yet I felt the violence in him, ready to erupt.

I was accustomed to violence from the men in my family. My father had whipped me often enough, and Selby had made no bones about boxing my ears when he thought the occasion warranted it. Yet Richard's unwonted, venomous assault frightened me more than my father's beatings had ever done.

I ought to have known this letter would provoke him. I ought not to have been so pleased to see the back of Margaret Smith.

My lying-in took place in London, attended by the celebrated accoucheur Mr Denman, and all was well. Determined to suckle the new babe myself, I resisted strenuously all attempts to employ a wet nurse along with the other nursery staff. I am pleased to say that on this point I had my way.

It is a bittersweet pain to recall those days. Henry, my precious son, was my universe, the moon and the stars and all the planets combined.

For three months, I was content to stay in London with my child. The world outside was filmy, unreal, viewed without interest through the cocoon of domesticity in which I wrapped myself. As soon as I could travel, I took him back to Seagrove with me and surrounded him with love.

My aunt came with me and stayed for a time, but complained that I was such dull company, always wanting to be with Henry, she might as well take herself off again. Adjuring me to build up my strength with blancmange, calf's foot, hartshorn jelly and isinglass boiled in milk, she left me to my obsession.

Summer came and went. Richard visited at the houses of various friends for a month, which stretched into two, while Margaret was with the dowager in Bath. I was glad of it; with both of them gone, life at Seagrove was ordered just as I liked it. I spent many hours in the nursery, playing with Henry, cooing over him, demanding that my friends, family, servants, anyone who was at hand, admire every gummy grimace that might be interpreted as a smile. What an utter bore I must have been!

In the fifth month of his life, Henry suffered for two weeks from fevers and chills, and I was in terror for his survival. The late-night vigils and lack of sleep, coupled with worry, took their toll on me. For that fortnight, I did not leave my apartments but to go to the nursery. Thank goodness for my dear Jane, who took charge of the nursery and shared the worst of those nights with me.

The joy I felt when the fever passed and my little one was out of danger cannot well be described. Once that elation spent itself, however, I felt horridly low. If my darling boy had been precious before, now he was my reason for living. I suffered nightmares in which he perished from that fever. I was obliged to check on him several times a night to make sure he still breathed.

Wrapped in these concerns, it took some time before I realised my husband, who had now returned from his visits, watched my absorption with increasing hostility and distrust. How a man who had practically ignored me from the beginning of our marriage now felt himself maligned and dismissed in favour of an infant was beyond my comprehension.

Perhaps foolishly, I had been content to let Margaret take command of the household again. Ever since her return from Bath, scarcely a morning had gone by without her reproaching me for some oversight or other. In time, I intended to re-enter the world, to return to my usual matter-of-fact efficiency, and to put Miss Smith back in her place. But for the moment, motherhood held me in thrall.

Margaret seemed to resent my single-minded devotion to my child. That made me wonder: did she long for children, a husband of her own? Her position at Seagrove was invidious. I supposed her to be in love with Richard – at least, she applied herself wholly to his interests. While I believed Margaret too prudish and staid to act on, or even fully recognise, the nature of her feelings for my husband, at the same time I rather despised her for repressing them. It could not be out of loyalty to me.

Had I been more patient, cleverer, less ignorant, I should have trod around Margaret with more care. Indeed, had I known what the future held, I would have kissed Margaret's hands and feet, given her everything I possessed, including my husband, if she'd wanted him.

The truth was that the weeks without sleep as Henry fought for his life, coupled with physical changes in me after his birth, had left me woolly-headed and vague. Had my aunt been on hand, she would have advised brisk walks in the gardens, or a turn in the Long Gallery if the weather continued inclement. She would have chivvied me back to my old self with that blend of kindness, astringency and good sense that never failed to have effect. Lavinia would have fallen into some scrape from which she needed rescuing, and I would have been obliged, perforce, to rouse myself.

However, I had given my aunt a life beyond her family now, and I had made Lavinia's scrapes Mr Burton's responsibility. Whatever Selby's troubles were, I had washed my hands of them. Now, all I lived for was the small bundle in my arms.

CHAPTER NINE

Liz

'Come on, Lazy-Liz.' Gemma padded into the cottage living room, waving her sparkly pink thongs in Gemma's direction. 'You need to get out of the house. We only have five minutes of summer in this country and you're missing them.'

Gemma wore a bikini top and flirty floral shorts that made her legs look long and slender. Liz thought of her own chunky frame and tried not to hate her friend. 'Where are you going?'

'To the beach, of course,' Gemma said, clapping a straw cowboy hat on her head that was very cute, even if it provided minimal protection from the sun. 'Sandown this time. I'm picking up Maddie on the way.'

When Gemma had first taken Liz to the little private cove immediately below the cottage, Liz had thought, You call this a beach?

One narrow crescent of sand, red with weed, spread between grey rocks and shale. Liz had made polite noises of appreciation and put up her deck chair, with a surge of regret for the blinding white sand of Koh Samui.

That led to wondering what Tony and Jess were doing now, a sure-fire way to kill any positive feelings a trip to the beach might have produced.

Sandown, which actually had proper sand, was a more enticing prospect than the Nashes' private beach, but Nick wasn't paying her to sunbathe or splash in the water. Well, actually, Nick wasn't paying her at all. But he was footing the bill for her accommodation and so forth.

She could lollygag at the beach back home. Right now, she needed to get on with the task at hand.

'Sorry,' Liz said. 'More research to do.' She hadn't yet finished the memoirs, but a few nights ago she'd begun one of Delany's novels, when she was too tired to decipher her handwriting. Liz had been so hooked on Delany's fiction that she'd read deep into the night, and had devoured the others in a matter of days. Now she was half way through the last one.

She held up *The Wraith of Harrowby Hall*. 'Got to finish this. Maybe tomorrow?'

'Fergus will be here tomorrow,' said Gemma. 'I'm clocking some sunbathing time while I can.'

Oh, right. And Liz had promised to help with the renovations. 'Is your man a slave driver, then?'

'Definitely.' Gemma grabbed her keys. 'Well, I'm off now. Sure you don't want to come?'

'Have fun.' Liz crossed her legs and sank deeper in the armchair to read.

THE WRAITH OF HARROWBY HALL

A ROMANCE;
INTERSPERSED WITH SOME PIECES OF POETRY
BY LADY NASH

IN FOUR VOLUMES

—

VOL. 1

—

LONDON:
PRINTED FOR GIBBS & REETH
PATERNOSTER ROW.
1832

The lantern swung in her clenched fist, its pale light waging a losing battle with the gloom. The sea fog rolled around her feet, making each step treacherous, but she pressed on, stumbling through the darkness and whipping rain.

She heard the harsh sough of each breath, the slap of her sodden skirts against her calves. Her half-boots squelched into the mud and sucked free. Ghosts, woken from their sleep by her desperate search, gathered themselves and howled with the wind.

Behind her, she dragged a shovel. In the way of dreams, it had come to her hand as if by magic – before she'd known she wanted it, before she'd known what she must do.

Her hair straggled down her back and shoulders, plastered to her skin like seaweed. Tears burned tracks over her frozen cheeks as she searched the graveyard for that fresh, small mound.

Sobs tore at her throat. She fought the urge to release them, to keen in unison with those restless souls whose life force was tethered to this place. If she did that, she would be mad indeed. Only a Bedlamite would come here on such a night. But she must know. She must find him.

Row upon row of headstones sagged; mouldy angels wept for the loss of their crumbling wings. Crosses lay prone or leaned drunkenly to the side, as if evil had infected the very ground, rejecting the Christian symbol, spewing it forth.

Turning down the next line of plots, she shone her lantern upon inscription after inscription. But no – she'd been this way before.

She made another turn. Again, the same carved blocks of weathered stone, the same names leaping out at her, taunting.

Desperate, confused, she tried to get her bearings, but the graveyard evaporated, dissolving into the fog. At every point of the compass, the ruined Hall rose up, grinning at her like a gap-toothed crone.

Abandoning method and reason, she ran, the lantern light skewing wildly, a single harsh note playing over and over in her ears. She threw a glance behind her before she realised that the odd music she heard was her own terrified whimpers.

The faster she ran from the Hall, the more she gained on it. The scorched ruins shimmered and expanded, flourishing, renewing themselves, growing into the blank-eyed mansion she'd first entered as a bride.

Then she saw it at the edge of a wood: a lump of newly turned earth.

The wood grew denser, closing in as she stumbled toward the tiny hillock. A tree root snaked out to trip her. A far-off cackle of laughter, the crunch of her twisted ankle as she fell hard on the ground.

Discarding lantern and shovel, sobbing with horror in the blackness, she dragged herself by instinct alone to the spot she'd marked out and clawed at the sod with her bare hands.

Her fingernails tore and filled with muck and rotten matter. The mingled scents of mouldering leaves and festering flesh filled her nostrils, clogging her mouth. Cold and damp and the taint of something evil seeped through her body and chilled her bones. But her heart blazed with longing and love and hope.

A sudden, thin wail echoed behind her.

She stopped and raised her head, straining to listen.

The slightest disturbance sifted the earth. A pale worm inched its head above the ground. Then another, and another, bending, flexing in concert, as if to some unheard, secret lullaby – until there were five of the creatures, each studded with a shell-pink nail. One was shorter and fatter than the rest; she remembered it ringed at the joint by plump, rosy lips.

With a brittle cry, she reached down into the hole she'd dug and touched the delicate whorl on the fattest worm with one reverent fingertip.

The tiny digits closed around her finger and squeezed.

Liz

Wow. That Lady Nash had a creepy mind. How did a woman of her privileged background even come up with stuff like that? But then, of course, the Brontës didn't exactly write about kittens and rainbows, did they?

The scene about the dead baby in the graveyard had given Liz the heebie-jeebies. What was it about people of that era and their love of the macabre?

Liz didn't understand certain references to people and events. They seemed like inside jokes that only Delany's contemporaries would appreciate. Had Delany satirised real people? Caroline Lamb had populated her novel *Glenarvon* with her acquaintances, most notably the lover who had spurned her, the poet Byron. Still, Liz found Delany's gothic tales so absorbing in their own right, she'd neglected the rest of her research while she focused on them.

She'd also taken up running again, rising early each morning to get a head start on the day. When she came back through the estate gardens, via one of the circuits Valerie had shown her, she'd see Theo, hard at work.

On the first day she'd nearly expired in front of him, panting, sweaty and bright red in the face.

'Water,' she gasped.

He handed her his squeezy-bottle and she squirted a blessed cold gush of water into her mouth.

She lay flat out on the cool grass while he worked around her, skirting her supine body with the wheelbarrow, until she recovered enough to be on her way.

The next day, he had an extra bottle of water waiting for her. Overcome with gratitude at his quiet thoughtfulness, she'd stolen his spare hat and joined in with his work once she'd drunk her fill.

He didn't object this time, simply put the tools in her hands. They didn't talk, just dug and planted and weeded. Whatever needed doing, she was up for it.

'You want to come back to the house for a late breakfast?' said Theo when she said she'd better get back.

'I have a lot to do. Thanks anyway.' They stood there for an awkward beat before she gave him back his hat and water bottle and shuffled on her way.

Parts of her still ached from her run that morning, but she made small inroads into her fitness each time. She had to walk at some points, but on each circuit she managed to improve. Before she left Seagrove, she aimed to run the whole distance.

Now Liz realised she'd been daydreaming, stuck for several minutes on the same page. She made herself a cup of coffee and got back to it, making notes in her laptop when something struck her as having a bearing on her quest.

It seemed like no time at all before Liz heard the clang of the gate and looked up to see Gemma and Maddie traipsing up the path. A glance at the clock told her four hours had passed since Gemma had left.

Liz put her book aside. 'Phew!' she said. 'I feel like I've been in another world.' She'd read the graveyard scene over twice. It seemed so real. Could it possibly be an allusion to Stephen, the son Nick claimed had died as an infant? She shivered.

'What's the matter?' said Maddie.

'Creepy book,' said Liz. 'Graveyards and ghosts.' She didn't tell Maddie about the baby.

'Want a drink, Mads?' said Gemma, tossing her keys on the counter and going to the fridge. 'We've got OJ, Diet Coke or water. Or wine, but your dad would kill me.'

'Water, please.' Maddie dumped her things in the corner by the door.

'Hang out your wet stuff, hon. Don't let it fester away in your bag.' Gemma raided the fridge, filling her arms with food. 'Maddie's here for a sleepover,' she explained as her niece came back in. 'Hope that's okay.'

'Terrific,' said Liz, grabbing a peeler and a carrot from the pile of stuff Gemma had laid on the kitchen counter. 'I love sleepovers. Will we watch movies and gossip about boys?' Then she smacked her forehead in mock dismay. 'Oh, right. No TV. Boys it is, then.'

'Yuck!' Maddie wrinkled her nose. 'I know! We should tell ghost stories. I don't want to talk about boys.'

Liz didn't want to talk about boys either, particularly her husband. Since the Facebook episode there'd been nothing to upset her – not that she'd been able to stop herself checking. But she was coping, throwing herself into work, forgetting Tony for whole chunks of time now.

Gemma said, 'Actually, Delany's buried on the estate. We should visit her gravestone tonight.' She handed Maddie a glass of water, then started arranging cheese, fruit and crackers on a large plastic platter, shifting aside to let Liz dump her load of carrot sticks. 'Might be getting too late to go after we eat, though.'

'I'm on holiday. I'm allowed to stay up,' said Maddie.

Liz and Gemma exchanged smiles. 'Let's see how we go,' Gemma said.

They dragged some chairs outdoors and gathered around the ancient, wobbly wrought-iron table. Liz poured glasses of crisp pinot grigio.

The garden might not have been tidy or cultivated, but it was a pretty, overgrown wilderness. With sun-warmed, grassy scents whipped away now and then by the wind, and the muted, endless hush-hush of the sea, the cottage seemed like the most peaceful spot in the world.

Liz sighed with contentment. 'You're lucky to have this place.'

Gemma's face was inscrutable for a moment. She raised her glass. 'Well, it's not much compared with Seagrove, but it's home. A holiday home, anyway.'

She clinked glasses with Liz, then with Maddie.

A brown and orange butterfly that had been flitting among the tangle of untended garden that edged the lawn winged toward them. For a moment, it hovered above Maddie.

'Don't move,' Liz whispered to her. 'There's a butterfly about to land on your head. Or maybe it's a moth.'

The girl froze, stifling a giggle, her eyes nearly rolling back in her head with the effort of trying to see the insect without frightening it away.

'Ah, no, it's gone,' said Gemma, as the butterfly seemed to think better of settling on a mop of damp, curly hair and winged away. 'You can breathe again.' She tilted her head. 'It *was* a butterfly, not a moth.

In fact I think that might have been a Glanville Fritillary.'

'Are you an expert?' said Liz, remembering the butterfly meadow Theo had mentioned at one point.

'No, but my father was,' said Gemma. 'He had all kinds of exotic specimens in the butterfly house but he sold the lot when the money ran out.' This seemed to be a common theme at Seagrove and from Gemma's bitter expression, a sore point with her.

To lighten the mood, Liz leaned forward to scoop up some home-made hot smoked trout dip with a celery straw. 'I could live on this stuff.'

'Mrs Jackson sent down enough for us to live on.' Gemma cut a chunk of oozing brie and trowelled it onto a cracker.

'She's certainly gone above and beyond the call of duty,' said Liz. 'Surely all of this wasn't covered in my accommodation package.' She'd been here over a week and still the tasty treats kept coming.

'Mrs Jackson's feeding you because she likes you,' Maddie said to Liz.

Liz smiled. 'I only wish I could help her out with this catering thing. I've tried tact and persuasion but nothing seems to work on Valerie.'

'Did you hear Raooouuul is coming on the weekend to do a taste test?' said Maddie.

Liz nodded. 'Can't wait to miss it.'

'Well, well,' said Gemma. 'I hadn't heard anything about this. Is my invitation in the mail?'

'You can have mine for the asking,' said Liz.

'Raoul de Martin is a berk.' Maddie seemed to be testing out a new word, probably borrowed from her aunt's vocabulary.

'But a handsome berk,' murmured Gemma. '*And* he was voted one of England's most eligible bachelors in *Woman* magazine.'

'Maybe I will go, then,' said Liz. Now *that* would be a photo for Facebook.

'And you just know Valerie is going to gush all over him in that sickening way she has,' said Maddie, pulling a face. 'Poor Dad.'

The question Liz burned to ask was why Theo stayed with Valerie when she behaved like that, but it was none of her business. Besides, she didn't want Gemma to jump to the wrong conclusion about the reason for her interest.

Liz said, 'He's a good guy, your dad.'

Maddie smiled. 'Yeah. He's the best.'

Gemma reached over and smoothed back Maddie's hair, which was ratty and tangled from the surf and wind. 'Why don't you go up and have a shower? Make sure you use lots of conditioner and comb the tangles out before you wash it off.'

When Maddie had gone, Gemma said, 'I'm glad you didn't ask the question. It's hard for all of us to understand that relationship, but especially hard for Maddie.'

'Why *does* he put up with Valerie?' Liz said.

Gemma selected a fat, ripe strawberry and turned it in her fingers. 'It's not as if he confides in me. I have my theories.'

'And what are they?' said Liz, who had a couple of her own.

'Two things,' Gemma said. 'First, he couldn't make it work with Maddie's mum, so he refuses to fail this time.'

Liz had gathered that the split with Maddie's mother had been amicable, but it had taken Theo several years to commit to another serious relationship.

'Okay, I get that. What's the second thing?'

'I think . . .' Gemma bit into her strawberry and pegged the hull into the tangled garden. She swallowed. 'Valerie's put so much work into Seagrove, if he broke it off now, it would seem like he'd been using her.'

Guilt was not a good foundation for any relationship, but Liz could understand that, too. 'What about Valerie?'

'She's so wrapped up in her own little world, I don't think she notices the way she affects everyone around her,' said Gemma. 'Not sure if she'd care, either. She loves being the lady of the manor.'

'Does she?' Liz wondered. 'Maybe she only thinks she does.' It was obvious that Valerie pined for London, and couldn't understand why

Theo didn't take more time away from the estate.

The Open Day would be a test, wouldn't it? If Valerie received a good dose of things to come and she didn't like the taste . . .

But it was none of Liz's business. She should stop thinking about it and concentrate on the matter at hand. Changing the subject, she said, 'Do you think it's okay to visit Delany's grave tonight with Maddie? I'm not familiar with kids and their tolerance levels for scary stuff.'

'She'll be fine.' Gemma grinned. 'Be more worried about yourself.'

It was after eight o'clock when they set out beneath a softly purpling sky. Liz loved the twilight here, although being such an early riser, sometimes she had to shut the curtains on the light to get enough sleep before her run.

'The island is terrifically haunted,' Gemma was saying. 'Not at all a good idea to walk in some places after dark.'

'Where, in particular?' said Liz. She wasn't sure she believed in ghosts. At least, she'd never come across one before but people on the island seemed to take them as a matter of course.

'A few places,' said Gemma. 'The Botanic Gardens used to be a hospital, so of course it's thick with ghosts. Then there are all the historic houses like Arreton Manor and Carisbrooke Castle. You should go on a haunted tour while you're here.'

Liz grimaced. 'I'll think about it.' She was really only interested in the ghosts of Seagrove. 'Any hauntings at your house?'

'Oh, no,' said Maddie. 'I told you, there's nothing interesting about our house.'

'My father said there was a ruin in the grounds where you could feel a cold spot,' said Gemma. 'We're pretty sure it was originally the fake Roman temple where Richard Nash was murdered, near Marine Cottage. But the site was bombed in the Second World War and eventually it became so run-down it was dangerous, so they removed the ruin completely. The site is all overgrown now. I don't think you could get to the haunted spot without a machete.'

As they walked the coastal path, the ocean breeze tossed their hair about their faces. Liz shivered. Even though the day had been a hot one, the nights often turned cool here. She rubbed her bare arms, and for a moment turned to stare out to the water, the white foam of its breakers like iridescent lace in the dying light.

'Here.' They turned inland, taking the path that Gemma indicated, which was more like a driveway. When they got to a gate, Liz realised they'd passed through private property, but it seemed to be the way of things here that the coastal paths traversed private land.

They crossed a road and continued to climb. By this time, Liz could no longer conceal her shortness of breath. 'So unfit!' she panted, as they climbed a stile and kept moving.

By the time they arrived at the small graveyard, the sun had slipped low in the sky.

There were only two gravestones, large but plain, without ornate scrolled carving or weeping angels above them. They faced the sea, as if to allow the inhabitants a good view.

Liz shone her torch on one of the mottled headstones. It read:

IN LOVING MEMORY OF
DELANY ROTHWELL,
AUTHORESS
1768-1840

The second stone simply gave the name 'Julian Nash' and his dates.

'He died one year after she did,' said Liz. Her throat closed up. She was glad it was dark enough to hide the tears in her eyes. 'So he was the one who made sure they were together.'

'We assume so,' said Gemma.

'He died of a broken heart,' said Maddie in a matter-of-fact tone.

'Tuberculosis, more likely,' muttered Gemma.

'No, he did so die of a broken heart,' Maddie insisted. 'Dad said.'

Liz was surprised. She'd never pegged Theo for a closet romantic.

'People don't die of broken hearts, Maddie,' said Gemma. 'Come on. We need to get back or I'll be in trouble with your dad for getting you to bed so late.'

Still arguing, Maddie followed Gemma back down the path.

Liz lingered for a while, looking at the two graves, side by side. Nothing in all the caricatures, scandal sheets, letters and texts she'd read showed how these two had truly felt about one another at the end.

If you read the press sheets of the day, it seemed like the most sordid, tawdry affair, carried on by two irresponsible, pleasure-seeking aristocrats against the background of serial bed-hopping that was commonplace among their kind.

Yet here were their graves, placed side by side decades after a tawdry affair would have grown ice-cold. It seemed that their love for one another had been real. Not only that, but their love had never diminished.

And yet, as far as Liz could tell, the two of them had spent their final days apart. Delany lived at Saltwater Cottage, which was part of her widow's jointure. But Julian . . . what had happened to him?

He must have married and had children, or he could not be Nick's ancestor, could he? But he never married Delany. How awful. How bloody tragic.

Stupid of her to feel so emotional about it all. Real as they had become in her imagination, she hadn't known these people. They'd lived as far away in time as if they belonged to a fairytale. Yet she was choking back tears of sympathetic grief at the thought of them, loving each other so dearly but doomed to be apart – until death and Julian's determined disregard for proper behaviour brought them together once more.

'Come on, Liz!' Maddie called. 'Or a spooky ghost will get you!'

Later that night, in bed with the photocopies of Delany's memoirs, Liz reflected on what it meant that those tombstones were side by side. The early days of Delany's marriage to Richard had been no picnic, by the sounds of it. Had her disappointment driven her into Julian's arms?

Delany seemed determined not to repine at her choice of husband, but the impact Julian's reappearance had on her was telling.

Wholly engrossed, Liz flipped to the next page – and hit the back cover of the bound photocopies Nick had given her.

'*What?*'

She was at the end of the memoirs. Yet she hadn't come to the end of Delany's story, not by a long shot. She wasn't even up to the part where the court case came in.

Had Delany and Julian truly indulged in an affair, as Richard alleged at the trial? It seemed unlikely, based on Liz's reading. Of course, a lot could have happened in the time between the birth of Delany's first baby and the criminal conversation trial.

Why hadn't Nick told her the memoirs were incomplete? She was stupid not to have thought of it. She'd been too engrossed in the story to think about how many pages she had left.

Frustration and disappointment sent her riffling through the rest of the pages she'd printed in Valerie's office but there was no sign of Delany's missing memoirs.

Liz blew out a breath. What was she going to do? She craved the rest of that story so badly, it was an almost physical ache. The gravestones side by side – clear evidence of Delany and Julian's doomed love – made it far more imperative for Liz to discover the truth behind it all.

There was more. There had to be. Didn't Delany say in her letter to her second son that her memoirs were the full story of his life as far as she was concerned in it? She must have covered the circumstances surrounding his birth and the criminal conversation trial, at the very least.

Liz desperately needed to know what happened next. She'd asked

Theo to dig out anything from the archives that might have a bearing on Delany. Would it be too much to hope he'd have the rest of Delany's memoirs there?

Liz was about to set off for the Big House the next morning to subtly question Theo about the memoirs when she saw a gleaming white utility pull up outside the cottage. A man in a polo shirt half tucked into a pair of chinos climbed out.

'Hi,' called Liz, propping her bike against the fence. 'I'm Liz, a friend of Gemma's. You must be Fergus.'

'Hiya,' he said, smiling at her. He was a rangy, olive-skinned fellow, with a mop of curly black hair and black eyes that gleamed like jet. Though it was morning, he sported a five o'clock shadow. Not one of those designer ones. The guy probably needed to shave twice a day.

'Gemma should be back any minute. She's gone up the road to check her messages.' Liz waved her hand. 'No reception here. But of course, you know that. Do you need a hand with anything?'

'Should be right, thanks.' As he unstrapped a ladder and lifted it off the roof, he called, 'But I'd love a cuppa if it's no trouble.'

The faintest of Irish brogues came through in his speech. No wonder Gemma was smitten! Liz said, 'I'll just boil the kettle.' She went back inside and got busy with the tea while he unloaded the rest of his gear.

'So you're the lodger Gemma was telling me about,' he said, taking off his heavy work boots before stepping into the house.

Liz carried the tea tray to the living room and set it down. 'Sorry to be in your way. I'll be out of your hair tomorrow night, hopefully,' she said to him. 'They're giving me a room up at the Big House.'

'Just as well,' said Fergus, reaching for a biscuit. When she gave a surprised laugh, he grinned. 'Oh, not that you're unwelcome, but we'll be living rough once the demolition starts.'

'I hope you'll let me help,' said Liz. 'I'm supposed to be renovating my own house back in Australia right now, but . . .' She trailed off. Fergus wouldn't want to hear about her marital troubles.

Gemma's cheery greeting cut short an awkward pause. 'Oh, that's *very* nice, that is!' she said, hands on hips. 'Stealing my man with tea and Garibaldis.'

'I may be cheap, but I'm not that cheap,' said Fergus. He went over to her, bent his curly black head and kissed her on the mouth.

Liz was happy for them. Of course she was. But seeing them so wrapped up in each other was a stab in the guts all the same. 'I'll, uh . . . leave you two to catch up.' Liz backed out of the room, grabbed her things and cycled up to the Big House.

On her previous morning run, she'd asked Theo about the archives and he'd promised her all the information he could dig up. Again that guilty feeling over all the lying she had to do reared its head, but by now she was curious about Delany for the woman's own sake. She needed to find out what had happened to her. She needed the rest of the memoirs.

Not for the first time, Liz wished she could be more direct and open with Theo about the reasons for her research. Perhaps if she could find a more effective way to help him than simply weeding the garden, she'd feel better about investigating on Nick's behalf. But what could she do? Theo was not the easiest man to get to know.

Maybe if Nick got what he wanted, it would be better for Theo in the long run. Maybe, given Valerie's preference for London life, they'd all be happier if Theo sold Seagrove and moved back to the city.

But Liz couldn't make herself believe it. Valerie was leading Theo and the rest of them a dog's life. They wouldn't have any peace until she was gone.

Stop, Liz told herself firmly and went to find Theo in the library. He was there, hefting dusty archive boxes onto the large library table. Valerie would have a fit if she saw all the mess in here.

'Hi,' said Liz when he looked up and welcomed her with a grin.

'Looks like you've gone to a lot of trouble. Thanks.'

As she slid her backpack off her shoulder and dug for her laptop, Theo lifted the lid from one of the archive boxes. 'Wasn't sure what you wanted so I brought everything I could lay my hands on from around the time you're interested in.'

Liz forced herself not to dive head-first into the boxes, searching for Delany's missing memoirs. Theo pulled out files and loose papers and she kept her eyes peeled for any books that looked like journals. None turned up, except for some rather dull appointment diaries belonging to Richard Nash.

'What *are* you looking for, exactly?' said Theo.

She didn't want to tell him about Stephen. 'Anything you can find that dates back to Delany and Richard's marriage will be great.' She hesitated. 'But most important would be any diaries, journals, that kind of thing. Particularly Delany's.' She didn't say she'd already read a couple of them. How would she explain that without involving Nick?

They spent several hours sifting through the documents. The papers were in only the roughest order, but at least most of them dated from the right era. Bundles of private letters and legal papers Liz put aside to look through later. Others that dealt with irrelevancies or concerned people she didn't know she placed in the discard pile. There were several account books and other household records that might be useful in a tangential way, but nothing to set Liz's heart racing.

Beyond disappointment, Liz sighed, sitting back in her chair and rubbing her tired eyes.

'Maybe we should take a break,' said Theo.

'My thoughts exactly.' Liz glanced at her watch. 'Wow. We've been at this a long time. I'm sure you have better things to do.' She shouldn't have kept him so long. He had enough on his plate without her commandeering his morning like this.

Theo tilted his head. 'Actually, there are a couple of other things in the house from that era that might interest you. Would you like to come upstairs and see them?'

'Now you're not going to offer to show me your etchings, are you?' said Liz, recalling a similar conversation with Nick. That seemed like a lifetime ago.

He gave her a bemused look and she muttered, 'Never mind.'

Mentally, she slapped herself. That kind of talk teetered on the verge of flirting. What was wrong with her? It was Theo and his mountain-like impassivity. She wanted to be the earthquake that shook him up. As if she didn't have enough problems already.

'Through here,' he said, when they'd reached the second floor and turned down a hall. 'Excuse the mess. I've been working on something.'

So this was Theo's private lair. 'Nice,' she said, looking around. 'Very cool man-cave.' And yet there was not a wide-screen television or a fussball table to be seen.

'Thanks.'

The room was fitted out like a gentleman's club, so comfortably masculine she half expected the whiff of cigar smoke to waft on the breeze. Ancient leather chairs, mahogany desk. A billiard table, even. If the room hadn't felt so strangely intimate despite its rugged charm, she might have challenged him to a game.

Plans were spread out over the desk. She thought of the stacks of similar papers she and Tony had at home and suffered a pang of loss.

Perhaps misunderstanding her expression, he said, 'I didn't bring you here to show you those. Don't worry, I'm not going to bore on about landscaping.'

Ignoring him, she smoothed out one of the plans that wanted to curl back into a tight cylinder. 'Is this for Seagrove?'

When she looked back at him over her shoulder, he shrugged. 'It'll never happen. Not worth talking about.' The expression on his face was oddly vulnerable.

'Well,' she said, straightening and rolling the plans back up, 'what *did* you want to show me?'

'Right.' He crossed to another door and opened it, switching on the light.

It was an internal room, much larger than a walk-in wardrobe, but with a similar feel. Only, rather than being lined with coat racks and drawers and shoe shelves, it was lined with floor-to-ceiling glass cabinets.

'Wow.' There was so much stuff here she couldn't take it in.

He explained some of it. Silver-gilt plate and Meissen ware stood cheek-by-jowl with fossils and feathers, moths and butterflies pinned to boards and art deco bronzes of dancing ladies.

'What *is* all this?' she said, glancing at Theo.

'It's called a curiosity cabinet,' he told her. 'Refurbished and expanded since the time you're interested in, but I believe Richard, the sixth baron, was the one who installed it.'

'I read that he was a keen collector,' Liz said. 'I have a digital copy of one of his catalogues. It's mainly bits of frieze from Roman temples, but there were some cameos too.'

She looked more closely at the fine carving on the cameos in the cabinet, wondering if these were the same ones. 'What are they made of?'

Theo took a key from his pocket and opened the cabinet. 'This one's supposed to be carved from the lava of Pompeii,' he said, tilting it to the light so she could make out the exquisite detail. 'Diana at her bath.'

She knew the story. Some fellow had watched the goddess skinny-dipping and she'd turned him into a stag for his impudence.

There were so many other, equally fascinating items in this collection, they'd spent an hour there before Theo reminded her of her purpose.

'Now, this,' he said, taking out an oddly formed piece of silver about the size and shape of an ice-cream cone, 'is what I wanted you to see.'

Tiny bells tinkled as he held it out to her. 'It's a baby's rattle that belonged to Richard and Delany's son Stephen, my ancestor.'

Liz couldn't help it. Her hand shook as she took the rattle from him.

'See that long pink tongue at the end? That's made of coral, a sort of teething bit.'

'Oh, my goodness,' said Liz, with a surprised laugh. 'I can see the tiny teeth marks in it.'

'Where?' Theo bent his head close to hers.

She caught his scent, a mixture of earthy smells and an astringent, like aftershave. Liz heard her voice go a little higher in pitch than usual. 'Here. See?' She ran her fingernail over the small indentations.

He laughed softly. 'Oh, yeah. Reminds me of one of Maddie's favourite toys, this hard plastic ring with a duck on it that she used to gnaw like a little lion cub.'

His hand closed around the rattle, turning it. 'And here are the initials.' S.E.N.

'Stephen Edward Nash.' Liz cleared her throat. This cabinet thingy was getting a bit claustrophobic. 'Can I borrow this, please?' She didn't know why, but she felt drawn to this small piece, intimately connected as it was with the very child she was trying to investigate.

'Of course.' Theo bent to a set of drawers beneath the cabinet. 'There should be . . . Here.' He pulled out a velvet box and cracked it open for Liz to put the rattle inside.

'Have you started the novels?' he said as they went downstairs again.

'Started. Finished,' said Liz.

He glanced back at her in surprise. 'That was quick. What did you think?'

'I know this sounds strange,' said Liz slowly, 'but I feel as if I know Delany, having read them. There's such an energy that comes through on the page, so much personality. Even though they are such dark books, there's that dash of wit here and there that takes you by surprise.' She smiled. 'Sorry. I probably sound crazy to you. Have you read any of them?'

'One or two, but it was a long time ago. I'll have to refresh my memory,' said Theo.

They headed back downstairs. In the library, he said, 'Feel free to get Valerie to copy anything here, but I'd prefer it if you didn't take anything away. Some of the documents are fragile and falling apart.'

'I understand. Thank you.' She smiled at him. 'I appreciate it, Theo.'

He dug his hands in his pockets. 'No problem.'

'Is it okay if I spend the rest of the day here?' said Liz. 'There's a lot to get through and Fergus just arrived at the cottage so I want to stay out of their way. Killing two birds with one stone.'

He nodded. 'That's fine. I have to go out but Mrs Jackson will get you lunch. Stay for dinner if you like.' Then he seemed to reconsider. 'Actually, it's Mrs Jackson's night off and my turn to cook so perhaps you'd better not.'

Liz laughed. 'Now I'm definitely staying. What's for dinner?'

He grinned back at her, a full-on smile that packed some serious wattage. 'Don't say I didn't warn you,' he said. 'See you at seven.'

CHAPTER TEN

Something smelled amazing. Something garlicky, spicy, possibly Italian. Liz felt her tastebuds shimmer into expectant awareness.

Neither she nor Gemma was an enthusiastic cook. They'd been eating well, thanks to Mrs Jackson, but simply, grazing on crudités and salads most of the time, with the odd bit of locally caught shellfish thrown in here and there. When they felt like a treat, they'd go to an authentic Spanish tapas bar in Ventnor called Delfina's, a regular haunt of Gemma's. But it had to be said, there was nothing like a home-cooked meal.

Liz followed her nose to the kitchen and found Theo there with Maddie. He was chopping a bunch of deep green continental parsley with a dexterity she wouldn't have expected in such a big man. All those heart-throb celebrity chefs weren't celebrities for nothing. There was, Liz admitted, something undeniably sexy about a man who could cook.

Maddie, who was shaving strips off a hunk of parmesan, turned around and caught sight of Liz.

'You're early,' she said in an accusatory tone.

'Sorry.' Liz glanced at the clock and realised that she'd arrived ten minutes before the stated time. 'But you can't fill the house with an aroma like that and expect people not to follow their noses.'

Theo glanced around at her. 'Grab the bread knife from that block over there and cut us some ciabatta, would you?'

Liz did as she was told. Maddie found her a wooden bread board and handed her the ciabatta loaf, then went to the massive stainless-steel fridge to pick out what looked like salad items.

'What are we having?' said Liz. God, she was starving.

'Whore sauce,' sang Maddie; at the same time, Theo said 'Fettucini puttanesca' with a very creditable Italian accent.

He frowned at his daughter, who spread her hands and shrugged in a gesture that reminded Liz of her aunt. 'Gemma says it.'

'Gemma says a lot of things,' said Theo. 'You know better than to repeat most of them.' But the gleam in his eyes told Liz he was amused. He glanced at the clock. 'Mads, why don't you wash up and get ready for our guests? They'll be here any minute.'

'But I need to do the salad.'

Liz said, 'I'll finish it if you like. Since I was so rude as to arrive early.'

'Okay, thanks!' Maddie took off her cute little apron with dancing cupcakes on it and made Liz bend down so she could jam it over Liz's head.

Ouch. The neck of the apron was a snug fit and caught on her ear on the way down. 'Thanks, that's great.'

Maddie scampered off. Liz pulled down the front of the apron so it wouldn't choke her. 'Guests? I didn't know it was an occasion.' She wasn't exactly dressed for one.

'It's not,' said Theo, tapping his wooden spoon on the side of a large pot. 'I'd say this is nearly ready.'

She looked over. A thick red sauce glugged away like hot lava.

'Hope you like anchovies,' said Theo.

'Love 'em.' Anchovies got a bad rap but she enjoyed the salty, strong, fishy flavour. 'Cracker, cottage cheese, anchovy. Perfect snack.'

'You lost me at cottage cheese.' Theo scooped out one flat length of fettuccine and bit down on it.

He held the remainder of the piece out to her. 'What do you think? *Al dente?*'

Liz had her hands full of knife and avocado. Without thinking, she leaned over to bite into the strand of pasta he dangled above her mouth.

Her lips brushed his fingertips, the smallest whisper of a touch, and she jerked back, nearly slicing her finger with the knife.

Talk about awkward. The pasta seemed to stick in her throat.

He watched her with a questioning tilt to his head. She was about to make some smart-alec remark to deflect his attention when she realised he was waiting for her verdict on the pasta.

'I don't know,' she said because she had no clue what the consistency of the fettuccine had been. 'Um, maybe give it another minute.'

He returned to the stove top and she dived back into her salad.

Liz decided to do her own thing here, ignoring the marinated peppers, artichoke hearts and marinated mushrooms Maddie had set out, in favour of a variety of fresh leaves, herbs and avocado, topped with a simple vinaigrette. With all the strong, complex flavours in the puttanesca, simple and crisp was best. A purist probably wouldn't add the avocado but who was judging her here?

In front of her was a bowl stacked with tomatoes. They had a depth of colour that laughed in the face of the anaemic tomatoes she usually bought in the supermarket back home. She'd always intended to grow her own, but as with everything else that wasn't work-related, her good intentions had fallen by the wayside.

She gestured with her knife. 'I assume those lovelies are from your garden.'

'We eat our own produce as much as we can,' said Theo.

No tinned toms in the puttanesca, then. Liz took the various salad leaves Maddie had already washed and dried out of the spinner – endive, radicchio, a handful of cress, all from the kitchen garden.

'The arugula is for garnish,' said Theo.

'A man who knows how to garnish,' said Liz. 'Lord Nash, you are full of surprises.'

A flicker of annoyance crossed his face.

After a moment, she said, 'Sorry. I didn't mean to offend you. Do you hate being called that?'

It was the first time since their initial meeting that she'd mentioned his title. In fact, she'd only said it because she would otherwise have said 'Mr Nash' and that wouldn't have been right. It was like calling her GP 'doctor', wasn't it? She hadn't meant any offence.

He didn't answer, but hefted the big pot and dumped the pasta in a colander that stood ready in the sink. Steam gushed upward and he turned away to grab a bottle of wine that stood open on the counter. 'Would you like some?'

'Please,' she said, glad to let the awkward subject drop.

Taking her glass from him, she sipped the wine. She wasn't a great judge but it tasted light to her, almost refreshing. Not her usual kind of tipple but a good complement for the spicy pasta dish.

'I'd better not have too much of this,' she said, taking another sip. It was a huge glass and he hadn't stinted. 'I forgot to eat lunch today.'

'You must be hungry.' He gestured to the antipasto platter that sat ready on the table. 'Have some.'

Obediently, she chose a fat kalamata olive dripping with garlic and chilli marinade and bit in. Theo leaned past her to snag a sliver of char-grilled zucchini. He popped it into his mouth, then went back to the stove. Tonight, he smelled like the ocean.

Suddenly, Liz didn't feel all that hungry. She wondered where Maddie was.

'Did you find anything interesting in the archives after I left you?' said Theo.

The kitchen door opened. 'We're here,' sang out Gemma.

She and Fergus came in bearing wine and a store-bought cake for dessert. Because, as Gemma loudly confided to Liz, Theo couldn't bake for peanuts and her own kitchen was in the process of being ripped out.

Gemma winked at Liz. 'There's a sledge hammer waiting for you when you get up tomorrow.'

Liz grinned. 'Now you're talking.'

Maddie came in, to great acclaim from Fergus. Clearly these two adored each other.

The family was noisy and talkative as they ploughed through the antipasto. Even Theo seemed to unwind as they moved on to the main course.

Liz was prepared to love any meal she didn't have to cook herself, but this puttanesca was a universe apart. 'Oh, my God, that's orgasmic,' she said, twirling another coil of fettuccine around her fork.

'What's orgasmic mean?' said Maddie, breaking her bread into tiny pieces.

'I meant *organic*,' said Liz, with a grimace of apology at Theo, who merely looked amused.

'Oh, I know what *that* is,' said Maddie. 'It means you've grown it without any nasty chemical pesticides and stuff.'

'Anyway, it's out of this world.' Liz pushed the pasta dish toward Maddie.

'A touch too salty for me,' said Gemma with a wink at Liz. 'Easy on the anchovies next time, brother.'

'Well, I, for one, need a trough to enjoy this to the full,' said Liz. She looked down at the flecks of red on her t-shirt. 'And maybe a bib.'

Theo laughed. God, it was a sucker punch to the gut when he did that. No man had a right to look that good when he laughed *and* be a great cook.

'You know this is the only dish he *can* make,' said Gemma, with a wicked smirk. 'It was his stock-in-trade seduction routine when he was single.'

'Lies, all lies,' said Theo on a sigh.

'Dad can make tons of stuff,' said Maddie loyally.

'Mainly Italian cuisine, right, Theo?' put in Fergus. 'On account

of that gorgeous girl he went out with for a while . . . Gina? Sophia?'
Fergus whistled, black eyes glittering with mischief. 'Legs up to her —'

'Thank you, Fergus,' said Theo, reaching for the bottle to pour his
sister more wine.

Gemma glanced around, as if she'd just noticed something.
'Where's Valerie tonight?'

Theo cleared his throat. 'London.'

'Valerie's gone to talk Raaaooouul into coming to Seagrove so we
can taste his disgusting rabbit food,' said Maddie. 'Can I have some
juice, please?'

'Sure.'

Maddie scrambled up from the table to get herself a glass.

Fergus said, 'And who is this "Growl" fellow when he's at home?'

'Raoul de Martin is the celebrity chef who came up with this stupid diet Valerie's on,' said Gemma, serving herself extra salad. 'She's
lost pounds and pounds she never needed to lose in the first place,
and now she wants the rest of the world to join her in demented stick-
figure land. She's going to ruin that cocktail party before the Open
Day and there's not a damn thing any of us can do about it. Except
you.' Gemma jabbed her finger at Theo, who was staring fixedly at the
pepper grinder.

Attempting to break the tension, Liz said, 'Speaking of the Open
Day, how's all that going?'

Theo didn't answer. Gemma shrugged. 'Ask Valerie. I'm sure she
could tell you to the last detail. Knowing her, she has spreadsheets.'

'Hey, don't knock spreadsheets,' said Liz. She wasn't naturally very
detail-oriented but she'd trained herself to be. A spreadsheet had saved
her bacon on more than one occasion.

'But you've been working hard on the Open Day, haven't you,
Gemma, my sweet?' said Fergus, no doubt trying to inject a positive note.

'I'm trying,' Gemma said. 'I'll start contacting media once I have
the okay from Valerie on the publicity plan. I've done the concept
designs for the flyers and the other advertising guff.'

She took out her phone and scrolled through some photos, then held it out to show Liz the designs.

Liz flicked through the images. 'Wow, they're terrific,' she said, and meant it. She glanced at Theo, but he was still contemplating the tableware.

'Want to see the animation I had made?' Gemma frowned, tapping at her phone. 'Can't get it to work on this thing but I'll show you on the computer when we get home. I made the lion and the unicorn on the family crest come to life and do a dance together. Then they each explain a bit about the family history.'

'It's so cool,' said Maddie. 'Only I bet Valerie won't let us use it,' she added, slumping in her chair. 'She'll think it's not dignified.'

'Dad would turn in his grave,' said Theo, coming to life again. He drained his glass and reached for the bottle. 'Do it.'

'Really?' said Gemma. 'I thought I'd make a special children's page for the website to encourage schools to visit. It can go there.'

'She's been working on that site for a year,' Fergus told Liz in a stage whisper. 'It's her baby, so it is. She's never going to let it go.'

'I want to get it right,' said Gemma. 'Anyway, it should be up and running, subject to Valerie's approval, in the next week or two. At least, that's the plan. Valerie always wants lots of changes.' Gemma pursed her lips at Theo. 'You ought to at least look over what we've done before it goes live.'

Her brother pushed his chair away from the table and stood up. 'I don't know anything about websites. I'm sure it's fine.'

He began collecting plates but Liz whipped them away from him, insisting that the cook must never clean up. With her customary efficiency, she cleared the table and went into the butler's pantry to rinse the plates and stack the dishwasher.

Liz was glad to remove herself from the tension surrounding the website, Valerie and the house in general. She wasn't surprised when Fergus joined her.

She handed him a tea towel. 'I'll wash, you dry.'

As the enormous rectangular sink filled with hot water, Fergus hefted over the large pots Theo had used for the spaghetti. Liz rummaged around, finding containers for leftovers and scraping vegetable scraps into the compost bin. She couldn't find rubber gloves, so she added a bit more cold water and started in on the washing up.

'All Gemma wants is a bit of a pat on the back,' Fergus murmured. 'He's hard on her.'

'I don't think he means to be,' said Liz. 'He has a lot of worries, what with the house and the garden, Maddie and so on.'

The 'so on', of course, being Valerie.

Liz wondered if Theo knew or suspected his fiancée might be infatuated with another man. Was Valerie up in London enjoying a cosy night in with her lover at this very moment?

None of your business, Liz, she told herself.

She hated cheaters. Loathed them. The Facebook photo of Tony and Jessica flashed into her brain. But of course, that was only cheating in the most technical sense. Through his refusal to answer her calls, Tony had as good as told her it was over. Presumably, that meant they were both free to see other people. That he'd moved on so quickly was a slap in the face, but there was no mandatory mourning period for the ten years they'd been together.

On the other hand, that photo could well have been innocent. She knew that, but something in her gut told her to prepare herself for the worst.

She'd taken off her wedding and engagement rings to wash the dishes: a not-quite-half-a-carat diamond solitaire and a plain yellow gold band that looked unassuming, maybe even a little scrawny, on her long fingers with their slightly squared-off tips. If she were honest, she wouldn't have chosen these rings in a blue fit. She never wore yellow gold and she preferred something less generic in design. But Tony had chosen those rings so she'd loved them anyway.

Having finished the pots and pans, Liz dried her hands and picked up her jewellery.

She hesitated. Then she slid them back on her finger and went to join the others.

'Now,' said Gemma, 'who's for dessert?'

After dinner, Liz went back to the library to do a video conference she'd organised with Nick, but when she checked her email she saw he'd cancelled and nominated another time.

She emailed back to ask him where he had found the two volumes of Delany's memoirs and whether he had any ideas where she might search for the rest? She'd got hold of a heap more documents from the Seagrove archives and she'd let him know when she'd gone through them. One thing was for certain – the missing memoirs weren't among those documents either.

The whole business left her ambivalent. The close relationship she'd developed with the Nashes made her simultaneously reluctant and more determined than ever to find out what had happened to the real Stephen Nash all those years ago. She needed to do her job and leave before she became too heavily involved with this family.

She suspected it was already too late.

Liz yawned. Fergus and Gemma were giving her a lift back to the cottage. She certainly couldn't ride her bike back in the dark after all that red wine.

She glanced around her. That couch looked comfy. In fact, the entire library, which before had seemed so grand and imposing, now seemed welcoming, almost cosy. She still wanted her ashes scattered in this room when she died. Maybe they'd rent her some space in one of those Japanese urns by the door.

Gathering up her bits and pieces, Liz was packing her backpack when Maddie padded in, wearing polka-dot pyjamas. 'Dad told me to come and say goodnight.'

She stopped when she saw the silver rattle in Liz's hand. 'What have you got that for?'

Liz wasn't sure. 'I'm doing a little research on it,' she said, which was true, in a way. She handed it to Maddie.

The bells jingled as Maddie turned it over, tracing the engraved initials with her fingertip. 'It looks new, doesn't it, all polished like that,' she said. 'Isn't it amazing to think it was there for hundreds of years?'

'There?' said Liz. 'Where would that be?'

Maddie's brow furrowed. 'In the park. Some man found it with a metal detector. Granddad paid him – can't remember how much – to hand it over.'

'Where was it found, exactly? Do you remember?' said Liz, wondering why Theo hadn't told her about this. Then she recalled he hadn't been close to his father. Perhaps he'd never heard this story.

Maddie shook her head. 'Sorry. But Mr Jackson will tell you. He knows everything about Seagrove.'

'Maddie, bed!' Theo was calling her.

'Oops, better go.' Maddie gave back the rattle. 'Goodnight.'

'Night, Mads,' said Liz.

To her surprise, Maddie put her arms around her. A little awkwardly, Liz returned the quick hug. 'Sweet dreams,' she called as the girl ran out, long curls fluttering like streamers behind her.

'Night, Dad!' Maddie yelled, speeding past as Theo came in.

Theo's face softened as he watched his daughter go.

Liz smiled. 'She's the best.'

He cocked his head at her. 'I might be biased, but I tend to agree.'

She noticed he had a bottle in his hand and two balloon-shaped glasses, which he set down with slightly exaggerated care on the coffee table in front of the couch by the fireplace. 'Is that brandy?' she said. 'I'm sorry, but I don't drink it.'

He sat down and reached for the decanter. 'You've never had brandy until you've tried this, my dear Ms Liz. It's from Cognac. Smooth as . . .' he poured some into a glass and handed it to her, 'silk. Try it.'

She wondered now if he was a little drunk. Not obnoxiously so. Not so that he slurred his words. Just enough to become slightly more garrulous. Almost as talkative as a normal person, in fact.

How could she say no? She moved to take the glass from him and perched on the arm of the couch. Playing for time, she swirled the brandy around, copying what he did, but not expecting to like the result. She felt a bit pretentious, to be honest.

Cautiously, she sipped, and her eyes widened in surprise. It was all velvety, smoky heat rolling over her tongue, with a slight sweetness in the aftertaste.

'I'm right, aren't I?' he said.

'Ooh, yes,' she breathed, never one to begrudge praise when someone introduced her to a new indulgence. 'This ought to be illegal.'

'It's prohibitively expensive,' said Theo. The fact that he could still say 'prohibitively' meant he couldn't be that intoxicated.

She, on the other hand . . .

'Where are Fergus and Gemma?' said Liz.

'Upstairs.' Theo waved a hand toward the ceiling. 'Fergus thought he might be over the limit so you're all staying here tonight.'

Liz put down her empty glass. She wished she didn't always have to be so sensible. She'd love to sit here drinking expensive brandy with Theo, then ask him with a sultry pout to show her to her room. But that would be ten kinds of complicated and she needed to get out while she was sober enough to remember that.

'Right,' she said, slapping her thighs and standing up. 'I'd best be off to bed, then. Early start tomorrow.' She sounded like the jolly sports teacher at her old high school.

'I'll show you to your room,' said Theo.

Yes. Fine. This shouldn't be awkward at all.

As they went upstairs, Liz felt slightly resentful. She had no right to expect Fergus to remain sober so he could chauffeur the three of them back to the cottage, but still . . . Why did it feel like the night had been ruined?

She was a married woman. She should not be appreciating the easy way Theo moved as he climbed the stairs, or the breadth of his shoulders, or the way his jeans — No, just stop. She shouldn't be imagining what might happen when they got to her bedroom door. She was not *that* woman. She did not cheat. She did not help men cheat.

Had it been almost any other man with her on that staircase, she would have known exactly what his motives were and sent him to the right-about. But she was terrified of giving Theo the brush-off only to find he'd never had the least intention of making a move on her.

After all, someone like Liz wasn't exactly a threat to someone like Valerie.

And then there was that other possibility. That if she let him come with her to the bedroom door, she might give in to temptation and throw herself at him. He might do the equivalent of a Rugby fend to hold her off and then she'd have to pack up and leave the island. There was no way she could face him again after that scenario.

'You know what? Just tell me which door,' she said, overtaking Theo when they reached the second floor. 'I'm good from here.'

When he didn't respond, she looked back. He stood with his arms by his sides, his face shadowed. The lines of his body seemed taut, as if he were waiting for something.

'Second on the left,' he said. He stayed where he was while she found her room and fumbled with the door knob.

'Thanks,' she mumbled. 'Goodnight.'

She went in and shut the door and leaned against it, one palm pressed against the wooden panels.

Tony. She needed to talk to Tony.

Without so much as switching on the light, she took out her phone and dialled.

Lord Kenyon

Mr Garrow, for the plaintiff, had the slightly bulbous, heavy-lidded eyes of a somnolent frog. However, looks could be deceiving. The young man's mind was acute and his advocacy vigorous – perhaps too vigorous for Lord Kenyon's taste, particularly when employed in the defence of criminals.

Presently, however, Mr Garrow was happily employed on the side of the angels, which was to say, appearing for the plaintiff in this criminal conversation trial. Lord Kenyon was well satisfied with Garrow's preliminary statements and the depth of feeling he had shown the court as he delivered them.

Mr Erskine himself could not have done better. He almost invariably appeared for the plaintiff in cases such as these. There must be some personal connection between Julian Nash and Mr Erskine – a political one, perhaps? Lord Kenyon resolved to quiz him about it over a bottle of claret in his club one evening.

Having so ably set the stage with his initial remarks, Mr Garrow continued. 'The defendant is the younger brother of the plaintiff. Until recently, the defendant, being Lord Nash's dependent, received a quarterly allowance of some £500 from the estate.'

Mr Garrow threw a look brimful of meaning toward the jury. Not only had Julian Nash betrayed his brother, he had bitten the hand that fed him.

Clutching at the edges of his robe and rocking on his heels, Garrow went on. 'The brothers enjoyed a close relationship. Their mother lived with the plaintiff, and Julian Nash would stay in the family home at Seagrove for extended periods, sometimes conducting his mother to Bath for her health.

'It seems that after his marriage, Lord Nash saw rather more of his brother than ever before. Lord and Lady Nash and Mr Julian

Nash were often to be seen together in society. During the months in question, Lord Nash, being greatly occupied with estate business, allowed his wife to travel to London and remain there in the care of his brother – secure, or so he thought, in the knowledge that his wife would come to no harm while under the protection of one so intimately connected and bound to him by the ties of familial affection.'

The Lord Chief Justice rumbled his agreement. 'As he had every right to do.' He glared beneath lowered brows at the jury, lest they think Lord Nash had been foolhardy in entrusting his lovely wife to such a notable womaniser as his brother.

Mr Garrow inclined his head. 'As your lordship pleases.' As if to emphasise the accord between himself and the judge, he allowed a short silence to fall. Then he called his first witness.

The gentleman was sworn in. Mr Garrow began. 'Would you state your full name for the court?'

'Mr Fitzgibbons,' mused Lord Kenyon, when the gentleman had obliged. 'Are you connected with Mr John Fitzgibbons of Roseberry Park?'

The witness bowed. 'I have that honour, my lord. He is my uncle.'

'Yes, yes, a most respectable and honourable gentleman,' said his lordship, making careful note.

Mr Garrow tucked his hands into the folds of his robes. 'Do you know Lord Nash, the plaintiff in this case?'

'I do, sir.'

'And how long have you known him?'

'Rather more than ten years.'

'Are you acquainted with Lady Nash?'

'Indeed I am. I met the lady on the occasion of her marriage and have supped with Lord and Lady Nash many times since.'

'In London?'

Mr Fitzgibbons nodded. 'Yes, although I have also visited them frequently at Seagrove.'

Mr Garrow glanced at the jury. 'That is Lord Nash's house on the Isle of Wight.'

'Yes, sir. A most handsome residence.'

Mr Garrow extended his arms and pressed his hands on the bar table. He leaned forward, all earnestness. 'In your opinion, what was the state of Lord and Lady Nash's marriage?'

The witness's brow furrowed beneath his neat powdered wig. 'I'm not sure I take your meaning.'

Garrow's forehead creased. 'Until the distressing events of last spring, did they seem to you to be a devoted couple?'

'Why, yes. Indeed they were devoted.'

'Did Lady Nash seem to you to be a virtuous wife?'

'Most virtuous. A paragon of virtue, I should say.'

'Mr Fitzgibbons, are you acquainted with Mr Julian Nash, the defendant in this case?'

'Yes, sir.'

'And what is your opinion of him?'

At this, the witness looked sidelong at the jury. 'I'm sure I could not say.'

'Oh, come now, Mr Fitzgibbons. You must have formed an opinion.'

The witness, with a puff of his cheeks meant to denote reluctance, said, 'I have, sir.'

When he did not say more, Lord Kenyon intervened. 'Your scruples do you credit, sir, but we must have the truth. Believe me, you cannot say more to discredit Mr Nash than this court is likely to hear from other sources.'

'My lord.' The witness made a slight bow and turned to the jury. 'My impression of Mr Nash is of a profligate, a womaniser and a hot-headed brawler.'

Mr Garrow paused, to let those words sink in.

'A profligate . . . a womaniser . . . and a hot-headed brawler,' Lord Kenyon repeated, making a careful note to that effect.

'And how came you by these opinions?' said Mr Garrow.

'By observation, sir. There is never peace when Mr Nash is at hand.'

'Did you ever observe Mr Nash and his sister-in-law alone together?'

'I did not make any observations upon them.'

'Thank you.' Mr Garrow sat down.

Lord Kenyon's pen scratched across his page for a full minute before he raised his gaze to invite Mr Erskine, for the defendant, to speak.

With a playful challenge in his tone, the judge said, 'Well? And what do you have to say to that, Mr Erskine?'

Mr Erskine was a dark man with heavy brows and an imposing nose. He was not overly large in stature, yet the force of his personality dominated the court room whenever he spoke.

'My lord.' Upon rising, Erskine bowed, then turned to cross-examine the witness. 'Mr Fitzgibbons, you intimated that you have *direct* experience or observation of Mr Nash's, ah, profligacy, womanising and brawling? Those were your words, I believe? In what circumstances did you have the opportunity to observe such behaviour?'

The witness fidgeted and glanced down at his toes before turning to the Lord Chief Justice. 'I must decline to answer that, my lord.'

'Yes, yes, you are not obliged to answer that,' said Lord Kenyon, with a heavy frown. Mr Fitzgibbons was not the man on trial here. Erskine was being mischievous, seeking to implicate the witness in Mr Nash's crimes.

Mr Erskine bowed. 'Thank you, my lord.'

The witness was stood down.

CHAPTER ELEVEN

Liz

Liz adjusted her safety goggles and squared up to the kitchen wall as if she meant business. Her head pounded like fury but the sledge hammer was a solid, hefty weight in her hands. She was not a violent person by nature, but this morning, she had a lot of aggression inside her that needed somewhere to go.

She hauled back the hammer and swung it with all her might.

The conversation with Tony had not gone well. First of all, Liz had dialled him in the dark, leaning against her bedroom door. It was more of a reflex action, really. She'd expected him to ignore the call as he'd ignored all the others she'd made.

She was still fumbling around for the light switch when Tony's voice said, 'Hello?'

She dropped the phone.

'Damn!' She crouched and felt around the floor. She hadn't thought she was that affected by the wine and brandy, but the world tilted. She overbalanced and landed hard on her hands and knees, sending the phone skittering under something solid, like a free-standing wardrobe.

Her hands slid over the plush carpet beneath, hoping to encounter her phone. She'd finally reached Tony and she'd lost him again. Would he think she was playing some juvenile game with him?

'Come on, come on. Where are you?' she muttered.

Panting with effort, she made great sweeps with her palms, connected with something hard and yanked out the phone.

'Hello! Tony, sorry, are you there?'

The line was dead.

Light. Calm down and find the light. If he answered a minute ago, he'd answer again.

She turned the light on and looked around. 'Crikey,' she breathed, in a totally non-ironic way.

This bedroom belonged to Lady Mary on *Downton Abbey*, not to her. The wallpaper was exquisite – a soft turquoise with chinoiserie trees, the flowers and birds so vividly painted they looked alive. The bed was a mahogany four-poster. Against one wall stood the most delicate dressing table she'd ever seen, complete with a gilded mirror. There was even an ensuite with marble tiles and a claw-footed tub.

Her phone jangled. Tony.

'Hi, I'm so sorry about that. I dropped the phone.'

'Do you know what time it is here? Liz, are you drunk?'

'Sorry. Sorry,' she mumbled. She had no idea what time it was there. 'But I wanted to ask you something. Something very important.'

All that wine and brandy had kicked in with a vengeance. She couldn't seem to crisp up her diction and her words were sliding into each other. She knew it but she couldn't seem to make it stop.

'Not a good time, Liz.'

'Then why answer, you berk?' Oops. Had she said that out loud? 'Are you sleeping with her?' Liz blurted out, overriding his response. 'That – that Jessica girl?'

'Who?'

'The one you're all cuddly with on your Facebook page.' You berk. That time, she only said it in her head. Maddie was right. 'Berk' was a good insult. A very good, very British insult.

A long pause.

Then Tony sighed. 'Actually, I suppose I'm glad you asked.'

'Oh. Glad, are you?' said Liz, ruffling her hair with one hand. 'Right, good.'

She had an awful, churning feeling in her gut and it wasn't from the alcohol.

'I *have* met someone,' said Tony. 'Not Jessica. Someone else. Someone special. Liz, I've never felt like this before about anyone.'

That ought to hurt more than it did. She rubbed her forehead. Maybe it was the alcohol numbing the pain.

Tony rhapsodised on while she faded in and out, wishing he'd stop, but powerless to say so or even to do the obvious thing and hang up.

His voice turned husky. 'You know, Liz, I keep thinking, what if I'd missed this? What if she and I had never met?'

What the hell? Did he think she'd be pleased for him? Excuse her, but she was not that civilised. Barely five minutes ago, she and Tony were planning a renovation. A family, for God's sake!

The name of the so-special woman was Leanne. Ordinary name, but when Tony said it, all breathy and reverent like that, Liz wanted to vomit. Come to think of it, she might in fact vomit. Her skin felt clammy and the nausea and dizziness didn't help.

She took the phone into the ensuite and sat on the Chinese garden stool next to the bath.

How could this be happening to her?

'I hope that you and I can be friends,' said Tony.

She gave a sarcastic laugh, but tears were leaking out of her eyes. 'You mean that, don't you?'

'Take care of yourself, Liz. I want you to be happy.'

He said it in such a gentle, patronising way that she knew it was over between them.

Desperate not to let him hear her distress, she held her breath and raised her gaze to the ceiling, trying to get herself together. She could

yell at him, but that would achieve nothing but her own embarrassment. Pride stopped her from making more of a fool of herself than she
felt already.

She managed to say, 'You too.'

'We'll sort out the house and everything when we get back, yeah?'

She was sobbing as she hung up.

The conversation played over and over in Liz's mind for the rest
of the night. It was a good thing the plasterwork on the ceiling was so
intricate and beautiful. She must have inspected every inch of it as she
lay there awake, replaying their friendly little chat.

In the morning she felt sluggish and wished she'd gone easier on the
vino, not to mention the brandy. The night had been long and miserable, but she had neither the inclination nor the opportunity to wallow.

She avoided Theo, letting the hours of her morning run and gardening session pass by. The last thing she needed was to face him in
her fragile emotional state, considering the tension between them
last night. Head pounding, she downed aspirin and drank water and
accepted gratefully when Fergus and Gemma suggested going out for a
greasy breakfast fry-up to soak up their hangovers.

Theo wasn't about, thank God. Part of her wished she had jumped
his bones last night, but then she would have been using him to boost
her ego.

She wasn't like Tony. She couldn't move on that fast. If you loved
someone, you couldn't just switch it off.

By late morning, rage had overtaken her misery. Despite the pounding in her head that seemed to strengthen with every hammer blow, she
threw herself into the demolition work on Gemma's cottage with grit
and gusto.

That wall was history. A lot like her marriage.

When they stopped for a break and Liz had chugged some of Mrs
Jackson's lemonade, Fergus said, 'For a girl, you pack a wallop.'

'I'll take that as a compliment,' said Liz. She massaged the back of
her neck. 'I'm going to feel it tomorrow.'

'Ladies, I have to go into town this afternoon for supplies, so I won't be needing you after lunch,' said Fergus.

'Good time to move you up to the house,' Gemma said to Liz. She and Fergus were renting a camper van so they could be on site, but Liz would stay in the Big House from tonight onward.

Great, she thought. How could she avoid Theo now?

Besides, she couldn't lose sight of why she'd come here in the first place. She'd better get stuck into all that material Theo had pulled out of the archives for her or Nick would think she was having a nice little junket at his expense.

It took no time at all to move her in. She didn't have a lot of belongings, after all.

When they'd carried her things into that gorgeous bedroom, Gemma said, 'Are you okay? You've been looking like death warmed up today.'

'Hung over, I think.'

'Mmm.' Gemma lifted a sceptical eyebrow.

Liz bit her lip. 'Yeah, well, it's not just the hangover. You know I've been having trouble with Tony . . .'

Gemma nodded.

'Last night, I was a bit drunk and I called him.' She took a deep breath. 'He told me he'd met someone else. Sounds serious.'

'The rat!' Gemma grabbed Liz's hands and pulled her over to sit on the bed. 'Why didn't you tell me? You didn't need to do all that work this morning. We would have understood.'

Liz shook her head and sniffed. 'No, I need to be busy. I can't let myself sit and think. When I do that it all becomes overwhelming.'

'Oh, sweetheart.' Gemma's eyes moistened in sympathy. 'Here's what we'll do. You need a big, hot bath. I'm going to steal some of Valerie's stuff. She'll have something beautiful and expensive and you can just lie there and soak in it for a while. Be good for your sore muscles, too.'

Gemma went into the ensuite and Liz heard taps running.

'Back in a tick.'

She returned from Valerie's room with all sorts of designer-brand unguents, most of which had functions Liz had never guessed a human woman might want or need. Weakly, Liz tried to object. Valerie would not be happy about this.

'She's not here. How would she know?' said Gemma. 'I'll put them back, don't worry. You just relax.'

'Okay. Thanks.' Liz rummaged in her backpack for her toiletries case.

Gemma put out towels and fussed about the water temperature like a mother with a new baby, then went to leave. At the door, she stopped. 'Do you want me to check on you later, or would you rather sleep?'

'Can't sleep,' Liz muttered. 'I've got work to do.'

Realising that had come out too abruptly, she made herself give her friend a smile. 'But thanks. I . . . This is really nice of you.'

The bath did improve her spirits a little. By the time she got out, she knew she wasn't going to cry any more. No festering in bed and gorging on chocolate, either. In fact, she'd make herself go for a run before dinner. Surefire hangover cure.

She put on the peacock-blue robe Gemma had brought her and was towelling her hair when she heard the muted roar of an expensive-sounding car engine. Glancing out the window, which overlooked the front of the house, she saw a black sports car – Ferrari, maybe? – skid to a stop with a small spray of gravel on the drive.

'Oh, no!' It was Valerie. The driver, all loose-limbed grace with a movie-star smile, could only be Raoul de Martin.

The stolen beauty products sat on the ceramic stool next to the bathtub. Liz needed to get them back to Valerie's room quick-smart.

She grabbed her phone and texted back and forth with Gemma, who was now in Ventnor, running errands. She was too far away to help, except to give directions to the master suite. Unsurprisingly, Valerie and Theo's suite was next to the curiosity cabinet Theo had shown her. Liz knew the way.

She hurled the phone onto the bed and raced down the corridor, arms full of beauty products, barefoot and naked but for the robe that billowed around her ankles.

Jeez, the house was like a rabbit warren. She must have taken a wrong turn somewhere, because she opened a door to find an empty space where the master suite should have been.

God, why had she listened to Gemma? Had she really needed that scented bath oil or that divine sugar body scrub? She retraced her steps, and, as she approached the gallery that skirted the entry hall, heard voices float upward. Good thing Valerie had Raoul with her; she wouldn't come up to her room immediately.

Liz realised she'd taken a wrong turn at the end of the corridor so she tried the mirror image of the way she'd just been. This time, her sense of direction didn't fail her. She opened the door to the left of Theo's study and peeked in.

No one there. Liz scarcely had time to do more than register the immense floor-to-ceiling windows and the enormous canopied bed as she scampered through. There were two doors on the left-hand side, opposite the communicating door to the curiosity cabinet. She wrenched one open and found a walk-in robe, with a stupendous number of orange boxes taking up space next to racks and racks of shoes. The other was the door to the ensuite.

Liz blinked. Bit of a pigsty, this bathroom. That was unexpected. The vanity counter was littered with Valerie's lotions and potions on one side. On the other sat mouthwash, a can of shaving foam, a razor and deodorant that she assumed were Theo's.

A couple of cleaners 'did' for them every second day, Mrs Jackson had told Liz. Clearly, today was not that day.

The mess seemed to clash with the opulent expanse of the bathroom, which, according to Gemma, had been renovated to Valerie's specifications before she would agree to move to Seagrove. Smoky marble tiles covered the floor and huge silver peonies rioted over the charcoal wallpaper. A glittering chandelier hung – against safety regulations, she was sure – over a massive claw-footed bathtub. The shower was so cavernous you could host a cocktail party in it; the jets and sprays and massive overhead shower rose looked like a lot of fun.

Liz didn't want to imagine the kind of fun Theo and Valerie might have in a shower like that. Back to the job at hand.

A bottle of shampoo hit the deck with a clatter as she unloaded her armful of products onto the gypsy stool by the enormous tub. She bent to pick the bottle up, put it back with the others and turned to go.

And almost crashed into Valerie, who was standing silently in the doorway.

Liz yelped. Then she laughed nervously, pressing one hand to her chest, clutching the edges of the robe together with the other. 'You scared me.'

She'd never seen that look on any real person's face before. Murderous, that was how she'd describe it. Cruella de Ville style.

'*What*,' said Valerie between clenched teeth, 'are you doing here?' Shock and outrage took the place of the cartoon villain expression. She jabbed Liz in the shoulder with a fuchsia fingernail. 'You *slut*. That's my bath robe!'

Oh, hell. 'This is yours?' Liz was going to kill Gemma.

Valerie whipped around and stalked back into the bedroom. '*Where is he?*'

Only then did Liz realise Valerie had leaped to a ridiculous conclusion. 'Oh, come on. It's not what you think. God, I would never . . . Theo is probably outside in the garden right now. He —'

'Theo?' Valerie opened the door and barked into the corridor. '*Theo!*'

Liz sidled out of the ensuite just as Theo came into the bedroom through the communicating door opposite.

'Oh, hi.' He started over to Valerie, presumably to kiss her hello, but the look on her face made him stop. Then he noticed Liz and scratched his head, making his hair stick up at oddly endearing angles. 'What's going on?'

'*What's going on?*' Valerie echoed, biting off each word. 'Why don't you tell me?'

Theo frowned, then glanced at Liz again, wet hair, robe and all. 'Sorry to say I have no idea. I wish I did.'

Valerie's up-cut nostrils flared. 'There's another woman. In our bedroom. Naked under that robe. *My* robe. And you're telling me you have *no idea*?'

Coolly, he said, 'That's what I'm telling you, Val.'

'Don't call me Val!' she snapped.

Incongruously, Liz found that old Paul Simon hit 'You Can Call Me Al' running through her mind. Only, rather than 'Al', it was 'Val'.

Valerie whipped around and pointed at her. 'Take that off. Now!'

This was a farce. An honest-to-goodness *Fawlty Towers* episode.

'Can't. Sorry.' Liz was almost starting to enjoy herself. 'I've got nothing on under here.'

In other circumstances, she'd bet Theo would have seen the joke, but he wasn't smiling now.

'You should think very carefully about what happens next, Valerie. I don't think you want to be the one to start flinging accusations around,' he said.

Was it her imagination or had the temperature in the room chilled to freezing?

'What I've been trying to explain —' Liz started.

He held up his hand, cutting her off. 'No, Liz. No explanations needed. Valerie either accepts the situation is innocent or she doesn't.' He shoved his hands into his pockets. 'Well, Valerie? What's it to be?'

He acted as if he didn't care which way she went. Maybe he knew she'd back down. But there was something unspoken here. To do with Valerie's trip to London, perhaps?

Unable to stand the tension, Liz said, 'I'm sorry to have used your robe, Valerie. I didn't know it was yours, or I wouldn't have. It's, um, difficult to explain.' Difficult to explain without landing Gemma in trouble, that was. 'I'll . . . I'll wash it and get it back to you.'

'It's dry-clean-only,' Valerie snapped.

Liz thought a dry-clean-only bath robe was the stupidest concept she'd ever heard of, but that was rich folk for you. 'I'll dry-clean it, then.' She took a few tentative steps toward the door. 'Think I'm just going to, uh, go and get dressed. Leave you to it.'

Back in her room, Liz called Gemma and told her the whole story. The incident should have sunk Liz with embarrassment, but Gemma's utter, unabashed delight made her smile. And the look in Theo's eyes when he'd seen her in that bath robe had not hurt her ego either.

Somehow, she thought, as she pulled on her running gear, she might just get through the bad stuff in one piece.

Contrary to Liz's fears and Gemma's hopes, Valerie did not pack her bags and leave Seagrove, taking Raoul with her. In the days following the bath robe incident, she seemed to focus exclusively on seeing that Raoul had everything he needed for the trial cocktail party. The rest of the preparations for the Open Day seemed to be on hold as far as Valerie was concerned.

To avoid conflict, Theo had suggested to Mrs Jackson that she might take the day of Raoul's trial cocktail party off, since Raoul would be taking over her kitchens to prepare for the taste-testing that night.

Mrs Jackson refused. 'She said she didn't trust a damned frog to take care of her kitchen, so she'd stay around to keep an eye on him,' Gemma reported to Liz later.

They were going shopping to buy something for Liz to wear that night. She was tired of slobbing about in the clothes she'd bought in Ventnor. Besides, the best thing to do after your husband declares his love for someone else is to get yourself a new outfit, quick smart. Maybe a drastic new haircut too.

'Do you think I'd look good as a platinum blonde?' said Liz as

Gemma backed out of the cottage driveway.

'Um, no,' said Gemma. 'Look at the eyebrows on you, for heaven's sake.'

Liz traced one admittedly thick, black eyebrow with her fingertip. More Brooke Shields than Tippi Hedren. 'I suppose so.'

'Actually, it's not the eyebrows, there are plenty of platinum blondes with dark eyebrows around. But you don't have the right skin tone. Trust me, young Jedi. I know these things. Dress you, I will.'

'Plus, there's the re-growth,' said Liz glumly. 'Couldn't be bothered looking after it.'

'You don't need to change anything,' said Gemma. 'We'll get you a great dress and I'll do your hair and makeup, that's all. It'll be fab.'

'Deal,' said Liz. 'As long as you don't use anything of Valerie's, that is.'

Gemma grinned, pulling into a parking space in front of a small vintage fashion boutique in Ventnor. 'Doesn't look like much, I know,' she said, 'but wait till you see what she has out the back!'

That evening, gussied up to the nines in pre-loved fashion, Liz and Gemma climbed out of Fergus's utility.

'Sure you don't want to come in with us?' said Gemma through his open window. Unlike Liz, Fergus hadn't received a formal invitation and he was using that as an excuse to stay home.

Fergus grinned and deepened his accent. 'Isn't it a thing of sorrow to me, to be going back to me steak and chips?'

'Grr,' said Gemma.

Liz sighed. 'Wish *I* was having steak and chips.'

'Come on,' Gemma said to Liz. 'We'll go this way.'

They walked around the side of the house and went up the shallow steps to the paved terrace at the rear.

Gemma nearly reeled when she saw the decorating scheme Valerie had chosen – or rather, the scheme she must have instructed her florist to use. Massive formal arrangements of flowers in red, green and orange fanned out behind the serving tables. Great, life-sized, standing cut-outs of Raoul stood sentry between each set of French doors that led into the house, and a massive banner advertising Raoul's latest cookbook hung above the bar. The only thing Valerie hadn't spoiled was the stunning view.

Liz murmured to her friend, 'I take it you had nothing to do with this.'

'I need a drink,' said Gemma. However, she didn't move, apparently paralysed by the awfulness of the decorations.

'Brilliant night for it,' said Liz, as the first guests began to stream in. 'Fantastic place for a party.'

'Yes,' agreed Gemma, falling in with Liz's attempt at distraction. 'When we were small, my parents used to hold huge, fancy parties here.' She made a wry face. 'Back when we could afford it. Theo and I used to watch from the upstairs windows and Mrs Jackson would send up plates of savouries.'

'She's a treasure, that woman,' said Liz.

Gemma frowned. 'I only hope this Raoul thing isn't the straw that breaks the camel's back.'

Just then Valerie appeared, firmly in charge, and looking expensive in a dress made from a draped silver jersey fabric that clung to her in all the right places.

'Hello! Good evening!' called Maddie, hurrying up to Gemma and Liz. She pulled up short as her gaze took in Liz from head to toe. 'Wow.'

Laughing, Liz said, 'Thank you – I think.' Clearly, Maddie was accustomed to seeing her in slob clothes.

All that running and healthy eating hadn't shaved off a dress size as she'd hoped, but Liz had found a flattering black beaded cocktail dress that shimmered subtly when she moved. As well as doing her hair and makeup, Gemma had lent her a gorgeous jet necklace to complement the deep V neckline.

'Hello, young lady,' said Gemma. 'Have you seen my niece?'

Maddie giggled and whirled so the bell skirt of her simple navy silk dress flared. 'I look nice, don't I?'

'You certainly do,' said Liz.

Valerie's head whipped around. She scanned Liz from head to toe, her face frozen for perhaps two seconds. Then she came toward them, smiling.

'Welcome, ladies,' she said. 'Let me get you a glass of champagne.' She turned to Liz. 'Will you help me? I need to open another bottle and my bartender seems to have deserted me.'

'Sure,' said Liz. She was wary but willing to let bygones be bygones if Valerie was.

Inclining her head graciously, Valerie let her arm hover close to Liz's waist, shepherding her along.

Where was Theo? Surely even he would have to be sociable tonight or risk Valerie's severe displeasure.

An enormous silver bucket filled with ice and champagne bottles stood in the corner. Valerie ran her fingertips over the various bottle tops that stuck up out of the ice, as if her choice would be made by touch.

In a low voice, she said, 'I want to apologise for that incident about the bath robe, Liz. I can't imagine what came over me.'

Surprised, Liz said, 'Oh, no. I understand completely. I shouldn't have used your stuff. I'm so sorry about that.'

Valerie yanked a bottle of Bollinger free. 'Yes, well, I know who to thank for that.'

Had Gemma owned up, then? Liz made a non-committal noise as Valerie ran her fingertips over the gold foil. 'Ugh, I always break my nails getting this wire off.'

'Here. My specialty.' Liz took the bottle. She denuded it of the wrapper and the wire, and with a twist of the cork, the bottle made a satisfying pop, releasing a festive coil of vapour. 'Glasses?' She looked around and spied some on the table.

While she filled them, Valerie said, 'Anyway, as I said, I'm sorry if I was rude.'

'You had every right to be mad. Let's forget it.'

Liz took Gemma her glass and was relieved when Valerie, spying a new group of guests, swanned off to greet them.

More and more people arrived. A few local friends, Valerie had said. Liz suspected she wanted as many people as possible to know about her connection with Raoul de Martin.

The man himself did not appear, sending his two assistants up from the kitchens with each dish. That allowed Valerie to explain each item to her guests and hand out small cards they could use to rate each dish on presentation and flavour.

'Come on,' whispered Gemma, 'let's try the foulest thing on the menu.'

'Looks like a hot contest,' said Liz out of the side of her mouth. So many unfamiliar flavours and textures – none of them terrifically appetising to a carnivore like her. And all of them red, orange, green, or some weird combination thereof.

Gemma popped something that looked like a knot of seaweed into her mouth and chewed. Her expressive eyes widened.

'Better than you thought?' said Liz.

Gemma swallowed then smiled sweetly. 'Tastes like vomit.'

Choking a little on her champagne, Liz approached the buffet. Valerie had thoughtfully put out cards with each dish, not only labelling them but listing ingredients.

Liz tried a relatively innocuous-looking mini red lentil patty. It had herbs and sundry other stuff in it, and it tasted like a hard ball of flavourless dhal. When she bit into it, the patty nearly fell apart in her hands. No binding agent, her mother would have said. No eggs, bread crumbs or flour of any kind in the tri-colour diet.

Liz searched the crowd for Theo but he was still nowhere to be seen. Maddie had taken one bite of a red pepper stuffed with something unidentifiably green, pegged it over the balustrade when no one but Liz was looking, and slipped away.

'What do you think, ladies?' Mr Jackson came over to them,

looking very distinguished in a navy blazer and tie. His kind eyes were dancing.

'Let's just say we don't think Mrs Jackson has anything to worry about,' said Gemma. 'Who are all these people?'

He glanced around. 'London rent-a-crowd, Mrs Jackson says.'

'I thought they were neighbours,' said Liz.

Gemma crumpled her rating card into a ball. 'She's stacked the trial with people who already like his food.'

A glance around told Liz Gemma might well be right. These people all looked disgustingly healthy. There wasn't a pot belly or a pendulous bottom to be seen. 'What price beauty?' she murmured. She eyed the sweating buckets of expensive champagne. 'I notice they don't exclude booze from the diet.'

Theo came up then, holding a highball glass of what looked like Coke – obviously contraband. He was wearing jeans and a collared shirt, which Liz supposed was dressed up for him, but hardly befitted the occasion. Valerie would not be pleased.

When he saw Liz he stopped, eyes widening. It took Gemma two attempts to capture his attention. 'Sorry, what?' he said, turning to his sister.

'Where did all these randomers come from?' Gemma demanded.

'Damned if I know,' said Theo. 'Don't even know why I'm here, frankly.'

'Well, you have to stop being all nothing-to-do-with-me and hands-off and everything, and get in there and fix this,' said Gemma. 'There is no way we can serve this crap to guests at the Open Day and make them pay for it. I've got all kinds of people coming to this thing. That bloke from *The Island Gazette*, editors of bridal and country lifestyle magazines, the lot.'

Theo stared into his drink and swirled it so the ice clinked against the glass.

'Valerie ruins everything around here,' Gemma blurted out.

Liz was concerned to hear the tremor in her friend's voice. She hadn't realised Gemma was so invested in the Open Day.

Theo shot his sister a searing glare. 'And what do you think we'd do without her here, Gemma? Valerie might not be your cup of tea, but she runs this place. She makes the bookings, looks after the house, the insurance, the licensing, council permissions, parking, all of it. There are so many boring details involved in running a place like this and even more in putting on an event, and you don't have the first clue.'

'Yes, I —' She shut her mouth, perhaps realising that she had not, in fact, thought of all the things he'd listed.

Liz didn't think Theo was being fair. Gemma had never had to run the house herself, but from what Liz could gather, she had never been offered the opportunity.

The fire seemed to have gone out of Theo now. He looked very tired. 'I'm just one man, Gemma. I can't do it all on my own.'

'But I . . . You know I'd help you . . .' Gemma trailed off, looking shattered.

'No. You've got your own life, your own career.' Theo shook his head, staring into the crowd of thin Londoners. 'If this is what Valerie wants, she can have it. After all, she's the one doing most of the work.'

'I'm sorry,' said Gemma in a low, stiff voice. 'I didn't mean it.'

Theo rubbed his jaw, as if feeling for stubble. 'Yeah, well, I'm sorry too. All of this gets to me. You know how I hate this kind of thing.'

She reached up and gave her brother a peck on the cheek. 'Hang in there. Screw the cocktail party. We'll make this Open Day the best damn event the island has ever seen.'

Her shoulders very straight and her head high, Gemma walked off quickly, setting her half-drunk champagne on the balustrade as she went.

'It had better be,' said Theo, gazing after his sister. 'We have a lot riding on it. If we don't get that funding, it'll be curtains for us. I'll be forced to sell to a property developer, of all people. God knows what would become of the place then.'

Liz froze. He meant Nick, of course. Something curdled in her stomach and she couldn't blame it on Raoul's cooking. The urge to tell Nick the truth nearly overwhelmed good sense.

But before she could respond, Theo seemed to remember he was confiding in a virtual stranger. 'Sorry, Liz.' He gave her a wry smile and clinked his glass against hers. 'Bet you're glad you came tonight.'

'I want to help.' The words came out before she realised what she was saying. It seemed like this Open Day was make-or-break for all of them. The more she came to know Seagrove and its people, the less she wanted to see it leave their hands.

And just what was her purpose here but to make sure the house *did* leave their hands? She cursed herself, wishing she'd never spoken. She hated feeling like a hypocrite. It was becoming increasingly difficult to remember whose side she was on.

Theo looked half amused, half horrified. 'God no. It's not your problem.'

She tried not to feel hurt that he was trying to shut her out. 'Of course it's my problem,' she said breezily. 'I mean, of course I don't consider it *my* problem but I've already promised Gemma I'd give her a hand with the preparations. You're helping me with my research. It's the least I can do. Anyway, it will be fun.' If you didn't count having to deal with Valerie . . .

He was staring at her with an odd expression

Liz hesitated. Should she say it? What did she have to lose?

'You know, I admire your loyalty and all. But just because Valerie works hard for this place' – a fact Liz, frankly, disputed – 'it doesn't give her the right to make poor decisions.'

Theo sighed. 'Not you too.'

Liz wasn't going to back down now she'd started. 'Do you want this cocktail evening to be overshadowed by Raoul and his weird, inedible food?' She swept an arm expansively, encompassing the terrace and the spectacular grounds beyond, the view of the sea below. 'I mean, look at this place! It's glorious. *That* is what people should remember, not the fact they were forced to eat rabbit food.'

Theo took a sip of his drink, then studied the bottom of his glass.

She knew she was being nosy and bossy and rude, but she owed it to Gemma, to Mrs Jackson, and most of all to Theo himself, to tell it like it was.

'You said this event is crucial,' she said quietly. 'If you can't stand up for Seagrove when it's something this important, you might as well sell up and move on.'

Liz was starting to loathe this lying business. She wasn't very good at it, and the more helpful people became, the more she wanted to chuck the whole thing in.

She almost blessed the lack of phone reception at the cottage because it had given her an excellent excuse not to contact Nick for the past few days. He didn't know she was staying at the house now and she'd neglected to share that information.

Nick could not be avoided forever, though, and the next morning, Liz went to a cafe on the Ventnor Esplanade, where they had free wi-fi. There was a series of booths toward the back where she could get a small amount of privacy.

Sipping her double-shot latte, Liz went through the rigmarole of setting up the video conference. Thank goodness it was a slow time of day. She'd feel like an idiot doing this with people around.

When they'd discussed a few ongoing business matters, Liz introduced the topic uppermost in her mind. 'Why didn't you tell me Delany's memoirs were incomplete?'

'Didn't I?' said Nick, frowning and a little distracted, she thought. 'I bought the memoirs at an auction at Seagrove along with the painting about five or six years ago. I asked at the time if they knew where the missing volumes were but I was told they were lost.'

'Oh, no!' Liz groaned. She'd hoped MJ had made a mistake with the photocopying or something. Would she ever find out what had happened to Delany?

'I know. Frustrating,' said Nick. 'I take it you haven't found the missing memoirs, then.'

'I'll keep looking,' said Liz. Why would some be preserved and others lost? Perhaps there was something in the missing volumes that someone didn't want known? She couldn't bear to think that the ending to Delany's story might never be discovered.

'What else have you got for me?' said Nick.

'Okay . . .' She took out the velvet box Theo had given her and opened it. 'First, get a load of this.'

She held up the baby rattle, turning it so that Nick could see.

'What is it?' he said.

'It's Stephen Nash's baby rattle.' She shook it, making the bells tinkle. 'Someone here told me it had been found buried somewhere on the estate. Man with a metal detector dug it up.'

'How do you know it was Stephen's?' said Nick.

'It's the right period and it has Stephen's initials engraved on it.'

'I'm not sure that's enough, is it?' Nick seemed a bit testy today. Was he getting impatient with her lack of progress or was it something personal? She didn't ask. She did not want to hear about the life and loves of Nick McCann right now. She had enough problems of her own.

'I can check if it's listed in any inventories,' she said. 'But anyway, supposing it is Stephen's, why was it buried? I'm going to ask Mr Jackson what he knows about it – where it was found and so on.' She should have done that last night but she'd had other things on her mind.

'Right.' Nick tapped his pen on the desk. 'Doesn't seem like a lot to go on.' He shifted restlessly in his chair. 'Anything else?'

'I got hold of Richard Nash's diaries but there's nothing much in them beyond appointments and such. They don't mention his sons at all. Still, I'll go through them more thoroughly now that I've finished Delany's memoirs. There are mentions of someone called Margaret, and I read in the trial report of the criminal conversation case that a Margaret Smith gave some pretty damning evidence against Delany and Julian. She might be worth looking into.'

'Was she a relative?'

'She was Richard's mother's companion, but stayed with the household after the old lady's death,' said Liz. 'There's very little written about her, and no records of anything she wrote. Except . . .'

She slid out the copy she'd taken of the dedication for the island history. 'Except there is a note in a history book that was written by Richard, published posthumously, to the effect that he had charged this Margaret Smith to see it through to publication. It must have taken her a few years, judging by the copyright date. That suggests she was with the family at the time both boys were born, right through to the end, doesn't it? And that she had a close working relationship with Richard.'

'Are you thinking the relationship might have been more than that?' said Nick.

'Unlikely,' Liz said. 'She was a companion, not a maid, and females who took those roles had to be extremely careful. Her status would have plummeted if she'd become Richard's mistress.'

'You seem to have gained a good handle on the period in a short time,' said Nick.

She wasn't going to tell Nick that it had all come from reading novels – Fielding, Austen, Thackeray, not to mention Georgette Heyer. Liz shrugged. 'Lawyers are trained to assimilate a lot of information and synthesise it quickly.' That sounded good, didn't it?

Nick grunted. 'What else can you tell me?'

She shuffled her papers and found her list. 'Theo has given me access to a heap of archival material. Inventories, household accounts, letters, stuff like that. When a person died, it was customary to return people's letters to the sender. So if I wrote to you, and you died, your next of kin would send me back all the letters I wrote.'

'I imagine a lot of them were burned,' said Nick.

'Yes. But maybe if I find a keen correspondent of Richard's or Delany's and search in their archives, I might come up with more. We could extend the search to Delany's sister, say.'

'You won't find anything from Julian's side of things,' said Nick. 'I looked into him pretty thoroughly when I was over there.'

She told him she'd seen Julian's headstone, and Delany's beside it.

'Sad, isn't it?' said Nick. 'They were never allowed to be together, except in death. They must have loved each other to the end.'

'Yes.' Liz felt a sweeping, unprecedented sense of envy. What would it be like to feel that all-consuming, desperate, enduring love? To be honest, she'd never felt like that about Tony. Maybe she was too ordinary to fall head over heels in mad, passionate love.

She cleared her throat. 'Right. Well, I think that's all I have for now. I'll let you know when I find out more.'

'It will have to be when I get back,' said Nick, looking as if the cloud of woe was descending upon him again.

'Back from where?' she said. 'Or is that secret squirrel?'

He rubbed his palm over his jaw and slid it behind his neck in a characteristic gesture that shouted reluctance. 'It's Yolande. She doesn't want a divorce after all.'

'Bummer,' Liz muttered.

'What?'

'Nothing.' She should not be so entertained by his marital woes. 'So that's good, isn't it?'

He tapped his pen. 'She wants to go to the Bahamas. Re-kindle the flame.'

'She actually said that?' said Liz, trying not to snigger.

'You're not helping.'

'Sorry.' She slid her papers into a neat stack. 'Bahamas. Sounds like paradise. So you're going to be off the airwaves for a while. How long, may I ask?'

He put his head in his hands. 'Two weeks. Two goddamn miserable weeks.'

Liz smiled at him sweetly. 'Ah, but who could be miserable in paradise?'

She went back to the cottage with a smile still teasing at her lips. Yolande would make Nick pay through the nose for his infidelity. She was going to torture him for a while before she put him out of his misery. Good for her. Liz couldn't feel too sorry for Yolande. She might not be your garden-variety gold-digger, but she didn't care as much about Nick as she did about his bank account.

Liz knew one thing for certain. She could thank her lucky stars that her own infatuation with Nick had been fruitless and brief.

Back at the cottage, she dumped her bag and went to see what was doing on the renovation front. More people milling around – an electrician, a plumber, and Theo was there too.

She looked at him uncertainly, wondering if he bore a grudge about her outspokenness the night before.

'Hi,' she said. 'What are you doing here?'

'Delivering the landscaping plans. Demanding client, that one.' With a jerk of his head, he indicated Gemma. 'She's cleaning me out of hydrangeas.'

So they were going to pretend last night had never happened; that she hadn't told him how to run his business, not to mention his life. Fine with her.

'You're not doing the exotic plant thing here, then,' said Liz, shading her eyes from the sun.

He shook his head. 'Traditional cottage like this wants an English country garden. Nothing too showy or bright, but we'll put in something special here and there.'

He glanced away from her, to where Fergus was studying yet another set of plans with the electrician. Theo seemed to have run out of things to say. She probably should apologise for her outburst, but she was damned if she would. She'd meant every word.

Abruptly, she said, 'Want to come and destroy stuff?'

He shrugged and followed her into the house.

They donned protective gear and Liz picked up the two sledge hammers, handing one to Theo.

'Are you sure we're supposed to be doing this?' said Theo.

She nodded. 'Fergus promised to save this wall just for me.' She hefted the sledge hammer. 'Ready?'

Theo nodded.

'On three. One . . . two . . .' Her 'three' was obliterated by the crash of the hammer heads against the wall.

Goodbye, poky little sitting room. Hello, big, welcoming, beautiful kitchen, complete with conservatory. Liz really wanted to see this when it was all done.

'Wait! Stop!' Theo grabbed her upper arm and put down his sledge hammer. He waved away a cloud of dust and took off his mask. 'Do you see that?'

They'd made an opening in the wall that was just smaller than Liz in height and about the width of two people.

He poked his head into the cavity, then ducked it out again. 'Is there a torch around here?'

Liz couldn't find one, but she asked around and the electrician gave her his pencil torch. Brimming with anticipation, Liz played the beam over what they'd revealed.

Panelled in oak and dripping with cobwebs, smelling coolly of dust and must, there was a secret cavity about the size of a small powder room inside the wall.

'Crikey,' said Theo.

CHAPTER TWELVE

'You are kidding me!' breathed Liz.

Ducking her head, she stepped through the hole they'd bashed in the living room wall to join Theo.

She gazed about her in a sort of delighted swoon. How many times had she read about priests' holes and secret passages in old English houses? But to discover one in real life . . .

'What have we here?' said Theo under his breath. He crouched, then kneeled in front of a large, rectangular chest. It had a curved lid, and certainly appeared old enough to have belonged to the pirates of the island's distant, romantic past. But what would pirate treasure be doing in Gemma's cottage?

'This is brilliant,' said Theo, excitement warming his voice as he ran his hands over the chest. He brushed aside dust and filmy cobwebs and turned his head to look up at Liz. 'What a find!'

He bent to examine the lock on the chest, then tried lifting the lid. 'It's either locked or stuck. Hand me the torch, will you?'

Liz passed him the electrician's torch. '*Is* it treasure, d'you think?'

He chuckled but shook his head. 'Doubtful. More likely contraband of some kind. The island has always been a playground for smugglers.'

A thought seemed to strike him and he sat back on his heels, slowly trailing the beam of the torch along the wall and all over the room, then the floor.

'Hang on,' he said. With a small grunt of effort, he shoved the trunk aside. 'There's a trapdoor under here.'

'Where?' Liz craned her neck.

He shone the torch light on a particular spot. She could just make out a large square of boards that didn't sit quite flush with the rest of the floor, and an iron ring, black with age.

She clutched Theo's shoulder for balance as she leaned over to peer more closely. 'What do you think is down there?'

'Cellars? A tunnel, maybe? Let's find out.' He shifted to reach for the ring-pull but the trapdoor didn't move, so he moved into a half-crouch and tried again.

'Hey, what's going on?' Gemma's voice came from outside the aperture.

Liz was too busy holding her breath to answer. Theo tugged hard at the ring-pull, the muscles in his arms standing out in thick ropes. He had one foot braced on the wall behind the trapdoor, and still he was straining with effort. 'Think I've . . . Got it!'

The trapdoor opened toward him with a bloodcurdling creak and a shower of dust. Theo let go of it, coughing. When the dust dissipated, he shone the torch into the space below.

'What was that? I can't see a thing!' Gemma complained from behind them. 'Will someone please tell me what's going on?'

Liz, realising that it was Gemma's house, after all, stepped away to let her see. 'We found a trunk and a trapdoor!' she told her friend. 'This is just like one of Delany's novels.'

'There's a passage down there,' said Theo, his voice tense with excitement. 'What's the bet it goes all the way to the cove?'

'Smugglers?' Gemma, who had been examining the trunk with interest, came over to grab the torch from him to see for herself. He stepped out to give her room.

'Theo, you're covered in cobwebs.' Liz laughed. Unthinking, she reached up to brush the soft grey strands from Theo's hair.

His eyes met hers and for a long, dangerous moment, she forgot to breathe. Then he cleared his throat and she snatched her hand away.

'I'll grab a ladder,' Theo said. 'Excuse me.'

Liz stood very still and released a long, shaky breath.

Fergus, equally excited about the secret chamber, brought an aluminium ladder, but with the cramped dimensions in the priest's hole, it was impossible to manoeuvre it into place.

'Too wide for that trapdoor, besides,' Fergus pointed out.

'It's not far to the ground,' said Theo. He clamped the pencil torch between his teeth. Before anyone could object, he braced his hands on either side of the square hole in the floor and lowered himself down.

'Be careful!' called Gemma. 'We can't afford to have you laid up with a broken leg.'

'Ah, he'll be fine.' Fergus handed a more powerful torch to Theo before he slithered down after him.

Liz cocked an eyebrow at Gemma but her friend crossed her arms and shook her head. 'Not me. They're crazy. Could be anything down there.' She shivered, retreating from the opening in the wall. 'I'll work on the trunk.'

Gemma was right, of course, but Liz was too excited not to go after the men. 'Someone get ready to catch me,' she called, and lowered herself down.

'Got you.' Just as Liz's arms gave out, Fergus caught her around the waist and swung her to the ground.

They were in a cold, cellar-like room with limed walls glistening with moisture. There was nothing but cobwebs, rat droppings and the skeletons of small creatures down there. It smelled musty and dank.

Liz was disappointed. 'Looks like a dead end,' she said. 'I wonder what it was used for? Priests? Smugglers?'

Theo hadn't given up yet. He played his torch light slowly over the walls. 'There.' He pointed. 'See? That's where the tunnel's been bricked up.'

Fergus examined the area Theo indicated, tracing his fingertips over the place where the limed wall ended and the bare brick began. The exposed wall was about the shape and size of a low doorway.

'Can we knock through the bricks, open it up again?' said Liz.

Theo raised an eyebrow. 'Fond of that sledge hammer, aren't you?'

'Delicate job,' Fergus muttered. 'Best to avoid it if we can. Don't forget we've lost bits of this cliff to landslip.'

Liz was disappointed but accepted Fergus's argument against knocking through. 'Do you think that if there was a tunnel it might have collapsed, then?'

'More than likely,' said Fergus, ever practical.

Other than the bricked-up tunnel entrance, there was nothing else of interest down there. When they all agreed they'd seen enough, Fergus boosted Liz up through the trapdoor and the men followed with little more difficulty than they'd had getting down there.

When they reached the top, they found that Gemma and the builder's apprentice had been at work on what Liz now thought of as the treasure chest.

'You got it open!' She hurried over to where they'd set it down in what used to be the living room, out of the way of all the wall debris.

'It was stuck, not locked,' said Gemma. 'But no treasure, I'm afraid. Not even contraband. Just this.' She held up a wooden container shaped like an oversized jewellery box.

Interesting. When Gemma wiped the dust off it with the sleeve of her shirt, the detail on the box emerged: a sort of fine marquetry work in a paler variety of wood.

'It's a house,' said Liz, delighted. Not as grand as Seagrove, but not as small as the cottage either.

'It's a tea caddy. See the lock?' Gemma traced the narrow border around the keyhole with her fingertip.

Once the grime was removed, Liz saw that the border gleamed white.

'I think that escutcheon is probably made of ivory,' said Gemma. 'It's fine craftsmanship.'

Liz had never heard of an escutcheon before but she knew that tea was such an expensive commodity in Georgian times that the mistress of the house kept it under lock and key, safe from petty pilfering by her servants.

'My gran used to collect tea caddies.' Gemma inspected the box from every angle. 'No damage that I can see. This might be quite valuable.'

'Do you know how old it is?' said Liz.

Gemma shrugged. 'Late Georgian would be my guess. I'm sure an expert could be more precise. Pity there's no key.' She and Liz felt around inside the chest for one, but came up empty-handed.

'Tantalising, isn't it?' said Liz. 'I wonder what's inside.'

'Probably just canisters of tea,' said Gemma. 'I'll see if I can get a locksmith or an antique dealer to open it.'

'Was that the only thing in the trunk?' said Liz.

'Oh, no. There were a couple of old books. I put them in my bag because I was worried they'd get damaged. What did I do with the blasted thing?' Gemma looked around, frowning. 'Hang on.' She went out and returned with two slim volumes.

As soon as she saw them, a thrill of something between anticipation and recognition ran down Liz's spine. The books were bound in brown leather crazed with age, each of them tied closed with a leather thong. Holding her breath, she untied one of them and opened it, then leafed past the blue marbled end pages.

And found handwritten pages in a familiar bold, flowing script.

Liz trembled as she read the first few lines. A surge of triumph flooded her chest. 'Oh, my God!'

'What?' said Gemma. 'Do you know what they are?'

'Yes, I . . .' Liz broke off, remembering she hadn't told Gemma about Nick, about the memoirs, about any of it. Lamely, she finished. 'I'm pretty sure Delany wrote these. Do you mind if I hold onto them?'

'Not at all,' said Gemma. She smiled. 'You looked like all your Christmases have come at once. You really are obsessed with Delany, aren't you?'

Liz scarcely heard her. She wanted to dive in straight away but she needed to clean up first. 'I'm sorry. I have to go,' she said, and left Gemma to stare after her.

Delany, Lady Nash

Lady Verena died in her sleep, and not of the horrid illness that had recently returned with a vengeance to plague her. The doctor said it was her heart, and so it might have been.

On a blustery autumn day, her funeral was held in the church at Godshill. Julian attended, sober as a judge, the sparkle quite gone from his dark eyes. He appeared so heartbroken at the loss of his mother I ached to take him in my arms. Yet I was forced to treat him as scarcely more than a stranger.

My husband, by contrast, could not keep the hint of a smirk from his lips. Perhaps it was only I who sensed it, but he seemed to radiate smugness.

That was, until he heard the terms of the dowager's will.

The family, Miss Smith, and some trusted servants gathered in the drawing room at Seagrove to hear the will read. We sat like a murder of crows, all got up in black, fresh from the wind-whipped church yard where Lady Verena had been interred in the family crypt.

I had ordered decanters to be brought and cups of hot negus to warm us, and a fire crackled in the enormous hearth.

Richard needed nothing but his joy at his mother's passing to sustain him. He took brandy anyway and tossed it back, refilling his glass once more before he offered a drink to any of his guests.

Julian put a hand on his brother's shoulder. 'Steady, old fellow.'

Richard shrugged his brother's hand away with a bark of a laugh. He went to join Miss Smith on a couch at the side of the room rather than coming to sit by me.

Julian took the place meant for Richard and I was grateful for his solid presence at my side. How had I been so lacking in judgement? Julian was supposed to be the more volatile of the brothers. Now, it seemed, he was the dependable one.

I looked up into his face. 'Awful business, isn't it?'

'Wish to God it were over.'

We watched the attorney, Mr Whittaker, who selected a document from amongst his papers and cleared his throat in a preparatory way.

Julian's jaw set, as if he braced himself for what was to come.

'Do you know something about the will?' I murmured.

'I might.' He glanced down at me, then jerked his head toward Richard. 'He won't like it.'

I felt the heat drain from my face. 'You mean . . .'

'Hush.' Julian stretched his legs before him and folded his arms. 'He's about to start.'

Richard was obliged to hold his rage inside him for hours before the last mourners left. I don't know how he managed it, but he must have exercised superhuman restraint. As soon as the final stragglers departed, he shut himself and his mother's solicitor in the library and screamed like a madman.

I bit my lip. 'I ought to rescue the poor man.'

Julian shrugged. 'Old Whittaker? Don't trouble yourself. He's been harangued by more formidable men than my brother.'

Sure enough, after some minutes, I heard the library door open and close and the butler conducting Mr Whittaker to his carriage. Relieved on that score, I still wondered what my husband would do when he finally accepted he'd been routed.

'I have something for you.' To my surprise, Julian reached into his waistcoat and drew out a letter.

'For me?' I said, recognising Lady Verena's writing. 'Why did she not post it?'

'She did not want it falling into the wrong hands, she said.'

I raised my brows. 'A little dramatic, surely?'

'Perhaps.' He frowned as he looked out the window, to where my husband now stood in muted conversation with Margaret Smith. 'Perhaps not.'

I puzzled over the letter, and over Julian's cryptic words, but I had no leisure to consider them. 'You will stay here, of course. I've directed Mrs Ludd to make up your apartments.'

Julian made a wry grimace. 'Given the humour my brother is in, I ought to put up at the Swan.'

'I wouldn't hear of it,' I said, 'and Richard will agree when he has calmed down. Of course you must stay here. Besides, as you are executor and most of your mama's effects are in this house, you will need to remain for some time, I expect.'

'Well, I will, then,' said Julian, still appearing troubled. 'If I don't, he might take out his frustrations in another quarter.'

I sent him a sharp glance. Did he suspect, then? But how could he?

I lowered my gaze, ostensibly absorbed in the seal on the dowager's letter. It was a dark, rusted red.

Richard's voice cut across the room, making me jump. 'Julian, I must . . . I must speak with you.'

Julian grimaced at me as if to say, Here it comes, and followed Richard out.

When they left, I turned the dowager's letter over, running my fingertips across the bumpy wax of the seal. A rush of sadness overtook me. I would miss Lady Verena, her caustic humour, the leavening in the lump of tedium at Seagrove. I'd miss her as an ally too. On rare occasions, she would bestir herself to come down on my side against Margaret and Richard. Those two were so often ranged against me.

The dowager had particularly supported my determination to keep Henry with me, rather than send him to a wet nurse in the village. 'I sent you off to be suckled, my boy,' she said to Richard, 'and look how that turned out.'

On glancing up from the letter, I noticed Miss Smith on the terrace, watching me. Had she seen Julian hand me the missive? An unreasonable sense of dread overtook me when I met her cold-eyed stare.

Hardly thinking about what I did, I picked up the closest book to hand, a copy of *Gulliver's Travels* I had been reading, and slid the letter between its leaves, then went out to join her.

Since she'd returned from Bath, accompanying the body of her erstwhile mistress, Margaret had not been herself. Now, her usually creamy complexion was ashen.

I did not think it was grief at her mistress's passing that ailed her. I rather suspected it was the news that Lady Verena had left the entirety of her vast fortune – amassed by her second husband, the nabob – to Julian.

Twenty thousand pounds.

Not one solitary penny to her elder son. To her companion, she'd left Pug and a sum of £50. Hardly a generous bequest. Really, I thought, I must persuade Richard to pay Miss Smith a suitable pension when she leaves us.

As for Pug, I made a mental note to take the dog myself, regardless of my mother-in-law's wishes. Much as I loved larger canines, I was not fond of pugs. However I had once observed Margaret give the poor little wheezer a kick when she thought no one else was looking.

As I reached her side, I said, 'You look pale, Miss Smith. Are you feeling quite well?' I rubbed my arms, for the wintry chill had set in. 'Are you not cold out here?'

Her wide gaze turned on me. 'I am perfectly well, I thank you, my lady.'

'You are quite at liberty to use your old room if you would like to lie down,' I said. 'Shall I tell Mrs Ludd to have the bed made up for you?'

She eyed me coolly. 'I have already instructed her to do so.'

I raised my eyebrows and waited, having learned by now that Margaret never overstepped the mark without solid backing from my spouse. She wanted to bait me into making an objection so she could override me, citing Richard's orders.

'Lord Nash wishes me to remain at Seagrove for the present,' she said. 'He means to work on his history over the next few months.'

'Of course he does,' I murmured.

Recently, I had inquired what span of time the history was to cover and how much of it was complete. That had been a most tactless question. After much blustering and prevarication, Richard admitted he was not even a quarter of the way through. At this rate, he would be doing well to finish the book before he himself belonged to history.

Margaret would be with us for the foreseeable future, then. On balance, I supposed I ought to be thankful for that.

Margaret

She had not slept, for when she slept, she dreamed, and then . . . Well, suffice it to say Margaret had nightmares enough to fill several gothic novels.

Ludicrous. Margaret's waking mind knew she could not afford a conscience. She must banish recriminations, for they were a waste of time. If only there were a way to keep her dream self from grubbing about in dark recesses.

The way Delany looked at her that afternoon . . . Was it her imagination? It must be. And yet . . . was there knowledge, accusation in those fine eyes?

Margaret had done everything Lady Verena asked of her. A loyal and true servant.

And look at her reward. Betrayal. She crumpled the dowager's letter to Delany in her fist.

She'd seen Julian hand Delany the note, known what it might contain. When Mrs Ludd had called Delany away to discuss arrangements for Julian's accommodation, Margaret had seized the opportunity. She'd slipped into the drawing room and snatched up the book in which she'd seen Delany hide the letter.

She'd been right to act. The letter was from Lady Verena, dated the day before she died. With a shaking hand, Margaret smoothed the paper out and read.

> My dear girl,
>
> First, do not be distressed or saddened by my passing. You are no doubt aware of the disease that riddles me, and that the death in store for those who contract it is an exceedingly drawn-out, painful and undignified one. The treatments for it are scarcely less so.
>
> If God sees fit to take me from this mortal coil before I lose my faculties, then at least I shall have something for which to be grateful.
>
> Goodbye, my dear. I like you too well to hold any real hope you will be happy with my son. But I do trust you will experience happiness one day, even if you must wait for widowhood – as I did.
>
> In all sincerity, one favour I beg. _Rid your household of Miss Smith._
>
> I considered granting her a generous pension but I doubt even that would tempt her away. She has her eye on a larger prize. You might guess what that is. And you might also guess what she is prepared to do to win it.
>
> If you are reading this letter, it is proof that Miss Smith is, indeed, the most determined female I ever encountered. That is to the good in my case, and the primary reason I kept her about me. But now she has served her purpose, banish her if you can.

If you have any compunction on this subject, pray put it out of
your heart. Much good your compassion will do you if she has her
way.

    I remain yours, etc.
    Verena Grant

Even now, having read the note more times than she could count,
Margaret could scarce believe the old harridan had served her such a
trick. After all she'd done for that woman!

What had she to show for it? A Judas letter, a measly £50 and a
putrid, snivelling mutt of a dog.

That was the final insult. At this moment the foul, drooling creature dozed on his pink satin cushion with nary a care in the world. She
sent him a glance of loathing. If the pug hadn't inherited a handsome
pension in his own right, she'd have tossed him to the hounds to be
torn limb from limb.

Margaret would not waste much time repining, however. Well
acquainted with the baseness of human nature, she had never expected
any great mark of appreciation from Lady Verena. She'd extorted as
much as she could from the woman before her death; she could hardly
complain now that the bequest was a mere bagatelle.

With a disdainful flick, she dropped the dowager's letter onto the
fire. The paper flared and blackened from the edges inward; the seal
melted and dripped like blood from a wound.

What rankled most was the great deception Lady Verena had
perpetrated on Richard, with Margaret as her unwitting instrument.
Margaret had been obliged to talk quickly – a smooth flow of self-
exculpation mingled with delicate flattery – to stop Richard flinging
her onto the street.

She gave a sour smile. Men never tired of hearing how wonderful
they were. Perhaps her greatest talent was shoring up the male ego. If she
could make Lord Nash think himself a god, she could achieve anything.

He was a difficult subject, though, for his moods were increasingly volatile and his self-loathing fathoms deep. She could not be with him always. Without the constant bolster of her fawning presence, soon enough self-doubt flooded him, corroding him from the inside like acid, diverting him from his purpose. Delany, of course, with her clever competence and her cutting wit, made him feel thoroughly inadequate.

In one way, that was all to the good. In another, the flashes of contempt Delany could not help but show him made Richard behave rashly, without careful consideration. Inconvenient, potentially disastrous now, when Margaret needed him to follow her plan.

She did not fool herself that Richard cared one scrap for her. Their alliance had served him while his mother lived; Margaret needed to convince him she was still useful now that the rancid old witch had cocked up her toes. Rid of one formidable obstacle to her ambitions, there was only one step more to be taken before she, Margaret, could become the next Lady Nash.

She must tread warily, for Richard's hatred for his mother would soon need a new focus. Margaret was determined that focus would not be her.

When Margaret had seen Julian with Delany that afternoon, a notion had struck her that was so brilliant as to dazzle her senses.

Certainly, Lady Verena had played Margaret and Richard for fools. But there was a way to recoup their losses. It would require careful strategy and nerves of steel. But if the cards played out the way Margaret intended, both she and Richard would get everything they'd ever desired.

Her first task would be to convince Richard to fall in with her plans. To that end, she decided to brave his presence later that evening. She approached him warily, unsure of his mood from one minute to the next. But his agitated pacing appeared to be the product of excitement rather than fury. A good sign? Too soon to tell.

'She's increasing again,' he said abruptly, before Margaret had even opened her mouth to introduce the subject uppermost in her mind.

'Did you know?'

'Lady Nash? I did not.'

That was unexpected. She narrowed her eyes. Perhaps it might be used to advantage. Ordinarily, the disparity between Delany's circumstances and her own would have been exquisitely painful. Now it made her even more determined to prevail.

'When is the infant due?' she asked.

Nash shrugged. 'July, or thereabouts. Another boy. I'm convinced of it.'

'Ah.' She lowered her gaze. 'Does Mr Julian remain with us long?'

Richard's expression altered from satisfaction to petulance. 'Damn the scaly fellow. I must suppose we are obliged to house him until he has arranged my mother's effects. Otherwise, the whole island will gossip.'

'You must be the bigger man,' said Margaret, soothingly. 'Show him it is a matter of indifference to you.'

He flung himself down on the couch, eyes stormy, and put his hand to his brow. 'I cannot bear it, Margaret. I could kill him with my bare hands.'

Margaret doubted it, but she rushed to sit beside him and gripped his arm tightly, as if to restrain him from leaping up to commit violence that very moment.

'No,' she beseeched him. 'Indeed, sir, you must not. Only think what would happen if you killed him, Richard.'

With a show of reluctance, he allowed himself to be restrained. Yes, she thought acidly, Julian would floor you at the first blow and you know it.

She bent her head and took a deep breath. 'No, dear sir. We must bear the humiliation. We must hope and pray that this child isn't . . .' She broke off, a swift hand to her lips as if she'd said something she ought not.

'Child?' Richard's brows knitted. 'What about the child?' Turning, he seized her shoulders and shook her. 'Tell me, Margaret. What do you know about this child?'

She stared into his cold blue eyes. 'Have you not seen how they are together?' she said softly. No need to explain who 'they' were.

'Ha! Yes, I've seen it, by God.' He relaxed, releasing her. 'But what you're suggesting is out of the question. Even my brother would not stoop so low.'

'He loves her,' she said. 'Love can be a very powerful thing.'

She put up her hand and stroked the fine fair hair from Richard's brow. 'People do all sorts of things for love. They betray their countries, their honour. Even their brothers . . .'

She saw that behind his denial, his mind was working. Margaret waited patiently. He might not be quick on the uptake but he would get there in the end.

A gleam of comprehension came into Richard's eyes. That was enough. For the moment, at least.

She had only a matter of months before she must leave him. She could not trust Richard to carry through her plan alone. Nor could she risk explaining her strategy to him explicitly, for she must have grounds to deny involvement if things went sour or circumstances changed.

She – *they* – had to act quickly.

Margaret made a small adjustment to Richard's cravat. 'I suggest that once Mr Nash finishes his business at Seagrove, you find some means to keep him here.'

He plucked at his bottom lip. 'I cannot abide the fellow, and he knows it. I can't possibly —'

'But my lord, only consider . . . He might have your mama's fortune, but you possess something infinitely more valuable. You have the love of your wife.' She smoothed the wide lapel of his coat. 'Just think,' she added softly, 'what torture it will be to him to see you together. Day and night.'

There was a tension about him she recognised, an avidity in his gaze. Good.

'I will come up with some excuse to keep him at Seagrove,' she promised. 'You need only play along.'

Delany, Lady Nash

For the first evening in recent memory, we dined *en famille*, without even the vicar or any of the local gentry in attendance.

Both Julian and I were sober and subdued, not from any false sense of piety appropriate to the occasion, but from genuine grief at the dowager's passing. Richard, on the other hand, seemed unable or unwilling to conceal his good spirits. His unfettered fury of that afternoon had undergone a complete transformation.

While I might not consider it appropriate for my husband to display such high spirits on the very day his mother was laid to rest, I cannot deny I was relieved he no longer frothed at the mouth with rage.

Eyeing Miss Smith over my soup spoon as I sipped, I marvelled at the woman. She must be the cause of this alteration. How had she done it? One could not deny that whatever her faults, Margaret handled my lord as a first-rate fiddler drives a team of finicky thoroughbreds. Regardless of my dislike of her, life at Seagrove was far less fraught when Margaret was here.

I thought of the letter the dowager had written to me, and my failure to relocate it after hastily secreting the missive in Mr Defoe's famous novel. I'd searched the couch and the floor near where I'd left the novel, thinking that in my haste I might have dropped it, but to no avail.

Had Margaret seen me hide it? Had she stolen the letter? Oh, but I should have read it on the spot, or taken it to my chamber for privacy. Would the secrets that missive contained go to the grave with Lady Verena? The darkest musings took possession of my mind. Try as I might, I could not shake free of them.

I spoke little throughout dinner, partly due to absorption in my own thoughts, partly for fear of disrupting the delicate balance of my husband's temper. Judging by his expression, Julian was lost to grief, and I noticed his glass was refilled often with the heavy burgundy Richard had chosen. Julian's appearance was rumpled. He ate little and spoke less. I worried his sorrow might send him headlong into a bout of dissipation and chafed at the considerations of propriety that constrained me from acting to prevent it.

When Richard said to him, 'You will stay for the hunt, won't you, brother?', Julian stared as if Richard had grown an extra head.

'The hare-coursing, you know,' said Richard, with the false jocularity of one who never made much more than a show of participating in the sport. 'I believe they're taking the pack out next week.'

'I don't hunt,' said Julian, his diction slightly thickened with drink. While a first-rate horseman, Julian's views on the cruelty of hunting ought to have been well known to his brother, as they were to me.

'Ah. Yes, yes, I'd forgotten,' said Richard with something of a sneer. Trust Richard to see compassion as weakness.

Miss Smith touched her napkin to her lips. 'What I believe his lordship is trying to ascertain, Mr Nash, is whether you will do us the honour of remaining here at Seagrove for the present? I am sure your dear mama would have wished it.'

Julian shot me a quick look from beneath lowered brows.

'Yes, do stay,' I said. Seeing Julian here every day would be painful, but at least I might try my best to alleviate his sorrow. Here, moreover, he would be well away from the fleshpots of Town. If left to his own devices he might well ride directly to the devil, as my brother would say. His remaining at Seagrove would be the lesser of two evils.

Still, I did not expect him to agree to such a delightful sojourn. No one was more surprised than I when Julian raised his glass to me with an ironic lift of an eyebrow. 'If that's *your* wish, my dear Rothwell, then of course I'll stay.'

In the days and weeks following that reckless comment at the dinner table, I avoided Julian as much as possible. With Henry now thriving and my own vigour returning, I took up my pen again, embarking on my second novel, *The Abbey at Inglesforth*. Into that novel I poured all of the frustration, longing, passion and tenderness Julian's proximity stirred in me, emotion I could not otherwise express.

For his part, Julian did not often dine at home. He might have asked for my help in sifting through his mother's effects. Instead, he accepted the assistance of Miss Smith.

An unforeseen consequence of Julian's prolonged stay was his effort to improve the lot of his brother's tenants. Richard had no intention of altering the practices of his father and grandfather before him when it came to running his estates. Rather than flying into a fury with his brother, however, he listened to and agreed with everything Julian said.

The morning after witnessing such an encounter, I said to Julian, 'What can you be about, interfering at Seagrove?'

I had found him leaning his elbows on the fence that surrounded the horse paddock, his hands clasped before him, watching one of the grooms exercise a grey mare. He turned his head and gave me a grim smile. 'You noticed it too, did you?'

'He seems to be taking your advice to heart.'

'Chilling, isn't it?' He set his foot on the lowest rail of the fence. 'He wants something. He wants something so badly I could piss on his boots and he'd thank me for cleaning them.'

As if a new thought occurred to him, he eyed me with a degree of intimate speculation that made me blush. Did Julian mean to make love to me to test how far his brother was prepared to bend? I decided to ignore the insult, whether real or imagined. He'd gain no ground with me if that was his plan.

'You are goading him,' I said. On the one hand, this pleased and relieved me, for I'd thought Julian displayed unwonted stupidity, not to say tactlessness, with his meddling. On the other, something told me it was a dangerous game to play.

'What do you think he wants?' I asked. 'He cannot possibly imagine you will give him the money.'

'Lord, no,' said Julian. 'Although he did manage to suggest I invest in certain improvements at Seagrove, re-building cottages and the like.'

'A worthy project.'

He gave a cynical bark of a laugh. 'Yes, and if I thought he'd put my money to that use, I would give it gladly.'

'He is like a child jealous of his brother's new toy,' I said. 'I suppose it is understandable. He might think it's all about the money, but deep down, he's hurt that his mama favoured you in her will and not him.'

'My brother was amply provided for by our father, as you are well aware,' said Julian. 'Besides, he would have seen Mama starve in a ditch if she hadn't been so monstrous wealthy on her own account.' He shrugged. 'She was clever enough to beat him at his own game. Allowed him to think that if he housed her and put up with her whims with a smile, she'd leave him her fortune. Do you know, she even had a false will drawn up that named him sole heir, in case that companion of hers went looking for it?'

I frowned. While that might have been a clever ruse on the one hand, on the other . . .

A suspicion too horrible to mention had taken root in my brain and this news only served to nourish it. The notion refused to be dislodged, no matter how often I told myself it was as absurd and fanciful as one of my gothic tales.

'Why don't you get rid of that woman?' said Julian. He'd been saying it since I'd told him my suspicions about the lost letter.

I sighed. I had little hope of ejecting Margaret from our home, and I wasn't at all sure I wished to do so. She had wedged herself into the re-ordered structure of our lives so tightly that without her, I feared all would come tumbling down.

Julian's presence seemed to throw the strangeness of life at Seagrove into high relief. I began to realise that the arrival of my firstborn had made me increasingly insular, retreating to the world of the nursery and leaving the household in Miss Smith's hands. I saw how much control I had lost during my confinement, and how little will I'd had to regain it.

I longed to confide in Julian, but despite his willingness to discuss his brother with me, he seemed hard and bitter and unapproachable on more personal topics. Our periods of accord were fragile and fleeting as butterflies. A full rapprochement seemed too much to hope for.

He still resented me for marrying Richard. I did not reflect on the irony that Julian had now inherited a fortune, because my refusing him had never been due to his improvidence alone.

The truth was that I did not deserve the relief of unburdening my worries to him. He owed me nothing, not even the small measure of sympathy he gave me. Yet I knew he understood how hard it was to be dependent on someone whose temper was so uncertain and whose power was absolute. Julian was free of that yoke now. I could not suppress a spike of envy whenever I thought of it. What would I do with £20 000?

But where was the use of thinking such a thing? I could never leave my husband. My love for our son tied me to Richard as securely as the strongest of shackles. As long as Richard lived, I would never be free.

CHAPTER THIRTEEN

Lord Kenyon

The plaintiff's counsel, Mr Garrow, mopped his brow with a pristine linen handkerchief and straightened his rather less pristine wig. The atmosphere of the court, packed with men of all ranks and conditions, was airless and thick with all manner of odours, from the scent of old sweat to the stifling mix of pomade and other scents worn by a group of macaronis who seemed intent on making a spectacle of themselves. The foppish bows they wore instead of cravats, the hair powder in shades of the nursery – lilac, blue and even pink – the silly hats and loud waistcoats were all calculated to disgust.

And amid the throng, Lady Nash, looking as cool and unruffled as if she'd lately emerged from her dressing room. What was her situation now that she'd been barred from her husband's house? One heard rumours . . .

The Lord Chief Justice turned from her to focus on the latest witness for the plaintiff: the housekeeper, a Mrs Ludd.

She seemed a respectable, no-nonsense sort of woman. Yet giving evidence in such a trial seemed to be trying her nerves. She clutched a voluminous reticule in both hands as if her life depended on it, her knuckles white.

Mr Garrow, who had established that the housekeeper had worked for Lord Nash since before his marriage, said, 'Mrs Ludd, was Mr Julian Nash a visitor to the house when you were in London last spring?'

'Yes, he was.' Keen to exculpate the defendant, the housekeeper turned to address Lord Kenyon. 'But there was no harm in that, my lord. He —'

'Thank you, Mrs Ludd,' said Mr Garrow, stemming the good woman's protestations. 'In fact, Mr Julian Nash made his home there for more than two months, did he not?'

'Yes,' said the housekeeper. 'Yes, he did.'

'And in that time, was Lord Nash in residence?'

'His lordship stayed behind in Seagrove and joined the family on the fifth of July, a week after the baby came,' said Mrs Ludd.

Mr Garrow's eyes widened. 'Do you mean to tell this court that from the eleventh of April until the fifth of July, the defendant lived at Nash House *alone* with Lady Nash?'

'Hardly that, sir,' said Mrs Ludd, reddening. 'Miss Smith, companion to the late dowager, was there the entire time. Mr Julian left the house on the same day as Miss Smith departed for Reading.'

'And was it your observation that Mr Nash and his sister-in-law were on terms of intimacy?' said Garrow.

'I know nothing of the matter,' said Mrs Ludd. She glanced toward the back of the room, where her master sat behind a curtain, and blinked twice. 'That is to say, I believe they liked each other.'

'*Liked* each other?' Garrow pounced. 'What leads you to this conclusion, Mrs Ludd?'

The woman pokered up at that. 'It is not my place to say.'

Lord Kenyon approved of the woman's discretion, but he intervened. 'Your reticence does you credit, madam. Indeed, I believe we should all be well pleased to have such a loyal servant. But you are here as witness to a very serious crime indeed, and it behoves you to answer those of Mr Garrow's questions that are pertinent to the matter without prevarication.'

The woman's mouth flattened into a line. 'Lady Nash and Mr Julian chattered to one another in a lively manner. They both liked books and horses and – and politics. That is all.'

Clearly dissatisfied with this assessment, Garrow moved on. 'Now, Mrs Ludd, I wish you to cast your mind back to the end of July. The thirtieth of that month, to be precise. Did you have cause to observe Mr Nash that day?'

'I did.'

'Where did you observe him?'

'I saw Mr Nash go into Lady Nash's boudoir, sir. But he —'

'And where was Lady Nash at the time?' said Garrow, cutting off her justifications.

'I do not know, sir. I was merely passing when I observed it.'

'Did you hear voices?'

'No.' That last with a flare of indignation.

'Are you quite certain of this, Mrs Ludd?'

'It is not my habit to listen at keyholes, sir.'

Mr Garrow, apparently accepting the rebuff, bowed. 'No more questions, my lord.'

Again, Mr Erskine rose to his feet. This time with a weary sigh. 'Mrs Ludd, did you ever observe any physical intimacy between Lady Nash and the defendant, Mr Julian Nash?'

'Sir, I did not.'

With an inclination of the head, Erskine said, '*Thank* you', as if they had at last got at the heart of the matter. 'I have nothing further for this witness.'

A chamber maid, Miss Betsy Baker, was called. Now, this was a young woman of considerably less discretion than the housekeeper, if Lord Kenyon did not miss his guess. A plump, pretty girl with a mane of glossy brown curls spilling from beneath her mobcap.

'You are responsible for cleaning the bedchambers at the London town house of Lord Nash, are you not?' said Mr Garrow.

'Yes, sir,' she mumbled.

The girl appeared avid, brown eyes wide and lips trembling with excitement. Kenyon had encountered many such young misses. Pert, they were, and brimful of garrulous mischief, if only one gave them a forum.

'Speak up!' he growled. 'Loudly, so the jury can hear you.'

The girl's shoulders lifted as she filled her lungs. 'Yes, sir!' She shouted like a drill sergeant, making the court rumble with laughter.

'Get on with it,' said Lord Kenyon testily.

'As you please, my lord,' said Garrow. He tucked one hand into the folds of his gown. 'Miss Baker, do you recall the morning of May the twentieth?'

'Yes, sir.'

'Did you have cause to visit Lady Nash's bedchamber that morning?'

'Yes, sir. It's my duty to make up my lady's bed every morning. *Was* my duty,' she amended scrupulously, a reminder to all that Lady Nash no longer resided in the household with her spouse.

'And when you made up her ladyship's bed that morning,' said Garrow, 'what did you observe?'

'The bed had been laid in by two people,' said Miss Baker.

'How do you know this?'

'It was mussed on both sides, sir. My lady always sleeps – *slept* – on the left side of the bed, sir.'

Garrow bowed. 'Thank you. Miss Baker, what time do you usually turn down the bed of an evening?'

'Depends on when the mistress is expected home, sir. But on the night before, I remember my lady dined at home. It was about half past ten when I went to visit her chamber but she was already abed.'

'Had her ladyship been ill?'

A giggle escaped the silly wench. 'No, sir. I shouldn't have said so, sir.'

'She dined in company?'

'Mrs Boddington, my lady's aunt, was there, and another lady of

Mrs Boddington's acquaintance, Mrs Wilton, who were to go with my lady's sister, Mrs Burton, to the opera that night. And Mr Julian Nash, of course. He were there too. Oh, and Miss Smith.'

'Your visit to the bedchamber, was that before or after dinner?'

'After.'

'Who remained in the house besides the servants when the ladies left for the opera?'

'Only Lady Nash and Mr Julian Nash. And Miss Smith also, but Miss Smith retired to her own apartments directly after dinner.'

'So my lady retired early, you said. And the next morning, the bed had been disarranged on both sides.'

'Yes sir.'

Mr Garrow bowed. 'No further questions, my lord.'

When Mr Erskine cross-examined, he made the girl look foolish and prurient, as was no doubt his intention, but he couldn't shake her certainty as to what she'd seen and the conclusion she'd drawn from it.

Finally, he said, 'On the morning of May the twentieth, did you observe anything else in my lady's bedchamber that was out of the ordinary, other than disarranged sheets?'

'No, sir.'

Upon Mr Erskine's releasing the maid, Garrow called yet another witness.

Frowning, Lord Kenyon said, 'Is this necessary, Mr Garrow? I should think we have sufficient from the testimony of the maid.'

'Vital, my lord,' Mr Garrow assured him. 'I call Margaret Smith.'

Margaret

Matters hardly progressed as Margaret had hoped. Either Julian and Delany had fallen out of love or they each possessed an inhuman amount of restraint.

Of course, Henry was not yet weaned. It was well known that nursing an infant could drain a woman of desire. Perhaps, love Delany though he might, Julian no longer wanted her in that way either. Some men were repulsed by the notion of the female body bearing children, or being used for any purpose but male pleasure.

Exasperated, Margaret blew out a breath between her teeth. She'd suffered endless nagging from Richard on the subject, worn herself to the bone with spying on the pair, hoping against hope for evidence that would vindicate her.

Truly, she felt ill with fatigue. She wished she, and not Delany, might claim an ague and keep to her own apartments tonight. Instead, she sat at the fortepiano, indulging Richard's fondness for Haydn and wishing her head would stop pounding in quarter-time so she could blessed well think.

Her fingers moved over the keys independently of her brain. From the corner of her eye, she watched Julian Nash prowl the room restlessly. He'd been trapped with them tonight, having committed to dine at home before he discovered Delany's indisposition.

Julian kept his cards close to his chest, but she sensed he would not bide much longer beneath their roof. That he had not left them long before this spoke volumes about his attachment to Delany. Ironic, was it not, that a man so experienced at seducing women would not so much as touch his sister-in-law's hand?

Something drastic was called for. Margaret brought her piece to a close with a flourish, then rose to her feet.

'I ought to see how Lady Nash does,' she said. 'She has been sadly pulled of late.'

That caught Julian's interest. He made no comment, however. Nor did Richard, to whom his wife's health was a matter of indifference at best.

'Do you know,' she mused, with a subtle flare of her eyes at her co-conspirator, 'I do believe Lady Nash needs a change of scenery. The Continent, perhaps?'

Richard pulled at his lower lip in that childish way he had. 'No, no. Not while she's increasing. Besides, think of the unrest there now. No, I won't have her ladyship gallivanting to the Continent with my babe in her belly.'

Margaret noticed Julian had paled a little at the news Delany was again with child. He said, 'Very wise, brother. But I confess I had not descried so much difference in Lady Nash. What is this illness you speak of? I thought she had a trifling cold.'

'Well acquainted with her constitution, are you?' Richard demanded.

Julian merely gazed at his brother until the flush rose to Richard's cheeks.

Smooth as cream, Margaret intervened. 'At all events, we must see what we can do closer to home. Bath, perhaps.'

Julian gave a derisive snort. 'Aye, I can well see Delany Rothwell doddering among the invalids. Good God, ma'am, she has a paltry sniffle and you must needs send her off to some watering place? Nonsense.'

'Her spirits have been much depressed since the baby was born,' Margaret said. 'Surely you have remarked upon it.'

Julian shrugged. 'She needs something to damned well do, don't she? Take her up to Town, do the pretty with all her friends.' Casually, he added, 'I'm for London myself shortly. I could escort you ladies if Nash here is too occupied with his, ah, history to join us.'

Before Richard could cavil, Margaret cut in, exclaiming in delight, 'An excellent notion, sir. Just what the doctor ordered.'

She bent a minatory look on Richard. 'Don't you agree, my lord?'

'Eh?' Three fraught seconds ticked by before Richard caught her intention.

He gave a start. 'Oh, er, yes.' He leaned forward to add, 'If you could see your way to cheering the old gel up, Julian, I'd be much obliged to you. Can't have my lady falling into melancholy when she's carrying my son, can I?'

Thank you, Margaret thought. Richard always got there in the end.

She turned voluble, sketching plans and listing acquaintances and family she must notify of their imminent arrival.

Frowning, Julian interrupted. 'Ought we not consult Delany herself about this? Presumably, she'll have her own opinion on the matter.'

'Oh, she'll do as I tell her,' said Richard, provoking his brother to deepen his frown.

His lordship, as he told her later, was more concerned at losing Margaret's company than he was bothered about Delany's objections.

'You won't be without me for long, my lord,' Margaret promised. 'What say you to my abandoning the happy couple somewhere on the road to London?'

His gaze lost focus. After a pause, he changed the subject entirely. Margaret wondered whether he hadn't heard her, or whether he merely pretended he had not.

Delany, Lady Nash

When I rose from my sickbed, I felt enervated and out of sorts. The weather was so blustery and inclement that it was the perfect day to curl up by the fire. I went to the library in search of a new book to read while Henry slept.

Julian sat at the chess board, playing against himself, with Pug asleep in a tight ball at his feet. A little lost since Lady Verena's death, Pug had taken to following Julian about the house. A most comical sight, the enormous man and the tiny, snuffling lap dog, but Julian did not seem to mind.

He indicated the board. 'Can I interest you in a game?'

I shook my head, crossing to the shelves. 'I am not in the mood for chess today.'

'You mean you don't wish to engage with me,' said Julian. 'On *any* point.'

He'd risen when I entered the room. I fixed my gaze on a row of tooled leather books as I felt his approach.

'Do I make you nervous, Delany? His tone had deepened, roughened somehow, and the hairs rose on the back of my neck.

Turning to find him too close, I struggled to speak. 'Why should you think that, pray? You of all people must know that I have nerves of steel.'

He shrugged one shoulder as he scanned the shelves beside me. 'You've been avoiding me. You have not been yourself since I arrived here.'

'Tosh! I've been occupied with the baby.' I hesitated, then added, 'Things are different now.'

'Delany.' That one word expressed everything unspoken between us.

'Don't.' I could not look at him. I could not afford to converse with him in such an intimate manner. Lately, my resolve grew weaker the more time I spent in his presence.

Recently, too, Richard had been caressingly affectionate toward me whenever his brother was near. Whether he sensed something between me and Julian and sought to stake his claim while torturing his brother into the bargain, or whether he simply wished to show me off to Julian the way he displayed me to his friends, I did not know. Fervently, I hoped Richard did not mean to offer Julian a private viewing of my charms. I shuddered to think of that humiliation. Moreover, the consequences to Richard might well be dire if Julian were to discover how Richard used me.

My lord's attitude towards my admirers had convinced me I was free to love outside my marriage now that our son was born. Indeed I had often wondered if Richard wished me to engage in such liaisons so that he might take his voyeurism a further step. But to give in to my feelings for Julian would be a betrayal Richard would never forgive.

Besides, my love for Julian ran too deep to treat him so lightly. An *affaire* that could never be more . . . that would be exquisite torture.

As if he sensed my discomfort, Julian stepped away. A current of relief swirled around me.

He said, 'Has Richard mentioned his plans for you?'

'He's sending me to Town.' Some interest in the world stirred in me at the thought. 'I must go to London, if only to see Mr Wilberforce speak.' Soon he would introduce his Bill for the abolition of the slave trade in the Commons.

'Yes, of course you must,' Julian said. 'How will you manage it?'

Ever since an incident years before, when some buffoon of a man could not find a seat due to the presence of females there, women had been excluded from the strangers' gallery in the House of Commons. There were held to be no exceptions; the Duchess of Portland herself had once attempted to gain admittance only to be turned away.

'There is only one solution,' said Julian, leaning back against the chess table with a gleam in his eye. 'You must dress as a man.'

I laughed. 'You cannot be serious.'

'It has been done before.'

'No, really?' I shook my head. 'You are joking me.'

Yet the idea appealed to me so strongly, I felt excitement rise in my veins like sap in a tree. I had not experienced such enthusiasm for anything but Henry in a long time.

'Hmm.' He looked me up and down. 'To be sure, there was never a form less like a man's than yours, my dear. Yet we shall contrive.'

Demurely, I said, 'Ah, but my lord would never consent.'

'Need you tell him?' said Julian. 'I know a lady – respectable and discreet, I vow – who will help us.'

I remained undecided on the matter. If I was caught dressing as a fellow, as other ladies had been, there would be no very dire consequences. Yet I did not relish attracting gossip. Moreover, I thought it ridiculous that I should have to go to such lengths to see a parliamentary debate.

Was it subversive and clever to go disguised as a man, or merely laughable? Ought I to go as a female, demand entry on principle and be denied? How desperately did I want to witness a great blow struck against a despicable, unchristian industry that caused misery to countless people? There seemed no easy answer.

I longed to see Mr Wilberforce speak, to carry all before him, as surely he must. The triumph and exaltation of eradicating a hateful, cruel practice would be sweet indeed. In the end, this keen desire weighed more heavily in the balance than propriety.

'I'll do it,' I said. 'I'll dress as a man if you will help me.'

Julian laughed, and the old glint returned to his eyes. It was the first time since his mother's demise that I'd seen him happy, free from the taint of cynicism that seemed to characterise him these days.

When I discovered Julian was to escort me and Miss Smith to London, I was bewildered. There could be no advantage to my husband in sending me to Town with his brother, could there? I knew whose company I should prefer, of course, but far be it from Richard to consult my wishes in the matter. However, I shrugged and accepted the gift horse. Margaret was to accompany us, so there would be no whisper of impropriety about our travelling together.

At all events, I became much occupied ensuring Henry's comfort for the journey, so Richard and his odd fits and starts ceased to exercise my mind.

Margaret and I almost came to blows over my taking Henry with me. She was adamant that he ought to stay behind at Seagrove, where the air was healthier than in London.

'Balderdash!' said I. 'He is better off with his mama, wherever that may be.' Ignoring her protests, I bundled my lusty little fellow into the coach with me. I took Pug, too, for good measure.

Margaret appealed to Richard and he added his objections to hers. However, when I pointed out that since Henry had yet to be weaned, I could hardly go at all if he did not come with me, I had my way.

Good God, why did they seek to separate us? Richard could not pretend he wanted Henry with him. He scarcely noticed the child existed.

Soon enough, we were on our way. Despite the calm crossing to the mainland, Henry, poor poppet, was violently sick, and I began to regret setting out at all. But as it turned out, his suffering was temporary and I need not have despaired. Once on dry land, he was right as rain.

Margaret, sullen as a thwarted schoolgirl, scarcely spoke but to complain of the smell of vomit and Pug's farts. Julian remarked he was glad he'd decided to ride – whether to escape the rank smells or Margaret's complaints, I could not decide.

My visit to Town this time was very different from the previous occasion. In Julian's company, I entered a rarefied world of politics, of intellectuals and essayists, poets and playwrights. I do not pretend to anything like the erudition of those celebrated thinkers, but I learned and read and debated the momentous topics of the day. My world expanded under their tutelage and guidance.

My earlier fears that Julian would find solace in the fleshpots of Town were allayed. His mother's death seemed to have sobered him rather than the reverse. Of course there is a side to a man's life to which a female will never be privy so I cannot claim his was a completely reformed character. However, no rumours linking Julian's name with another woman's came to my ears during those months and his demeanour showed no sign of dissipation.

Since Lavinia and my aunt refused to accompany me, I dragged Margaret to political salons, ignoring her claims of boredom. How could anyone be bored among the very people who ruled England, whose opinions and philosophies influenced policy both at home and abroad? When they might meet Mr Fox, exchange witticisms with Mr Sheridan, be dragooned into Whig campaigning by Lady Duncannon and receive a proposition from the Prince of Wales, all in one evening?

I'd been warned about the Prince, so his grovelling at my feet was not as embarrassing as it might have been otherwise. I tactfully refused him. Say what you will about 'Florizel', he did not bear the slightest grudge, but appeared to have forgotten the matter entirely when next we met – and, to be sure, he most probably had.

In the event, I was present when Mr Wilberforce gave his famous speech. I was not, however, obliged to don a boy's clothes, for I'd been fortunate enough to fall into the company of ladies with influence, and we managed to inveigle our way in. Upon payment of a hefty bribe, we were guided to a gallery so high as to give but a bird's-eye view of the Commons. We had to squint down through a grille to glimpse the proceedings, but I was so buoyed by emotion at the momentous occasion that the indignity of our position, caged high above the fray, hardly rankled. Despite our uncomfortable and inadequate vantage point, no one cheered as loudly as we ladies when Mr Wilberforce had said his piece.

Surely, I thought, no man on earth could fail to be swayed by Mr Wilberforce's words. I came away exultant, only wishing to share my elation with Julian. Had I known the reprehensible practice would still go on decades later I would not have felt quite so triumphant. But of course, where money and power are involved, men commit every kind of atrocity – or turn a blind eye to it, which is equally bad.

Julian's fury at the subsequent stalling of Wilberforce's Bill, and the obstinacy of so many men in failing to see truth when plain evidence was thrust under their noses, made for a tense atmosphere at Nash House that spring.

Yet, despite Julian's dark moods and darker predictions, I had not felt so enlivened since before my marriage. As ever, Julian listened to my opinions and argued his own.

We discussed our hopes for the liberation of those hapless individuals who had been stolen from their homes and shipped to the Indies like cattle, who had suffered disease and deprivation, only to be sold to harsh masters and put to back-breaking work without hope of ever returning home. For Julian, the abolitionist cause was an obsession, a religion. He gave it his all and he continues to fight for true abolition alongside his brethren to this day.

As for me, I am sorry to confess that commitment to my own survival soon took precedence over worthier causes.

My second lying-in was easier than the first. Stephen was a bouncing, healthy boy, and no less dear than his elder brother.

I'd fought strenuously against Richard's edict that my new baby be given direct to a wet nurse once he was born. How was I to guess he did it for any reason but to wound me? I'd taken such joy in nursing Henry that it seemed criminal to abandon my second child to another woman's care. Moreover, I was fiercely jealous of this unknown wet nurse who would never treasure my son as his own mama would.

My distress at Richard's intransigence brought on my labour; it was with tears of rage and frustration drying on my cheeks that I felt the first pangs warning of my baby's imminent arrival.

I was frantic to have my way, and the knowledge that I was powerless to stop my husband acting as he thought fit in the matter first enraged, then disheartened me. How would the babe know how dearly his mama loved him if he were taken away and given to a stranger to raise?

I would have fought for my child like a tigress, but for a time after the birth, I became ill of a fever. I lay for what seemed like years in delirium, shivering and sweating and crying out for my children. When, at length, I came to my senses, Jane told me they'd feared for my life. More than that, my lord had worried my disease would infect the boys so he'd sent both of them away.

The illness left me weak as a kitten, without the energy to fight for my sons. Racked with the most exquisite pain – of the body and of the heart – I believe I would have continued to decline but for the fierce love I bore my children. And, perhaps, that indelible streak of stubbornness that was native to my character.

I had no ally in the household. For once, even Jane sided with

Richard, though of course she would have been powerless to stand against him if she had not.

Miss Smith had left us some weeks before to visit relatives. Surely Margaret would feel for me in this predicament and help me persuade Richard. I discovered later, however, that the letters I wrote to her begging for help were never sent.

My aunt did not seem to grasp the seriousness of the matter. She wrote to me, advising me not to make such a fuss – that it had always been the fashion among high-born folk to send their infants away, that perhaps it was for the best as I'd been so ill. Indeed, I was inordinately attached to my children and must learn to separate from them . . . and so on. I would never forgive my aunt for this letter. Never.

Lavinia, my brother Selby . . . worse than useless. In desperation, I sent for Julian.

I tried to make myself look presentable for his visit – or at least, I ordered Jane to help me do so – but I cannot say she achieved success. My illness had left me hollow-eyed and gaunt. My skin had lost its lustre and my tumble of black curls had thinned. I did not care for any of that, but I expected Julian, being a man, would.

I asked him to call at a time when I knew Richard would be at his club. Jane feared that I might catch a chill and refused to let me leave my over-heated private chambers. Had I been able to walk, I would have ignored her decree, but I was too weak to take a step. Though I trusted my invalid status would exempt me from accusations of impropriety, I asked Jane to sit by the fire with her sewing during our interview, just in case.

It seemed three ages before Julian's heavy tread sounded in the corridor outside. The butler, with the avuncular air of the old retainer, showed him into my boudoir and shut the door behind him.

'Rothwell,' Julian said softly, tossing his hat and gloves on a table and striding forward to kneel by my couch. He took my hands in his, then, seeing the misery in my face, he drew me with heartbreaking gentleness into his arms.

I had no tears left. I trembled violently as a wave of the utmost relief washed over me.

Deaf to Jane's half-hearted remonstrances, Julian kissed the crown of my head and folded me closer and murmured soothing nonsense in his deep, resonant voice. His breath warmed my hair, the skin behind my ear. Such a sensation of homecoming flowed through me that for one moment – just one – I felt at peace.

I shut my eyes, unutterably grateful for his presence. Julian would make this right.

'I'll kill him,' he muttered when he'd heard the full story.

After the lack of sympathy I'd met at every turn, his compassion almost overwhelmed me.

'What the devil does he mean by it?' demanded Julian.

Bitterly, I said, 'He would do anything to thwart my happiness.'

'But to keep a mother from her child . . .' Julian gripped my hands again. 'It is a cruelty. Particularly so, in your case.' His gaze softened. 'I saw how you were with Henry, my dear. No child could wish for a more tender mother.'

At his words, grief flooded my heart. What tenderness would my sons receive from whomever kept them now? Visions of a gin-swilling wet-nurse treating my sons with cruelty or neglect crowded my mind. 'Julian, I need you to find my children for me. He won't let me visit them. He won't even tell me where they are. Please. Help me persuade him.'

'I'll deal with Richard,' said Julian. 'You must devote yourself to recovery.'

Julian set the household by the ears, ordering all manner of accommodations to be made for my comfort. He mixed me a hot rum punch, redolent of spices and lemon, and helped me raise the silver punch cup to my lips, his hand steady on mine. He declared the brew a panacea for all ills, and perhaps it was. But his presence, his protection, were better for my spirits than any tonic.

He seemed to sense the improvement, for he said, 'Now, Rothwell, we shall have no more of this languishing about on sofas with tea and toast. You must eat a nourishing meal tonight.'

He glanced questioningly at Jane, who nodded eagerly. 'The doctor said mistress can have a morsel of solid food now. Boiled chicken or mutton, perhaps.'

'Good God! No wonder she looks thin as a rail,' said he.

'Thank you,' I replied in what I hoped was a withering tone.

He grinned and gave orders for an impressive array of small delicacies to be served. They were my favourites, most of them, but, 'Oh, not boiled tongue, I beg.'

'That's not for you. It's for me,' he responded. 'I'm staying here until we get to the bottom of this. Can't have you wasting away to a shadow, can we? You must think of your boys, ma'am. You must regain your strength so that they have a happy mama to come home to.'

I would not be happy until they were with me, but I took his point and applied myself to his carefully chosen meal with diligence, if not with gusto.

The following day, I was too anxious to remain in my bedchamber, so I had a footman carry me down to the drawing room, where I stayed with Pug for company. The little dog regarded me with those bulbous eyes of his, the wrinkles above them all bunched, as if in concern for my distress.

I stroked his creamy fur. 'Dear Pug.' I knew the silly animal only thought of his dinner, but he comforted me all the same.

I chafed at my helplessness, but I'd agreed to leave it to Julian to see what he might do to persuade Richard to retrieve the boys now that I was out of danger. Where such a matter as my children's welfare was at stake I did not lightly give up my place at the negotiating table. However, as Julian pointed out, I was too weak and distraught to deal effectively with my husband. I insisted Julian divulge his strategy but he shrugged and said he had none, that it would depend on the circumstances.

Soon enough, I heard Julian's voice raised in anger. Pug stood up in

my lap, on high alert, curly tail wagging. He leaped off me and scampered out, to sit whining outside the library door. I rather wished I could
do the same. It was pure torture to wait quietly while the men argued
back and forth. The volume of Julian's voice dropped once more, as if
calm had prevailed, and my hopes raised their heads.

The wait seemed to go on forever, and I cursed my incapacity a
thousand times over. If I had not contracted this stupid fever, I might
have my boys with me now.

I heard the doors to the library burst open and a hasty step on the
marble floor. 'Where is she?'

I sat up, clutching the arm-rest of my chair, wishing my infernal
legs would carry me to meet him.

Julian erupted into the room with scant regard for my invalid
state. 'He's impossible. Close as an oyster. I can't get a word out of him
regarding their whereabouts.'

I had expected as much, but the knots in my stomach tightened to
a hard, painful mass.

'I'll find them.' He set his hat on his head. 'I'll find them and fetch
them back to you.'

'Let me come.' I scrambled to get up, but blackness seeped into my
vision. My knees buckled, and in two strides, Julian had caught me in
his arms.

The darkness receded as he hoisted me up, the blood pounded
unpleasantly in my throat and my head swam. I struggled to suppress
the urge to cast up my accounts all over Julian's cravat. Oh, but I could
have screamed with frustration. 'Put me down!' I snapped, struggling
ineffectually. 'I'm coming with you. Only tell Jane to fetch my pelisse
and bonnet, and get one of the footmen to carry me to the coach.'

With a curious twist to his mouth, he complied with my direction
to release me. Having deposited me on the sofa again, he stood before
me, the great mountain, with his arms akimbo. He made no move to
follow my other orders.

'We'll take my landau,' I said with a blazing look.

'No.'

I all but growled at him. 'I won't argue with you. If you don't take me, I shall order my carriage and follow you.'

'Don't be ridiculous. I'd be half way to Hampshire by the time you got out the door.'

'Hampshire? You think that's where he's sent them?' My poor infant, travelling all that way in a draughty carriage . . .

Julian slapped his gloves against his palm. 'Richard owns several estates in different parts of the country, but I think he'd be most likely to choose Lamerton Hall.'

'You don't think he sent them back to Seagrove, do you?' I asked. 'To a woman in the village, perhaps?'

He shook his head. 'He says not, and I believe him. Besides, Seagrove is too obvious if he doesn't want them found.'

'You cannot ride all over England searching for them,' I said. Neither of us mentioned the glaring difficulty that even if Julian did find my boys, we were both powerless to compel their return.

'Do not concern yourself with that,' said Julian. 'I'll go myself to the most likely places and send inquiries elsewhere.' He set his large hand on my shoulder, a warm, comforting weight. 'I'll find them. You must devote yourself to getting better. Put some flesh on your bones, m'dear. I've no fancy for skeletons.'

It was a deliberate goad but I was too agitated to reply in kind. I took his hand and fervently kissed the back of it. No words could express my gratitude. I stared up at him, still clinging to his hand. 'Julian, I —'

'Yes, yes,' he said abruptly, extricating himself. 'You're most obliged, aren't you?' He sighed and shook his head.

I hardly heard him, scarcely saw him go.

I would get better. I would gather every ounce of my strength. And by God, I would fight tooth and nail to bring my beloved sons home.

Three weeks later, through determined effort, I had almost regained my customary vigour. I'd given Richard little respite from my pleas, threats and cajolery during that time. Nothing worked. The man was like one of his own marble statues: emotionless and immovable.

'You are worn to the bone, my love,' he said, with an air of great patience. 'Overwrought. When you are yourself again, you will see I have done the right thing.'

'I will never forgive you for this, Richard.' I could have killed him, but then I'd never find my children.

He ignored me and glanced over my head at Jane. 'See that she gets some rest.'

'Yes, my lord.' Jane, grim-faced, dropped a curtsy.

Margaret. I needed Margaret. She could always talk sense into Richard when no one else could. But where *was* the woman?

I asked Julian to call on her in Reading, where she said she would be staying with her family. He wrote to say there was no sign of her there – nor, indeed, of any family bearing her name. She had directed me to send her mail to the King's Arms in that town, but when Julian inquired at the inn about her post he was told her letters had been re-directed to a London address.

My suspicions roused by what seemed a clear subterfuge, I called at that address in Upper Wimpole Street. There, I was told someone – a boy, not a lady – collected letters on behalf of a Miss Smith. No one knew whence he came. I paid the landlady a handsome sum to send word to me if the boy returned, but I waited for news of him in vain.

Where in the world was Margaret Smith? And why would she lie to us about her whereabouts? Could it be that she had my boys with her? But she'd left for Reading long before I was brought to bed with Stephen.

Conscious that I needed to rebuild my strength, I began riding again as soon as the doctor allowed it. The fresh air and exercise ben-efited me greatly. Little by little, my appetite returned.

I would not give up hope. Julian had yet to try several places. Aside from that, there must be some means of persuading Richard that I had not considered.

Even so, a strange conviction gripped me: finding Margaret was the key to the business. Either she knew where my children were or she could persuade Richard to bring them back.

If she wasn't with the children, where was she? Could she be with a lover? I blinked, unable to imagine it. Sifting through memories of our recent sojourn in London, I tried to recall any gentlemen who had paid her particular attention, and failed. She herself had never shown the slightest interest in anyone except Richard.

Seeking solace from my troubles with someone familiar and dear, I called on my sister in Clarges Street.

So much for solace. I found Lavinia pouting prettily, tears making silvery tracks down her alabaster cheeks. She clutched at the lapels of my black redingote and wailed. 'I hate him! I hate him, I hate him! Oh, Delany, he is so cruel to me. Tell him he is cruel!'

I sighed. Lavinia was having one of her tantrums. How unbecoming. Glancing over her shoulder at Mr Burton, I raised my eyebrows in mute inquiry.

My brother-in-law wore an expression of long suffering. Nevertheless he was quick to seize the opportunity my presence afforded. 'I am late for an appointment, my dear Lavinia. But see, here is your sister come to call, and you can have a nice, comfortable prose together.' With a strangled farewell, Mr Burton made good his escape, leaving me with a lachrymose mess of muslin and brown curls.

'You see?' she demanded when the door closed behind him. 'He speaks to me as if I'm a child.'

'Well, if you insist on behaving like one, what would you have him do?'

'You don't understand!' She threw herself face down into the sofa cushions and sobbed.

'Lavinia,' I said, 'you cannot lead Mr Burton such a dog's life. He will tire of you and take a mistress, and then where will you be?'

She sat up at that, dashing at her eyes with the back of her hand. 'A *mistress*? He has a mistress?'

'Rest assured,' I said dryly. 'I am sure he cannot afford one with you as a wife. What is it now?'

'Oh, Delany,' she breathed, her tear-stained face brightening as if at a cherished memory. 'I saw the most exquisite pearl and diamond chip bracelet yesterday, and I am so utterly desperate to have it I could die. Only Burtie says I have masses of bracelets I never wear, and why should this one be different? But oh, I was so taken with it. You can have no notion.'

When I thought of our hand-to-mouth childhood, when I thought of the bad marriage I'd made to give my sister her chance at happiness, when I thought of all I'd suffered this past month, I could have shaken her until all notion of bracelets tumbled from her woolly head.

With what patience I could muster, I said, 'Lavinia, listen to your-self. You have a husband who loves you, one who is kind and gentle and generous. No!' I held up a warning finger to stem her objections. 'Don't tell me he isn't generous, because that is nonsense. I'm intimately acquainted with your wardrobe, don't forget – not to mention the contents of your jewel case and the amount of pin money he gives you.'

She slumped in her chair. 'I never thought you'd be in league with him against me.'

'I am not in league with him. I am trying to make you see that you've turned into a spoiled child, pushing and pushing for brighter baubles you neither need nor truly want. Soon you will make Mr Burton forget why he married you, my dear. Do not be one of those women who is forever grasping for more.'

She picked at her sleeve. Her lower lip – an item to which a man had once written a very bad sonnet – wobbled. Aghast, I watched as her face crumpled in unfeigned agony.

Had I misjudged Mr Burton? Was he, in fact, one of those men who hid a cruel disposition behind a pleasant mask? I could not credit it.

'What is it, sweetheart?' I gathered her into my arms, for when all was said and done, she was still my little sister. Surely she could not be so miserable over a piece of jewellery.

'Oh, Delany,' she murmured into my shoulder. 'I am so utterly undone. Burtie and I have been married all this time and still I have not conceived! His parents have never needed a reason to slight me, but I feel their condemnation in every word they speak to me, every look. And Burtie never says a word in reproach, but I know he f-feels it as keenly as I.'

'Darling,' I said, stroking her hair in my old way. 'It's still early days. Give it time.'

'I don't *want* to give it time.' She pushed away from me, hunted in her pocket and took out a handkerchief. 'I want a baby. I want a son.'

Though already worn as a dish rag, my heart was wrung.

She must have sensed my pain, for she said, 'Oh, I know that you have your problems too, Delany, but at least your boys are born and they are alive. At least you have given your lord an heir. You have done your duty and no one can say you haven't. Whereas I . . .'

Oh, yes, Lavinia, I thought wearily. You are always the more pitiable of us.

'Confide in Mr Burton,' I said to her. 'Tell him the cause of your distress and I am certain he will reassure you. The worst thing you can do now is to set him at a distance.'

She choked on a small sob and dabbed at the corner of her eye with her handkerchief. 'Do you think he would take a mistress?' Lavinia was one of those fortunate females who looked even prettier when she cried.

'I don't know, darling. But I do know that you cannot go on like this. Continue with this behaviour and you will drive away one who loves you dearly.'

I walked home from Lavinia's house deep in thought, and not a little angry with my sister for her wanton attempt to fling away her happiness. Surely Mr Burton would not reproach her for failing to give him a son after a bare year of marriage. I could name any number of couples who had waited several years for their first child.

When we arrived home, Jane went up the front steps ahead of me. Before she had lifted the knocker, the door opened to admit her. I followed at a more leisurely pace, girding my loins for a possible encounter with Richard.

To my surprise, when I reached the top of the steps, our butler stood in the entrance, blocking my way with his large, stooped body. Ordinarily, the porter, a far less exalted personage than Pargeter, was in charge of opening the door. Was something amiss?

'Good morning, Pargeter.' I searched his face in concern. He did not appear at all well. His skin looked clammy as a corpse's and his expression was grave. 'What is it?'

'My lady . . .' His lips trembled as if the words were difficult to speak. 'My lady, I have orders that I am not to admit you.'

'What?' I frowned at him. 'Pargeter, are you drunk?'

That most respectable of butlers recoiled. 'No, my lady!'

'Then let me pass.'

He looked as if he wished the ground would swallow him up, but he did not move. A cold feeling crept through my veins.

'Pargeter?' I said, more uncertainly.

The kindly servant's eyes moistened. In a voice that was infinitely gentle, he said, 'My orders are not to admit you, my lady. Not now, nor never again.'

CHAPTER FOURTEEN

Liz

Having committed to helping Gemma with the renovations and Theo with the mammoth task of preparing the gardens for the forthcoming Open Day, Liz could not simply hole up somewhere with Delany's memoirs and refuse to come out until she'd finished them.

There were two volumes filled with tightly packed script. Liz forced herself not to flick to the end to make sure she had the full story now. She read the memoirs in the library at night in an orderly fashion, transcribing them onto her computer as she went. It slowed the process but it helped her absorb the information. Now she could do a search any time she wanted. It also meant she had a copy of the memoirs. They weren't hers, obviously, and she felt a deep reluctance to leave Delany's world behind when she left Seagrove.

As before, deciphering the text was hard going. Her reading limped along with frustrating slowness. Still, the memoirs made entertaining reading. Delany did not waste words on trivia. She was a stiff-upper-lip sort, for she seemed rather to skate over times of great tragedy and she rarely wrung her hands over her lot.

Her observations on the people around her were wry, clear-eyed and unsympathetic. Liz could imagine Delany as a formidable woman, even at the tender age of seventeen, when her memoirs began.

Despite her sketchy knowledge of the way the criminal conversation case had been conducted, the revelations in the third volume shocked Liz. Delany's pain on losing her children seemed as fresh on the page as on the day she'd experienced it. How powerless she'd been, even with all that beauty, intelligence and spirit. Liz hated to think of Delany, weak and ill and frantic over her children's wellbeing.

The boys' removal did seem to support the circumstances in which the nursemaid alleged the baby swap took place. If the switch was made when Stephen was a newborn living away from his family, it was easier to see how the imposture might have been accomplished with no one the wiser but the perpetrator and the baby's nurse. But wouldn't Delany have discovered the truth? Would she have recognised her son upon his return? Perhaps she had not been part of the household by the time Stephen returned to it.

With all of this conjecture floating around in her brain, Nick's enforced vacation came as a blessing. She knew he'd be over the moon about the discovery of the last two volumes, convinced it would lead to vindication.

Liz wasn't so hopeful. Or rather, what she hoped for ran directly counter to Nick's objective. If she could find evidence that Stephen *was* Delany's legitimate child, Nick might abandon his plans to buy Seagrove.

Why hide the last two volumes? Had Delany secreted them away, or had someone else? Saltwater Cottage had been part of Delany's jointure, and considering her final resting place nearby, she had probably lived there until she died.

Liz was considering taking a break for a bite of dinner one evening when Mr Jackson strolled into the library.

'So, these are the famous memoirs,' he said, smiling at her. 'How are you going with them?'

'Getting there,' said Liz. 'It's a colourful era. And she's a fascinating woman. I'll be sure to send you a copy of the transcript when I'm finished.'

Something hovered at the edge of her mind. She frowned, trying to grasp it. 'There was something I meant to ask you. Do you mind if I check my notes?'

Jackson smiled and sat down beside her. 'Happy to help.'

Liz riffled through her notebook – she'd tried to discipline herself into keeping a record of her theories and queries in one place.

She tapped a page with her index finger. 'That's right, I wanted to ask you about the baby's rattle. The one that was dug up somewhere on the estate.'

'Oh, yes,' said Jackson. 'Have you seen it? Beautiful specimen, isn't it?'

'Yes, it is. I wanted to ask you where it was found,' said Liz.

'Ah.' Jackson pushed his glasses up his nose. 'Well, now. That's quite a poignant story, actually.' He stood up, gesturing towards the window, from which they could see the soft blanket of twilight settling over the landscape. 'Let's go for a walk and I can show you, if you like.'

Liz shut down her computer and followed him out.

They set off in the direction of Nash's Folly, the stunted remains of a tower on the northern Down. In fact, Jackson said, the tower had never been complete. Richard Nash had it built on purpose as a ruin, as was the fashion at the time.

'It was damaged by a bomb blast in the Second World War,' he said, panting a little as they climbed, 'or it would not be quite so decrepit as it is now.'

Liz was pleased to find her own breathing came easily, despite the hill. She was getting fit enough to run up here now. Of course, the grass and soggy ground made it much harder than the road-running she did at home. But before she left Seagrove, she meant to tackle it.

They reached the summit and Jackson said, 'Here we are.'

The ruin was only foundations and a waist-high wall now. Beside it, a shadow box displayed an engraving that showed how the ruin would have looked when it was built.

Liz peered through the cloudy glass at the line drawing of the crumbling tower. 'It could have come straight out of one of Delany's novels,' she murmured. 'Funny to think they made it that way on purpose.' She glanced at Jackson. 'So this was where they found the rattle? When was that?'

'Late seventies or thereabouts,' he replied. 'There was a bit of a craze for those new metal detectors, you see. One of the mechanics who worked here for Theo's father found quite a lot that way.' Jackson squinted. 'Not knowing the history of the place, one of the first areas he tried was around the folly. He thought it was a genuine medieval ruin.'

'And this is where he found the rattle? Do you know the exact spot?'

'Yes, as a matter of fact, I do.' He bowed his head and his mouth worked, as if the notion upset him.

Liz peered up into Jackson's face. 'Is everything all right, Mr Jackson?'

He gave a rueful half-laugh and shook his head. 'Ah, don't mind me. I'm sentimental. The past is more with me than with some, I suppose.' He turned and pointed to a large oak tree by the folly. 'The rattle was found at the base of the tree there.'

They walked over, and on the tree trunk Liz saw that a crude cross had been carved into the bark. In spite of herself, she felt a cold, ghostly hand clutch at her heart.

'When they excavated properly, they found something else,' said Jackson softly. 'The bones of an unknown infant, probably not more than a year old.'

Liz stared at him. An infant. Buried with Stephen Nash's rattle . . . 'What happened to it?' Liz said. 'The, er, the bones, I mean?'

Jackson reached out and traced the carved cross. 'The remains were put back where they were found and never spoken of again.'

But this might mean . . . 'Could the bones have belonged to Stephen Nash?' said Liz. 'It was his rattle buried here, after all.' She thought of Delany's novel, of that awful scene where the child's hand reached up from the grave.

'Oh, no,' said Jackson. 'Stephen Nash lived to middle age. We never could work out what that baby was doing here, or even when the child had been buried.'

She couldn't share the source of her doubts, so Liz said no more. She wondered how she might broach the matter of identifying the baby's remains with Theo. On the one hand, such a find might be of historic significance, quite apart from its bearing on Nick's quest. On the other, that poor little soul deserved to rest in peace.

The discovery was at the forefront of Liz's mind when she returned to the library and read Delany's memoirs with renewed purpose.

The question was, if Henry, the elder son, had died in his late teens and Stephen, Delany and Richard's younger son, had grown up to father children of his own, then who was this other baby? And why was Stephen's rattle – an expensive trinket, and clearly identifiable – buried with this child if the child wasn't Stephen?

She did not want to believe what she suspected might be the truth. If the baby buried at the folly was Stephen Nash, then Nick was the true heir to the Seagrove estate.

After much poring over maps and drawing of diagrams, Fergus and Theo reluctantly concluded that the entrance to the Saltwater Cottage tunnel had caved in years before in one of the landslips that had occurred since the tunnel was made.

Meanwhile, preparations for the Open Day continued. The family met in the library every evening to discuss their progress. All except Valerie, who was still communing with Raoul somewhere. Rather than return to London, he was staying on for a holiday until the night of the cocktail party.

They'd seen little of Valerie since the tasting trial, which was a bit of a reprieve. It might have been her imagination, but Liz thought Theo seemed a lot more relaxed without her around.

While the others planned the Open Day, Liz kept working on the memoirs, glad of the company but lost to their discussions. She'd always had the ability to turn off background noise like a tap, and it helped that Delany's story was so absorbing. The woman came alive in her writings, like the best fictional characters always did. Yet Delany had been real. She turned many of Liz's preconceptions about fine aristocratic ladies on their head. Ultimately, Delany might have been ridiculously privileged, but she was still a woman, with all of a woman's concerns, ordinary and vital.

She could hardly believe it when she read about Delany's banishment from her own home. 'Listen to this!' Liz said to the others. When no one answered her, she turned around. 'Oh.'

Of the three others, only Theo was left, reading – or, more accurately, dozing off over a book in a comfortable armchair.

Liz checked the time. Nearly eleven. Theo would have to be up in a few hours. Maybe she should give him a nudge and send him off to bed.

But he'd roused at the sound of her voice. He blinked, set his book aside and came to read over her shoulder.

He chuckled. 'Firebrand, wasn't she?'

'Indomitable. I can't imagine what it must have been like for her to suffer all the embarrassment and speculation around the court case.'

'I'd assume she carried it off in style,' said Theo. 'It must have been a blow to her when Julian married, though.'

Liz sighed. 'I'd like to believe she was constant to him even if they couldn't be together.' She looked down, a bit ashamed that a terrible sadness welled in her at the thought. 'They are buried side by side. I like that idea.'

He cocked his head. 'You think she was faithful to Julian after he married and had children? Seems unlikely.'

Shrugging, Liz said, 'Maybe I'm a romantic, but in my experience, if a woman is deeply in love with a man, no one else will do.'

He was silent and Liz realised what she'd said. 'I mean, in those days. Now, it's different.'

Was it? Was that how she reconciled her attraction to Theo with her love for Tony?

Since Raoul's arrival had removed Valerie from their orbit, the atmosphere around Liz and Theo seemed to have become increasingly charged. She felt the solid mass of Theo's presence behind her, the space between them filled with a kind of gravitational force she was finding more and more difficult to resist.

She couldn't look at him. She couldn't think of anything to say that would break the tension.

'There you are!' Valerie walked at a clipped pace even at eleven at night.

Thank God for that, thought Liz, as Theo stepped away from her. She hated feeling like this.

'Gemma has only just told me about Delany Nash's memoirs,' snapped Valerie, ignoring Theo's greeting. 'Though why I'm only hearing about them now, I can't imagine. They're exactly what we need for the historical display at the Open Day.'

Oh, no. Liz couldn't give up the memoirs. Not to Valerie. She forced herself to be conciliating. 'Would it be all right if I give you the one I've finished transcribing? I can always put the one I haven't finished into the display when the day itself arrives.' She was not going to mention the photocopies of the first two volumes that Nick had given her.

Valerie held out her hand in a peremptory way that set Liz's teeth on edge. 'No, I want both of them and I want them now. I'm bringing in an expert to . . . to authenticate them and I need to have them both.'

'What's this about a historical display?' said Theo. 'I haven't heard anything about it.'

Valerie gave a put-upon sigh. 'Darling, I never trouble you with minute details, you know that.'

Liz thought Valerie was lying and she knew Theo suspected it too. He had that granite-statue look about him that made Liz decide she should get out of the way.

It was a wrench to part with the memoirs but she didn't see that she had a lot of choice. If Theo stood up for her, it would only make things more awkward. The last thing she needed was to become a further cause of friction between him and Valerie.

'Here.' With bone-deep reluctance, she handed Valerie the two volumes. 'I – I can wait until after the Open Day.'

But could she? The Open Day was more than a week away. She'd been so close . . . She could have screamed with frustration. 'What about a photocopy?' she said desperately, but Valerie shut her down. 'Certainly not! You might damage the spines if you lay them flat.'

Liz wanted to argue, but she realised Valerie wouldn't give in, no matter what. She left the couple together, torn between anger at Valerie and confusion over her feelings for Theo. Unreasonable to expect him to side with her against his fiancée, but she had.

As she showered and got ready for bed, she tried to come to terms with all that had happened since she'd come to Seagrove.

On the one hand, she was drawn to Theo. His dry sense of humour, his kindness, and his willingness to work his tail off to preserve Seagrove for his family, made him even more attractive to her than his undeniable good looks. On the other hand, there was Tony and the rawness of their break-up.

She wasn't in a position to make a good judgement about her feelings. With Theo already involved with Valerie, there was neither room nor time to explore the possibility that something might develop between him and Liz.

Not forgetting, of course, a major stumbling block: Theo didn't know the real reason Liz was at Seagrove.

Ultimately, proving that the real Stephen Nash had died in infancy was unlikely to have much practical effect. Even assuming they *could* prove it. A buried rattle wasn't evidence. What about DNA testing? She didn't know how that might work, or how precise it would be.

Yet she knew that any weight her investigations lent to Nick's theory would make him that much more determined to wrest Seagrove from Theo and his family.

She didn't want that to happen.

Lack of capital made Theo vulnerable. He needed investors sympathetic to his aims and he needed them quickly. The Buildings Trust people and a couple of other organisations were visiting on the Open Day to judge the estate's potential for generating income. It would be a test of the Nash family's competence in managing the place as well. These organisations weren't investing in the house alone; they were investing in the people who ran it too.

Everything depended on making a good impression. With Valerie hell-bent on running up costs left and right on things for which there would be little return, Liz wondered how on earth it would all come together.

She had just showered and put on her pyjamas and was considering how she'd plan the Open Day if she were in charge, when she heard an angry voice – Valerie's? – and feet stomping down the corridor towards her room.

Hell! Were they going to come right in here? Liz dived for the grey marle hoodie she'd left draped over a chair and pulled it on.

The footsteps stopped outside her door.

In a low voice, Theo said, 'Valerie, you are blowing this out of proportion.'

'Am I? *Am* I?' Her voice was shrill. 'I'm working, Theo, driving myself into the ground over this event, all for you. And I come in after a hard day to find you cosying up to *her*.'

'Whatever you think you saw, there was nothing in it. I shouldn't have to explain that to you.' He paused. 'But that's not the issue here, and you know it.'

'She's made trouble here from the start,' fumed Valerie. 'You trusted me before she came.'

What was this? Liz didn't even try to avoid eavesdropping. After all, they were right outside her door.

'Look, leave Liz out of it,' said Theo. 'I want to be more involved in running the Open Day, that's all.'

'No, you want to interfere. I've worked my fingers to the bone for this, made all the arrangements, and you want to come in at the eleventh hour and ruin it all.'

Mildly, Theo said, 'I asked to see the outgoings, that's all. At the end of the day, it *is* my money, Val.'

She burst into tears.

'That's done it,' muttered Liz. Theo was not the kind of man who could stand to see a woman cry.

She didn't hear any more. After some muted conversation, receding footsteps told her the show was over.

If anything had been needed to convince her that both Theo and the estate were a lost cause, that conversation had been it. This scenario, or something like it, would play out over and over until Valerie scuppered their chance of attracting investors and drove the estate into the ground.

Maybe it would be a kindness to Theo if Liz helped Nick buy Seagrove. He'd no longer be beholden to Valerie, for one thing. He could go back to running his landscaping business instead of wrestling with all the myriad difficulties inherent in running a house of this size. And Nick would preserve Seagrove for future generations to enjoy.

But something inside her went hollow at the thought. Nick wouldn't live at Seagrove. He'd use it as a holiday house once a year, if that. The rest of the time, it would be shut up, useless, or left with a skeleton staff. That wasn't what this sort of house was for. It was for family and community, to act as a solid reminder of the past.

But if Valerie was allowed to ruin the Open Day and the Nash family lost this golden opportunity to attract investors, they didn't have a hope of holding out against Nick.

Mindful of Valerie's outburst, Liz tried to stay out of everyone's way as the preparations for the Open Day grew increasingly frantic.

That turned out to be impossible, however. After only a few weeks at Seagrove, everyone except Valerie treated Liz like one of the family, and depended on her willingness to help out in any way she could.

Theo had brought in volunteers to shift plants and create displays. He trusted Liz to oversee them for a couple of hours each day while he conferred with Fergus about the temporary structures that were at various stages of completion. Then there was Gemma, who enlisted her and Maddie's help styling the tea and gift shop they'd set up in the old stables near the house.

Liz had never heard 'style' used as a verb before. In practical terms, it meant tying strips of green raffia around a hundred tiny bud vases shaped like milk bottles, tacking up lots of pale green and white bunting, sewing patchy table cloths together out of material scraps and raiding cupboards and attics for old silver candlesticks and mismatched china.

'The Witch Queen wouldn't give me a budget for decoration so we have to mend and make do,' said Gemma.

'I love it,' said Maddie. 'It's more like home this way.'

Liz knew she meant to compare the pretty clutter of the tea room with the uber-sophisticated decorating that was going on inside the house and on the terrace. All avant garde art and hard surfaces. But there was no telling Valerie.

Part of the charm of visiting a country house was feeling that the family invited you to be part of their lives. This Open Day was all about creating a welcoming atmosphere.

Personally, Liz was interested in modern art and admired a lot of the pieces Valerie had brought in. But they didn't complement the house. To her mind, Seagrove should be the star attraction at the cocktail evening. The house itself shouldn't be overshadowed by the art.

When she'd suggested putting the collection of classical statues from the Gallery on display instead, Valerie had shot her down. '*That old tat*,' she said with a sniff. 'No one rates that stuff any more.' She added that they did modern installations at Chatsworth all the time, and that was the end of that.

'I've got the local ladies coming in to do the flowers for the tea room,' Gemma said. She handed Liz a sheet of paper. 'If you're going out, would you ask Theo to look at the list of flowers?'

Liz hadn't intended to go to the gardens, but after all that sitting making a billion paper rosettes, she could do with the walk.

She used the walkie-talkie Gemma had given her to contact Theo. 'Where are you?'

'Australia,' came the reply.

When she reached the Australian part of the gardens, the clean burn of eucalyptus scent transported her back home. Suddenly she missed all of it. Her friends, her mum, her shabby old Queenslander, the sticky, shimmering heat and the wide blue skies. Strangely the one person she did not miss was Tony.

'Oh, no.' Liz pulled up short. Valerie was there with Theo.

She looked out of place in this slice of the Australian outback, in her elegant charcoal suit, high heels and blonde French twist. In fact, now she thought about it, Liz couldn't remember having seen Valerie in the grounds before. She was always bustling about indoors. Another reason she should not be with a man like Theo.

Valerie followed the direction of Theo's gaze and saw Liz. 'Theo doesn't have time for you now,' she snapped.

'I asked Liz to come down here,' Theo said coolly. 'Why don't you tell her what you told me?'

Hmm, more trouble in paradise. Things had been increasingly tense since that night they'd argued outside Liz's door.

'You know what you need here?' said Liz, squinting up into the trees. 'Kookaburras. You're definitely missing kookaburras.'

Theo was breathing hard through his nose. 'Valerie has seen fit to cancel the catering for the Open Day.'

'Raoul is going to do everything,' said Valerie defiantly.

'Oh, hell,' said Liz.

'My thoughts exactly,' said Theo.

'You have *no* idea what an honour this is!' The tendons in Valerie's neck stood out, she was so tense. 'Anyway, it's all a *fait accompli*. I can't get those bookings back now.'

Liz suspected she was lying about that. With less than a week until the big day, the catering company would be unlikely to get another booking at such short notice.

Theo said, 'Surely if you speak to them and tell them you've changed your mind . . .'

Valerie flicked a stray leaf off her jacket sleeve, avoiding his eye. 'Well, I can't. That Phyllis Green woman was so rude to me I was forced to give her some home truths about the quality of her food and customer service.'

'Of course you were,' Liz said under her breath.

'Just how much money did we lose on that?' demanded Theo. 'They'd be mad to give us refunds at this stage.'

'It will be worth it,' Valerie insisted. 'It's an investment in Seagrove's future.'

Theo glared. 'We weren't supposed to be *making an investment*. We were supposed to be showing investors we could run an event and turn a profit.'

'Well, you know what I think about *those* investors,' said Valerie.

But Theo was on a roll. 'Oh, and I suppose Raoul's going to offer sausage rolls and hot dogs for the kids, is he? And fairy floss and hot chips. And what about the drinks? What about . . .' He broke off, shoving both hands through his hair. 'I depended on you to have this sorted, Valerie.'

'I *do* have it sorted. You'll see.'

'No.' Theo shook his head and grabbed her by the wrist. 'You're coming with me. And we're going to fix this. Now.'

Valerie shook off his hold, spots of colour glowing on her high cheekbones. They glared at one another for a moment, but she must have detected a new implacability in Theo, because she huffed a dramatic sigh and stalked up the path ahead of him.

Watching them go, Liz could have cheered.

Theo turned back. 'You too!' he barked at Liz.

'Yes, *my lord*,' she muttered, and followed them up to the house.

By the time they reached Valerie's office, the woman was blinking damp eyelashes and protesting shakily at the injustice of Theo's accusations. But this time Theo was too furious to notice her tears. He went directly to the computer and demanded to see Valerie's spreadsheets.

To Valerie's credit, she turned off the waterworks as soon as she realised Theo was not going to fall for that tactic again. Holding on to her dignity by a thread, she went through the details of her plans for the Open Day and her expenditure.

The entire event was a mess.

It was only when he saw the black and white figures that Theo hit the ceiling. 'We're paying that jumped-up gigolo *how much*?' he roared.

Liz tried to sidle out the door.

'Stay!' said Theo.

She'd had quite enough of this master-of-the-universe tone he was directing at her. 'Watch it. I'm not a puppy.'

'No, Liz. Please. Stay,' said Valerie, with ominous calm. 'I know you're behind all this. It's you, poisoning Theo's mind against me. Before you came he wouldn't have dreamed of questioning how I run things.'

'Which just goes to show what a bloody idiot I've been. Valerie . . .' He broke off with a shake of his head, as if the enormity of the disaster had just hit him. He took a deep breath. 'Liz, maybe you *should* leave us, actually.'

He was going to do it. He was going to break up with her.

'No, *I'll* go.' Valerie snatched up her purse and keys from the desk return. 'It's perfectly clear to me what's going on here. Raoul tried to tell me but I wouldn't listen. I've given my all to this place, and this is the thanks I get.' She threw back her shoulders and stuck up her chin. 'I'm leaving you, Theo.'

An expression of weary relief washed over Theo's face. 'I think that's probably for the best.'

'Don't try to stop me!' Valerie swept past Liz and out of the room.

With a grim 'Goodbye, Val', Theo sat down at the computer and started tapping the keys.

They worked all afternoon on the Open Day, joined later by Fergus and Gemma, who had seen Valerie speeding off up the drive with Raoul in his Ferrari.

'What's her problem?' said Gemma, flopping down on a hard Lucite chair. 'God, I hate this room. Why are we here?'

Theo said nothing, frowning in concentration over Valerie's spreadsheets.

Liz filled her in as briefly and tactfully as possible.

Gemma was half furious, half jubilant at the turn events had taken, but catching a severe look from Liz, she put her hand on Theo's shoulder. 'Sorry. It's tough on you.'

'Yeah. Thanks.' He reached for his coffee, not taking his eyes from the computer screen.

'He's really broken up about it,' said Gemma in a stage whisper to Liz.

Liz scowled at her and shook her head. Just because Theo kept his feelings to himself it didn't mean he wasn't in pain.

Rather than put her arms around him as she would have liked to have done, Liz set about redistributing Valerie's responsibilities. 'We're going to make this work.'

Mrs Jackson broke off her baking and jam-making to bring them sandwiches and coffee.

'How much notice do you think you'd need to put on cocktails for one hundred, Mrs Jackson?' said Liz.

'Never say we've seen the last of Raoul,' said Mrs Jackson, very dry.

'I regret to say that we have,' said Liz. 'I have very little in the way of cooking skills but I'm happy to be sous-chef if that helps.'

'Bless you, you've got more important things to do,' said Mrs Jackson. 'Leave it to me. My daughters and Mr Jackson will help me with the shopping and preparations. We'll see if a good old-fashioned cook can't do every bit as well as some fancy-pants London chef.'

'Thank you,' said Theo, taking Mrs Jackson's hands and gripping them warmly in his. There was a grave note of apology as well as relief in his tone.

Gemma and Liz swamped Mrs Jackson with hugs and thanks until she was waving them off, all rosy-cheeked and misty-eyed. Everyone went on with their assigned tasks, eventually moving operations from Valerie's office to the library so they could spread out more.

'No luck with any of the catering companies,' reported Liz that evening when they met after dinner for a debrief. 'I used every tactic in the book but I couldn't get Phyllis Green to calm down. I don't know what Valerie said to her but she's adamant she won't lift a finger to help.'

'Why would she? She's been paid in full for work she hasn't even done,' said Gemma. 'Ooh, I could murder Valerie.'

Theo glanced over at Liz. 'Isn't there anyone else? Maybe on the mainland?'

'I've called everyone who seems half way decent.'

Liz bit her lip, unsure whether to stick her neck out. She didn't want to be blamed if her idea didn't work. On the other hand . . .

'What?' said Theo, reaching for a sandwich. 'Come on, spit it out.'

She sipped her coffee, then plunged in. 'What if we did themed catering for the Open Day?'

'Themed?' Theo looked doubtful. 'What sort of theme?'

'Nuns and hookers!' said Gemma.

Liz threw a screwed-up ball of paper at her, but it went wide. 'I was thinking about tying in the food with your gardens. We could do a sausage sizzle and meat pies for the Aussies, maybe a couple of those enormous paellas for the South American bit. People love paella and you've got the fresh seafood suppliers right on your doorstep. Individual Greek mezze platters using your own olives and local cheese . . .'

Gemma sat up. 'That's a great idea. We'd have a garden room for each nation. Huge floral and plant displays to match. Maybe some themed entertainment too.'

Liz nodded. 'We can showcase your plant business and the event spaces at the same time, show people the possibilities for staging their own functions here.'

'And who is going to supply all this food?' said Theo.

Liz sat forward. 'Delfina's can do the paella. That's what gave me the idea. We don't need to be involved in that. They can set up a stall like they do at the markets and we charge them a license for the day. We can make up cold mezze plates ourselves beforehand; the sausage sizzle is easy. Anyone can do that. Do you have a barbecue?'

'Yes, but it's about this big,' said Gemma, putting her arms in a circle as if she were hugging a tree.

'That's not a problem,' said Liz. 'We can hire one. Two, maybe.' Simple, good food, and lots of it.

'I like it.' Theo nodded, taking notes.

Liz updated Valerie's spreadsheets and assigned everyone their tasks. Theo knew some local musicians who might be willing to provide entertainment. Fergus would be in charge of building stalls and ordering seating and marquees.

'Everyone give me their email addresses and I'll send you your list of jobs. You can tell me anything I've missed, but I want the plans all nailed down by close of business tomorrow.'

When the others had gone, Liz said to Theo, 'What do we do about the financial situation?'

His expression made her heart sink. 'Let me worry about that.'

Liz doodled on her notepad as she considered. 'You know, I think we should open up the house as well. Just this once. It will bring in a lot of money for little outlay, and drive traffic to the tea room as well. I'm sure Mr Jackson would come back and conduct the tours for us, maybe even train up a couple of volunteers from the historical society to help.'

She didn't know if he was listening to her. She couldn't blame him. It had been a hell of a day.

'I'll say goodnight, then.' She hesitated, thinking that he needed to get away from the worry of it all, if only for an hour or so. Then she remembered the butterfly meadow. She'd wanted him to show it to her since he'd mentioned it but there never seemed to be the time.

'Do you think the butterfly meadow might be another attraction at the Open Day? Maybe tomorrow, you could show it to me and we could come up with a plan.' She thought it sounded quite restful, wandering around a grassy field, identifying different species of butterfly. A great way to recharge the batteries before the final push.

Theo shook his head. 'You're right that we should use it as an added attraction at some point, but I don't think it's a good idea to have that many people traipsing around the meadow at once.'

'Oh, no. Of course,' said Liz. Stupid of her. 'I really want to see it, though. Maybe you could show it to me another time. When things are less hectic.'

Theo sighed, as if he couldn't imagine when that might be. He looked defeated and weary. She wanted to urge him to go to bed but that might sound suggestive. The last thing she wanted to do was to give the impression of moving in the second Valerie was gone. A serious relationship simply wasn't on the cards for her, and that was the only kind she could envisage having with Theo. Liz made herself pat his shoulder in a nice, platonic gesture of support and went out.

She wondered how on earth she'd get to sleep tonight. Her brain teemed with ideas and plans. She wished she'd thought to grab something to read from the library before she left.

The memoirs. She stopped short. What had Valerie done with them?

Liz sped back to the library and found Theo still sitting where she'd left him. He turned his head and Liz saw the look on his face.

'What's wrong?' Liz wanted to kick herself. Stupid question.

Theo bowed his head and shaded his eyes. It was awful seeing him look like that. She had the sense she'd caught him out giving in to his emotions and he'd rather she hadn't.

She couldn't leave him to it, though. 'Come on, Theo. Talk to me.' She went to kneel on the floor in front of him.

'Nothing for you to worry about, Liz.'

'But . . .'

He sat back in the chair, staring at the ceiling. 'No. Go to bed. You must be exhausted.'

'I'll never get to sleep now anyway.'

Theo sighed. 'Look, I appreciate your help with all this. I should refuse but I know we won't get through it without you.'

'Hey, I am more than happy to —'

'But at the end of the day, you don't live here, do you? When the Open Day is over, you'll leave.' She saw the ripple of his throat as he swallowed hard. 'And I'll still be stuck with this mess.'

Funny how someone you'd known for a bare few weeks could knife you in the guts. Liz didn't know how to respond. All the things she wanted to say sounded too much like commitment. Too much like stepping onto the next sinking ship when she'd only just caught the lifeboat from the last one.

She settled for, 'I'm here now. Use me.'

He didn't respond.

She got to her feet. It was either that or put her arms around him, and she didn't want him to take the gesture the wrong way. 'Listen, you have enough to worry about, what with untangling Valerie's mess on the accounting side of things, dealing with the investors and the bank. Not to mention the gardens. Leave the event itself to the rest of us.'

He stopped staring at the ceiling. 'Why should you spend all your time on this?' he said. 'I mean, I'm grateful, but that's not what you're here for.'

She shrugged. 'Until I can get my hands on those memoirs again, I'm pretty much at a standstill as far as my research goes.'

'Memoirs?' said Theo. 'What happened to them?'

'Valerie took them for the historical display.'

He frowned. 'Oh, right. I forgot.'

'What would she have done with them, do you think?'

'I have no idea,' said Theo. 'Her office, maybe? Though if she was putting together a display she'd need somewhere bigger than that to store everything. Only, I thought she wasn't letting anyone inside the house itself . . .'

'Do you think the display was mythical?' Liz had suspected as much at the time, but had been too polite to call Valerie on it. They weren't her memoirs, after all. 'Hold on,' said Liz, as a sudden thought occurred to her. 'Didn't she say she was getting an expert to look at them?'

'That's right.' Grim-faced, Theo said, 'I think I can guess who that will be. I'll call him in the morning and get them back.'

She would have told him not to worry about it, except that in anticipating the call he seemed to have regained some of his usual energy.

'Theo, I've been dithering about whether to say this but I'd never forgive myself if I didn't, and . . . well . . . you should call your bank and freeze the accounts Valerie had access to.'

'Already done,' he said, which surprised her.

He'd always seemed to believe the best of Valerie. Had he seen through her the entire time?

'I've saved everything from the computer she used to an external drive too, in case she decides to wipe all her spreadsheets remotely. They're all synched with her tablet.'

Liz stared at him.

'Don't look at me like I'm some sort of genius,' he said. 'Just about the first thing she must have done when she walked out that office door was to clean out the event account.'

'*What?*' If she ever saw Valerie again she was going to wring that woman's scrawny neck. Freezing accounts was a precaution she'd always advised clients to take in this situation back when she was a solicitor in a law firm, but she hadn't seriously thought Valerie would stoop to stealing.

'How much?' demanded Liz.

He shrugged. 'Fifty thousand, give or take.'

'Call the police.'

He shook his head. 'I've thought about it, and you know, it's about right. I knew it wasn't working with Valerie, but I couldn't tell her because of all the effort she's put into the place, over and above the salary she draws. Well, it's a generous golden handshake, but it gives me some peace of mind.'

Would it stop there, though? A woman like Valerie could suck a man dry.

Well, that was a problem for tomorrow, she supposed. 'Please promise me you'll talk to a family lawyer tomorrow. You need to get your legal position sorted out properly, before she ruins everything you've built here.'

'Yes, ma'am,' he said, with a glint of humour. 'Ah, Christ, you're right. But at the end of the day, it's only money, isn't it?'

Money they sorely needed. 'Speaking of which,' said Liz, 'how are we going to fund the Open Day now?'

'I can move some money around,' said Theo. 'The budget will be tight, though. I like your idea of charging licence fees. That means cash in from the food vendors, rather than cash out of our pocket.'

'Some local businesses might donate goods, as a promotion,' said

Liz. 'It's still all doable. We can't forget that the main attraction for people is that they can finally come and see the place. You're so used to it, you probably lose sight of how spectacular Seagrove is.'

'She's a grand old dame,' said Theo.

Liz smiled. 'I think we can do her justice.'

CHAPTER FIFTEEN

Liz

Liz could not help scanning the crowd for Valerie that night. She felt light-headed with tiredness after a week of fourteen-hour days, so when a waiter headed towards her with a tray of champagne flutes she smiled and shook her head. One glass of champagne and she might fall asleep on her feet.

Thanks to the efforts of their tight-knit team, everything was ready for the Open Day tomorrow.

No one poked fun at Liz's spreadsheets any more. Everyone had their schedules, planned down to the last minute. Nothing ever ran like clockwork, but it didn't need to. They were as prepared as they could be, with several contingency plans in place; they had to be flexible enough to deal with things they hadn't yet foreseen. All part of the fun.

Having stepped inside to check that Mrs Jackson and her staff had everything they needed, Liz paused for a few moments in the doorway that gave onto the terrace.

Gemma had outdone herself with the 'styling' tonight. Nothing outrageous or particularly fancy. They couldn't afford fancy on their budget, anyway. Rather than make the decorations the focus of attention, Gemma had used them to highlight Seagrove's best features.

Because the purpose of the evening was to showcase the house's desirability as a wedding venue, Gemma had cleverly chosen white as her theme. Table cloths, flowers, gleaming silverware – all had a subtle whiff of 'bridal' without being over the top.

Maddie was in charge of filling goody bags for each guest that included the printed program for the next day, various tasteful items donated by local businesses, and a flyer describing the house and its suitability as a beautiful setting for all kinds of events.

Mrs Jackson's *hors d'oeuvres* were the perfect combination of spectacular presentation and bursts of delicious flavour. She'd used fresh, local produce with an emphasis on seafood. As a special treat, she'd even deconstructed Liz's favourite crab pasties, placing the filling in dainty tart shells made of pastry so light, Liz's mother would have swooned with envy.

Liz left the magazine editors and other glamorous types to Gemma while she homed in on the investors. They seemed impressed so far, but as one of them, Nathan Miller, said, 'We'll see if the figures stack up. Cocktail parties are all well and good, and you've done wonders with the place, I'll grant you that, but I can get everything I need to know about a business from the numbers.'

Liz wanted to tell him that this house was about much, much more than a balance sheet and projections, but she knew she'd gain nothing by it. She made a confident response and moved on to other guests.

After another hour, she slipped away to check her messages and saw that Nick had called. That was all she needed, to have him on her case again. She'd speak to him tomorrow, though when she'd get the time was a good question. She dealt with a few last-minute inquiries that had come in, then looked for Theo.

He was nowhere to be found. Having done the obligatory meet and greet, he'd taken himself off somewhere, no doubt working on last-minute details for the Open Day. The trouble was, he was the one people had come to see and his absence would soon become conspicuous.

Catching Gemma between conversations, Liz murmured, 'Have you seen him?'

'Nope.'

Liz blew out a breath. 'He drives me insane. I read him the Riot Act about tonight but he's playing the invisible man again.'

'It's not his scene,' said Gemma, shrugging. She seemed far more relaxed about her brother's lack of interest in the cocktail evening now that she and Liz were in charge.

'Half the people here paid to hang out with the lord of the manor,' said Liz, exasperated at the way the family did not seem to understand this point.

'No, they didn't,' said Gemma. 'Most people here think the nobility are all in-bred tossers, or at best, obsolete. These people don't care about Theo. They're here for a booze-up and a sticky-beak at the house, that's all.'

Unconvinced, Liz texted Theo, and when her message wasn't delivered, tried him on the walkie-talkie.

'I'm at the orchid house,' he told her. 'Why don't you come down? I want to talk to you about something.'

He sounded serious. Instead of demanding he return to the party, she made her way down to the gardens.

It was dark out here, and quiet so far away from the party. She had to be careful not to trip over anything on the way. The light was on inside, however, and beneath its glow the orchid petals gleamed like rare jewels.

Theo, his suit coat off and his bow tie undone, was busy shifting pot plants around.

'I thought you had all this sorted,' she said.

He looked up. 'Hi.'

'You know there's a party you're supposed to be hosting up there,

don't you?' said Liz, frustrated. 'I can never decide whether you're naturally shy or you simply hate people.'

'I hate people,' he said.

She tilted her head. 'Did you ever think the event business might
not be your bag?'

He finished what he'd been doing, washed his hands at the sink
and dried them on a ratty old towel. 'We had to do something. I'd be
crap at running a B and B.'

'You would have given Basil Fawlty a run for his money,' she
agreed.

'We had a plan, and I think it would have worked if Valerie
hadn't . . . well . . .' He shrugged. 'But I can't do it without an events
co-ordinator. I don't know the first thing about all that.'

'Gemma could —' Liz began, but he shook his head.

'Gemma is excellent at certain things but she's not interested in the
nitty-gritty details that can make or break a business like this. Besides,
I can't go into partnership with Gemma. It wouldn't work.'

'So . . . what are you saying?' said Liz. Something about the way he
looked at her made the back of her neck tingle.

The corner of his mouth twisted up. 'I was wondering if you would
consider taking the job.'

'Me?' Liz tried to laugh but it came out in a nervous huff of breath.
'You're not serious.'

'Think about it. The deal is, we do a maximum of ten large events
a year. Wednesdays to Sundays through spring, summer and a bit of
autumn we open the gardens and the tea shop, sell plants to the public. Late autumn and winter, we're closed. That's when we take our
holidays.'

'You? On vacation?' said Liz. 'I'd like to see that.'

Theo grinned. 'They do tend to be active. Surfing, skiing, that sort
of thing. But you don't need to do that. You could have an Australian
summer every year.'

Imagine that. Her life could be one endless summer. Who was he, the devil? It sounded pretty darn perfect to her.

All except for the money. The truth was, he couldn't afford her. He had no hope of matching her current salary, and she was a rank amateur at event management, so she couldn't command much of a salary doing that anyway. If she took him up on his offer, it would have to be for the love of it. Did she love Seagrove that much?

And what would happen if it didn't work? She'd have thrown away her legal career – not to mention the chance at an executive role – on a whim, out of some crazy Good Samaritan wish to help these people out of a crisis.

'There must be any number of great events co-ordinators you could get,' she said. 'People far better qualified than I am.'

'Maybe,' said Theo. 'Yes. I suppose you're right.' He sighed. 'It's just that you seem to understand the place. You know me . . . us. I don't have to explain things to you, or show you how to do something twice. You fit in here. The Jacksons like you. Gemma likes you. Maddie likes you.' He paused, and his green eyes met hers. 'And I like you too.'

For a man as reticent as Theo, that speech was momentous. Liz knew it, and despite the rush of pleasure she felt at hearing him say those things, alarm bells clamoured in her head, urging caution.

Everything was moving too fast. In an effort to calm herself, slow it all down, she drew a deep breath, then blew it out. 'Look, Theo, it's a huge step. Moving jobs, moving countries. I hadn't even thought about it.' She paused, not wanting to reject the idea outright but unable to see how it could work. 'Let's get through tomorrow first, and then we'll see.'

He shoved his hands in his pockets and bent his head, as if he were studying something interesting on his shoes. 'Yes. Okay. Fine.'

'Come back to the party,' Liz said. 'You're the host, after all.'

'Right.'

'You need to fix your tie, by the way,' she said, with a flick of her fingers in its direction.

His eyebrows rose. 'Isn't this where you offer to do it for me?'

'I would, but I don't know how,' she said. Her father had been more than competent at doing his own and the couple Tony possessed were ready-made.

He shrugged. 'Then it will have to be the sloppy look. I can't do them either.'

She considered him. He looked like James Bond after a fight in the casino stairwell. 'Actually, it's sexy like that. You'll start a trend.'

He laughed. 'Among those stuffed shirts? Not likely. Come on, then. We'd better go.'

They walked side by side in the moonlight, neither of them needing to talk to fill the silence. The night was fragrant with the scent of jasmine, alive with the creak of crickets, the rumble of laughter and music from the party, the ever-present sigh of the sea.

'Theo?' she said. Something about the soft darkness gave her the courage to ask.

'Mmm?'

'How are you? Since Valerie left, I mean?'

He didn't answer for a few moments.

She squirmed at the awkwardness but made herself go on. 'I feel partly responsible.'

'You?' He sounded genuinely surprised. 'Why should you feel responsible?'

'Oh, you know. The bath-robe incident, and my urging you to stand up to her. I was hoping you didn't regret it, that's all.'

Of course, any sane man would have jumped for joy. The woman had all but ruined his life, not to mention an event that meant the world to him and to the house. Besides running around with celebrity chefs and upsetting his family . . . The list went on.

'I know it's none of my business,' she said in a rush. 'I know that gentlemen don't discuss their break-ups and all that. I . . . I'm feeling guilty, that's all.'

Mostly, she felt guilty because while she'd wanted Valerie gone for the family's sake, she'd also wanted Valerie out of the picture for her own. She liked Theo. A lot.

After a while, he spoke. 'Ahh, I shouldn't say this. Wouldn't say it to anyone else. But since she left, it's as if a crushing weight has been taken off my chest.'

Relief washed over her. 'Thank God for that.' When they arrived at the steps to the terrace, she hesitated. 'If I'm going to consider your job offer, I need a commitment from you.'

'Sounds ominous,' he said.

'Go up there and show your guests a good time. Show them you were born to this place, to this role. Show them what a fantastic investment Seagrove is going to be.'

He glanced down at her in amusement. 'Bossing me around already, are you? I haven't hired you yet, Ms Jones.'

But he was still smiling as he moved into the fray.

The morning of the Open Day, Liz woke shortly before dawn with energy to burn.

There was a lightness in her chest and a spring in her step as she took off for her run. What a life. Who wouldn't want to live and work at Seagrove?

She'd run the same course since she'd arrived, but she no longer walked any part of it. The first ten minutes still felt like hell every time, but she knew that if she pushed through the burn, she'd get to the good stuff on the other side.

She'd taken to finishing her runs by picking her way down the cliff to the Beach Shack, a fish cafe right on the beach. It served brilliant coffee and hearty breakfasts in the mornings and scrumptious dishes made with freshly caught seafood the rest of the day. The crab pasties were out of this world and the chowder was the best she'd tasted since visiting San Francisco a few years before.

She'd drop into one of the wooden folding chairs set out on the deck, with a view of the water lapping at the beach. She'd read the paper, take a long, cool guzzle of water and top it all off with a coffee.

Even now, at seven in the morning, the place was buzzing with early morning hikers and some regulars too. Regulars like Liz. The notion filled her with quiet satisfaction.

'Liz!'

She looked up and nearly fell off her chair. 'Nick? What are you doing here? Aren't you in the Bahamas?'

'Change of plan. Yolande decided on Cannes instead.' Nick pulled up a chair. 'Thought I'd pop over, see how you're going. I called last night but it went to voicemail.'

She'd meant to return his call later this morning. 'Sorry,' she said. 'Last night was crazy. Where are you staying?'

He grinned, cracking open his tomato juice. 'My yacht. You'll have to visit. I thought I'd hang around until you've finished your research.'

The milky coffee seemed to curdle in her stomach. Well, there went her lovely morning. Was Nick here to cause trouble? She couldn't imagine his presence would help her quest. Not when they both wanted to keep their association secret.

'I'd love to, but I have a lot to do today. I'm helping run the Seagrove Open Day.' She licked her lips. 'They're counting on me.'

He settled back in his chair, the rims of his sunglasses glinting in the sun. 'Is that so? Didn't I say you were good at getting people to trust you? I'm sure you've got everything in hand.'

She felt that nasty twist in her chest when he said that about people trusting her. It made her feel a fraud. She said, 'How do you know I've got everything in hand?'

He smiled and toasted her with his drink. 'I know you.'

She supposed that was a compliment. Before she could reply, he added, 'I'm here for the Open Day, actually. I hear it's going to be huge.'

Liz stared at him but it was impossible to tell what went on behind those sunglasses, what was in his mind. Was it that old sense of mischief, or something else?

Carefully, she said, 'You didn't want anyone to know you'd sent me to Seagrove. If you suddenly appear, won't that jeopardise everything? Why take the risk?'

Nick watched a curvaceous, bikini-clad girl walk past. 'I want to see the family in action. This is the perfect opportunity.'

'I don't think that's a good idea,' Liz said. 'We're both Australian. They'll guess we know each other.'

'Australia's a big country,' said Nick.

'But we *do* know each other,' Liz pointed out. 'And I don't want to lie to them. Any more than I have to,' she added lamely, sliding her gaze away.

So much easier to forget she was a dirty rotten traitor when she thought Nick was on the other side of the Atlantic. She stared out to sea, trying to reconcile her conflicting emotions.

It was a bright blue day and the sea was a mesmerising shift of colours – aquamarine, grey and a dark, moody teal. A gull hovered on the wind, its wings chevrons of blinding white.

She'd been floating in some dreamland until Nick's arrival knocked her back to earth. How could she have thought even for five minutes that she could take up Theo's offer to run the events at Seagrove? How could she build that kind of career, that kind of relationship, on lies?

Let's not kid ourselves here, Liz, she told herself. She'd been tempted partly because more time with Theo might help her sort out her feelings for him.

'I hear there are some investors interested,' said Nick.

She forced her mind back to business. 'Only one who is likely to come to the party – that's Bill Roberts. He fancies himself as an angel investor but he's an amateur and I don't think he quite understands the costs involved in running a place like Seagrove. The other one, Nathan Miller, is too hard-nosed, cares only about the bottom line. The Heritage Lottery Fund is another thing they need to pursue but

Gemma told me something went wrong with the application.' No doubt that was Valerie's doing.

Liz gave Nick a precise rundown on the players, much of which she suspected he already knew. 'There's a lot riding on today.' She pursed her lips. Whatever path she chose, she'd feel guilty. Of course, it was in Nick's interests that the Open Day fail. 'That's why I agreed to lend a hand when Theo's fiancée Valerie left them in the lurch.'

He nodded. 'I'm glad you did.'

Surprised, she scrutinised him more closely. Damn those sunglasses. She couldn't read his expression.

Was this the ruthless businessman she knew and loved? Ordinarily, she would have teased him over this about-face, but he seemed remote today, almost a stranger. A certain melancholy seemed to cling to him, a solitary, untouchable quality that forbade her customary quips at his expense. She'd had that impression a few times back in Australia too. Sometimes, Nick seemed like a modern-day Great Gatsby, surrounded by people but forever alone. She wondered how the holiday with Yolande in France had gone. Not well if he was here with Liz, presumably.

She remembered she had other news. 'Oh! I would have told you this but you were incommunicado. We found the rest of Delany's memoirs. Two more of them! They were in a secret chamber, of all things.'

'What?' Nick sat up and leaned forward, and even with the barrier of those tinted lenses, she felt the intensity of his interest. 'Why didn't you say so? What's in them? Did you find anything?'

She grimaced. 'I'd only just begun reading them when Valerie snatched them away. Unfortunately, Theo broke up with her and she stormed off, and now we can't find the memoirs. She probably took them with her out of spite.'

Theo had called the dealer he knew to ask for the memoirs back but the dealer hadn't heard a thing about them. They'd turned Valerie's office upside down but no luck there either.

'Damn!' Nick's hand smacked the table. 'Why did you let her take them?'

'I could hardly stop her,' said Liz. 'They're not my memoirs.'

'Why did Theo let her take them, then?'

'It's complicated,' Liz said. 'She was doing so much work for the Open Day and the house that he kept letting her have her way out of a sense of obligation.'

Not a failing Nick would suffer from, or even understand. He sat back, shoving his hands through his hair. 'Geez, this could be our answer. Who is this Valerie person?'

Liz filled him in on the background and Nick jotted down some notes.

'What are you going to do?' said Liz. She was of a mind to practise a little judicious blackmail herself – after all, there was that missing £50 000 – but Theo had asked her to leave it to him. She had to respect his decision, but it bothered her more than she'd admit that he was going so easy on his former fiancée.

Nick slouched in his chair, stretching his legs out before him, crossed at the ankles. He dug his hands into his pockets. Inwardly, Liz sighed. Even when he slouched, there was something about Nick that commanded attention. The women at the next table hadn't taken their eyes off him since he'd arrived.

'So, apart from all of that,' he said, 'what do you think of the place?' His tone was carefully casual, as if her answer mattered to him very much but he didn't want to show it.

'I can see why you love it,' she said. She was tempted to try to talk him out of his plans but she suspected it would do no good. Seagrove was in his blood, however far back in the family tree the connection might be.

She ought to tell him now that she'd switched sides somewhere along the line. That she'd certainly do everything in her power to find out the truth of Nick's ancestry, but that she also hoped like mad to prove his theory wrong. Not only that, she wanted to show him Seagrove was better off with the Nash family in charge.

Liz didn't know quite how she intended to do that. She'd thought

Nick was in the Bahamas. She'd thought she had more time.

Changing the subject, she said, 'You will be discreet today, won't you? I mean, I know it's a waste of breath trying to persuade you not to come to the Open Day, but can you at least try to be inconspicuous?'

He looked at her, genuinely puzzled. 'But I'm always inconspicuous.'

Liz couldn't help it. She laughed.

'What?' Nick started to laugh with her, a little uncertainly, as if he truly didn't understand the joke.

'Never mind,' said Liz. 'Just stay away from me. You don't want to blow my cover, now, do you?'

The Seagrove Open Day did not pass without a hitch. Liz spent most of the day putting out fires. They'd been forced to compromise here and there with the arrangements, of course. Some things Liz and Gemma had wanted needed to be ordered months in advance and no amount of persuasion could shorten the lead time.

However, the essentials were covered. Despite small emergencies and oversights, no major disaster occurred. They had over a thousand visitors throughout the day, far more than they'd expected.

A beaming Delfina sent her handsome sons off for more ingredients before the paella ran out. The dish was so popular she was having trouble keeping up with demand. Lines were long at the house, too, and Liz sent entertainers and mobile vendors over there to make the wait more fun. Despite the delays, there was a festive, positive atmosphere overall. No one seemed to mind queuing.

Liz had just finished sorting out a minor fender bender in the car park when her walkie-talkie crackled. 'Meet me?' said Theo.

Liz ran a hand through her hair and looked around. Everything seemed to be under control for the moment. She could probably spare a few minutes. 'Okay, where?'

'Australia.'

She smiled, gave directions to the lavatories to a mother with three whining children, then helped an elderly lady who needed transport down to the gardens. She made a note that they should hire more golf buggies next time and hurried off to the Australian bushland garden.

They'd set up the main entertainment stage here among the gum trees, and as she got closer, Liz heard the thump of music.

'Hey,' she shouted to Theo as she caught up with him in front of the stage. 'Where's the fire?'

He was looking far more relaxed today than he had last night, dressed in faded jeans and work boots and a green polo shirt that intensified the colour of his eyes.

'No fire,' he said, with a nod to the performers. 'That's my mate Joe's band up there. Thought you might like to hear them.'

Was that all? She was about to say she didn't have time when the lead singer stopped playing mid-song. He leaned close to the microphone and said, 'Folks, this one's for Liz.'

She laughed, looking at Theo, who lifted his shoulders in an unconvincing shrug.

The introduction was a confused jangle of chords. Eek, was she supposed to appreciate this?

She didn't know what on earth the music was until she heard the lyrics. Joe's band was playing a thrash version of Peter Allen's 'I Still Call Australia Home'.

'Damn it,' she muttered, biting her lip. No matter who played it, or how they murdered the score, that song choked her up every time. How had Theo known?

She tried to stop the tide of emotion that swept over her but it was no good. That lump in her throat, the goofy, nostalgic, patriotic burn in her chest. She kept smiling, though, aware that there were a lot of eyes on her and Theo.

For the final verse and chorus, the band slowed down, playing the anthem the way it was meant to be played. By that time, much of the audience was singing along, and the tears were sliding down Liz's cheeks and she couldn't stop them.

She thought of all she'd left behind when she came here. The pain and sadness, the triumphs, the disappointments, the friends and colleagues, the people she loved. The husband she would not be going back to whether she returned to her home town or not.

Theo put an arm around her shoulders, and she laid her head against his big chest.

'I'm getting your shirt wet and it's all your fault,' she said, sniffing and wiping her eyes with the back of her wrist.

She felt his laugh reverberate through his chest.

When the song had swelled to a finale, she yelled and whistled and clapped her appreciation along with the rest of audience, noticing that a small section of the crowd were particularly raucous in their acclaim. Looked like some expats were here. She must go and have a quick chat.

Then she noticed who was at the centre of that noisy Australian crowd.

So much for staying inconspicuous. Nick caught her eye and raised his beer at her in a silent toast. Then he grinned and turned away, his arm slung around the slim, tanned shoulders of a blonde woman in a printed pink halter top and denim cut-offs.

'Liz . . .' said Theo. She looked up at him and her heart stopped, all thought of Nick falling from her head.

He stared down at her with a tinge of amusement in his green eyes, but not only amusement. Tenderness lurked there too. Whatever she'd been about to say evaporated from her tongue.

He took her face in his hands, wiped the tears from her cheeks with his thumbs, and kissed her, for all the world to see. That garnered a bigger ovation than the band.

Liz knew she was blushing when he let her go.

'Sorry to keep you from your work,' he said softly.

'Work?' she said, feeling fuzzy and embarrassed and all-round wonderful. 'What work?' She wanted to forget all the noise and activity of the Open Day and go away with him somewhere quiet. She wanted Theo all to herself.

The corners of his eyes crinkled, as if he understood. He looked away from her to their surroundings and back again. 'Not the best timing.'

She found her voice. 'The worst.'

Gently, he tucked her hair behind her ear, making her skin tingle. 'To be continued.'

'Yes.'

Not even the possibility that Nick had witnessed that kiss could puncture her delight. She floated through the rest of the day.

By nightfall, they'd rounded up the last stragglers and closed the gates to the field they used as a car park. Liz was dog-tired, and happier than she'd ever been in her life.

They built a bonfire in the field next to the gardens and put on beer and pizza for all the workers and volunteers. A slight chill descended with the night. Holding her paper cup of beer, Liz moved away from the group of garden volunteers she'd been chatting with and stood gazing into the flames.

She'd had the time of her life today. Counting the takings and roughly calculating their profit had been a triumph matched only by the promise in Theo's kiss.

Unfortunately, if the ridiculous sums Valerie had wasted were taken into account, they hadn't made a profit. That would be all that mattered to investors like Miller. He was only interested in the bottom line, after all.

Despite that, Liz couldn't help feeling a crazy sense of optimism. The day ought to have exhausted her but she didn't feel tired in the least. Her blood hummed in anticipation. She wouldn't sleep at all tonight. She hoped Theo felt the same way.

She was going to say yes. Turn her back on her legal career, tell Nick she could no longer help him. She was playing for the other team now, and she would give them everything she had.

But first she needed to complete her quest. If only she could get those memoirs back from Valerie. She didn't believe they would reveal anything that would help Nick's case. On the contrary, perhaps something in them could help her prove the nursemaid's tale of impostors was a fabrication. In her letter to him at the beginning, Delany seemed to tell Stephen that he *was* legitimate, rather than the reverse.

How to make Valerie give up the memoirs without a great deal of unpleasantness was a difficult problem to solve. The woman wouldn't answer Theo's calls or respond to his texts.

Regardless, Liz had made her decision. She was staying. The world would not end if there was one less corporate lawyer in it, and Nick could find any number of talented people to fill her role. A seat on the board seemed like an empty ambition now that she'd embraced life at Seagrove. Working to preserve this house, its gardens and grounds and most of all its history, was a worthy goal, one to which she would happily devote a lifetime.

As far as her relationship with Theo went . . . well, she'd take that slowly and see what happened. She needed to be sure she was doing this for herself and for Seagrove, not solely to be with its owner.

Maddie, who had been toasting marshmallows on a very long stick, closely supervised by Gemma and Fergus, came over and offered one to Liz.

'Thanks,' she said, taking the stick. She touched the char-grilled puff of sugary sweetness with the tip of her tongue, then gingerly bit into it.

'Ha! That's hot,' she said, fanning her mouth with her hand.

'But delicious, right?' said Maddie.

'It is that,' said Liz. She threw the stick into the blaze and slung her arm around Maddie's shoulders. 'Did you have a good day today? I didn't see much of you.'

'I was helping with the kids' section,' said Maddie.

'I hope you had time to enjoy yourself as well,' said Liz.

'I like working. I helped Mrs Jackson in the tea shop, too. She said she's going to ask if she can open an online shop, selling Seagrove jams and chutneys to the public.'

'Great idea,' said Liz, thinking that people who discovered the produce online might then come to see where it was made.

Maddie giggled. 'Another change to the website. Gemma will have a fit!'

'Did I hear my name taken in vain?' Gemma came over, sleek as a cat in black. She waggled a bottle of champagne she'd conjured from goodness knew where. 'Want some?'

But Liz had registered Gemma's companion. A tall, broad-shouldered man, with that familiar, million-dollar smile. A jolt of apprehension shot through her. Her gaze locked with Nick's.

Don't expose me, Liz prayed silently. Please don't.

'Oh, this is Nick McCann,' said Gemma carelessly. 'He's trying to buy Seagrove from us.'

Yes, I know, thought Liz.

And suddenly all the reasons why she couldn't possibly stay at Seagrove with Theo hit her like a club to the head.

To cover her confusion, Liz said, 'Is that Bollinger? I'd love some.' She poured the rest of her beer on the ground and held out her cup, signalling Nick with her eyes to tell her how the hell she was supposed to react. 'Where did the champagne come from? Not out of tonight's proceeds, I hope.'

Gemma poured her a generous amount, causing a huge head of froth to bubble to the brim. 'Of course not. Nick brought it. Cheers.'

They clinked paper cups then Gemma said, 'Oh, sorry. Nick, this is Liz Jones. She's here researching a book.'

'Yes, we've met. How are you, Liz?' said Nick. His smile didn't reach his eyes.

For one long moment, Liz thought Nick was going to ruin

everything. He had that air of recklessness about him that spelled danger.

A stray thought speared her mind. Had he seen her kissing Theo this afternoon? A sick, slimy feeling writhed in her stomach. She'd betrayed everyone. Not only Theo and his family with her lies, but Nick, too, with her belated switch of loyalties. She'd meant only the best, but she doubted any of them would see it that way.

Nick said, 'You must be pleased at how the day went. Lots of traffic through.'

'I think we can all agree it was a huge success,' said Gemma.

'See?' Liz tried to act naturally, but it was hard with Nick there. 'I told you that you could do it.'

Gemma shook her head. 'Not on my own. I see that now. I'm not good with the big-picture stuff. We need you for that.'

'Don't sell yourself short, Gemma. I'm sure you'll manage.'

Nick was facing away from the bonfire, so his features were in shadow. Liz couldn't read his expression. His presence brought her two worlds into collision. She couldn't sit on the fence any longer. She needed to choose a side.

Gemma didn't seem to notice anything wrong, though. 'Have you seen Theo?'

'Maybe he's still talking to Bill Roberts,' Liz said.

Gemma sighed. 'He's better than that Miller fellow, but even though this is a business, it's still our home. I don't know if I like giving a stranger a say in how we do things.'

If only they could find an angel who would be prepared to let them run the house their own way. They shouldn't give up on the Heritage Lottery Fund. That was still a possibility, but they needed to review the application Valerie had made. No doubt she'd managed to mess that up too.

'I'm going to look for Fergus,' said Gemma. 'I'll be back.' She topped up her champagne and drifted away.

'So . . .' Nick said when Gemma was out of earshot. 'When were you going to tell me?'

'Tell you what?' Suddenly Liz's mouth felt dry. She took a hasty sip of her drink and nearly choked when Nick said, 'That you're in love with Theo Nash.'

'I'm not in love with him,' she spluttered. 'Even if I were, it doesn't follow that I've acted against your interests. I would never do that.'

'To hell with my interests,' said Nick. 'What are you doing, Liz? You haven't even sorted things out with Tony.' He paused. 'Are you sure it's Theo and not the house you're in love with? It's a special place.'

She wiped her mouth with the back of her thumb. 'Hey, you're the one assuming I'm in love. Don't put words into my mouth and then grill me about whether they're true.'

She hadn't wanted any of this. She hadn't asked to meet someone like Theo hard on the heels of her marriage falling apart, but there was no such thing as perfect timing, was there? 'The truth is, I don't know how I feel. But I've decided to stay here to find out.' She sighed. 'I'm sorry. I was going to tell you but things have happened so fast.'

'You want to resign and move to Seagrove,' said Nick slowly. Staring at her as if she'd turned into a stranger, he shook his head. 'I don't believe this.'

Liz gazed into the flames of the bonfire, trying to apply reason to what was clearly a crazy, emotional decision she might well regret. But Nick was right about one thing. She wasn't chasing after a new man. She was chasing a new life. At Seagrove, she felt healthy and happy and fulfilled in a way she'd never felt while working for Nick. She had so many plans for this place. A house like Seagrove needed to serve the community, not remain coldly aloof.

'Liz, you're rushing into this. You're throwing all your training and experience away. And for what?' said Nick. 'Did you break even on this event today?'

'We would have, if not for Valerie's ridiculous expenditure.'

'But surely you can see the Nashes have a long way to go to raise the kind of figures the house needs,' said Nick.

'You're right,' she said. 'But now they have me on their side, they have more than a fighting chance.'

She didn't have any contacts over here but she'd work every angle she could until she found that money. Of course, the perfect candidate stood right in front of her, if only she could persuade him to let go of his need to own the place.

Gently, she said, 'Nick, Theo's never going to sell. Not to you, not to anyone. The house means too much to him and to his family. I think you need to accept that.'

His face shuttered. Too much, too soon. Maybe neither of them was ready to hear home truths.

'You ought to know me better than to think I'd give up just like that,' Nick said. 'If you won't help me, I'll find another way. I always do.'

The last thing they needed was Nick working against them. Without thinking, she put her hand on his sleeve. 'I promise, I will do my best to find out about Stephen and about your ancestry, okay? Until then —'

'Well, isn't this cosy?' Valerie seemed to appear from nowhere, stalking up to them with that familiar clipped gait, a clearly reluctant Theo following in her wake. She shot a look at Theo so filled with triumph that Liz felt nauseous with fear. What had she been telling him?

Valerie's lips curved into a superior, feline smile. She looked pointedly between Nick and Liz. 'I didn't know the two of you were acquainted. Or at least, I didn't until I saw you having a nice little *tête à tête* at the Beach Shack this morning.' She widened her eyes. 'And then I did some internet research and guess what I found out?'

Damn the woman! So much for going under cover. Liz Jones was a common enough name, but pair it with Nick McCann's and Valerie would have found ample evidence of their association – from the company website, prospectuses and digital pamphlets, to photographs of her and Nick at everything from ribbon-cutting ceremonies to conferences and social events.

She watched Theo, willing him to look at her, but he stared, stony-faced, into the flames of the bonfire.

Liz realised she was shaking. 'I was going to explain everything tonight.' She spoke to Theo, willing him to look at her, to say something. Anything.

He seemed to come to life then. 'You mean it's true?' Theo gestured toward Nick. 'You work for him?'

'Theo . . .'

He shook his head as if to clear it. In a flat voice, he said, 'I didn't believe it. I thought there must be some mistake.'

Guilt clawed at Liz's insides. She hated to think she might have hurt him. This blow had fallen so swiftly after he'd shown his feelings for her today – and all of it hard on the heels of Valerie's betrayal. He must be reeling.

'So, tell us why you're here, Liz,' invited Valerie, her finely plucked eyebrows arching. Tonight she was over-dressed, as usual, in one of her ubiquitous twin-sets and pearls. She might as well have been wearing the skins of Dalmatian puppies.

Fergus and Gemma hurried over, perhaps scenting an emergency. 'Hello, Valerie,' Gemma purred. 'Come to make off with the takings?'

'*I'm* not the villain here,' said Valerie.

'Oh, I wouldn't say that,' said Liz. Now she wished she had called the police over Valerie's theft.

But the woman's triumph refused to dim. The firelight flickering over her face seemed to heighten the avidity of her expression. 'Gemma, why don't you ask your friend Liz here what she's been doing at Seagrove all this time? It wasn't research for a book.'

Liz flinched. 'No. It wasn't.'

Gemma stared at her. 'What, then?'

Nick came forward, spreading his hands in his usual oil-over-troubled-waters gesture. 'I think there's been a bit of a misunderstanding here and I'm sure I can clear it up. You see, I sent Liz here on a working holiday, of sorts. She was to research the family history.'

He smiled in a self-deprecating way. 'It's something I never mentioned when I offered to buy the place, but in fact, it turns out that I'm distantly related to the Nash family.'

Liz stood by numbly, as Nick gave his stunned listeners a rundown of the history of the Nash family and the centuries-old allegation that Stephen Nash, who succeeded Richard Nash as baron and owner of Seagrove, was an imposter.

'Ridiculous!' snorted Valerie. 'It's a fabrication. A fairytale.'

'And it's none of your business, actually, so you can take yourself off,' retorted Gemma. 'I'm sure no one invited you.'

Valerie ignored her, folding her arms and tapping her fingertips against her biceps in an irritatingly superior manner. Theo's engagement ring scintillated on her finger in the flickering light. Was that a signal they'd made up or merely a declaration that Valerie intended to win him back?

Nick said, 'I only wanted Liz to find out the truth. And, incidentally, to see if there was some way I could make my offer to purchase the house more attractive to you.'

'He sent you here to spy on us?' demanded Gemma. The expression of stunned hurt on her face made Liz cringe.

'It wasn't like that,' Liz said. 'Please believe me. At first I came here for those reasons, but as soon as I met you and the Jacksons and – and Theo, all I wanted to do was help. I wanted to find out about Delany Nash, but I knew Nick couldn't reclaim the estate on the basis of some long-lost heir. It's too far in the past.'

'How can we believe you?' said Theo. The rest of his face was expressionless but his eyes shone with pain and disbelief. 'You've lied to us from the start.' He glared at Nick, then at Liz. 'I told you about McCann. You could have given me the truth then. You could have told me when I offered you the job here, or at any other time. Was all this help you gave us just a way of getting us on side? A way of finding out our financial situation?'

'Mate, I already knew everything I needed to about the financial situation here,' said Nick. Unhelpfully, in Liz's view. 'You're struggling. You need capital and you need a lot of it, and you won't find that kind of money putting on open days.'

'Tell us something we *don't* know,' growled Fergus. 'The nerve!'

Nick shook his head. 'This place is an albatross around your necks and you know it. You'd be better off letting it go, getting out before you're so deep in debt you're forced to give it away.'

But they weren't listening to Nick now. Fergus, Gemma, Theo – they were all watching Liz, the Judas in their midst, with pained disbelief.

She took them in, the shocked, accusing faces of people she'd come to love. It was so long since she'd harboured any false motives, so long since her loyalty had been divided in any material way, that their horror and disgust came as a devastating blow.

But when she forced herself to see her actions from their point of view, she knew any justification would ring hollow. She had placed her career advancement above her friendship with these people – even above common decency, really. It was facile to tell herself or them anything different.

Liz swallowed hard, beating back tears. She curled her fingers in her palm, dug her nails into the smarting flesh. Her voice scraped painfully. 'I'm so sorry. Sorry for everything. I'll pack my bags and be gone in the morning.'

She walked quickly into the darkness. When she was out of sight of the bonfire, she broke into a run.

Delany, Lady Nash

For what seemed like endless days and sleepless nights, I struggled to understand why my husband had taken such a drastic step as to bar me from our house. He made no explanation to me or to anyone else.

He refused to see a soul, including Mr Burton, who called in Berkeley Square on my behalf. My brother-in-law and my sister had taken me in, thank God, for I had nowhere else to turn. There were friends, of course, but no one I trusted to be discreet about the circumstances surrounding my exile.

Tormented by images of the recent past, I examined my conduct with the attention of Bowdler combing Shakespeare for vulgarity. Or perhaps that is a bad analogy, for I found no incident for which I might reproach myself.

After a week spent in this torment of uncertainty, I managed to smuggle a message to Jane. My maid had been as shocked and surprised at my banishment as I. Why Jane had not been turned away, I didn't know. Unless in his spite Richard sought to keep even the comfort of my maid from me.

We met at an unfashionable hour in Kensington Gardens, like two lovers conducting an illicit liaison. My heart was so glad to see her I nearly wept.

Gripping her hands like a lifeline, I said, 'Pray, Jane, tell me all you know. Why has he sent me away? What have I done? Is it because of the children?'

'I don't know, my lady. That I swear.' Jane's face bore the same marks of worry that I knew must be graven on my own. 'His lordship has locked himself up in his rooms and won't see anyone.'

She returned the clasp of my hands. 'Oh, my lady, he gave orders I wasn't to bring you your gowns or your books or anything, and that anyone who took so much as a hairpin to you would be had up for stealing.' She set her mouth into a line. 'But I'll do it if you wish.'

At her news, my consternation multiplied, but I hastened to reassure her. 'No, oh, no, Jane. I would never expect you to run such a risk. Pray do not. I am well situated at my sister's house.'

Left with only the clothes I stood up in and a few coins in my pocket, I relied on my sister for every last item of food, shelter and clothing. Lavinia was too self-absorbed to spare me the indignity of asking for every item as I required it. The necessity of relying upon her humbled and infuriated me, but I'd persuaded myself it was temporary. Surely Richard must come to his senses soon.

Jane's news dashed my hopes. My husband seemed intent on punishing me. But for what transgression? Even a murderer is told the crime for which he is charged and convicted. What had I done to merit such treatment?

Had Richard run mad? I thought of poor King George, attacking members of his household, the Prince of Wales, his queen. Madness knew no boundaries of decency, no bonds of affection.

Yet, since he'd sent the boys away, Richard had seemed serene, almost unnaturally calm. Looking back, it seemed to me that my continual blandishments over my children had pleased, rather than angered him.

I'd sat down to breakfast with him on the very morning of my exile and we'd conversed with our customary careful politeness. Had he been hugging his intentions tight to his chest even then? He'd given not the slightest indication that mere hours later he would banish me from our house.

Perhaps something had occurred in the intervening period. It had been impossible to judge from his demeanour that day.

'Tell me, Jane, what . . . what do people say?' I asked her the question with marked hesitancy. Though I would trust my dear maid with my life, I never stooped to gossip with her. I licked my lips. 'Do the servants know anything? What about his lordship's valet?'

'No, my lady.' She glanced about her and lowered her voice. 'But they do say . . .' She broke off, a muscle working in her jaw.

I fixed my earnest gaze upon her, nodding at her in encouragement. 'Do not scruple to be frank. This is no time to spare my feelings. Tell me.'

Jane looked as if she might burst. 'They do say that you was mighty friendly with his lordship's brother, ma'am.'

'What!'

Every interaction I'd had with Julian flashed before my mind. To me, our encounters had been thick with constraint. I could not think of a single overt impropriety.

What had they seen? What had there been for anyone to see? The only time I had ever behaved with more than a distant sisterly affection toward Julian was when he had attended me in my boudoir upon my illness.

In my boudoir.

I passed a shaking hand over my eyes. 'For pity's sake, what a coil.'

Oh, the irony. How often had I wished with all my heart that there was more between me and Julian! We had held so steadfastly to the moral high ground, yet now we were the subject of scurrilous gossip over a perfectly innocent exchange.

'Do you think Lord Nash believes the rumours?' I asked. 'Surely he knows you were there the whole time when Julian was with me in my boudoir that day.'

'I think the rumours are sprung up to explain my lord's behaviour,' said Jane. 'I cannot say what the master believes. He sees not a soul but his valet, and you know how close-mouthed Simmons is.'

I considered this. Jane was a shrewd woman and I respected her opinion. It was true that if rumours of an affair between Julian and me had pre-dated my banishment, they would be rife by now. There would be cartoons in print-shop windows, salacious winks and nudges among my acquaintance, references to 'Lady N—' and 'Mr N—' in all the scandal sheets.

I'd quizzed my brother-in-law on the subject, urging him to be plain with me, but he claimed to be as baffled by my husband's actions as I was. He'd heard not a word about it in the clubs. I believe Mr Burton concealed nothing from me on that score. His story tallied with Jane's surmises.

Jane said, 'Shall I come to you, my lady? His lordship forbade it but I mean to stand with you, come what may.'

'You are a good, dear creature,' I said. 'But I believe you will be of far more use to me in the household, if you can bear to stay, and as long as my lord treats you with kindness.'

'Yes, my lady. I'll send word to you if I discover anything.'

I am not and have never been a person given to the physical expression of my feelings, but my gratitude for such a staunch friend overwhelmed me. I embraced Jane and kissed her cheek. 'Thank you,' I said. 'I do not know what the future holds, but I promise you, I will never forget how you stood by me.'

Confirmation of my worst fears did not come until Julian called in Clarges Street. He was pale, his dark eyes dull with fatigue, as he strode into Lavinia's drawing room.

He was dressed for riding. Mud spattered his boots and his disarranged hair added to the bone-weary look of him. He had been searching for my boys for weeks, in vain.

'Will you leave us, Lavinia?' I said.

'No. Better not,' said Julian with a swift, significant glance at Mr Burton. 'It is bad enough that I am here.' He handed me a document. 'Read this.'

Puzzled, I took it from him and scanned it.

My senses swam. It was a writ issued on behalf of Richard for the prosecution of Julian for criminal conversation, for having carnal knowledge of . . . me. The amount of damages Richard claimed was £20 000.

Days spent in apprehension of looming disaster had not softened the blow when it came. At first, I could not speak.

'Delany?' Lavinia said. 'What is it? Why has she gone so pale?'

My whole body flamed with humiliation. 'How could he? How could he do that to me? To us! To his own flesh and blood! Good God, this beggars belief. Does he hate us so much?'

'He hates me that much, in any event,' said Julian.

I turned my horrified gaze on him. 'Do you think his wits are deranged?'

Mr Burton said, 'May I?' and took the writ from my nerveless fingers. 'Good God!' His gaze snapped back and forth between Julian and me. 'Is it true?'

'No, of course not,' said Julian impatiently. 'This is my brother's clever notion to prise my inheritance from me. But that he'd sacrifice Delany's reputation to do it . . .'

Lavinia said, 'What is it? What has happened? Oh, pray, someone tell me at once or I shall scream.'

Briefly, Mr Burton explained.

'For shame!' cried Lavinia. 'How could he malign his own wife so? His own brother? But then I suppose any man heartless enough to send his sons away and never let their mama see them no more is *capable de tout*.'

Lately, Lavinia had taken to peppering her conversation with French phrases. Just now, such affectation made me want to strangle her. I struggled to bite back the cutting retort that sprang to my lips. After all, Lavinia's unquestioning loyalty meant a great deal to me.

'What are we going to do?' I said, addressing the question to the room at large.

'I've engaged an attorney,' said Julian. 'We must be clever about this. We must try to contain the scandal as best we can.'

I sent him a derisive look. 'If he has indeed brought such an action it will be all over Town soon enough.'

Mr Burton said, 'Might I be of assistance as an intermediary? Perhaps there is room for negotiation.'

'There is no room for negotiation,' I said. 'Julian is innocent.'

Even as I spoke the words, I knew no one would believe me. Julian's reputation with women was bad, and he and I had made it clear to all this past spring that we enjoyed each other's company. Who needed evidence, or even a trial, for that matter? The gossipmongers had destroyed reputations with far less cause. The very fact my lord had brought this action damned both Julian and me – but most especially me.

'I'm going with my attorney to see counsel now,' said Julian, putting on his hat. He looked down at me. 'Come with me. I need your help with strategy and the barrister will want to hear your side of the matter.'

'Ah, is that wise?' said Mr Burton. 'For the two of you to be seen alone together would rather lend credence to the accusations.'

'Indeed.' Julian bowed. 'Perhaps Mrs Burton will join us to lend her countenance.'

'Oh.' Lavinia looked from us to Mr Burton and back again. 'Oh, no, I couldn't . . . That is to say, I should be terrified.'

'Terrified of visiting a barrister's chambers?' I demanded. 'What do you think will happen to you there? Death by dust inhalation?'

'Well, I don't know, but I shouldn't like it,' said Lavinia. Her lower lip trembled and she looked again to her husband to rescue her.

He said, 'It is perfectly proper for you to accompany your sister to the Inns of Court, Lavinia. Indeed, I think you must.'

Later that day, Julian, Lavinia and I, along with Julian's attorney, Mr Black, presented ourselves at the chambers of the famous Mr Thomas Erskine.

Besides his vigorous defence of unpopular causes, including the ongoing impeachment of Warren Hastings, Mr Erskine was renowned for his histrionic speeches in the court room. Indeed, some wag had dubbed him 'The Oratorical Swooner'. He had obtained fantastical sums in damages for husbands in criminal conversation cases such as this one. We could only hope he was as adept at defence as he was at prosecution.

Julian had become well acquainted with Erskine during the Whig campaign of '83 when Erskine had won a seat in the Commons – albeit for a short time.

'He is a trifle eccentric,' Julian warned us. 'Don't be alarmed, for Mr Erskine has swayed more juries than you've had hot dinners. We must trust him to see us safely through.'

Julian gestured for Lavinia and me to precede the gentlemen as Erskine's clerk showed us in.

At first glance, Mr Erskine's chambers looked like the library of a gentleman's house. Then one noticed the trappings of his profession: pigeon-holes full of rolled-up briefs tied with red ribbon, shelves and shelves of thick legal tomes, and a red damask bag embroidered with what I took to be his initials hanging on a hook by the door. A large table dominated the room, around which ranged several Chippendale chairs. Upon one of these chairs sat the largest, shaggiest dog I had ever seen.

I gave a start and choked back a laugh, for not only did the dog have his forelegs on the table, as any man might do, but around his throat were the white linen bands of the advocate, and on his head a neat periwig of the style barristers wear in court. His breed, I believe, was Newfoundland; his expression was magisterial. Indeed, this particular canine was far more dignified than many magistrates I'd encountered.

'Come in, come in,' said a voice, which seemed at first to emanate from the dog himself.

The Newfoundland turned his head at his master's greeting, shattering the illusion. I turned also, to see Erskine emerge from some sort of ante-room, hurriedly doing up the top button of his coat.

Greetings were exchanged, introductions made, and Mr Erskine added, 'May I present Phoss? He will sit in, if you don't mind.'

The rest of my companions blinked. I said, 'Good afternoon, Phoss. How do you do?'

The dog regarded me severely beneath the curls of his wig. I could see he was not here to be patronised.

I adore dogs. In ordinary circumstances, I would have made friends with this one by letting him sniff my hand and scratching him behind the ear. However, the dignity of Phoss was such that I didn't dare pat him or tell him what a great, handsome fellow he was.

'Do sit down,' said Erskine, taking his own seat and looking over the writ. 'By God, what a bad business it is, Nash. Shocking, shocking. We must see what we can do about it.'

The attorney, Mr Black, shuffled his papers. 'I have here a list of possible witnesses.' He passed over the paper to me. 'Lady Nash, would you be so kind as to review it? No doubt you will have names to add.'

I took the paper. The list was longer than I'd expected. My stomach roiled as I thought of all these people being questioned about my personal habits. The porter would be interrogated about Julian's comings and goings, the chamber maids about the state of my bed linen and conversations in my private apartments, not to mention other, more intimate sounds. With a shiver, I wondered how much might emerge about my relations with Richard himself. I hoped that side of things would not be considered germane to the issue.

Margaret Smith was on the list. 'Miss Smith?' I looked up at Julian. 'She wasn't in London that day.'

Everyone stared at me as if I'd betrayed myself. I lifted my chin. 'I am thinking of the only occasion upon which there might have been the least misunderstanding about the nature of my relationship with Mr Nash.'

The solicitor cleared his throat self-consciously. 'The writ specifies the months between April and May. Moreover, witnesses are called for all sorts of reasons – to provide evidence as to the state of the marriage, the characters of the parties, that sort of thing.'

Of course. I ought to have known. I'd never been present at such a prosecution but I'd read many accounts of them. How I regretted my prurient interest in these reports, now that I was to be the subject of one. My chest tightened. Every time I thought of the humiliation in store, a wave of revulsion washed over me, hot and putrid as a fever.

A thought occurred to me. If Miss Smith was called as witness, that meant she was somewhere to be found. Even if I could not discover her direction beforehand, at court, I would at last have the opportunity to speak to her. Surely Margaret would not fail to help me find my children. Though not a mother herself, as a woman she must feel for my plight.

Much of what followed at the meeting passed in a blur while I planned what I would do if I found my boys again. Clearly we could not stay in England. I would be obliged to kidnap my sons and take them to the Continent, and hide away where Richard could never find me.

I'd have to orchestrate my escape carefully, for I must not let any repercussions hurt Julian. I fell to scheming, and had to remind myself that my children's recovery was by no means certain. I must not raise my hopes too high. But with every day that passed, I'd become more convinced that Miss Smith held the key to their whereabouts. Her continued absence, her elusiveness, while they were gone also, was too pointed a coincidence.

'Lady Nash?' Erskine's deep voice recalled me to the present.

My head jerked up. 'I beg your pardon, I was not attending.'

They all stared at me. I did not wonder at their astonishment, for what could possibly be of greater moment than the conversation taking place in this room? They could not conceive that scarce a moment of the day passed when I did not think of my children and long to be with them.

Kindly, Mr Erskine reiterated his explanation. 'In any action of this nature, there are two things the plaintiff must establish to the jury's satisfaction. First, that the act of debauchery itself took place. Second, the amount of compensation due to the plaintiff. In general, the trial takes a day and the verdict is returned immediately.'

One day to decide our fate.

'Is there no way to avoid a trial?' I said. 'My husband's allegations have no basis in fact. He can have no proof of wrongdoing, for there was none.'

Mr Erskine fixed me with an unwavering gaze that was at once compassionate and perceptive. 'We will, of course, test every piece of evidence with rigorous cross-examination. But I must warn you that a verdict of guilty is no longer very difficult for a plaintiff to secure. In times past, a judge required at least two witnesses to the act itself for the matter to be considered proven. Now, circumstantial evidence of the flimsiest nature may be taken as satisfying that requirement.'

I seemed to recall that Mr Erskine himself had contributed his might to this development. How many cases had he fought and won on the basis of a few tender gestures and time spent alone behind a locked door?

Infidelity was common among the upper classes. In remaining faithful to Richard, I was an anomaly. Where aristocrats were concerned, juries presumed the defendant's guilt as a matter of course. The only question was how much the wife's virtue was worth.

'However, I urge you not to despair,' Erskine continued. 'We have won far more difficult cases, haven't we, Phoss?'

The dog lifted his muzzle into the air as if to preen himself. His wig slid back a little. I expected it to fall off and ruin his dignity, and was relieved on his behalf when it remained in place. It might have been the sheer hopelessness of my circumstances, but I had a hysterical desire to laugh. Did no one else think it ridiculous to have our meeting presided over by an enormous chocolate-coloured dog?

'We must examine the evidence carefully,' continued Erskine. 'And there are several factors that will certainly go toward mitigation of damages, should the jury find for the plaintiff.'

He went on to outline the kinds of circumstances in which the injury suffered by a cuckolded husband might be diminished and consequently worth less in compensation.

He ticked off his fingers. 'Previous affairs of the wife, a bad marriage to begin with, the collusion of the husband in the affair, the husband's entrapment of the hapless lover for monetary gain . . .'

I exchanged a significant look with Julian. We both knew Richard's motive; the question was whether we ought to air that dirty laundry in court. I would leave that for Julian to decide.

At this point, Phoss leaned over and sniffed at his master's collar, appearing for all the world as if he were whispering in his master's ear.

'What's that, Phoss?' Erskine's heavy black brows drew together. 'Ah, yes, my learned colleague has recalled to my mind a case in which the lady's husband actually encouraged the defendant to look upon her while she bathed and was held to be well aware of her liaisons with other gentleman. Damages of a shilling awarded in that case.'

That trial was well known to us all, but I had no parade of lovers to call as witnesses to my loose character. Tom did not count, because our affair had occurred long before my marriage.

I did, however, carry a secret, one I did not intend to divulge to Mr Erskine. It was not shame alone that prevented me from disclosing the array of male eyes that had leered at me through peepholes at my husband's behest. If I aired such scandalous behaviour, society would hold me to blame as much as Richard, perhaps more. I could not afford to lose my reputation beyond redemption. If I did, I would never see my boys again.

'Surely we do not need to go into such intimate details,' I said. 'The fact remains that there is no case to answer. The only time Mr Nash and I have been in anything approaching a compromising position is when he visited me while I was on my sick bed one afternoon. My maid was there the entire time and can attest to the fact that nothing untoward occurred.'

'Ah.' Erskine glanced at the attorney, who diligently wrote this down. 'Is your maid a reliable sort?'

'Yes, of course. She would never forsake me.'

'Very well, then.' He fingered his chin and exchanged a glance with Phoss so pregnant with meaning that for one moment I could have believed the dog an extremely hirsute member of the Inner Temple. 'They must have *something*,' Erskine said at last. 'A collection of circumstances from which the inference might be drawn.'

As I puzzled over this, a number of incidents came back to me: Richard's insistence on Julian's remaining at Seagrove after their mother's funeral, his encouraging me to travel to London in Julian's company. If I had not taken Henry with me, what might then have occurred? Would Margaret have slipped away discreetly, and left Julian and me alone together at an inn one night? Now that I looked back at Richard and Margaret's behaviour, I realised they had thrown Julian and me together at every opportunity. How frustrating it must have been to be thwarted at every turn!

The barrister addressed Julian. 'You say you inherited a fortune from your mother that your brother covets. That is a powerful motive. We will hammer this home. In cases such as these, there is a narrative, you know. Pleading a case before a jury is like telling a story to a child. Capture their imaginations, sway their sympathies, and they will leap to acquit you.' He glanced at me. 'I will need to see you again, Lady Nash. You and I must explore this matter further. It will be better, perhaps, to do it without others in attendance.'

I glanced at Julian, silencing his objection with a look. 'I will do everything I can to help,' I said. 'Do you require a sworn statement?'

'That will not assist us, I'm afraid,' said Erskine. 'Neither of the parties nor the wife is permitted to give evidence. The case must rest on the testimony of third-party witnesses.' He leaned forward. 'It will be an experience that is far from pleasant for you. I suggest, too, that you retain counsel on your own account, Lady Nash. Do not forget that I act for Mr Nash, here. His interests might be served best by tactics that do not serve you.'

Grimly amused, I said, 'But I have no power to object to anything you choose to do or say in court on behalf of your client, Mr Erskine. I have no voice at all in the matter, not even through my counsel, though I'll wager mine is the only reputation that will be thoroughly destroyed by it.'

'Erskine, I won't countenance any strategy that injures Lady Nash,' said Julian. 'You will act in all things as if she is your client. I insist upon it.'

Julian had leaned forward in a way Phoss must have found threatening, for the dog emitted a low growl.

'Quite right, Phoss,' said Erskine in a soothing tone. 'Utterly misguided, but one must forgive him. He is under a great deal of strain.'

Julian's expression turned thunderous. With a nervous tug at the
black stock around his neck, Mr Black murmured something placa-
tory, but Erskine raised his hand to arrest the flow.

'Mr Nash, how I run the trial is entirely at my discretion.' He
smiled. 'It must be, you know. Allow me to do what I do best and I
assure you we will carry the day.'

Later, before we parted, Julian detained me. 'I meant what I said,
Delany. I'd rather hand the entire fortune direct to Richard than subject you to such humiliation.'

I felt responsible for Julian's predicament. If only I had never married Richard! I, who had thought myself such an excellent judge of
character, had made the worst mistake of my existence by giving my
life and liberty into the hands of such an amoral viper.

I held fast to one notion. 'We did nothing wrong, Julian. And he
cannot prove we did.'

'That's true,' he said. 'But I have the most God-awful feeling,
Delany. There's more to this affair than either of us knows.'

CHAPTER SIXTEEN

Margaret

Margaret tossed and turned in her bed, ready to scream with frustration. She'd longed for this moment all day and half the night. Now it had arrived she couldn't seem to take advantage of the brief, blessed quiet. She'd never been so exhausted in her life, yet she'd lost the habit of sleep.

Delirious with fatigue, foul-tempered and lacking her usual self-control, she'd abused the nursemaid for some minor error, she couldn't remember what. She'd boxed the girl's ear and dismissed her.

Now Margaret regretted her action deeply. Not because she felt remorse over the blow she'd dealt the nursemaid, though in fairness the girl had not deserved it. No, she regretted her hasty action because it left her without any help whatsoever. Though she'd written to Richard at his club begging him to hire a new girl, he had not troubled to meet her request.

He hadn't called on her at the small house in Cheapside for weeks. Or perhaps it was only days. She'd lost count. She had no notion of time any more, only that every twenty-four hour period seemed an eternity. Her brain was sluggish. Thoughts waded through sludge try-ing to reach her, only to disappear before they arrived.

Two babies to feed. Two babies, waking in the night and scream-ing. One would start, then the other, howling as if they knew no one here cared tuppence what became of them.

Now, as she lay there straining for sleep, the wailing started again. She ignored it for as long as she could, but already she felt the surge of milk rushing into her breasts, the ache that made her think of the piti-ful lowing cows made when they missed a milking.

That's what she was. A cow. A walking set of udders. By what madness had she agreed to this?

As she dragged herself out of bed to answer the infant squall, Margaret thought of the first child, the one Lady Verena had made her give up. She'd called the little girl Daisy in her mind, though she'd never spoken the name aloud. She'd never even seen the infant who was taken away from her as soon as it was expelled from her straining body.

She'd endured in cold, dead silence when they'd taken Daisy from her. Later, she would wonder, picture that little girl living somewhere far away – in the countryside, perhaps, or in Italy or France. But those imaginings had ceased long ago. Lady Verena had refused to tell her Daisy's whereabouts, even as Margaret had stood over her with a pil-low gripped between her shaking hands. Margaret hated her for that most of all.

Now, she longed for someone to take these babies away from her, though one of them was her own flesh and blood. Her second child with Richard. William. A son conceived within a month of Delany's Stephen.

She shuffled into the nursery. William was the one making the rum-pus this time. Little Stephen slept on.

Margaret would never forget the anguish and fury she'd felt when Richard had brought Stephen to her. Suckle the babe of her rival as well as her own? Was he inhuman? To add insult to injury, later he'd thrust that slavering, snuffling dog of Lady Verena's on her too.

But as always, she'd done what she must. Delany was insensible with fever, Richard said, and the babe was lacking nourishment. It was brought home to Margaret that the only time he'd recalled her pregnancy at all was when he'd needed her as a wet nurse.

The screaming grew louder at her approach. She snatched William up and took him away with her to her own bedchamber. Already she felt the tension in her own body rise as she tried to arrest William's flailing limbs. Of a sudden, he flung himself backward, spine arched as if racked with pain, and she nearly dropped him. Was he hungry? If she could but settle him down a little and nurse him, he might stop crying.

But he did not want to be fed. His little face turned so red he looked about to burst from outrage at being so misunderstood. She checked, but his clout was clean and dry.

She paced the floor with him, desperate to soothe and quiet him, but his screams went on and on, filling her head until she could have shaken him.

'*What is wrong with you?*' she shouted, scarce making herself heard over his din.

He gathered himself, clenched his little fists and yelled harder.

Margaret couldn't bear it. Her own chest crowded with dry, racking sobs. She was unwilling to love this child, knowing that she must give him up. Yet, even through the dead weight of her tiredness, she could not help feeling his distress as her own.

She laid him down on her bed and walked outside the room, where his wails no longer pierced her to the marrow.

She squeezed her eyes shut and stoppered her ears with her fingers, and for a few, precious moments, her senses swam in the blessed silence.

She took several deep breaths. Then she steeled herself and went back to William. In a soft, calm voice, she said, 'There, there, my darling. There, there.'

Scooping him up, she snatched a clean clout from the chair and put it over her shoulder, then nestled William against her shoulder in an upright position. Just as the nurse had done, she rubbed his lower back to soothe him.

How could such a small thing have such an inexhaustible capacity for wailing? Still unhappy, he squirmed against her, feet kicking. What did he want? She had no idea – until he tucked up his legs before him like a small frog, dug his little toes into her ribs, and unleashed a tremendous fart.

She looked down at him in surprise. He looked up at her, muddy blue eyes wide, as if equally astonished. At that moment, all the love that had been locked tight inside her broke free, pouring out of her, showering this precious child.

He gave a contented sigh and cuddled into her, as though he, at least, had never doubted her affection. Then he turned his face up, his eyes rolling a little before his eyelids fluttered shut. Black lashes resting in damp spikes on his flushed cheeks, he dropped like a stone into sleep.

Worn out though she was, Margaret couldn't bear to part with him. Moving carefully, so as not to disturb him again, she dragged the coverlet off her bed and placed it over herself as she sat down in the armchair by the fire to enjoy her baby.

She must have drowsed after a while, because when she opened her eyes again, Richard stood before her.

'My lord!' God in heaven, what a slattern she must look. She put a hand to her hair, which was falling out of its night-time braid. 'You should have sent word you were coming.'

Aware of the warmth of William against her chest, she glanced down in fright, lest she'd managed to suffocate or harm him while insensible. But the babe was content, the steady flickering beneath his purple-tinted eyelids telling her he was deeply asleep.

She rose, coverlet, baby and all, and managed an awkward curtsy.

Richard said, 'There has been a development. I need speech with you.'

Stung that he'd barely acknowledged the baby, she said, 'Will you not kiss your son, my lord?'

He eyed the child but made no move to oblige her. 'In fact, it's partly about the child that I've come.'

Uncertainty gripped Margaret. He'd not taken the least notice of Daisy's arrival a little over three years ago. Indeed, Lady Verena had warned her never to mention the babe in his presence. To Richard it was as if she had never been with child. Such was the freedom of men!

She must not let that old wound preoccupy her now. The air of suppressed excitement about Richard told Margaret she needed to remain alert. What had he done?

Cautiously, she said, 'Pray, sit down, my lord.' Of course, he might do as he pleased here; he needed no invitation. It was his house, after all.

She wished she might offer to ring for a cold collation to be brought, as she would if they were at Seagrove. Most of Richard's acquaintance would be sitting down to supper at this late hour. But she had no servants. Her own meals came from the chop house down the street, delivered by the boy who laid her fires and did the heavy work about the house.

Ever mindful of his own comfort, Richard kept a set of decanters here. He crossed to the sideboard and poured himself a brandy. He raised the decanter with a look of inquiry at her.

'No, I thank you.' She needed all her wits about her for this conversation, and precious few of them she had left.

At the sound of her voice, William turned his head in his sleep and gave a whimper. After a few wavering attempts, he succeeded in lodging his tiny thumb in his mouth. Perhaps she ought to return the baby to his cradle. But that might wake him and she didn't want her conversation with Richard complicated or postponed on account of a crying infant.

She need not have worried. Richard seemed to forget the babe's existence. He took a chair on the other side of the fire and brought her up to date on recent events, including his banishment of Delany from Nash house.

'You served a writ upon Mr Nash!' she exclaimed. 'But we haven't any evidence yet!'

Oh, the fool! She could have wrung his neck for it. Hadn't she known he'd ruin her plans if left to his own devices? But she'd been helpless, tied down, marooned on an island ruled by small tyrants.

Now she understood why he'd removed not only Stephen from Delany's care, but Henry, the elder boy, too.

'No evidence.' Richard pulled at his lower lip, a sure sign of impending trouble. 'And who do I have to thank for that? Your scheme to throw them together didn't work, did it?'

'It was only a matter of time.' Her words and her tone were measured with the utmost care. If she gave full vent to her feelings, she'd alert Richard to her utter contempt for him. With superhuman effort, she regained control of her temper, which seemed to simmer just below the surface these days, apt to boil over at any moment.

Richard's handsome face had contorted into a snarl but his eyes were clear and cold. 'They were too clever for us, hiding their filthy incestuous liaison so well that we never caught them at it. But I know, Margaret. I *know*. They have been at it like rabbits for years.'

He glanced down at the baby in her arms.

She felt a twinge of unease. Margaret pulled the coverlet closer about her and the baby. 'That may be, but my lord, we have no proof. Surely our case must be flimsy at best. Why, they have scarce spent a moment alone together these past few months.'

'Ah.' His expression lightened. He drew from his coat pocket a folded document, which he smoothed out and handed to her. 'This, my dear Margaret, is our evidence.'

It was an affidavit in which she, Margaret Smith, outlined – in lurid detail – no fewer than three occasions on which she had discovered Delany and Julian having carnal relations.

'This is all lies,' she said. 'Expressed in the crudest, most ungenteel fashion. You would have me swear to this?'

It showed how little Richard respected her that he would contemplate such a thing. No matter what had happened between them, she'd always been scrupulously careful, fearfully discreet. Lady Verena had taken good care to shield Margaret from any suspicion when Daisy was born. None knew better how to conceal an incriminating pregnancy. There had never been a whisper of a question about her modesty and good character. Why, Julian had nicknamed her 'the Quaker' for her sober dress and unimpeachable virtue. Better to err on the side of prudishness, she'd thought. That way, no one would suspect what went on between her and Richard.

She'd taken extraordinary pains to conceal her ongoing affair with the master of a large household, not to mention her two pregnancies; she'd agreed to give up her two illegitimate children, sending them away to be nurtured and raised by strangers. All in the pursuit of one day becoming Lady Nash.

When she thought of the things she'd done to that end . . . But this! This affidavit could jeopardise everything she'd worked for.

It was not that she baulked at breaking her sworn oath in court. Compared with other sins she had committed to shore up her position, perjuring herself seemed a bagatelle.

No, if she gave this evidence of Delany's infidelity, Margaret herself would become tainted by association. That affidavit would be but the beginning. She would be obliged to stand up in court and repeat her allegations in full view of the gossipmongers, undergo detailed cross-examination without a waver. Describe things a respectable spinster shouldn't know existed, much less speak of in public.

She'd never intended her name to be mentioned in the prosecution at all. Now, she was to be the key witness. Her name would be bandied about Town, spelled out in the scandal sheets. She'd become almost as notorious as Delany.

Richard must have sensed the refusal on her lips, because he said, 'Perhaps I ought to remind you that if I do not win this case, I cannot obtain a divorce. If we do not prevail here, there will be no other chance.'

She nearly laughed at his telling her what she had known and worked for since the day of the dowager's funeral. But hadn't she always said it? Richard's thought processes might be slow, but he always got there in the end.

This time, he'd moved precipitately. While Delany was exiled from her home, Margaret could not return there. With no well-born female to lend Margaret countenance, she could not live with Richard without the world's assuming she was his mistress. Once that connection was made, he would never marry her.

Then there was the matter of survival. Margaret had hoped to return to Seagrove when the babies were weaned. Now, Delany's absence made that impossible. How would she live?

Once she'd served her purpose at trial, would Richard cut her adrift? There was nothing to stop him, was there? Once divorced, he might look about him for a second wife who would add to his consequence, bring with her wealth or position or both.

Margaret played for time. 'Could we not set a watch on Delany and Julian now? Left to their own devices, they would provide us with real evidence very soon, I know it.'

'And in the meantime, my bastard brother will spend my mother's fortune on good causes,' snapped Richard.

The way he spat out the words 'bastard brother' made Margaret want to hold William closer, and stopper his small ears.

Richard swirled his brandy in his glass. 'Much as I'd like to see Julian clapped up in the Fleet, I want the money more.'

Margaret saw that he wouldn't be moved, and indeed, it would make him look weak if he withdrew his allegations now. Moreover, she was too weary to attempt the campaign of flattery and persuasion that might change his mind. The best she could manage was to say, 'I'm afraid this affidavit won't do. It is demonstrably false.'

Richard sat up. 'What? What do you mean?'

She consulted the document. 'I mean that on the twenty-eighth of May, when you have them both stealing away to a boarding house in Kensington, I distinctly recall Lady Nash was visiting her aunt in St Alban's overnight. And Mr Nash dined with us, then accompanied us and the Burtons to the play.'

Pointing out Richard's deficiencies was always a risk. 'Of course,' she added in honeyed tones, 'the mind of a great man like yours is far above trivial matters such as the dates and times of social engagements. I, however, being a mere woman, have kept detailed diaries of small doings all my life. I have but to consult them to construct a credible tale.'

She waited, her breathing suspended, for Richard to throw one of his tantrums.

She sensed it was a near-run thing. But at length, he said, 'Very well. Have a plausible draft done by tomorrow afternoon. I'll collect it then.'

When did he think she would have time to do that? 'Shall we rather say in three days' time, my lord? I fear I am much occupied until a new nursemaid may be found.'

He looked her over critically. 'You must give evidence in court, you know. It is vital to make a good impression.'

Did he mean to imply she'd best improve her appearance? Good God, it was after midnight. She was in her night rail and she'd been struggling to care for two babies on her own for more than a week.

She forced her lips into a smile. 'As to that, my lord, might I trouble you to hire a new girl? And perhaps a maid of all work, as well. If you recall, the last nursemaid is no longer —'

'Yes, yes, that's the other thing I need to talk to you about.' He gestured to the sleeping bundle in her arms. 'I'm taking the boy.'

'What?' Her hand came up to rest on the back of William's head.

'I've decided to send Stephen down to Hampshire,' Richard said. 'I have a wet nurse waiting downstairs, a most respectable female. She'll take Stephen and Henry to Lamerton Hall with her and set up a household for them there.' His eyes gleamed in triumph. 'Now that Julian has already searched the place, he will not think to look for them there again.'

It occurred to Margaret to wonder where Henry, Richard and Delany's elder son, had been all this time, but she didn't ask. She was far more preoccupied with the misunderstanding Richard seemed to have formed about the child sleeping in her arms. He thought William, his bastard, was Stephen, his legitimate son.

To a mother, the two children were chalk and cheese. Stephen was a chubby, fair-haired infant. William was smaller and finer boned, with darker hair and a more sallow tinge to his skin.

True to form, however, Richard took no notice of that which did not concern him directly. His children were no more to him than pawns in a game. Sometimes she wondered if he remembered William's existence. He had an uncanny talent for wiping undesirable subjects from his mind. That lack of feeling chilled her far more than his treatment of his wife.

His hatred for Delany ran as deep as his loathing for his brother. Delany was too quick-witted, too often impatient with him. She belittled him by her very competence. This was a man who imagined slights at every turn, who required careful handling. Delany, forthright and unaccustomed to male fragility, offered him every opportunity to take offence.

He had concealed it well, maintaining a veneer of husbandly solicitude – at least when they were in company. But now he struck, fast and sharp as a viper.

Margaret marvelled at his viciousness. Removing the children from Delany's care, locking her out of the house, had been his idea alone. Oh, Margaret had fanned the flames of his irritation when he'd complained of Delany's besottedness with baby Henry. She admitted that. The aching reminder of her own loss as she'd watched Delany dote on her firstborn had made Margaret lash out in retaliation. She'd even hinted that Stephen might be Julian's bastard, though if any reasonable man considered the matter, he would see the timing wasn't right.

But she'd never expected him to move with such swiftness and decision, and without her counsel. Perhaps, she thought now, she had underestimated him all these years. Just as Delany had.

Clearly, it behoved Margaret to clear up this misunderstanding about William's identity. Richard's legitimate son would be brought up with all of the wealth and status that were his privilege and birthright. She ought to put William safely to bed, remain here with him until he was weaned, then hand him over to that nice couple in Somerset who so longed for a child of their own. They would be kind to him, she knew. She'd interviewed them herself to make sure.

She'd also extracted Richard's solemn promise to support William financially, though she did not know what reliance she might reasonably place upon the oath of such a man. Had he not sworn to love and protect his wife, all the while using her as an instrument with which to torture his brother?

'Well?' demanded Richard. 'Is there something amiss?'

She ought to ask him to wait while she fetched little Stephen. Yet somehow, other words seemed to flow from her mouth. 'Yes. Of course. Will you summon the wet nurse to take him while I pack his things?'

Blood throbbed in her ears. In a haze, she saw the nursemaid enter the room, bob a curtsy. The woman was as plump and freshly pretty as a dairy maid, with a kind, competent manner. Richard did not tell her Margaret's name. Though she knew he did it out of a wish to avoid gossip, it rankled, being treated as a nobody.

She looked down at William for a moment, steeling herself. Then she eased the precious bundle into the nursemaid's arms and went out.

Deliberately, she avoided glancing at the innocent child sleeping in his little cradle. She packed a valise with all the tiny garments she had made for her baby in the last few months of her confinement.

Her hands stilled. No. That wasn't right. She scooped the clothes out and dumped them in a pile on the floor, then gripped the edge of the valise to steady herself. A wave of regret swept over her for the plain, serviceable garments she'd made William, resentment stitched into every seam.

She eased open the drawer that held Stephen's belongings. His gowns were of the finest lawn, lovingly worked in exquisite white-on-white embroidery by Delany's elegant, talented fingers. Margaret swept them up and laid them in the valise, along with all the other items Richard had brought for his son.

She looked around to see if she'd missed anything. Something bright beside Stephen's sleeping form caught her eye.

His silver rattle. The one Delany had given him at birth, engraved with his initials. Attached to the rattle section was a tongue of coral about the size of a child's finger, on which Stephen loved to suck.

She crept up to the cot, feeling like a grave robber but steeling herself for what must be done. Holding her breath, she took hold of the rattle's silver end and tried to ease it out from under Stephen's cheek.

The bells tinkled. Stephen frowned and whimpered. 'Hush,' she said softly, as she stole the rattle away.

When she'd finished packing, Margaret breathed in deeply, then let out a slow, steady exhalation. Courage, you weak fool! she told herself. Do not fail your son now.

She returned to the bedchamber with the valise and handed it to the nursemaid. She knew her agitation must be palpable and suspicious, but Richard didn't notice. The nurse's expression did not alter, though surely she must be curious about this odd situation.

'Wait.' Reluctant to let them go, desperate to hold her son one last time, Margaret said, 'We should wrap him more warmly.'

She went to her travel chest and drew out her precious cashmere shawl, a gift from Lady Verena.

She made as if to reach for the babe, but the nursemaid took the shawl from her hand and wrapped it with practised dexterity around the infant.

Margaret stifled a whimper of pain, just as a faint cry came from the nursery. She felt it in her body, rather than truly hearing it – that uncanny sixth sense of mothers.

Oh, God! What if Richard remembered now that he had two sons? What if he asked to see the other child and somehow recognised him as Stephen?

She darted a glance at both Richard and the nursemaid, but neither seemed to register the fretful murmur. At least, the nursemaid might have heard it, but it was none of her business, so she didn't react. A most discreet creature, Margaret thought. How on earth had Richard found such a jewel?

The pain was too great. If she must part from her son, let her do it quickly. 'I – It is late,' she said, with less tact than truth.

'Yes, we'll go.' Richard drained his brandy glass, then picked up his hat and gloves from the sideboard.

As he set his hat on his head, he added, 'I'll call again tomorrow afternoon for that, ah, document.'

With her heart pounding so hard she was sure her companions must hear it, Margaret nodded and showed them to the door.

Farewell, little one. We shall meet again soon.

Excerpt from The Trial at Large of Mr Julian Nash, Esq., for Criminal Conversation with the Wife of the Right Honourable Lord Nash His Brother; with the whole Pleadings of the Counsel, *viz.*, Erskine, Garrow, &c.

EVIDENCE FOR THE PLAINTIFF.
MISS MARGARET SMITH, SWORN.
EXAMINED BY MR GARROW.

—

Q. Miss Smith, you were employed as companion to the late dowager?

— *Yes, sir. After Lady Verena died, I stayed on as companion to the Plaintiff's wife Delany, Lady Nash.*

Q. When the events outlined in the writ occurred, were you a member of Lord Nash's household?

— *I was, sir, until the thirtieth of May, when I travelled to Reading to stay with family.*

Q. And have you returned to Lord Nash's household since?

— *No, sir.*

Q. Miss Smith, what is your opinion of the relations between Lord Nash and his wife, Lady Nash?

— *At the beginning, they were devoted to each other. I have rarely seen a more felicitous match.*

Lord Kenyon. We have heard similar encomiums from other witnesses. The happiness of the marriage seems to me to be indisputable. Move along, Mr Garrow.

Q. Miss Smith, when did Mr Julian Nash first become acquainted with Lady Nash?

— *I do not recall. I believe I first saw them together at my mistress's funeral.*

Q. And what did you observe when Mr Nash and Lady Nash were together?

— *I do not understand the question.*

Q. Were their relations amicable, would you say?

— *Oh, yes. They would argue for hours about politics. In the spring, Mr Nash stayed with us in Town and they went everywhere together.*

Q. And were you with them when they went about?

— *Sometimes.*

Q. They went often alone?

— *No, Lady Nash's aunt, Mrs Boddington, or her sister, Mrs Burton, was always with them.*

Q. And where was Lord Nash?

— *Lord Nash was at his estate on the Isle of Wight. He had important business there.*

Q. Did Lord Nash express qualms about leaving his lady in the care of his brother?

— *No, none. He had the utmost trust and confidence in Mr Nash.*

Q. During your sojourn in Town before you left for Reading, did you observe any behaviour between Mr Nash and Lady Nash that might tend to show Lord Nash's confidence had been misplaced?

A pause.

— *Your lordship, must I answer?*

Lord Kenyon. You must give the facts as you know them. Keep to the
   facts and you will have nothing to be ashamed for.

Q. On the night of April the fifteenth, what did you observe?
— *I do not like to say. I left Lady Nash with Mr Nash in the drawing room
   alone. I intended to retire for the evening but I had left my handkerchief
   behind. Upon returning to fetch it I discovered Mr Nash and Lady Nash
   sitting side by side on the sofa.*

Q. Is that all?
— *They were in an intimate embrace.*

Q. I'm afraid I must ask you to be more precise.
— *Mr Nash had his arms around Lady Nash and he was kissing her on the
   mouth.*

Lord Kenyon called for order.

Q. Was there another occasion on which you observed similar
   intimacies?
— *There was but one.*

Q. Do you recall the date?
— *To the best of my recollection, it was the nineteenth of May.*

Q. And what did you observe?
— *I heard voices coming from Lady Nash's bedchamber.*

Q. What time was this?
— *I do not recall. It was after the household had retired. Quite late, I
   think.*

Q. Could you identify the voices?
— *Oh, yes. One was her ladyship. The other, Mr Nash.*

Q. Do you know what they were doing in the bedchamber?
— *I do not know, of course, for I did not see them.*

Q. You heard them.
— *Yes.*

Q. What did you hear?

A pause.

— *I am too ashamed to say. Must I answer?*

Lord Kenyon. Yes, you must answer.

— *I heard moaning and panting, your lordship.*

Q. Indicating that the couple were engaged in intercourse?
— *I know nothing of it.*

Q. One more point as to that evening, if I may. Miss Smith, did you
observe anything about the bedchamber afterwards?
— *I did not. However, the chamber maid described the bedding —*

Lord Kenyon. Yes, thank you. We have heard from that witness.

Cross-examination by Mr ERSKINE.

Q. Miss Smith, were you aware of any prior acquaintance between
Lady Nash and Mr Nash? Before Lord and Lady Nash married,
I mean.

— *I never troubled to inquire.*

Q. Did Lord Nash's marriage seem sudden to you?
— *It is not for me to make judgements on my employer's affairs. I made no observation upon it.*

Q. Miss Smith, when Lady Verena died, you were in a precarious position, were you not?
— *I shouldn't say so. I knew Lord Nash would provide for me.*

Q. Why so certain?
— *He is an honourable gentleman.*

Q. On the evening you heard sounds from her ladyship's bedchamber, why were you there?
— *Her baby was ill. I came to inform her ladyship.*

Q. She is devoted to her children?
— *Yes. But on that occasion —*

Q. Thank you, Miss Smith. Would you say you are on good terms with Lady Nash?
— *Of course.*

Q. Did you know that if his lordship succeeds in proving his case, he is a step closer to obtaining a divorce from his wife, should he wish to do so?
— *I've given no thought to it.*

Q. I suggest to you that you found yourself in a precarious position when Lady Verena died. Lady Nash is not in her dotage, far from it. She had no need of a companion. Your continued position in the household is in truth at Lord Nash's insistence, is it not?

— *No. I am employed as companion to Lady Nash.*

Q. Miss Smith, I put it to you that you have a fancy to become the next
Lady Nash upon Lord Nash procuring a divorce, as would be his
next step if successful in this trial. That you are lying to this court
about the events you witnessed. Moreover —

— *No!*

Q. *Moreover*, Miss Smith, I put it to you that you agreed to give false
testimony against Mr Nash in return for Lord Nash's continued
protection. That from the moment Lady Verena left the Defendant
her fortune, you have schemed with the Plaintiff to take
possession of that fortune, by fair means or foul.

— *I have not lied. Certainly not. It is with the greatest reluctance that
I have appeared here today . . . My lord, I must beg to be excused.*

Lord Kenyon. You are excused.

Delany, Lady Nash

Margaret's testimony left me reeling.

I tried not to care about the stares and lewd remarks of the men
around me. Who were they to me? But the press of bodies, the ocean of
leering faces, made me tremble with fear. There was something preda-
tory about this crowd, as if once the trial was over they would descend
upon me *en masse*. Once a woman lost her reputation, she was fair
game for any man.

Attending here today had been necessary, but not wise. Mr Erskine
had counselled against it, warning me that I had no notion what sorts
of inquiries and suggestions might be made.

I'd believed the truth would safeguard me, that counsel might ask the questions but there was nothing damaging to tell. How could I have known that Margaret, of all people, strait-laced, mealy-mouthed Margaret Smith, would utter so many shocking, bare-faced lies before God, judge and special jury? Richard must have bribed Betsy besides.

As Margaret made her way out of the court, I was too stunned to move. My mind was blank. I did not recall until much later that I'd intended to follow her, that begging her to bring my children back to me had been my primary reason for appearing here today.

When my dearest Jane took the stand to give evidence for Richard, I felt it as a dagger to my stomach. Struggling to breathe through the pain of betrayal, I forced myself to remain impassive. I would not give in to my emotions. I must not let them see how her defection pained me. Richard was her employer, after all. She had no choice but to testify on his behalf.

They went through the palaver with the swearing in. At the judge's insistence – it was close to the day's end and no one wished to be obliged to return tomorrow – Mr Garrow came straight to the point.

'Miss Long, you have been Lady Nash's personal maid since she was a girl, have you not?'

'Aye,' said Jane. 'And her nurse before that.'

'You know her well.'

'As well as any servant might.'

Mr Garrow extracted a document from his papers and held it out to the bailiff. 'Will you look at this document, please, Miss Long? What is it?'

Jane took the paper from the bailiff, who handed it up to her. She barely glanced at it before saying, 'It is the beginning of a letter, sir, from my mistress to Mr Nash.'

Mr Garrow folded his arms and tucked his hands into his sleeves. 'How did you come by it?'

'I discovered it in my lady's escritoire.'

'Does it bear a date?'

'No, sir.'

Mr Garrow glanced at the jury. 'Will you read it aloud so that the court can hear?'

Jane swallowed. I thought for a moment that she would refuse. But she raised the paper and read:

My dear Julian,

Forgive me. There is much to say, and my usual concision deserts me at times of great emotion.

You tell me you love me. But what is love to a man but a temporary affliction? A mixture of desire and admiration that ignites, hot and bright as a firework, only to fizzle and fade.

I am a pragmatist. In my lucid moments, I cannot but believe that my love will long outlive yours. I cannot bear the thought of it.

And yet, when I was with you yesterday at Mouse's picnic, a madness overtook me. At such times, I think it would be worth all the heartache to be with you, body and soul, for as long as the fire of your passion burns.

Jane looked up. 'The letter ends there.'

'It is unfinished and unsigned. How do you know your mistress wrote it?'

'I recognise her hand,' said Jane.

I felt the weight of regard upon me. Even the stuffy old judge stared and stared. Was I blushing? Good God, what on earth must Julian think of me now? I'd never have actually sent such mawkish nonsense to him. That letter ought to have been burned.

Jane's distress showed in the rigidity of her pose, the wooden quality of her answers. Poor Jane. She must be suffering several shades of torment.

Then I remembered something. The letter was undated, but I knew precisely when I'd written it: after the picnic at Richmond, when Julian had kissed me.

I took out my little notebook and scribbled on it frantically, tore out the page and waited for Mr Erskine or one of his minions to turn around.

None of them did. They conferred together, shuffling papers and doing nothing to the purpose. In the end, I was obliged to march up to them and tap Mr Erskine on the shoulder.

Irritation twitched his beetling brows together when he saw who accosted him but he took my note. In a low voice, he said, 'You cannot give evidence, my lady. It is immaterial that *you* know when the letter was writ if your maid does not.'

Frustrated, fuming, aware that all eyes were upon me, I thought quickly.

'Mouse,' I said. 'The letter speaks of Mouse's picnic. That was Mrs Townsend's picnic in the summer of '87. *Before* I married Lord Nash.'

'One must assume, however, that it was not the only picnic Mrs Townsend hosted,' said Erskine. 'It is imprecise.'

Lord Kenyon rumbled. 'Mr Erskine, we are waiting for you to cross-examine the witness.'

'Yes, my lord.' Mr Erskine bowed and turned back to the bar table.

In desperation, I tugged on his gown, but he ignored me.

Lord Kenyon said, 'I believe I warned you about this, Lady Nash. Sit down.'

I couldn't bear to be ejected from court at this juncture, so there was nothing for it but to obey. I wanted to scream in frustration.

I'm not sure why it mattered so much to me. They had sufficient from Margaret's testimony with which to convict Julian. Quibbling about when I had written that letter would make little difference.

However, to his credit, Mr Erskine followed that line of questioning. 'Miss Long,' he said to Jane, 'the letter you read out is undated.'

'Yes, sir.'

'Have you any notion when it was written?'

'No, sir. At least, I never thought about it.'

Erskine fingered the watch chain on his waistcoat. 'The letter mentions that Mouse's picnic took place the day before the letter was written. Who is Mouse?'

Jane frowned. 'I believe it was Lady Nash's nickname for a friend of hers, a Mrs Townsend, sir.'

Mr Erskine said, 'Does that aid your recollection?'

Jane straightened, a light kindling in her eye. 'Indeed, sir, it does. For Mr Townsend sold their house at Richmond soon afterwards, and moved to Bath, and there were no more picnics after that.'

'Was this before your mistress married Lord Nash?'

'Yes, sir.'

'And had your mistress known Mr Julian Nash for very long at the time of that picnic?'

'My lady first met Mr Nash in the winter of 1787, sir.'

'I have nothing further, my lord.' As Mr Erskine sat down, he shot me a glance brimful of triumph beneath his heavy brows.

Hope surged inside me. I no longer had the least hope of salving my reputation but I trusted we might yet thwart Richard's fell purpose – and, most importantly of all, save Julian.

Had I known the line of argument this latest development had inspired in Mr Erskine's mind, however, I would not have been so optimistic.

CHAPTER SEVENTEEN

Mr Erskine called witnesses attesting to my sterling character, that, to their observation, nothing untoward had ever occurred between Julian and me, and that Lady Verena had left a large fortune to Julian, the amount of which happened to coincide with the amount of the plaintiff's claim.

All very well, but one could not prove a negative. While several trusted servants reported having seen no misconduct on my part, that scarcely weighed in the balance against Margaret's damning evidence, ably seconded by the chamber maid.

I sensed the audience becoming restless during this accumulation of benign testimony, and indeed, after sitting so long on the hard pew, my own arse had all but fallen asleep. However, the assembly was in for a treat when Mr Erskine made his closing speech.

How skilfully he wove the disparate threads of evidence to form a narrative tapestry! With what poise did he enumerate the merits of Julian's case, and annihilate the arguments of the other side!

In writing this account, I have used the report of the trial to aid my memory, but mere printed words – so bland and dry in the reports themselves – fail to capture the mood in that court room as he spoke.

The atmosphere was electric, as if holding its breath before unleashing a storm. Indeed, the room had darkened as clouds rolled overhead, shrouding the sun and throwing the court room into darkness.

Through the gloom, all eyes focused on Erskine. His white collar and bands gleamed; his teeth flashed. Though he was not above average height, his presence was wholly commanding. Such was the strange fascination of the man.

'My lord,' he said, when he had allowed a pause for dramatic effect, 'I should be loath to condone or palliate the offence with which the defendant is charged. To violate the trust and confidence reposed in him by so near a relation is a matter of the most serious consequence. The charge is a shocking one, indeed – so shocking, and so contrary to the manners and morals of our country, that without the strictest and most positive evidence of his guilt, the defendant ought to be acquitted.'

A fine beginning, but Margaret had given the jury a surfeit of evidence, surely, from which to infer guilt. Erskine had done his best to cast doubt on that testimony. Would that be enough?

Counsel for the defence swept his arm in a graceful arc. 'As to the plaintiff's case, it rests on the evidence of two witnesses. One who might well be mistaken. Another whose motives and reliability must be closely and thoroughly examined.

'The maid saw but one thing.' Erskine raised his index finger and shook it for emphasis. 'A bed that had been slept in on both sides. There might be any number of explanations for this circumstance – including . . .' here, he set his doubled fist on the bar table and leaned toward the jury, '. . . *contrivance by a third party*.'

I glanced upward, fully expecting a bolt of lightning to punctuate this statement. None came, but the graven images of kings seemed to glower down at me from their sconces in the wall.

With a flourish, Erskine continued in a more moderate tone. 'But let us be generous. The maid is most probably mistaken. She says she came to make up her mistress's bed the morning following the incident in question and found it had been slept in on both sides. She made no *other* observations on the state of the linen, which she was in every position to do, being the person employed to make up that bed . . .'

Here, there were murmurs and a few jocular remarks from the audience. Mr Erskine waited for them to subside before he continued. 'Thus, the evidence of the maid may be disregarded.'

Erskine held the jury in the palm of his hand. Looking back, the performance was almost ridiculous in its theatricality. Yet, at the time, even I, who possessed first-hand knowledge of the truth, was spellbound.

'If the evidence of Miss Margaret Smith, the companion, is true,' said Erskine, 'then you must convict. However, we have uncovered here today a most diabolical plot, perpetrated by three clever people to defraud the defendant of his inheritance.'

I straightened. Three people? *Three?* What nonsense was this?

'As one of the defendant's friends of long standing attested, the plaintiff, Lord Nash, has always been jealous of his younger brother. In the winter of 1787, Mr Julian Nash had the infinite misfortune to meet and fall in love with one Delany Rothwell, as the plaintiff's wife then was.'

Erskine made one of his sweeping gestures – this time toward *me*. 'Ah, but Miss Rothwell hunted bigger game, did she not? She set her sights on wedding Lord Nash.'

I sucked in a breath. Of course, everyone stared at me. I suffered Erskine's words as someone in the stocks must suffer the mud and refuse flung at them – powerless to defend myself. The one saving grace was that my hat shielded my expression from all but a few.

Oh, dear God, what a fool I'd been! Had Erskine not warned me it was not his role to safeguard my interests? Had he not recommended I stay away from the trial?

Heart pounding in my chest, I was torn between a longing to escape and a desperate need to hear in what manner I was to be slandered. The effort of maintaining my cool demeanour nearly broke me, but I was determined not to crack now.

Erskine went on. 'Like a spoiled child, Lord Nash was forever snatching away what his younger brother had, even if he himself did not truly desire the thing. On this occasion, the prize was Mistress Rothwell, with whom Mr Nash was deeply in love. In this, Lord Nash, with his superior wealth and position, succeeded.' The advocate spread his hands. 'But was that enough for the plaintiff? No! When Lady Verena, the parties' mother, left Mr Julian Nash a fortune, the plaintiff was livid that he had been overlooked.'

Amid the buzz of conversation in the court room, Mr Erskine raised his voice to a thunderous pitch. 'Between them, Lord and Lady Nash and Miss Smith concocted a cold-blooded scheme to cheat Mr Nash out of £20 000. Indeed, it is no coincidence that the amount claimed on the writ is the precise sum Lady Verena bequeathed to Mr Nash.'

These statements caused an uproar. Lord Kenyon called the court to order several times before Mr Erskine could proceed.

Gently, but with deep resonance, Mr Erskine continued, 'Whether or not the act of criminal intercourse itself occurred – I leave the gentlemen of the jury to weigh the evidence.'

He fixed the said gentlemen with his dark, intense gaze. 'If you decide the act *did* occur – whether once or on successive occasions as alleged – then the amount of damages must be determined. It is well established that a husband who colludes in his own cuckolding is not entitled to compensation for it. Yet, even if he had not orchestrated this entire, shocking affair, Lord Nash is not entitled to damages.

'Mr Julian Nash did not insinuate himself between a loving, happy couple and seduce his brother's wife away. We may see from the letter read out by my lady's maid that Mr Nash loved Miss Delany Rothwell and she returned his affection long before Lord Nash stole her out from under the defendant's nose. If anyone is entitled to compensation, it is Mr Julian Nash, who was forced to relinquish great love and future happiness to his brother's jealousy and spite.'

For perhaps a minute at the conclusion of this impassioned address, you could have heard a pin drop in that crowded place.

Then pandemonium broke out. What deliciously scandalous entertainment! It was better than a play. I wondered how I would make my escape from this place without being molested by the mob.

But that was a question for later. The judge summed up, clearly so swayed by Erskine's oratory that his lordship practically directed the jury's findings in the defendant's favour.

The question of whether the 'act' had occurred, however, did not seem to be in serious doubt. I realised then that once Margaret had given her evidence, Erskine knew that part of the cause was lost. He changed tack accordingly.

To me, the verdict was everything. A finding that Julian was innocent would, I hoped, leave my reputation tarnished but intact. A finding of guilty and it would be smashed to smithereens.

By contrast, Erskine would consider the case won if he could limit the amount of compensation his client had to pay for his transgression.

The jury huddled together to deliberate.

By now, everyone seemed to have surged to their feet, milling about while the jury considered their verdict. I was in such a daze as my world crashed down around me, and there was such noise in that court room, that I did not at first notice Julian, trying in vain to reach me through the crowd.

Over the heads of other men, he shouted something to me. He might have been mouthing the words for all I could hear of them. Yet his expression communicated far more than words ever could. I realised that in that unsent letter Jane had read out in such wooden tones, I'd said what I'd never told a living soul, including Julian himself.

What more proof could I need of his constancy and affection, than when his livelihood and independence hung in the balance in this court room, all he thought about was me and the message of love contained in that unsent letter from long ago?

'Delany!' He elbowed his way towards me, ruthlessly thrusting men out of his path. 'We must get you away from here.' He held out his hand to me, clearly expecting compliance, oblivious of the prurient interest surrounding us.

'Are you mad?' I yelled back. 'People are staring. Julian, you must go. Call on me afterwards at Lavinia's house.'

'You'll be eaten alive,' he shouted.

I shook my head, refusing his help. Whatever the verdict, I *must* think of my children. I must maintain my innocence, both of this plot Mr Erskine had outlined, and of any wrongdoing with Julian.

Of course, I wasn't stupid enough to think society would believe me, not after the revelations of today. But I trusted that if I continued to protest my innocence and remained scrupulously careful of my virtue from that day on, at least my family and close friends would not shun me.

Above all, I must find Margaret and beg her to tell me where my children were.

A bare fifteen minutes later, the members of the jury expressed themselves in agreement.

His lordship demanded their verdict and a solid-looking citizen in a brown coat stood up.

'Not guilty,' pronounced the solid citizen.

The court room erupted into chaos.

The triumph of that moment cannot well be described. Julian's supporters raised a great whooping cheer. I was elated, my head full of possibility for the first time since my eviction.

However, the reality of my situation was brought home to me almost at once. As I skirted the court room in an attempt to avoid Julian, several unpleasant individuals accosted me.

One woman called me whore and spat at my feet. A man clutched himself and made a suggestion I did not understand, but I could well infer the meaning. Had it not been for the large man I had displaced from his seat earlier that morning knocking heads and shouldering through the crowd to clear my path, I believe I might have been injured. I bestowed another coin upon him and expressed my gratitude once we were safely out of the fray.

I was badly jostled and bruised by the time I hailed a hackney to take me home. Despite the jury's finding, the world had judged me guilty. I ought to have been prepared for that.

Richard had not succeeded in the court room but he had succeeded in ruining me.

Deep down, I'd known the verdict would not save me. After Margaret's testimony – good Lord, who had known she was so skilled an actress? – no one would judge me innocent. The verdict was intended as a slap in the face to Richard for his scheming, not vindication for me.

Now, half the world believed I had colluded in my husband's scheme. Not only was I a whore, but a clever, scheming whore to boot. Was there a more contemptible species in the world?

Thank God for Lavinia, I thought, and dear Mr Burton.

I found my sister in her sitting room, sewing. Like me, she was an adept needlewoman, and stitched the tiny garments for the baby she expected with swift skill.

Her happiness ought to be complete now that she was to be a mother. The disconsolate droop of her mouth said otherwise, but I did not feel adequate to a conversation about the latest gimcrack she wanted and was not permitted to buy.

'Have you heard?' I said, going over to her and dropping a kiss on her brow. 'We won.'

Delight broke over her face. 'Oh, Delany, that's marvellous! Will you go back home now?'

I stared at her. Had Lavinia no common sense at all? 'Tired of my company, sister?' I said it lightly, but the notion troubled me. Had I outworn my welcome?

Mr Burton emerged from his book room, looking grave, and

suddenly realisation clicked into place. Ought I to pretend I did not know what that expression portended? Undignified to protest the injustice, of course. Why stoop to defend myself when no one would listen? Yet how it pained me to have a man I respected believe so ill of me.

Blast it, I *would* defend myself. 'It was all lies, you know. Truly, I am innocent.'

He gave a curt nod, but his tension did not ease.

Very well. There seemed nothing for it but to give in gracefully. I knew then what I must do. I looked away to hide my distress, saying airily to Lavinia, 'I believe I shall hie me to St Alban's. Aunt Boddington is due for a visit.'

Silence. I turned and caught Lavinia exchanging a glance with her husband. They'd discussed the matter already, it seemed.

My sister said, 'You had best read our aunt's letter, I think.'

She made as if to retrieve it from her escritoire but I held up my hand to stop her. I pressed my other hand to my stomach, as if to hold myself together. 'No, don't. I don't want to read it.'

Without a word, I went up to my bedchamber to pack. A trunk and a valise stood ready and waiting at the foot of my bed. How thoughtful.

I would have given anything to avoid further conversation with my sister, but hard on my heels there came a scratch on the door.

When she slipped inside the room, I said, 'Lavinia, you don't have to —'

She burst out, 'Delany, you must understand how impossible it would be for me to continue our association, now that you are . . .' She gestured helplessly.

'Branded a whore?' I supplied. 'My dear sister, you needn't explain. If I remain here, you will be tarred with the same brush, guilty by association. Mr Burton has persuaded you to forsake me to save your own fair name.'

'Burtie wishes it were otherwise,' said Lavinia. She hesitated. 'He says you are to take all the gowns and such that you need.' Of course it would never do to offer the thing I chiefly needed – money – and I could never accept outright financial assistance. While staying with my sister I had managed to earn a small amount from writing poetry and songs but I feared my savings would not sustain me for long.

I bowed my head and accepted my sister's cast-offs, but oh, how I longed to refuse them! Practicality won out over pride, however. What on earth would I wear if I did not take them? The *chemise à la Reine* that I'd worn to Lavinia's house on the day of my banishment was as flimsy as a butterfly's wings. It would be poor covering come winter.

Some remnant of dignity came to my rescue. If nothing else, I would look my sister in the eye. 'It is best if we do not see each other again. At least, not until the talk dies down.'

She agreed with more alacrity than tact. Perhaps she'd been wondering how to broach the subject. Well, it had ever been my mission in life to ease her path.

I considered applying to Selby for help. However, it is a curious phenomenon that often those men who are the most deeply steeped in vice are the most judgemental of their womenfolk. Most likely, my brother would box my ears for bringing scandal on the family name. And what assistance could he be, after all? He was never in funds, nor was he in the habit of providing sage counsel.

No, I must strike out on my own. There was a cheap boarding house in Kensington where one or two ladies of my acquaintance conducted their illicit liaisons. I'd try my luck there. Most would say it was my proper milieu, after all.

Suddenly, I wished that I had been *that* sort of woman. At least I would have had the amusement for which I now bore the shame. At least I would have had Julian for a time.

When I had composed myself, I rang for a maid to help me pack. To my surprise, it was Jane who came. Dear, loyal Jane, beside herself with anxiety over her part in the trial.

I said to her, 'You had no choice. I know what it is to be at the mercy of such a man. I must suppose he is in a rare taking about the verdict.'

Jane shook out a petticoat and folded it with trembling hands. 'He dismissed me, my lady. Turned me off without a character. Said I should have kept my mouth shut about the date of that letter.'

I was no longer surprised by the depths to which Richard might stoop. 'Lavinia will give you a place until I can send for you,' I said. 'I will insist upon it.'

'No, my lady. I go with you and that's flat.'

Lavinia would have pulled a maid's hair for such insubordination. I could only blink back tears. My meagre funds would run out soon enough. They'd scarcely keep me, much less a servant.

'I cannot afford to take you with me, Jane. And before you say it, I will not suffer you to share in my misfortune. I shall come about, but until I do, I need to be on my own. It will be a comfort to me to know that you are here.' I tried to smile. 'Perhaps you might bring me news now and then.'

My dear, faithful maid finished packing my trunk and my valise.

When she tried one final time to persuade me to take her with me, I snapped at her, and nearly broke at the unaccustomed pain in her expression. 'One day, Jane . . .' My voice cracked and I couldn't go on.

The knocker on the front door pounded. Even before I glanced out the window, I knew who it would be. 'Quick!' I clutched Jane's arm. 'Tell the porter to deny me.'

Too late. The front door opened and I saw him disappear inside.

I bit my lip. 'The garden, then. Will you . . .?'

Jane was gone on the words.

I went to the looking-glass and gazed into it. I picked up the silver-backed, monogrammed brush Lavinia had lent me and passed it slowly through the fat ringlet that spiralled to my clavicle. As one in a dream, I set the brush down and surveyed the rest of myself critically.

How odd. Not a pin out of place. Yet I felt thoroughly trampled.

I found Julian pacing the terrace, his hands clasped together behind his back. When he saw me, his features lightened a fraction and he started toward me. Stopping short, he frowned. 'What is it?'

Blast and damn. 'What is what?'

'You appear distressed, Rothwell.'

I gave a snort. 'I am hardly likely to be dancing a jig, am I?'

'No, it's something . . . Something's happened since I saw you last.'

'I cannot think what you mean, sir.' I forced myself to smile at him. 'You ought to be out celebrating.'

He caught at my hands. 'Delany, you —'

'Don't.' I pulled away, squeezed my eyes shut. This was even more excruciating than I'd imagined. I had nowhere to go. The thought of seeking shelter with Julian tempted me almost beyond reason.

'I cannot see you,' I said in a stifled voice. 'This must be the last time.'

He waited.

'My children. My boys. I have not – *can*not – give up hope of seeing them again. If I go with you . . .'

'Who said anything about going with me?' he demanded.

I smothered a gasp. Dear God, I'd nearly betrayed myself. If he knew Lavinia was casting me out he'd sweep me away this moment to take care of me.

The notion was so tantalising that I lashed out. 'There is no understanding between us. Do not pretend that there is.'

I turned from him, gazing out over the ordered prettiness of my sister's garden. Why couldn't I stay here? Why did my choices always have to be so hard?

'Delany.' His voice shimmered down my spine. I clenched my fists tightly.

He stood very close to me now, so close that I could scarcely breathe for longing, remembering with pinpoint clarity that kiss we'd shared so long ago. I made myself rigid and unyielding, fighting the urge to turn into his warmth.

His voice, so rich and caressing, deepened. 'In that letter, you said you loved me.'

'I was young and foolish.'

'You love me still.' Julian's breath whispered over my nape. His hands settled on my shoulders, then slid to my arms. He turned me to face him and the depth of emotion in his dark eyes stripped my pretence away.

'I *do* love you,' I said, my voice trembling. 'It's true. But my love for my children is . . .' Tears filled my eyes. Could he ever understand? 'I think about them every minute of the day. I wonder if they are warm, if they are hungry, if they are well tended, if their keepers are kind. I am afraid for them, Julian, constantly afraid.'

His grip on my arm firmed with purpose. 'We will find them, Delany. I promise you.'

'And if we do? What then?' I shook my head. 'There is no earthly means by which I might keep them.'

'We would take them away with us,' he said. 'To Austria, to Italy.'

But if we did that, none of us could set foot in England again as long as Richard was alive. Julian would give up everything he'd worked for. The powerless and downtrodden depended on his fighting for them. He was a man with a brilliant future, with much good to contribute to the world.

'I can't abide foreigners,' I said pettishly, pulling away.

'Be serious, love.'

I bit my lip and shook my head. 'It's impossible, Julian. You must see that.'

His face seemed to age before my eyes, as finally he comprehended. 'You will go back to him.'

'I must try.'

Though it would kill me a little each day to subject myself to Richard's rule, if I could but see my sons again, have them with me, it would be worth any sacrifice. But to win back my place at Richard's side, I must remain above reproach. I must never see Julian again.

'Please . . .' I whispered, my fingertips brushing his arm. 'Please understand.'

Lavinia chose that moment to fly out to the terrace, wrapping her shawl around her. 'Good God, Delany! What can you be about to have him here?'

'Go,' I whispered to Julian. 'You must go.'

Julian's face froze. His lips parted as if he would say something. Then he turned on his heel and strode away.

No. We would not end like this. I started after him but Lavinia caught my arm in a vicious grip. 'What are you doing? Are you mad? Have you *no* consideration for what people will say if they know you met with him here, under *my* roof?'

I stared at her. My world had crashed about my ears. I'd lost my children, my home, I'd given up the man I loved for the second time and she was concerned for a bit of *gossip*?

'Go to the devil, Lavinia,' I said, and wrenched myself from her grasp.

CHAPTER EIGHTEEN

Liz

The morning after the Open Day, Liz did not go for her usual run. She woke with a splitting head, which she hadn't drunk nearly enough to deserve. Then reality hit her.

In one night, she'd lost her job, her friends, the man she — Theo. In short, she'd lost her future. Now she had to get herself away from here fast, back to Australia. Take a job in a legal firm, or at another company as in-house lawyer, where she'd have to prove herself all over again.

Only this time, her heart wasn't in it.

Liz felt like a balloon cut adrift. Not a kid's balloon, all happy and light. One of those cumbersome hot-air balloons, with a heavy load in its basket, an incompetent pilot and nowhere to go.

A knock on the door and the muffled sound of Gemma's voice reached her. She took a few seconds to steady herself, then went to open it. She grimaced. 'Hi. Wasn't sure you'd still be talking to me after last night.'

'I'm not sure why I am, but I'm here.' Gemma walked past her to perch on the four-poster bed. 'Maddie wants to see you. I needed to come up first.'

Gemma's eyes still smouldered with resentment. Liz couldn't blame her.

'Look, I don't deserve forgiveness,' Liz said. 'I just wanted you to know that all the good things were real. I love Seagrove. Once I got to know you all, the reason I was meant to be here seemed not to matter any more. I was going to stay. I was going to quit my job and tell Nick to go to hell and help you raise the money to keep this place afloat.'

Gemma's mouth turned wry. 'I *want* to believe you. It's just hard.'

Hard to forgive. Yes. Liz supposed it might well be impossible, particularly for Theo.

She tried to smile. 'It shouldn't really matter, should it? I mean, I'll probably never see any of you again now. But if you can ever bring yourself to forgive me, would you drop me a line? It would mean a lot to me.'

'I can forgive you right now on my own account, for what it's worth,' said Gemma. 'But it's not easy to forgive what you've done to Theo. He doesn't deserve that, Liz.'

'No, you're right.' She hadn't meant for things to get so complicated with Theo. She hadn't meant to become so deeply attached to the house and the people here. It had just happened. 'I wish to God I could go back and change it all but I can't,' she said.

She wasn't going to cry, was she? Quickly, she turned to open the wardrobe, trying to compose herself. She reached in and yanked a dress off its hanger.

A hand touched her shoulder. Liz paused, the black dress she'd worn to Raoul's cocktail party dripping from her arm. She sniffed.

'Oh, darling,' said Gemma. 'Don't cry.'

'No, don't,' said Liz. Waving Gemma off, she slipped past her and hurried to the bed, rolling up the cocktail dress and shoving it in her bag. 'Don't be kind. I don't deserve it. And you'll just set me off again.'

There was a pause. Then Gemma said, 'Okay, then. Tough-love time. If you really want my forgiveness, you need to go to Theo and tell him how you feel about him before you leave.'

That was the last thing she wanted to do. Give him her heart so he could throw it on the ground and wipe his boots on it.

'What would that achieve?' Liz said bitterly. 'He thinks I'm a liar. He won't believe me.'

'Maybe not. But you need to say it and he needs to hear it,' said Gemma.

Liz fiddled with the zipper on her backpack. She'd asked for penance and this was what she'd been given. The promise of forgiveness from Gemma, at least, was a powerful motivator.

She blew out a long breath. 'Okay. Yes. I'll do it.'

There was a knock on the door, then Maddie came in, carrying a set of three loom bands. 'I made these for you.' Gemma must have told her Liz was leaving, but from Maddie's open expression, Liz concluded that her aunt hadn't told her why.

With a watery smile at Maddie, Liz slid the bands onto her wrist. All different colours and patterns, they clashed beautifully. Maddie got her sense of style from her aunt. 'Thank you, Mads. That's brilliant.'

She hugged the girl and kissed her cheek. She smelled of shampoo and milk. 'Be good to your dad for me,' she whispered.

'I'm always good to him,' said Maddie.

When she was all packed and the others had gone, Liz picked up the case that held the silver rattle. She'd keep her promise to Gemma. She'd return this to Theo in person and tell him how she felt.

Her heart beating hard, she contacted Theo on the walkie-talkie one last time. 'Where are you?'

There was a long pause. She wondered if she'd lost contact. At last, 'South America,' came the reply.

She found him trimming back bougainvillaea, a shower of thorny canes and deep pink blossoms around his feet.

'Hi,' she said.

He shut his clippers and laid them in the wheelbarrow.

'Hi.' He met her eyes, then quickly transferred his frowning gaze into the middle distance, as if he couldn't look at her. His jaw was tight. She saw the convulsive movement in his throat when he swallowed.

'I'm so, so sorry . . .' she said. 'I've ruined everything.'

But she'd apologised last night and it had sounded hollow then. It wouldn't carry any more weight with him now. Better to get it over with. She'd keep her promise to Gemma and be done.

She stared up at him, at the sunlight glinting in the gold streaks of his hair, at the hurt buried in the depths of his green eyes. The breeze stiffened. The bougainvillea canes ruffled and swayed like flamenco dancers. She stood with the man she — with Theo in this paradise, a place she'd felt so strongly that she belonged, and tried to summon the courage to tell him how she felt.

Every stupid impulse, every beat of her heart, urged her to fight for him, to stay and to strive to win back his trust.

'Theo, I . . .' Her voice faltered, then seized up. Damn Gemma! She couldn't have prescribed a worse punishment.

Liz cleared her throat. 'Before I go, I wanted you to know that I . . . I care about you. Very much.'

His gaze snapped back to her.

'At least,' she hurried on, scarcely able to force herself to meet his eyes, 'I think I might have . . . have loved you if we'd had a chance to be together . . . I don't know.' She shrugged. 'Maybe.'

Lame, Liz! She heard the sing-song of Gemma's voice in her head. But truly, it was the best she could do. Hardly the kind of declaration that would make him sweep her into his arms and tell her all was for-given, but it was the truth.

He came alive then. 'And what am I supposed to do with that, Liz? What do you want me to say? You lied to me for weeks and now I'm supposed to believe you when you say you might, sort of, maybe, love me? How do I know what to believe?' His voice roughened. 'I believed Valerie and look how that turned out.'

That was like a punch to the kidneys. Liz couldn't breathe for a moment, winded by the comparison.

She wanted to tell him there *was* no comparison, that she might have begun with lies but they'd all fallen away long ago, like dead leaves in autumn.

Yet even she, who'd lived the lie, couldn't tell where pretence left off and truth began. Only that she must almost love him, because this conversation was killing her. Leaving him was killing her. The future that stretched before her would be a wasteland compared with what she might have had with him.

'Yes. No. You're right,' she said, turning the box she held in her hands. The infinitesimal hope that he might forgive her here and now, beg her not to go, fizzled to nothing.

It seemed unjust that he'd been so amazingly tolerant of all Valerie's faults for so long and yet he was so hard and unforgiving toward Liz. Perhaps it was because he cared more this time. She hoped so, and then got mad at herself for hoping it, because it was all over now and she was almost gone.

She tried to smile but it was a weak effort. She remembered the rattle, then realised this wasn't the appropriate place to return it to him anyway.

She held up the box. 'I'll put this back in your study before I go.'

He nodded. 'Right. Thanks.'

'Goodbye.' On impulse, she placed her hand on his shoulder and went on tiptoes to kiss his cheek. He was rigid, unyielding, but she couldn't seem to stop herself lingering there, with her lips against the brush of stubble on his high cheekbone, breathing in his masculine scent.

He drew a ragged breath. 'Liz —'

'Take care of yourself,' she whispered, before he had a chance to reject her verbally as well as physically. The faint tinkle of the rattle sounded as she turned and walked away.

She couldn't bring herself to confide in Gemma about what had happened between her and Theo, not even in the hope of her friend's promised forgiveness. Gemma's demand might have prompted Liz to go to him, but that hadn't been the reason she'd told him her feelings. She'd told him because she hoped he'd come to believe it for his own sake. With distance and time he might not feel as if he'd been a fool to place his trust in yet another deceitful, conniving woman.

The thought that in his eyes she was no better than Valerie – worse, in fact – hurt more than she'd thought possible.

After she'd said her stilted farewells, Liz went out to wait for her taxi. She hoped she wouldn't have to wait too long. Standing alone on the drive outside the quiet house, her sense of being an outcast sharpened.

About ten minutes passed before the drone of a car engine and the crunch of tyres on gravel reached her ears. Relieved, she grabbed her bags and stared up the avenue.

The car that approached was far too expensive-looking to be a taxi. A blue Aston Martin zoomed out of the trees, swung around the fountain and came to a stop beside her.

Ordinarily, she would have laughed at Nick's absurd flamboyance, but today she could barely raise a smile. 'What are you doing here?' she said. She thought he'd never speak to her again after last night.

He got out and came around to get her bags. 'I heard you were leaving so I cancelled your taxi. Thought I'd give you a lift while we debrief.' He stopped when saw her face. 'Christ, you look awful.'

'Gee, thanks.'

'Yolande's left me, if that's any consolation,' he added, as if it wasn't a complete non sequitur. 'Ran off with a Swiss banker she met in Cannes.'

Liz was still trying to understand Nick's attitude towards her. She'd thought he'd accept her resignation gladly after the debacle at the bonfire. She'd told him in no uncertain terms where her loyalties lay. And as for Yolande —

'Travelling light, I see,' Nick said, grabbing her backpack and tossing it into the trunk to join several Louis Vuitton cases. 'Have I taught you nothing, Jones?'

And it was such a relief, after the absolute mess she'd made of everything else, that Nick was still talking to her, already letting bygones be bygones, when her attempts at making amends with Theo and Gemma had foundered.

'Who are we today? James Bond?' she said, trying to match his mood. She wedged herself into the car beside him and settled her handbag on her lap.

'Why not?' He shoved on his sunglasses and grinned at her as they sped away.

It was a glorious summer's day and Nick had left the top down. Hedgerows and fields whizzed by in a green blur, and Liz wished she had one of those gorgeous scarves she could tie around her head, Grace Kelly style. Tendrils of hair kept plastering themselves over her mouth and whipping into her eyes.

'I assume you're coming back to work now,' Nick yelled over the noise of the motor and the wind, shifting gears with the expert precision of a racing-car driver.

'You should be so lucky.' The sassy quip was instinctive and completely without foundation, since she'd failed to achieve the objectives of her Seagrove visit and was feeling very fortunate to have kept her job. Particularly considering she'd resigned the night before.

However, she knew Nick had no time for losers and whiners, and she wasn't surprised when he laughed. 'I have big plans for us, Jones. Just you wait and see.'

It came to her then that Nick, too, might be relieved if she didn't leave the company after all. That he would miss her – and her work ethic – if she left.

She realised how much she'd envied Nick over the years. His success in business, his no-strings lifestyle, his work-hard, play-hard attitude. That was what she'd hankered after. That was why Tony's neediness had always made her a little claustrophobic. More than a little, in fact.

That was what she could have, if she worked hard and grabbed opportunities when they were offered. There would be other chances to prove herself besides the Seagrove deal. She could stay single, please herself always, be successful, charmingly ruthless – in business and in her personal life. She could be the female version of Nick.

'How big are these plans?' she said to him now. 'I might have big plans of my own.'

He raised an eyebrow. 'Are you saying I can't tempt you?'

She shrugged. 'It would take a lot.'

He laughed, as a startled pheasant shot up from the hedgerow, flapping madly into the trees. 'Come on, Jones. Name your price.'

Liz had arrived home to a space empty of Tony, in every sense. She didn't know when he'd returned from Thailand, but he'd been in Brisbane long enough to clear out his things.

Their house, with its overgrown yard and white paling fence, seemed tiny to her. Well, of course it would, after Seagrove. How could it match the scale and grandeur of Lord Nash's country estate?

Without much ado, she and Tony cancelled all their orders for the renovation and put the house up for sale. The younger couple who'd bought the Queenslander as their first home were all shiny in their new love and bubbling with plans of their own. She hoped they'd give the house the love the old lady deserved.

'Are you okay?' she'd asked Tony when the sale went through. Truthfully, she'd thought all of this would hurt a lot more than it did. Tony was like a stranger to her now, a passing acquaintance, someone from another life.

'Yeah,' he said, scarcely hiding his enthusiasm as they left their solicitor's office. 'Better than okay, really. Leanne and I are moving in together.'

Gently, Liz cut him off before he could hike too far down that track. She'd wanted to keep it civilised, but she was only human, after all. She tried to be happy for him but she was torn between envy and relief. At least Tony's happy ending meant she had one less thing to feel guilty about. She hadn't heard from anyone at Seagrove since she left six months ago.

Nothing could have been easier or less contentious than her separation from Tony, despite the down-payments they'd lost on the renovation. She ought to be grateful. How ridiculous to feel a pang of sorrow that it was all too easy to disentangle two lives.

Now, she rented an apartment in the city, close to the office, which was a blessing, because her work days seemed to get longer all the time as she threw herself back into the world of property development. The economic situation meant it was that much harder to get projects off the ground, yet Nick managed to ride the ups and downs of the market better than most. And after six months, he'd made her the offer she'd hoped for. An executive role, more money, share options, the works. She'd even bought a beach shack of her own at the Sunshine Coast for the odd weekend when she could get away.

She'd achieved more success than she'd dreamed possible a year ago, but the truth was, nothing in her life seemed to fit any more. If she'd never had that time at Seagrove with Theo, she'd never have known what she'd missed. But now she did, and she didn't know how she'd ever get that back. Her deception had ruined her chances forever.

Knowing she was living a second-best life now made it that much harder to give her all to her job in the way that she used to. But what was the alternative? It wasn't as if she'd wanted to become an events co-ordinator per se, was it? Her interest had been in Seagrove and nowhere else.

For now, she'd have to play the cards her stupidity had dealt her. It wasn't so bad, after all. She had her house at the beach, and she couldn't complain about the salary that went with her new role.

After a Friday lunch made tedious by the fact that everyone there was tipsy and she was stone-cold sober, Liz packed up her things, ready to take off early for the beach. They'd settled a huge contract today and Nick had given her Monday off, so she was looking forward to a solid long weekend of rest and recuperation before throwing herself back into the fray.

She located the latest version of her manuscript on her laptop and hit the print button. Satisfaction filled her as she watched the printed pages mount up.

Funnily enough, one lie she'd told Valerie and the others had come true. She had decided to write Delany's story – or at least, a fictionalised version of it. She might never have the chance to read Delany's account of events after Richard banished her from their home, but for her own satisfaction she'd decided to give Delany the ending she deserved.

On her way back from the printer, Liz noticed a package in her in-tray. She picked it up and turned it over. The return address said 'Seagrove'.

Adrenaline shot through her as she hurried back to her office. Her fingers trembled so hard she couldn't get the sturdy envelope open, and nearly dropped it when a loud knock on the door made her jump.

'Hey,' said Nick, coming into the room. Cursing his bad timing, Liz hurriedly shoved her manuscript and the package into her work suitcase and sat down. Her fingers itched to rip open the padded brown envelope but she didn't want to do it in front of Nick.

Like everyone else after their boozy lunch at a swanky riverside restaurant, Nick was a little drunk. He was all rakish and rumpled, a look that did him all kinds of favours in the attractiveness department.

'Good work today, Jones,' he said, toasting her with his Crown Lager bottle. 'Excellent.'

'Thanks, boss. Plans for the weekend?'

His shoulders hunched a little. 'Off to Sydney tonight with Greta.'

He sounded restless, almost disconsolate at the prospect, and her heart sank. Gorgeous Greta had occupied a lot of his extra-curricular hours lately, but it seemed his fascination with her had begun to fade.

Liz sighed. Well, it had been good while it lasted. It had been so nice not to be woken in the middle of the night to hear about another of Nick's mad schemes.

She was desperate for him to go away. First, because she needed to know what was in that package. Second, because she wanted to leave the office before he found a reason for her to stay. However, she knew from experience that the harder she tried to get rid of him, the less likely he was to leave. She had to let this play out and stifle her impatience.

'You know,' said Nick, settling himself comfortably on the edge of her desk, 'I think we can rescue that Seagrove situation.'

That got her full attention. What were the odds that he'd mention Seagrove the same day she received this parcel? But she supposed she ought to have expected something like this. Greta had been a distraction while his infatuation lasted. As his interest in her waned, his hyperactive brain was focusing on other passions.

Or possibly, he'd gone through Liz's mail.

He filched a small rubber ball from her silver dish of office toys and started throwing it with a flash of white shirt-cuff in the flick of his wrist. The ball bounced first onto the carpet, then onto the wall, and sprang back to his hand. *Dock, dock, smack.*

'What are you thinking?' said Liz.

Nick leaned back to get a better angle on his throw. 'You thought you failed in the mission over there. But it struck me that the ancestral thing was the least important part. You, my dear Liz, have the inside track on all their operations.' *Dock, dock, smack.*

Such as they were. The way he talked, you'd think the Nashes had perfected a new franchise system or discovered a cure for cancer.

'Most importantly,' said Nick, 'you established a rapport.'

She grimaced. 'Um, Nick, did you miss the part where they banished me from their house and haven't spoken to me in months?'

Well, to be honest, she and Gemma kept in touch, but Theo certainly hadn't forgiven her.

'So, I've been thinking,' said Nick, ignoring this technicality, 'they've probably been through a tough winter over there. They're still paying all the outgoings but the event business has closed down, and no one much will be buying exotic plants.'

Liz had thought of that and wondered how they were all getting along. Gemma hadn't been forthcoming about the financial situation but while she and Fergus had finished the renovation on Saltwater Cottage, they didn't seem to be in any hurry to leave the Seagrove estate.

'So,' Nick continued, 'they're probably feeling the pinch. Perfect time to play the white knight.' *Dock, dock, smack.*

'And you want me to be the . . . what, the herald?'

'Harbinger of glad tidings,' Nick agreed, spreading his arms wide. 'What do you think?'

Liz licked her lips. 'I think I'm probably the worst person to make this happen.'

'My dear Liz, that's where you're wrong. You're absolutely the best person.'

'I can't,' she said. How could she represent Nick's interests against Theo's? And why on earth would Nick think any of the Nashes would listen to her?

'Look, I'm not going to exploit them,' he said. *Dock, dock smack.* 'I'll give them a fair price.'

'But what would you *do* with Seagrove, Nick?' said Liz. 'Would you move there?'

'Of course not.' He threw the ball again. 'I'll restore it and put in a skeleton staff, keep on the Jacksons if they agree. Stay there during Cowes Week, of course, go sailing in the summer.' He frowned. 'Not the best location on the island for that, of course, practically speaking, but I can make it work.'

Quietly, Liz said, 'I just don't think that's what a house like Seagrove is for.'

Nick might have had a few drinks but he knew what he wanted and his mind was razor-sharp. 'Look, Liz, frankly I don't care if you

approve of why I want the house. I would like you to handle the negotiations for me. That's all. Think of it as your last job as company
lawyer before you make the move to the executive floor.' He shrugged.
'If you feel you can't do it, no hard feelings. I'll ask the new guy.'

Liz didn't like the sound of that. 'Let me think about it over the
weekend, okay?'

'Fine. We'll talk next week.' Without warning, he flicked the ball to
her. Automatically, her hand shot up to catch it.

'Now that,' said Nick, 'is why you and I are a perfect team.' He
stood, dropped his empty beer bottle into her waste basket and saun-
tered off, whistling.

Liz waited until he was out of sight. Then she grabbed her bags and
headed out the door.

After a frustratingly slow trip up the roadwork-infested motorway,
she arrived at the beach house in darkness, unlocked the ugly security
screen and let herself in.

She turned on the lights, dumped her bags and went through the
kitchen to the carpeted living room. She flopped onto the fat old couch,
not even bothering to change, kicked off her heels and ripped open the
package from Seagrove.

She cried out in shocked surprise. Delany's missing memoirs! Or
photocopies of them, anyway.

The note accompanying them read:

> *I hear you're writing the book after all. Thought you could use*
> *these.*
> *Theo.*

He'd managed to get the memoirs back from Valerie, then. How had
he done it? Please, she thought, don't let them be back together. No,
they couldn't be. Surely Gemma would have told her if they were.

Liz ran her fingertips over the brief note and closed her eyes. That
Theo had thought of her made something inside her sing. A reaction

out of all proportion to the gesture.

Or maybe not. Could this be the first sign of thaw in what had been to her a very harsh winter? It was not much to hang her hopes on, but it was better than nothing.

Liz flipped through the pages until she came to the place she'd left off, and settled in to read.

Delany, Lady Nash

I wonder if you know how low a female might fall in this world, though her lawful husband be a wealthy lord?

Though her sister lives in a mansion mere streets away, and spends an entire day choosing which of her silk gowns to hand down to her maid. Though her brother lays out thousands of pounds on the turn of a card; though her aunt lives comfortably, housed and fed through that female's efforts to secure her aunt's future. Though the man who loves her is as wealthy as a nabob.

This is how it happens. Her husband refuses her everything she once considered her own – even possessions she brought to the marriage, which he never paid for. Her clothes, her undergarments, her jewels, her shoes, her horses, her dogs: all his.

Did you know that until there is a formal separation deed, a husband must pay his wife's debts, even if he has turned her from his house for adultery? That is the law.

This is what happens: for a time, the wife may run up debts on her husband's account. Oh, not for extravagances such as she might have been accustomed to purchase during her marriage, but for bread and board and clothing – sober clothing, of course. She would not wish to give the impression that in her desperation she has turned to the only trade she is now fit for.

However, when her lord refuses to pay those bills and turns

tradesmen away from his door empty-handed, when he posts adver-
tisements in the newspapers that he will no longer pay his wife's debts,
the law becomes irrelevant. Tradesmen do not sue the great lord for
payment. They simply stop extending credit to his lady.

For a time, I managed to stave off eviction from the room I'd taken
by writing poems and songs for Mr Gibbs, as I'd done in years past.
I longed to recover the pages and pages I'd written during my marriage. One and a half novels and several stories and poems remained
yet in Richard's possession; could I but sell those to Mr Gibbs it would
give me some breathing space to write more.

At my request, Mr Gibbs paid me direct, and in coin, telling me
frankly that my notoriety made my work wildly popular. If only I
would write about the trial, break my silence and give my side of the
story, I would be a rich woman.

I demurred. For the sake of my children, I must endeavour to
remain on amicable terms with Richard. I must not give him cause to
keep them from me by feeding more fuel to the fire.

Despite his behaviour, I had not yet despaired of reconciling with
Richard. It seemed to me that he would have found some way to insti-
tute divorce proceedings against me if he truly believed me guilty of
adultery. No word of such an action came.

Months passed. This first winter had been hard, but I dreaded the
one that would come next. Swallowing my pride, I wrote to my relations, begging for assistance. With varying levels of politeness and
self-exculpation, they refused.

Despite the anguish I had caused him, Julian sent me a bank draft,
but I could not accept it. If it became known that he kept me, the scandal of our supposed affair would flare up again. Moreover, Richard
would seize upon the circumstance as an excuse to continue to refuse
me access to my children. I returned the bank draft and the rest of
Julian's letters unopened.

When I was obliged to move to meaner accommodation, I told no
one where I'd gone.

Shortly after the trial, Richard spent some months abroad, presumably to escape the worst of the gossip. Upon his return, from time to time I wrote to him, begging for reconciliation. He knew I had done nothing wrong! Would he have the grace to admit it?

The tone of my letters swung from cordial, to threatening, to abject supplication as my circumstances grew more desperate. None made a dent in his determination to shun me, though he toyed with my hopes as a cat with a mouse.

All of this correspondence was carried on through an intermediary. Mr Black, Julian's attorney, was a man I had grown to trust. Through him, I begged and begged to be allowed to see my sons. Richard would agree, nominate a time and place, then renege at the last minute. How it must have amused him to torture me so!

One day, when I called at Mr Black's office to inquire of any developments, the attorney had received papers for me to sign – a deed that would effect Richard's and my formal separation.

Thank God! In this document, my alimony and jointure would be spelled out and at last, I might have the means to drag myself out of a desperate situation. Most important, the deed would secure my right to see my children.

I read the document Richard's attorney had drafted with growing horror. Richard conceded nothing to me – not my jointure nor any alimony beyond a nominal amount that would not keep a cat, much less a woman. He would allow me to visit my children, but any meetings between us would be wholly at his discretion.

Furious, I wanted to reject the bargain outright, but Mr Black persuaded me to let him counter my husband's proposal.

'I don't care about the money but I must see my boys.' By this time, I had accepted that reconciling with Richard, or indeed obtaining custody of our sons, would never happen.

'It is his duty to provide for you,' counselled Mr Black. 'You must not surrender your entitlement.'

The worried frown in his eyes told me what he scrupled to say:

I looked scrawny and underfed, and if I did not get some sort of pension from my husband soon, my children might not have a mother at all.

Initially I had thought, as is the general misconception, that a mother was entitled to custody of her children until they reached the age of seven. That is not the case. Only women whose children are born out of wedlock have custody of them. Oh, the irony.

The pity in Mr Black's expression was like a slap in the face. I'd fancied him half in love with me at the time of the trial. To have become such a poor creature in his eyes stung my pride.

'Tell him I don't want alimony,' I said. 'Agree to anything as long as you have his assurance that I'll see my children – once a month or whatever you think appropriate, but *not* at Lord Nash's discretion.'

'I do not think that is wise,' said Mr Black. 'My lady, forgive me, but is there no one nearer to Lord Nash who would speak for you?'

'There is no one,' I said.

Lacking the funds to sue my husband, and without powerful allies who might shame him into good behaviour, I could only hope some shred of humanity might persuade him to let a mother see her beloved children.

In the meantime, I must make my own way. To do that, I must retrieve my manuscripts. I considered those servants who remained in my husband's household. Which of them might be most sympathetic to my cause?

After some thought, I sent Mrs Ludd a note begging her to smuggle my papers to me. If I could sell *The Romance of the Moor* and *The Abbey at Inglesforth*, I might at least gain some income on which to live while I wrote more.

To my joy, the housekeeper wrote her agreement, desiring me to come to the house and fetch what I could. His lordship was away at Newmarket for the week and she was sure the other servants would turn a blind eye if it was only my papers I wanted.

Filled with trepidation, under cover of darkness and with my face heavily veiled, I presented myself at the house that had once been my home. I scratched on the door and the porter opened it. Crossing his quick palm with a coin I could ill spare, I slipped into the hall. Thank God for Mrs Ludd!

A voice floated to me from the book room to my left. 'Ah. There you are, my dear. Come in.'

The voice was not the housekeeper's. It was my husband's.

CHAPTER NINETEEN

I froze. Fear dried my mouth. Fear, and shame, too, for how could I be so afraid of a weakling like Richard? Only weak men enjoyed flexing their might against women.

Pride had always been my besetting sin. Instead of cowering there in the shadows or bolting for the street, I forced myself to step into the doorway of my husband's library.

It was a sharp February evening but the room was warm, for a fire roared in the Adam fireplace. The scent of burning – something other than coal – filled my nostrils.

Richard stood by the mantel. In the crook of his arm, he held a stack of foolscap pages. A manuscript – one of mine. I watched, unblinking, with the bile lurching to my throat, as he peeled the top few pages off, bent with an elegant flourish, and fed them to the flames.

A voice in my head screamed with agony. No, no, no! Not *The Romance of the Moor*. Not *The Abbey at Inglesforth*. Not those pages and pages of poetry and fragments of stories and . . .

I did not move. If I'd had a loaded pistol, I would have put a bullet through that cavity my husband called his heart. But I did not have a pistol and he was far stronger than I. The only defence I possessed was a show of indifference.

He destroyed not only my livelihood, but my creation, the product of my mind and my toil – the one thing I had in the world that was wholly mine, independent of him.

Of course, that was why he did it.

By prosecuting Julian and losing, Richard had become the villain of the piece, not the hero he considered himself to be. That was inexcusable, infuriating to my husband, who had expected that public opinion would side with him. He would be vindicated and his brother would be shunned.

Everyone liked Julian. They knew Richard's prosecution to have been motivated by rivalry, greed and spleen. When the case came to court, only those sticklers who had previously disapproved of him thought the worse of Julian for bedding me. Most of his peers were frankly envious. I was a tasty morsel, after all, a paragon who had held herself above the fray of adulterous affairs and so more worth the conquering.

Julian had been obliged to withstand some gossip and snubs, but already the heat had gone out of the scandal. Very soon, all would return to normal. He might then enjoy his fortune, go on as before. Blessed with such affluence, he might even marry some respectable young lady and settle down to family life as if nothing had happened.

Such understanding did not extend to me, of course. I was snubbed everywhere, branded a harlot and a whore. But the public had more than enough scorn to spare for Richard, the vindictive schemer, the willing cuckold. That, he could not bear.

As I watched my thoughts and dreams, my livelihood, go up in smoke, all became clear. Despite his vacillations and prevarications, Richard would never let me see my boys. Why would he? That would argue a compassion he did not possess. He cared for nothing and no one but himself.

A very great recklessness came over me as I watched him take up another manuscript and feed it, chapter by chapter, to the flames.

I said, 'You will burn them. I cannot stop you. But while there is breath in my body I can write more.'

And you won't like what I write when I do, I added silently.

He turned to look at me. Then he threw back his head and laughed. I waited for his paroxysms to finish, despising him, wondering if he had, in truth, gone mad.

Finally, he grew calm enough to speak. 'My attorney told me something fascinating today, my dear. He said —' He broke off to clutch at his side as he shook with a fresh wave of mirth. 'Oh! It is too rich. He said that everything you have, whether you live under my roof or not, is mine.'

Richard waved the remaining sheaf of paper in the air. 'Everything you have ever written is mine. Everything you will ever write —' he broke off to toss more pages into the fire, 'is mine.'

Again, he could scarcely speak. 'The royalties f-from everything you published *before* we married are mine.' With a flourish, he sent the final pages spinning into the hearth. There was a puff and a whoosh. They curled at the edges, blackened, and disintegrated to ash.

'*You*,' he said, turning slowly to face me, blue eyes avid, 'are mine.'

I still see it in my nightmares, the unholy glee of him. I should have turned tail and run. I should have screamed for one of the servants to save me – but then, what could they have done?

Even now, I can picture his triumph as he took hold of me, as he reminded me in ways forceful and cruel that he was still my husband. That he owned not only the clothes I stood up in, the product of my mind and my labour, but every inch of my body as well.

My children. My reputation. My family. My home. The only honest means by which I might earn a living. He'd taken everything I had, even my gaunt, tired body, which he discarded with disgust once he had used me.

But he could never take my mind, my will, or my heart.

At my lodgings, I sat alone in darkness, I know not for how long. I searched deep inside myself for that spark of defiance I'd felt in Richard's library, but it had snuffed out.

At night, I huddled on my narrow cot, staring into nothingness, a handful of my coarse wool blanket clutched in each fist. The pervasive smells of poverty were forever present in this house, but above that came the reek of my own body: an odour I did not want to think about, yet had not the will to remove. The scuffle of rodent feet in the walls, the stomp of footsteps above, the sounds of slammed doors, of people fighting, shouting, laughing, echoed around me, and grew to a threatening clamour.

Every day since I'd been barred from my home, I had taken up my pen to write. Solace was to be found only in the escape of my mind to that place in the story. Nothing from the real world could touch me there.

Now, Richard owned those imaginary kingdoms, not I. What was the use in making more of them?

Yet an all but buried instinct told me that if I did not go back to my work I would be lost forever. There was just enough spirit left in me not to desire oblivion. I dragged myself to the page. I wrote. In anger, self-loathing and misery, I scribbled gibberish, unreadable raging scrawls of sorrow and pain. The cough that had been in abeyance over the warmer months now returned to plague me, but I kept on. If I did not write to expel the agonies and passions that threatened to engulf me, I would go mad.

I sat all hours at my little table scribbling, scarcely taking food or rest. By and by, such aimless meanderings no longer satisfied. I had only so much ink, so much paper left to me. I would not waste them on pointless drivel.

Forsaken by my family, disgraced and driven to desperation by my husband's hypocrisy, greed and corrosive resentment, I would give in to Mr Gibbs's urging. I would give the world the truth.

In poetry, songs and scandal sheets, I detailed everything about my marriage to Richard that he would not wish to become known, his follies and aberrant quirks, the injustices I had suffered at his hands regarding my children and the maintenance he owed me. I omitted his most recent brutality, for I knew public sympathy was never with the wife in such cases. Moreover, should the incident come to Julian's ears, I shuddered to think what he'd do.

Aside from this, I knew no constraint. I composed a barrage of letters to the newspapers and articles for scandal sheets, an arsenal of accusations thinly disguised as allegorical tales. And when the fire of revenge had burned down to a smoulder, I set them aside and embarked on my *roman à clef* and called it *Widow's Peak*. The word 'widow' seemed ineffably sweet.

I sent everything to Mr Gibbs, hardly caring whether Richard might step in and snatch my earnings away. The world would know the truth and the consequences be damned. Mr Gibbs and I discussed the best way to release the information to the public for maximum effect and came up with a plan.

I was unable to resist the temptation to watch Richard's reaction when the full catastrophe of my disclosures burst upon him. Knowing Richard's habits, I settled on Vauxhall Gardens as a likely venue and set to work.

With Mr Gibbs's collaboration, I stationed boys around the gardens to sell scandal sheets that read: 'The True History of the Crim. Con. Case between Lord N— and Mr N—'. The evening could not have been finer. A persistent drizzle throughout the day had dried up, leaving the stars whitewashed and the pavements slick with damp.

Loath to miss the entertainment, I donned one of Lavinia's old gowns and sallied forth. Arriving at the gardens a little early, heavily veiled, I stationed myself opposite the box my husband usually reserved for supper. Rack punch and shaved ham . . . How long had it been since I'd sampled such delights?

The boxes at Vauxhall were well illumined and wholly exposed, designed less for the purpose of taking refreshment than for showing oneself and one's guests to the passing throng. That evening, I was pleased to see Richard's party enter the box beneath the orchestra gallery, and that Richard was seated with utmost prominence in the place facing the crowd. The ladies, with their fine silks and feathers, and the gentlemen in more sober hues, made an elegant *tableau vivant*.

At my signal, my urchins went to work, bawling their almost unintelligible cries, hawking their single sheets of sensational journalism to the interested public. It was not long before the boys were chased off the premises by Vauxhall employees. The lads pelted for their lives and slipped into the dark anonymity of the infamous walks.

By that time, however, I rejoiced to hear several members of the fashionable crowd exclaim, 'By Jove!' and 'Shocking!' and 'Too sordid for words!' As more and more people read the news and passed it on to their neighbours, word of Lord Nash's depravity spread with lightning speed.

The buzz of conversation turned into an uproar when it was discovered that Richard was present that very evening, unaware of the cause of the tumult and wholly exposed to the rude public glare.

'For shame!' scolded one ostrich-feathered lady, who planted herself in front of Richard's supper box. 'Fiend!' cried another, shaking her fist.

Richard was aghast, his companions scarcely less so. What on earth had precipitated this riot, and made him the focus of the crowd's wrath?

Missiles of food and dirt and other detritus started hurling into the box, smacking wetly into Richard's forehead and chest, pelting his arms and elbows as he held them in front of his face to defend himself.

The orchestra above Richard's party were half hanging out of their gallery to see who had occasioned such a fuss, their notes falling awry. My husband's guests, who had received the brunt of the flying rubbish along with their host, fled. Richard himself, half blinded by panic and covered in debris, crawled under the table to hide, until two burly Good Samaritans braved the mob and dragged the soiled, gibbering nobleman away.

The satisfaction of that moment could never be pure, given my continued estrangement from my sons. Oh, but it was something, at all events.

The furore at Vauxhall provided fodder for gossip in its turn, and so the wheel of the machine that Mr Gibbs and I had set in motion ground on. Richard blustered that he would sue Mr Gibbs for libel, but that was an empty threat. To proceed with such an action would only fan the flames of scandal. He could not, of course, sue me, for I had no legal status as long as I was married to him. I was literally a non-entity.

How that made me laugh.

For his part, Mr Gibbs paid the anonymous author of these scandalous tales handsomely for her work and steadfastly rebuffed Richard's attempts to prove the identity of his source. Eventually Richard gave up the fight and scuttled back to Seagrove to lick his wounds.

Thus, I survived. At the expense of everything a noble English lady holds dear, I grew stronger and healthier once more.

Despite the insistence by the author that 'Lady N—' had been an unwilling participant in the acts of voyeuristic depravity carried out by her husband, no one believed me innocent. By broadcasting the truth, I had set the seal on my fate. I was banished from good society forever.

It was either that, or perish. What would you?

I resolved to follow up the advantage I'd so dearly gained over Richard to win back access to my children. My silence in return for my sons. It did not even occur to me to balk at blackmail, so desperate had I become.

Without a male protector, however, a woman's position is ever precarious. If I went to Richard alone, there was nothing to stop him using me as he had used me last time we met. But I needed a stronger man than Mr Black, my trusty attorney, to broker this deal. I needed a fierce champion who would not bow to Richard's orders, a man who would fight *with* me, not ride roughshod over my wishes.

'*Julian*,' I whispered, closing my eyes tight, as if I might will him to me. Julian Nash was my only hope.

CHAPTER TWENTY

Margaret

Margaret reached Seagrove to find Richard absent, the furniture draped in Holland covers. 'What has happened here?' she asked Mrs Ludd, as she freed Pug from his leash. 'Where is Lord Nash? I heard he'd returned from his travels months ago.'

'You'll find him down at Marine Cottage,' said the housekeeper. 'Never stirs far from it, not since he got back.'

Delany had taken her revenge. Each week, a new and scandalously frank account of Richard's habits and sexual quirks appeared in the scandal sheets. She'd made a mockery of her husband. He faced ridicule and derision on every side.

Initially Richard had renewed the hunt for his wife, but she was nowhere to be found. She'd left the mean boarding house his vindictive treatment had brought her to and not left a forwarding address, not even with her publisher or her attorney.

Thwarted of the object of his torment, Richard had raged and ranted and foamed. Thanks to Delany's scurrilous lies, he could not show his face around Town. One might think the world had run mad, he fumed, but in truth, Margaret thought it was Richard who might be mistaken for a Bedlamite if he did not mend his ways.

For her part, she had weaned her charge and delivered Stephen (William, as she now called him) to his adoptive parents. She'd entertained few qualms about leaving Delany and Richard's son to their care. He would grow up housed and shod and doted on by two kind people and never want for life's necessities. It was more than Margaret had ever had.

No matter how easily she dismissed Delany's son from her thoughts, she could not help longing for her William. Yet it would be dangerous for her to visit him without Richard's sanction. She had no pretext upon which to call at Lamerton Hall. Besides, she might betray her connection to her baby if she saw him again. Since his birth, her emotions simmered ever closer to the surface.

She'd not heard from Richard for some weeks. Did he mean to cut her adrift now she'd served her purpose? She had no intention of letting him discard her. She was not above using blackmail if it were required. She'd do anything to live at Seagrove as its mistress, as Richard's wife, as mother to her own son. She'd come here today to demand that he divorce Delany and marry her instead. His wife was not the only one privy to his lordship's secrets after all.

Still careful of her reputation, she'd engaged a respectable female to accompany her to Richard's house. Mrs Brodie was a genteel Irishwoman who had fallen on hard times. In return for the bed and board Margaret promised her, she was willing to live with Richard and Margaret at Seagrove while they resumed their work on Richard's history of the island. Margaret knew a thing or two about Mrs Brodie and trusted her to keep her mouth shut, should she suspect anything untoward about the arrangement.

After speaking to Mrs Ludd, Margaret went down to Marine Cottage in search of Richard. The estate was large, and Richard owned several houses on the Undercliff. Another of them, Saltwater Cottage, was traditionally used as the dower house, though Lady Verena had refused to move there in her turn.

It was a long walk to Marine Cottage, and a muddy one, but after the stuffy closeness of London, Margaret was glad to breathe in the clean air. She climbed a stile, hardly caring that the hem of her gown was edged in mud, or that the heat of the day had made perspiration gather beneath her bonnet at the forehead and temples.

Finally she reached the site of Richard's latest obsession and took in his version of Arcadia with a jaundiced eye. She had no interest in classical architecture, though due to Richard's interminable lectures, she knew a great deal.

Before his marriage, Richard had begun work turning this cliffside property into a slice of ancient Rome, with terraced gardens, marble statuary and faux temples. The countryside was too verdant, and the unbroken, classical lines of the buildings too perfect for realism, but she supposed that mattered little to him.

This part of the estate was like another world, intended as an escape from the formality of the Big House. Now that it was complete and furnished to Richard's satisfaction, it was the perfect haven from a world that despised him.

She picked her way down the terraced slope with its exotic fruit trees, now heavy with produce, and past the cool quiet of the olive grove. Around a bend and into a sudden clearing, she came upon a breathtaking vista. The sea, all glassy turquoise and teal, stretching to the horizon. Below, the crescent of rocky beach, the sheer cliffs thickly fringed with grass.

Margaret lifted her face as the cleansing sea breeze cooled her cheeks, then looked about her. A small, terraced vineyard striped the slope to her right. There she saw Richard, a broad-brimmed straw hat on his head, talking to a larger man. As she picked her way along the path to meet them, Margaret realised who the larger man was.

She gasped. *Julian Nash*.

The two brothers strolled in her direction, heads bowed, so deep in conversation they didn't notice her. How odd to see them together, and even stranger to observe Richard's demeanour. There was a distinct bounce in his step.

Dismay clutched her chest. What scheme could Richard have come up with now? What had made him so jubilant all of a sudden? Nothing good from her point of view, that was certain. She'd ceased considering him an ally long ago.

With a curt bow, Julian left Richard and headed in the direction of the stables, his long legs negotiating the steep path up to the crest of the cliff with ease. Richard stood very still for a few moments, watching him go. Then he snatched off his hat, flung it into the air with a boyish whoop and caught it again.

Margaret hurried towards him. 'My lord? What's to do?'

He stared in her direction with a sudden scowl at the unwonted intrusion. When he recognised her, however, the light of welcome dawned on his face.

'Margaret? Is it you, indeed?' Richard jammed his hat back on his head. 'Come. You must celebrate with me.' He grabbed her arm and hauled her back the way she'd come.

'But what is it, my lord?' she said, stumbling after him, her skirts and the uneven ground impeding her.

'It is beyond anything. The damnedest thing. A bargain!' he pronounced, blue eyes feverishly bright. 'Julian will sign his entire fortune over to me if I —' he stopped short, then resumed more casually, 'if I will let Delany see the boy.'

Such a bargain seemed ludicrously unbalanced. She wondered if she'd understood it properly, or if Richard was keeping something from her.

Then it registered. '*The* boy? Which boy?' said Margaret, trying to keep pace, both with Richard's steps and with his garbled speech.

'Henry, of course,' he said. 'Who else?'

'Only Henry?' Margaret halted, but he kept going, hardly seeming to notice her hesitation and surprise.

Brow furrowed, Margaret quickened her steps to catch up with him. As they neared the olive grove, she glanced up at him, trying to keep her voice calm, disinterested. 'What about the baby? What about Stephen?'

He sobered. 'Did you not hear the news? Ah, no. Well, I did not suppose you would mind it. The infant died, I'm sorry to say.'

The world seemed to fold in upon her. *William. Her William. Dead!* Her knees buckled. 'No,' she whispered. 'Oh, no.'

Richard caught her, one arm around her waist, his other hand gripping her elbow. 'Easy now. Come, Margaret. It's the sun. We must get you out of this heat.'

'When? How?' she whispered, as she limped along with him, drowning in a sea of agonised confusion.

'What's that?' he said, puzzled.

'How did . . . how did Stephen perish?' She couldn't comprehend it. There must be a mistake.

'Oh, one of these mysterious infantile ailments, I believe.' An odd, false note in his voice stroked a cold fingertip of dread down her spine. She pulled away from him and stared.

Richard's brows, pale and thin against his ruddy skin, drew together. 'Why do you look at me like that? Surely you cannot have forgotten who spawned that child.'

Who spawned . . . She couldn't think. Several moments passed before she untangled the various threads of her many deceptions enough to understand.

He thought the baby who had died was Stephen. And he believed Stephen to be Julian and Delany's illegitimate son.

He lowered his voice. 'I would *not* bring up that bastard's bastard as my own.'

With a stifled cry, Margaret turned from him and dug the heels of her hands into her temples, as if to crush the thoughts that now teemed in her brain like maggots in a rotting carcass.

Richard had murdered William. Her darling boy. Margaret's face buckled in pain. Dear God, oh, God, what had she done?

It was *she* who had planted that barb in Richard's flesh, questioning the legitimacy of his second son. *She* who had swapped babies, giving her own precious child into the keeping of a monster, while Delany's son grew up fat and happy on a farm in Somerset.

'Where is he now?' Margaret's voice came hoarsely from her dry throat. She turned to face him again, the man who had murdered their child. 'What did you do with him?'

'What *should* I do with him?' He frowned and shot her a sidelong look. 'Why do you want to know?'

'I . . .' Margaret clutched at her throat as if to loosen the invisible noose that constricted it. She shook her head. She would not ask. She couldn't bear to deal with him on the subject. She would go to Lamerton Hall herself. 'Did you tell Mr Nash the boy is gone?'

'No, of course not. Ostensibly, he and his elder brother remain at Lamerton Hall.' He rubbed the side of his nose. 'I think Henry is better off there for the moment. I do not trust Julian, nor Delany, neither. We must remain vigilant. I would not put it past them to steal the boy away and abscond with him to the Continent.'

Other mothers had attempted similar kidnappings when denied custody of their children, Margaret knew. And there was no doubting Delany's determination when she set her mind to a thing. Margaret was tempted to help her.

'So you will renege on your bargain with your brother,' Margaret said. She had neither will nor energy to pander to this despicable creature any longer. He horrified her.

But he seemed not to hear, merely expressing solicitude for her health, telling her she must rest in the shade and she'd be right as a trivet in no time.

Right? How could she ever be *right*? She had the strangest urge to give way to hysterical laughter.

In a waking nightmare, she went with him to a pleasure pavilion made of sandstone. She passed through the portico, with its Corinthian columns, and into the cool interior, which was about the size of the South Parlour at Seagrove.

The walls were painted eau de nil, and studded with white plaster cherubs and oval cameos of Roman gods. Light streamed through long sash windows with views to the gardens and the sea. A rich Persian carpet sprawled over the floor. Silk chaises longues and chairs were arranged in a pleasing group, and occasional tables with ormolu legs and intricate marquetry tops were scattered throughout. A young African manservant in green livery stood to attention beside a sideboard groaning with all kinds of fare.

Richard must have seen her eyeing the page, for he said casually, 'Do you like him? I . . . acquired him in Turkey. Fine specimen, ain't he?'

Margaret could not bring herself to reply. She'd guessed, of course, but for Richard to confirm her suspicion so casually turned her stomach.

As he passed the sideboard, Richard swiped a bunch of grapes from a gigantic silver bowl, then threw himself down onto a large silk divan by the window. He lounged on his side in the manner of a Roman emperor at a feast.

His relaxed attitude while she still stood showed her that even now, he neither honoured her as a lady, nor considered her status higher than that of a servant. After all she'd done.

'Scipio, a glass of wine for Miss Smith,' he ordered the page.

Margaret would have preferred water but knew better than to argue. She subsided onto a Chippendale chair that sat at right angles to Richard's divan.

Plucking one fat red grape, Richard turned it over between his long, thin fingers. 'You must stay, Margaret. When Julian brings Delany, I want you here.'

Every fibre of her body urged her to refuse, to abuse him and scream that he was a murderer. But in the face of his inhuman insouciance she found herself reverting to the habit of a lifetime. She boxed up her grief and pain and presented a smooth, polished surface.

Besides, she'd sacrificed so much. Too much to give up now.

'Of course,' she said, taking the goblet of claret the servant offered and drinking deep. She'd not forgotten how pleasant it was to be waited on.

With his kerchief, Richard dabbed at a trickle of grape juice on his chin. He reminded her of one of the weaker, less sane Roman emperors. Nero, perhaps, or Caligula. Caligula had killed babies too, if Suetonius were to be believed.

Hatred burning in her heart, she watched as he gestured imperiously to Scipio. Automatically, the page held out his gloved hand so his master could spit the seeds into it, then closed his hand into a neat fist and retreated to his station.

'My lord, I believe I might serve you also by taking charge of Henry's household,' said Margaret. 'I cannot foresee any benefit to leaving him in the care of a mere nursemaid, however competent she may be.'

He popped another grape into his mouth and chewed ruminatively.

'Perhaps you're right,' he said at last, leaning over once again to spit the seeds into the page's waiting hand. 'You must guard the boy and send word to me at once if anything untoward occurs. But not yet.' His gaze was distant now, and his mouth curled ever so slightly at the corners, as if he pictured an anticipated scene. 'I need you here when Delany arrives.'

'Indeed, I would not miss it, my lord,' Margaret said.

Delany, Lady Nash

I lost no time inquiring for Julian at his lodgings so that I might lay out my plan before him, but I was told he had gone out of town for a stretch and that his landlady did not know when he'd return. Heedless of my reputation – what had I left of that now? – I haunted the place, until one evening, my vigilance was rewarded. Julian's manservant, a knockabout villain if ever I saw one, answered my knock and told me his master was from home. Upon hearing who I was, he asked me to stay while he sent word.

Hours passed and I was drowsing in a chair when finally Julian burst in with that familiar, impetuous stride, shaking the rain from his hat.

'*Delany!* What —' He stared as if he thought me a vision or a ghost.

'Julian,' I whispered, rising and stretching out my hands to him.

He took them in a warm, encompassing grip. 'Oh, God, Delany. Where were you? I've been searching high and low.'

'You were looking for me?' I asked. 'Why?'

'Because . . .' He seemed to struggle with himself. Then he swore under his breath and stepped back, releasing me and turning away. 'You shouldn't be here.'

'Don't be ridiculous,' I said in a voice that was deceptively calm, for my heart hammered in my chest. 'My character cannot be blackened more than it already is.'

'The devil it can't,' he muttered. 'I need a drink.'

He poured the brandy, slopping a little over the sides of each glass, for his hand was a trifle unsteady. 'Come. Let us sit by the fire. You are cold.'

I realised this was true. Obediently, I settled deep in a wing chair by the hearth and sipped my brandy while Julian stoked up the blaze.

He perched on the arm of the chair opposite and watched me with a strange, hungry light in his eyes. Suddenly I remembered the bodice of my sister's blue and silver gown was cut very low.

'God,' he breathed. 'I must forever be shooting myself in the foot when it comes to you.'

'Why? What is it?' I said, alarmed at his tone.

He drained his brandy, pressing his lips together as he swallowed the fiery stuff. 'I've been to see Richard at Seagrove.'

His gravity told me it must be terrible news. Steel bands closed around my throat. My fingernails dug into my palm. 'Tell me. What has he done now?'

'I have made a bargain with him,' Julian said. 'If you consent, he will take you back as his wife and let you bring your boys home to live with you.'

'*What?*' I sat up, half horrified, half hopeful, and wholly incredulous. 'After all I've done to make a public spectacle of him? I don't believe it. How? What could you have said to make him change his mind?'

Once I'd published those embarrassing details about my husband, I knew I'd ruined any chance of reconciliation. Yet here was Julian telling me Richard would now have me back under his roof and let the boys return to me as well.

'I'm giving him the money,' said Julian. 'I should have done it from the start. That £20 000 has brought us nothing but trouble.'

Now I understood. 'But it's too late for that.' I went to him and gripped his wrist to emphasise the point. 'Oh, Julian, you must not! Richard is mad, and cunning with it. You cannot believe he will honour his promise. He'll take your money and you'll be left with nothing.'

Grimly, Julian replied, 'I will make sure that he fulfils his side of the bargain, never fear. I've enlisted our uncle to act as trustee. Richard will listen to him. He will not get a penny unless he complies with the terms of the agreement.'

I stared up at Julian, frozen in wonder, scarce able to believe he'd do this for me – forsake his future and his freedom to give me what I most desired in the world. The mere thought that I might have my children with me again made all of my longing for them return in a flood of agonising joy.

The small, unselfish part of me knew I should refuse to let Julian make such a sacrifice. But what would happen to my boys if I did not? I shuddered to think of leaving them to Richard's tender mercies. Could I be ruthless enough to agree to Julian's proposal? For my children's sake, perhaps I could.

The full implications burst in upon me then. If I returned to Seagrove, Julian and I could never see each other. Not tonight, never again. And I would be Richard's wife, with everything that implied.

When I thought of what going back to Richard would mean, panic clogged my throat. The image of a happy reunion with my darling boys blacked out, and the vision of relentless humiliation and degradation replaced it.

'No. I can't,' I said, releasing him and turning away to pace the floor. 'I can't do it. I won't go.'

'But Delany, think of your boys,' said Julian. 'How can you bear to be parted from them forever?'

'I cannot bear it,' I said, forcing down the rush of pain his words brought. 'But nor can I live with Richard as his wife.'

Julian frowned over this. Of course he did not know about his brother's violent behavior toward me. No one did. 'I told you,' he said, 'I'll force him to toe the line. I have it all in hand.'

How could he do that? Julian could not spend his life standing over his brother. And was it likely Richard would bow to their uncle's dictates? I wondered if my husband cared for anyone's good opinion after all that had occurred.

I saw the future clearly. Richard might adhere to the letter of his agreement with Julian, but there were any number of cruelties, large and small, that he might inflict upon his family and still keep his word.

How could I explain it without going into detail about Richard's treatment of me? I threw out a hand. 'I am his wife, Julian. Once he has me in his power again there is little you or your uncle can do to interfere. Richard is the most cowardly, devious, manipulative, cruel fiend of a man and I will not trust him.'

'Then trust *me*,' Julian urged. 'Trust me to make it right. You're not alone, Delany. You don't have to do everything on your own.'

I stared into those dark eyes, so hot and fierce with resolve that my heart flooded with joy. 'Oh, my darling,' I said, smiling through threatening tears. 'I know.' Julian was the one man on earth I trusted. The one person who never had, never would, forsake me. 'And I do need your help, but I have a different scheme in mind. One that does not involve parting from you.'

I knew I'd made the right decision. More than that, I knew I could not live another day without Julian by my side.

'Let's speak more of that later,' I said. Gathering my courage, I added, 'The truth is, I want you too much to wait any longer.'

The stark shock on his face swiftly turned to something harrowing. 'No. Delany, don't.'

'*Please*,' I whispered, setting my hands on his lapels, wishing he'd take me in his arms.

Grey with pain, he freed himself and moved to stand at the mantelpiece, his back to me. 'You must not toy with me. I cannot suffer this again.'

I longed to draw my fingers through the dark hair that curled at his nape. 'I'm not toying with you, Julian. I've never been more serious in my life.'

I went to him and he turned to face me with such naked longing in his expression that I gasped. Reaching up, I pressed my hand to his cheek. His entire body was taut with strain.

'How I love you,' I breathed. The warmth of his skin, the faint roughness of stubble beneath my palm made heat shimmer down my spine. 'I wish I deserved you but I doubt I ever will.'

On a groan of surrender, he turned his head to press a burning kiss to my palm, squeezing his eyes shut. 'Delany. My dearest love.'

He drew me into his arms and kissed me with such tender passion, such mounting desperation, that I grew dizzy. I felt like a prisoner freed from her bonds, cast suddenly into the sunshine – drunk on pleasure and freedom but struggling to find my footing, blinded by blessed, unfamiliar light.

Yet I found my balance in the gentle strength of him. By and by, I craved more than gentleness, and met him with every ounce of the passion that had been trapped inside me for so long.

We loved each other through the velvet hours of the night. There would never be enough time to make up for the years we'd lost. As dawn broke the following morning, I silently mourned those wasted, painful years. I'd done my duty by my family in marrying Richard, but I'd betrayed myself.

That long, bleak period was over now. Hope unfurled delicate petals inside me. I had Julian. And I had a plan.

There was no question of Julian's handing over his fortune. However, I would agree to cease publishing details about Richard's intimate habits and sign away my alimony in return for the right to visit my children once a month. If Richard would not tell me where he'd hidden them and insisted on a neutral meeting place, I would have the children followed home when the visit was over.

Then Julian and I would spirit the boys away, take them abroad with us. To Vienna, perhaps, or even the Americas – somewhere far beyond Richard's reach. It was a desperate plan, but it was the only way I could have both my sons and Julian as well; the only way I would not be forced to choose between them.

Shivering, I donned my shift and wrapped a swath of coverlet around my shoulders. I sat propped up against the headboard, my brain weaving plans as my fingers braided my hair, when the sheets rustled and a deep, masculine sigh filled the silence.

Finally! I thought he'd never wake.

Julian's eyes cracked open, then blinked as he seemed to register my presence beside him. His gaze travelled from my elbow, along my arm to linger on my bosom, then lifted to my face.

Silently, he stared up at me, a faint crease between his brows, as if he were puzzled to find that his long-held dream had manifested in the night. Then his expression cleared, the frown replaced by a lazy, wicked grin.

'Good morning, Rothwell.' He caught me by the braid and tugged gently, pulling me down against him, all rumpled, sleepy male.

I sighed with satisfaction, revelling in his strength and his sure, clever touch.

CHAPTER TWENTY-ONE

Liz

The sun was rising when Liz looked up again. She'd read all through the night.

Delany's account had riveted her, made her so mad she wanted to punch a wall. Such an energetic, proud woman, so full of wit and determination. Yet with all of her advantages, she'd been brought to her knees by a weak, insecure, despicable man, because the law was on his side.

She wondered about the novel Delany had described as a *roman à clef*, which meant that she would have used real people and events in the story. Presumably she had related some of the true circumstances surrounding the criminal conversation trial. *Widow's Peak* was not among the collection in Theo's library. Perhaps some Nash ancestor had deemed it too scandalous. She'd have to hunt it down some other way.

Rubbing her neck, Liz stretched, suddenly flooded with fatigue. She'd been so absorbed in Delany's tale that hours had passed by like minutes.

She padded into the kitchen for coffee, then realised she was out of milk. She drank it straight, wincing a little as the scalding espresso hit her dry mouth.

Unlocking the sliding door, she took her coffee out onto the deck. She leaned on the wooden rail, watching the sun rise over the ocean, a fiery orange ball against a spreading flush of pink.

The events Delany described – being locked out of her house, shunned by her family and friends, unable to accept help from the only man who offered it – seemed too dramatic to be real. Yet, from Liz's reading on the era, she knew such things had happened to women of that time. Perhaps, as she'd warned in her introduction, Delany had fictionalised her experiences to some extent.

· Much of it must be verifiable. Liz would do her best to find the facts to support the story.

And still the memoirs had not resolved the doubt over Stephen's legitimacy. By her own account, Delany had scarcely given birth to her second son before he and his elder brother were taken away. Would she have recognised him again once he was returned to the family?

True, she had told the adult Stephen that Richard was his father. But was that because she knew him to be the real heir, or because she knew no one alive could prove otherwise? Liz didn't see why Delany would choose to have an imposter inherit ahead of Julian, whom she loved.

Liz thought of Nick and his plans for the estate. Of course, there was no guarantee that Theo would sell, but Seagrove must be struggling. Liz knew he hadn't tried to replace Valerie with a proper events co-ordinator. Surely the Open Day would have brought them a flood of bookings. How on earth had Theo coped? She supposed he might have hired an external events company but that would have eaten up all the profits.

Gemma had told Liz repeatedly that she couldn't step into that role. 'I'm no good with details,' she'd complained when Liz had told her to use the spreadsheets from the Open Day as templates. 'I like having my discrete area to deal with, stick to what I'm good at. The big picture scares me. Too many balls to keep in the air, you know?'

If Liz negotiated with Theo on Nick's behalf, she'd feel like a traitor. No two ways about that. But if Nick intended to go ahead anyway, wouldn't it be better for Theo if Liz handled it? She'd do her best to rein Nick in where she could.

Well, then. Back to fundamentals. She took out a notebook and started doodling, always an aid to her thought processes. The key to any good negotiation was to dig down deep. What did each party really want? She had a fair idea of Theo's deep, if reluctant, attachment to Seagrove. What motivated Nick's determination to buy the estate?

That's when it hit her. Why hadn't she seen it before? So blinded by her need to advance her career, to satisfy Nick's demands without compromising her own loyalty to the Nashes, she'd overlooked something vital, something she should have seen from the beginning.

The idea was so brilliant she nearly spilled her coffee in her race to the phone. If this solution worked, everyone would get what they wanted.

Everyone, that was, except Liz.

So here Liz was again on the Isle of Wight. Coming back had been harder than she'd expected. For the hundredth time since she'd left Brisbane, Liz wished she hadn't resolved to see this through.

'Drop me at the gate, will you, Nick? I want to look in on Mr Jackson at the Lodge.' Since it was a Saturday morning, he might be at home doing the *Times* crossword.

'Sure you don't want me to come with you?' said Nick, not for the first time. 'I will if you like.'

That was all she needed: confronting Theo again with Nick breathing down her neck. 'No, off you go. I'll let you know what happens.'

The Lodge squatted beside the large stone gates at the beginning of the drive, its freshly painted door and window frames gleaming white against its lichen-covered walls.

Liz shivered. Though it was early spring, a cold wind whipped through the trees, piercing her light pullover.

She knocked at the Lodge and called out, but there was no sign of either of the Jacksons. She was stalling, she knew. Much as she wanted to see Theo again, she dreaded it too.

Unable to put it off any longer, Liz started down the drive toward the house, the leaves of the chestnut trees rustling above her in the wind.

The dell that cradled the Big House seemed shrouded in silence. Ancient cedar trees towered overhead, spreading their branches low and wide.

Daunted in spite of herself, Liz made her way around the back to the kitchen door, and was relieved to see that it stood open. 'Hello? Mrs Jackson?'

The cook came bustling out, wiping her hands on a tea towel, dispelling the aura of quiet gloom that had seemed to hang over the house's exterior. When she saw Liz, Mrs Jackson flung her arms wide and hugged her. 'Come in! Come in! What are you doing, standing there in the doorway like a stranger?'

Liz happily accepted a cup of tea and settled in for a chat – yet another means of delaying the inevitable.

'Jackson will be put out to hear he missed you,' said the cook when Liz said she didn't plan to stay. Mr Jackson was out for the day, fishing, and wasn't likely to return until evening.

'I'm sorry too,' said Liz. 'But I'm here on business, as it happens. It sort of depends on Theo whether I'll be around beyond today. Is he about?'

'In his study,' said Mrs Jackson, with a roll of her eyes. Liz wasn't sure what she was supposed to gather from that, and didn't ask.

Liz found Theo standing at the desk with his back to her, leaning down to make notes on a set of plans. She hesitated in the doorway, watching him intently, the tall, muscular figure poring over his work. The strength in his arms, the hands, so large yet so gentle, the quick, precise movements of his pen.

She waited for him to finish writing before she said, 'Hi, Theo.'

He tossed down his pen and turned around. When he registered who had interrupted him, a guarded expression came into his eyes.

She never failed to react to the sight of him, but the churn in her stomach wasn't pleasurable this time.

Then she saw the change in him.

'You've cut your hair.' It came out like an accusation.

No longer a shaggy tangle, Theo's wild mane had been hacked into a conventional short back and sides. The only hint of its former glory rested in the fringe that still threatened to flop into his eyes at every opportunity.

His guarded expression didn't alter. 'What are you doing here, Liz?'

'It's not what you think,' Liz said carefully.

'You have no idea what I think,' said Theo. His voice was neutral. Not welcoming, but not angry or bitter, either. That was something, she supposed.

'I'm here on business.' Better make that clear.

'Oh, yes?' said Theo, folding his arms. 'Still working for McCann, then.'

'Yes. But it's more complicated than that.'

His face was as responsive as a slammed door. She took a deep breath, gripping her hands together, trying to ignore the way his cool manner hurt.

She'd presented projects to tough audiences before – builders, property developers, merchant bankers and some highly nasty venture capitalists – but she'd never played to a tougher audience than Theo.

'You're wasting your time,' he said, forestalling her well-rehearsed speech. 'I'm not selling to him. Under no circumstances whatsoever.'

'I'm not asking you to,' she said. 'Just listen to me, will you?'

Not the most diplomatic opening, but she'd worked feverishly on the proposal and turned herself inside out trying to convince Nick to give it a chance. It had taken a lot of persuasion for Nick to drop everything to fly back to Seagrove with her to present their ideas.

Theo dipped his head and leaned back against his desk. 'All right. I'm listening.'

'I'm going to be blunt, Theo,' said Liz.

'Now, there's a surprise.'

She bit her lip. 'How are you going for money now that you've been through winter?'

'Pretty well, thanks.' His speech was clipped.

'Really?'

'Yes. Really.' He blew out a long breath. With palpable reluctance, he added, 'I've taken a job in the city.'

'What city?' said Liz, confused.

He scowled. '*The* city. The business district of London.'

'*You?*' said Liz. 'In pinstripes and a bowler hat?'

'Pinstripes, anyway,' he muttered. He shoved his hands into his pockets and dug the heel of his boot into the old carpet.

The idea was so ludicrous that a snort of laughter escaped her. 'Sorry. I was picturing you sniffing the red carnation in your buttonhole and twirling your brolly.'

'Glad to be the source of amusement.' But he couldn't help it. His eyes warmed and the corner of one mouth quivered in response.

'But what do you *do*?' she asked.

He sighed. 'Stockbroking.'

Crikey, she thought. Did he even know how? Didn't he need a licence or something?

He cleared his throat. 'They like it that I'm . . . they like to use my name. Basically, they pay me to go to lunches and parties and chat up their clients.'

This seemed unlikely to Liz in these days of tightening belts and cutting costs. In fact, now she thought about it, she remembered Gemma mentioning Theo had an economics degree from Cambridge – a discipline his father had insisted he pursue. As usual, his lordship was being self-deprecating.

Still, stockbroking was about as far removed from landscape design as she could imagine. 'God,' she said. 'You must hate it.'

'I don't hate the money.'

'But . . .' It pained her to picture it. Theo loved the outdoors and loathed schmoozing with every fibre of his being. He must be worse than miserable. 'Is this a permanent thing, then?'

He twisted to pick up his pen, not meeting her eye. 'It pays the bills until we can get more income from the events business.'

According to Gemma, Theo hadn't even interviewed for a new events co-ordinator.

'What about the gardens?' asked Liz. 'Who's looking after them now that spring is here?'

There was a long pause. 'I don't want to let them go but I simply don't have enough time to devote to them these days, and we can't yet afford to pay a full-time gardener. We have to make do with the groundsmen and volunteers. I come down on weekends whenever I can, but it's not enough.'

She stared at him. How could he discuss the neglect of his beautiful creations so calmly? He'd put his heart and soul into those gardens. They weren't just a miracle of nature, they were works of art.

'Liz, look, I appreciate your concern, but . . .' He glanced away from her, his throat shifting as he swallowed. 'You've come all this way on a wild goose chase. I wish you'd let me know so I could've saved you the trip.'

A dismissal if ever she heard one. It hurt, though she knew she deserved it. Theo was in the right. He was protecting himself.

Whatever nascent hopes she might have had for their passionate reunion died. Well, at least she could try to make it up to him a little by shepherding this deal to its conclusion.

She made herself focus on the job at hand. 'I'm here to propose a compromise.'

'I'm not selling,' Nick said again. He came closer to her, as if to emphasise the point. 'Do you think I'd take on that bloody joke of a job if I wasn't prepared to do anything to keep this place?'

'Listen, Theo —'

He gripped her by the arms in a firm, determined hold, his gaze burning with intensity. 'No, *you* listen, Liz. You were the one who made me realise the house was more than a millstone around my neck. You made me see that it was worth saving, not just for future generations but for me and my family, here and now. And I'm going to do that if it means wearing pinstripes for the next twenty years.'

'I don't think you should sell it to Nick.' Her voice trembled a little. Even if it was an impersonal gesture, the feel of his hands on her made her pulse race, made her long for things she couldn't have. 'I think you should take him on as a silent partner.'

'*What?*' He let go, stepping back.

She rubbed her arms. 'He has a solid connection to this house. He might even be its true heir. You owe it to him to at least listen to a proposal that will benefit you as much as it will him.'

'Nick McCann has no claim on this house.'

'You don't know that for sure,' Liz said. 'There was an affidavit from a nursemaid that stated positively Stephen Nash died. You have to at least admit it's possible she told the truth.'

'You don't know the full story,' said Theo. 'I need to talk to you about that.'

'What do you mean?' she said.

'In a minute.' Theo glanced out the window, then fixed his attention on her. 'Look, we're straying from the point here. The state of play now, in the twenty-first century, is that we own this house and we're determined to make a success of it without interference from any bottom-line, balance-sheet-bashing business type.'

Liz couldn't help smiling a little at this description of Nick. 'If you would just listen to me, Theo, you'd know that's not what this is about now.' She spread her hands. 'All Nick wants is to have a place in the country, an ancestral home he can call his own. So let him. Let him play host at the house during Cowes Week, when all his sailing-freak friends will come to stay. Believe me, he'll pay through the nose for the privilege. Even better, you'll get the time off from the house to race your own boat.'

Theo's surprise was evident. Then he frowned. 'What about the rest of the year?'

'Nick's business concerns are on the other side of the world. He's far too busy to bother you. So this is my proposal. Nick invests in the infrastructure and the events business. In return, he gets to take over the house for a set period every year. Yes, he'll want some sort of return on investment but it won't be a crippling amount. He's not in this for the money. All Nick wants is to belong.'

This was the realisation that had hit her with stunning force when she'd dug deeper into the reasons for Nick's obsessive desire to own Seagrove. He didn't truly want the house. He wanted a family, a history. He wanted to be part of something greater than himself.

Nick had never known a stable family life beyond the brief time he'd spent living with his stepfather. He might be all charm on the surface, but a deep-seated insecurity sent him constantly drifting from one woman to another in search of a safe haven. Simply buying Seagrove wouldn't give him the acceptance and security he desired, but involving himself in the Nashes' fight to restore the house and gardens just might.

Theo was silent for so long that Liz nearly tied herself in knots trying to guess what he was thinking.

At last, he said, 'A silent partner. With an emphasis on "silent"?'

'Well,' she said slowly, 'I'd be lying if I said Nick won't have opinions, but we can frame the agreement so that you have the final say.'

She watched him consider it, a faint frown between his eyebrows. 'Would you at least look at a proposal?'

He nodded. 'Yes, that's a good idea. I want to make sure there's no catch.' He glanced at her. 'It seems too good to be true.'

Trust me, she wanted to say. She needed to convince him that this time he could.

'Well, I admit Nick is not entirely sold on the idea, either,' said Liz. 'But he'll be taken aback when he hears you've joined the bowler-hat brigade.'

'He's been waiting for us to fail, hasn't he?' said Theo. 'Like a vulture ready to swoop.'

Liz shrugged. 'He's a businessman, but at heart he's not a bad guy.'

It was hard for her to say it, but she'd do it for Theo's sake. 'Look, I know you have very little reason to trust me. I wish I could go back and wipe out all the lies I told. But I can't, and . . .' Her voice wavered a bit but she made herself hold it together. 'I wish you could believe me when I say that I want what's best for you and for Seagrove. I happen to think this will be the best thing for Nick, as well.'

She hesitated, knowing Nick wouldn't like her to say more. Nevertheless, she owed it to both men to try to forge a link that went beyond business. 'You have to understand Nick's background,' she said. 'His father was out of the picture before he was born. His mother is a superficial socialite who divorced the stepfather Nick cared about and cut him out of Nick's life. He has no other family.'

Theo frowned. 'I don't see what —'

'He chases women and hooks up with one vapid trophy girlfriend after another. He thought his most recent wife was different but she turned out to be like all the rest. He's . . . I think he's lonely. I think what he wants more than anything is a connection to family. I *know* that if you invited him to stay with you at Seagrove, showed him what you've achieved here and your plans for the future, you could come to an agreement in no time.'

Theo cocked an eyebrow. 'You seem to know this guy well.'

'I went to university with him,' she said. 'We've been friends for longer than we've worked together.'

'Sure it's not more than that?' said Theo.

Was he jealous? She regarded him steadily. 'Yes. I'm sure.'

She cared about Nick. She hoped he'd see the light eventually and expect better, both of himself and for himself. One day, some strong, smart woman was going to set him back on his heels. But that woman was never going to be Liz.

'Hmm,' Theo said. 'If I ask McCann to stay here, would you stay, too?'

It was a moment before she answered him. 'No,' she said. There was a lump in her throat. 'Once we've nutted out the heads of agreement, I'll hand over to Nick's solicitors here and be on my way.'

Theo looked down at her with the hint of a smile playing about his mouth. 'I'd like you to stay.' He grimaced. 'I have a feeling I'm going to need a buffer between me and Nick McCann. Besides . . .' his voice dropped to a husky note, 'I'm going to want you close by in case I need to wring your neck for getting me into this.'

The sudden lightening of his demeanour left her confused. Staying here would be excruciating, a constant reminder of what she'd lost because of her dishonesty. The longer she stayed, the harder it would be to leave.

Before she could reply, Maddie burst in. 'Liz!' She ran to Liz and wrapped her skinny arms around her. 'Mrs Jackson said you were here but I didn't believe it! I'm so glad you've come back. Mrs Jackson said to tell you there's tea on the terrace. Come on, Dad!'

'Take Liz down. I'll be there in a minute,' said Theo. 'I need to get something.'

Maddie chattered away as she hauled Liz downstairs and out onto the terrace, where an ancient wrought-iron table setting had been placed overlooking the back lawn and the woods, with a glimpse here and there of the sea. The scene was just as she'd pictured it should be when she'd first arrived and suffered through afternoon tea with Valerie.

When Theo came out, he was carrying a wooden box, which Liz recognised as the tea caddy they'd found in the secret chamber at Saltwater Cottage.

'Did you get it open, after all?' Liz shifted plates of cakes and sandwiches to make room for the caddy.

Theo set it down in front of her. 'Gemma sent it to a specialist locksmith and he made a key. There was nothing inside. Not even the usual canisters you might find in a complete set like this. Maddie wanted it for her treasures, so Gemma gave it to her.'

'Lucky girl,' said Liz. 'It's a valuable heirloom.'

Maddie nodded, plopping a glob of damson jam onto a piping-hot scone. 'Yes, and it belonged to Delany, the lady who wrote the novels, you know, so it's extra special.'

'Really?' said Liz, but she'd guessed as much. 'How can you be sure it belonged to her?'

'Well, you know how the caddy is in the shape of a house? Mr Jackson remembered seeing a house like that somewhere before. He managed to track down a family portrait of Delany and her brother and sister and their parents with that house in the background. It's called Selby Park. So we thought Delany must have brought the tea caddy with her to Seagrove.'

'Tell Liz what you found,' prompted Theo.

Maddie licked jam off her finger and reached for the cream pot. 'Well, I was making a card for Mum with purple glitter on it and I knocked over the glitter and it all fell out over everything everywhere, even into the tea caddy.' She shot a guilty look toward her father. 'I'd left the caddy open on the floor.'

'Oh, dear,' said Liz.

Maddie grimaced. 'You know how glitter gets inside everything? Yeah, that. Well, I turned the box upside down and shook it to get the glitter out and you know what? The whole velvety inside bit fell out! And guess what?'

'What?' said Liz.

'There was *paper* inside it. Really old, like it was a letter dated in the 1800s.' Maddie bit into her scone with relish, leaving a dab of cream on her freckled nose.

'Wow! What a find,' said Liz, trying not to burst with anticipation. 'Come on. What did the letter say?'

'I don't know. I couldn't read the handwriting,' said Maddie. 'I haven't learned the sort of running writing they did in those days. Dad said it was just boring business stuff. But I want to know, if it was boring business stuff, why was it hidden in the bottom of the tea caddy?'

'A very good question,' said Liz, raising an eyebrow at Theo.

Losing interest in the mysterious correspondence, Maddie said, 'Oh! I should ring the cottage and tell Aunt Gemma you're here.' She shoved the second half of her scone in her mouth, giggling at Liz's exclamation of dismay and sending a small shower of crumbs everywhere.

'See you later.' She scrambled out of her chair and shot toward the open library door.

Laughing, Liz turned back to Theo. 'Your daughter seems happy as a clam.'

He smiled. 'She loves it here. I've been bringing her down every second weekend.'

Theo pulled the tea caddy towards him and plucked out the 'boring business letter', all mottled brown and brittle with age. He handed it to her.

Sensing that this was momentous, Liz met his gaze questioningly as she took the letter. That familiar jolt of awareness shot through her, and she wondered if she'd ever get used to being here with him without wanting more than he was prepared to give.

'Brace yourself,' he said, as she bent her attention to the letter. 'It's dynamite.'

Excerpt from the
Confession of Margaret Smith

In writing this confession I am confronted with an overabundance of sins – of dark acts terrible enough to feature in one of Delany's novels. Each one of them seemed necessary at the time, even inescapable. Perhaps that is why my conscience has seldom been troubled by them. Moreover, it seems to me that I have been punished severely on this earth for my misdeeds.

There is one matter that haunts me. A bright, sunny day at Seagrove in the summer of 1790.

Though I'd known Delany would accompany Julian to negotiate access to her sons, I was astonished to see her in such high spirits when she and Julian called at Seagrove that day.

'Margaret!' She took my hands in hers and beamed at me as if I were a long-lost friend. 'How do you do?'

I will not scruple to say that I was astonished. I had expected abuse and accusations. How could Delany forgive or forget what I'd done to her in that court room? How could she view with equanimity my taking her place by Richard's side?

While struggling for equilibrium, I rang for the tea tray – as if this were any normal morning call; as if I were the mistress of this house and not she.

'Is my brother at home?' said Julian, not one to waste time with idle chatter.

'He'll return soon.' I gave no further information, and invited Delany to refresh herself upstairs after her journey.

She was usually impatient with niceties, so I expected her to need persuading. However, she thanked me and followed the housekeeper out. Now was my chance.

Alone with Julian Nash, I watched him move restlessly about the room. 'I suppose you know why we're here?' he said, over his shoulder. 'You were ever in his confidence.'

'Yes.'

He took a paperweight from the escritoire and turned it in his hands. 'Do you know where he has hidden those boys?'

I hesitated. 'I know they are not here.'

'Where are they?' Julian set the paperweight down. His tone was pleasant, but I detected an undercurrent of menace.

I did not answer.

He started towards me, brow darkening. '*Where are they?*'

I held up my hand. 'If I told you, Mr Nash, your brother would make my life a misery. You'll forgive me if my fear of him is greater than my fear of being shouted at by you.' Unlike his brother, Julian was a gentleman, through and through, despite his unconventional ways.

He hesitated, no doubt seeing the truth of this. With a snort of disgust, he swung away and stared out the bay window, to sea. A fine figure of a man, I'd always thought. He'd spent far too many years mooning after Delany. What a waste.

'You must not leave him alone with her,' I said softly. I paused. 'He used to hurt her, you know.'

'*What?*' He turned to stare at me. 'How did he hurt her?' he demanded. 'In what manner?'

'I did not witness it, of course, but I recognised the signs. Bruises, scrapes. There is a certain look a woman gets in her eyes.'

'I'll kill him.' Julian strode towards the door.

That would not suit my purpose. I raised my voice to stop him. 'He is not here.'

'Why the hell isn't he? He knew we'd arrive today.' Julian turned back, and the expression in his eyes made my heart smack hard against my ribs.

I managed to modulate my voice. 'Do sit down, Mr Nash.'

He ignored my invitation but strode back into the room. 'You did nothing to prevent his ill-treatment of her? Noble of you.'

My smile was wry. 'When one is a mere woman, and a poor, dependent one at that, honour and nobility are luxuries one cannot afford.'

Julian shoved his hands through his hair, revealing the blue veins that pulsed at his temples. He breathed as if he'd run for miles, and when he raised his head, the fury in his dark eyes was so violent I became almost giddy with satisfaction.

His voice grew ragged. 'She should have told me.'

Delany had been wise not to do so, of course. She would have taken this secret to the grave to prevent his seeking vengeance on her behalf. I, however, had no such qualm.

Julian Nash went back to pacing, striking his palm with his fist, loudly berating himself and Delany. Why had he not seen? Why had she not come to him at once? How could she think he would stand by and let that happen? How could he have been so stupid, so blind?

He was like a caged bear in breeches, with so much anger and aggression toward his brother boiling inside him that I suspected if Richard had been here Julian might have carried out his earlier murderous threat.

I said, 'Be sensible, Mr Nash. If Richard were to die, who is the first person everyone would suspect?'

'What do you mean, "suspect"? It would be no secret. Word of a duel always gets out.'

Saints preserve us, the man was a noble idiot. 'A duel is not the answer. He won't fight you.' I shrugged. 'Why should he? There has been no breach of honour, no insult to you. A man is perfectly entitled to beat and rape his wife.'

He gave an inhuman cry of anguish. If I had not known it already, I should have been convinced that he truly loved Delany and felt her pain as his own.

For many minutes, he struggled to bring himself under control. His face was a mask of agony and fury as he came to loom over me. 'And all the while *you* were there, scheming and lying! You perjured your-self at that trial. To what purpose? Why should I believe a thing you say?'

I glared at him, fierce as a cornered animal. 'I'll thank you to step back, sir. Or is it a habit with men in your family to bully women?'

He didn't retreat but his aspect grew less threatening. 'If what you say is true, my brother is a dead man. But you give me no reason to believe you.'

'Ask him,' I said. 'I am sure he would delight in telling you the way he used her upon their last meeting. He certainly delighted in telling me.'

His chest was heaving now but he had himself in hand. 'Tell me where – where is he?'

It was time. 'Inspecting his vines,' I said. 'I believe you know the way.'

Julian would not carry out his stated intention to kill. He was inca-pable of such an act. But he would dole out severe punishment with his fists, of that I had no doubt. It would not bring back my William, but it would be retribution of a sort.

Having despatched my avenging angel, I sipped my tea and waited for Delany to return. And waited.

By the half-hour mark, I became concerned enough to go myself to the chamber I'd allocated her and scratch on the door. On hearing nothing, I opened it. The room was empty. She'd gone – to speak with Richard alone, if I did not miss my guess.

Curse the woman! She would ruin everything. I hastened toward the vineyard, keeping to seldom-used paths so as not to be seen.

Richard wasn't among the vines, where he'd told me he would spend the morning. There was no sign of Delany or of Julian, either. Damn and blast. I retraced my steps along the path Richard would have taken back to the house.

Finally, I found him at the pleasure pavilion, sitting alone. A din-ing table had been brought and laid for a light luncheon, all gleaming silver candlesticks and family plate.

'Where's Delany?' I said, breathless and sticky with perspiration from my prolonged search.

'Delany?' He started up. 'Is she here? Has Julian brought her?'

'Yes, but they left the cottage some time ago. Where can they have gone?'

If Delany had found Julian and was even now persuading him to calm down, I would box her ears.

Richard seemed unconcerned. 'If they return to the cottage to inquire, they'll find us. Scipio knows where I am.'

He poured himself more wine but did not offer me a glass. Nor did he invite me to sit when he resumed his chair. He pulled at his lower lip. 'I am thinking of removing to Seagrove again.'

'Indeed?' I was pleased to hear it. The cottage was a pleasant escape from the formality of life in a large country house, but it lacked prestige. If I were to become Richard's wife, I wished to preside over the family seat, not be tucked away in this place.

Oh, yes, even after all he'd done, I intended to wed Richard once he'd divorced Delany. Indeed, I'd sacrificed so much in pursuit of this end that it was inconceivable to me that I might not achieve it. Delany's indiscreet scribblings had made her marriage to Richard untenable. Moreover, surely now that Delany and Julian were reunited there'd be no shortage of evidence with which to prove their adultery, giving Richard ample grounds for divorce.

'Seagrove must be opened up,' Richard said. 'I am resolved upon it. I do not wish to share this place with Delany. It has ever been a retreat for me. I won't have her spoil it.'

'What do you mean, share it with Delany?' said I. 'There is no question of that.'

'Oh, didn't I tell you?' He gazed up at me with those limpid eyes. 'I am to take Delany back to wife. I made that a condition of my agreement with my brother. If she wants to have her son, she must return to me.'

'*What?*' His words struck a mortal blow to my vaunted composure. '*What* did you say?'

'Julian agreed to it that day he came to the vineyard, don't you recall?' Richard gave a crow of laughter. 'How it must have stuck in his gullet! But he said no one knew where she might be. He was searching for her, and when he found her, he would bring her here. So. He must have found her.'

'You will *not* agree to this,' I said, pacing, my hands twisting together. 'Not after all she's done. Why, she's made a mockery of you. She —'

'Thank you, madam,' said Richard with a snarl. 'I'm well aware of that. And I shall make her pay for it, *every second of the rest of her life.*'

At long last, the truth dawned. For all his promises and lures, Richard never had the least intention of marrying me. He'd used Delany to bear an heir and torment his brother. Now, he was using her to wrest Julian's fortune from him at long last. Torturing Delany for the rest of her days would merely be an added boon.

All this time, I'd played Richard for a fool. I'd thought I held him in the palm of my hand. Yet he never did anything that did not suit him. It did not suit him to divorce Delany now. It never would.

When I thought of every sin I had committed, every betrayal . . . when I thought of both the children I had borne him . . . Daisy, the daughter Lady Verena had taken from me years before, and William, my dear, sweet son . . .

The rage that came over me swamped my vision with red, became a thing so great that my poor, meagre body could not contain it. All those years of bowing and scraping, scheming, manipulating, all the while concealing my passion, my pain and my scorn, heaved up within me like lava in a volcano, until they exploded into action.

I snatched up a heavy silver candlestick from the banqueting table and hefted it high. Before Richard could cry out or act to save himself, I brought it down with all my might on his head.

For the rest of my life, I shall remember the quality of that silence. It seemed to throb in my ears like blood through a vein.

And his face. I will never forget the way he appeared, ludicrous in his startlement, staring out at me from those shocked blue eyes. Blood matted his golden hair, and trickled down his high forehead in a dark, sluggish ooze.

Cold as a January morning, I dropped the candlestick onto the carpet at his feet and returned by stealth to the cottage. It was fortunate that I always wore dark colours; my gown did not show the spatters of Richard's blood. I told Scipio to attend his master, knowing what he would find.

Then, I worked quickly, convincing the poor lad that he'd be taken up for murder, and that I was his only means of escape. I helped the young African hide in the vacant Saltwater Cottage for several days, then to leave by the secret way once his passage was arranged. He escaped through one of the smugglers' tunnels and thence to a boat that sailed for France.

Simplest if the page was blamed for that murder but never brought to trial. His life with Richard had been hellish, anyway, for he'd been bought as a slave, and treated like one, despite his fancy livery. I trusted he'd find sanctuary and freedom far from these shores.

Irony of ironies, Julian and Delany had been too busy arguing over what I had told Julian that day to seek out Richard. Drawn by the commotion when the servants raised hue and cry, they came upon the scene far too late.

It has never been my habit to be truthful when falsehood would better serve me. Yet what is the point of confession if one lies? Presumably, our Maker will discern the truth, whatever we say in print.

Truthfully, then, I feel no remorse for ridding the world of a man who was little more than a monster. Everyone but me benefited from his demise – Delany was granted her widow's jointure, free to write novels and earn her own income. Julian might pursue his own future untainted by his brother's malice. As brother- and sister-in-law, Delany and Julian were forbidden by law to marry. Though Julian did eventually wed and have children at Delany's insistence to secure his family line, I believe his heart was always with her.

In all the confusion in the wake of Richard's death, it was a simple thing for me to fetch first Stephen from Somerset where I'd placed him with the adoptive parents meant for poor William, then Henry from Lamerton Hall, where Richard had left him, and bring them home again.

Richard had dismissed the nursemaid at Lamerton and fooled the other servants there into thinking he had moved the baby elsewhere, when in fact he had buried William's remains just outside the Godshill churchyard. Thus, the nursemaid was the only one who knew that the child now called Stephen Nash was not the same baby who had been in her care.

She returned in later years to plague us, but her tale was fantastical, after all. Who in the family would believe Stephen had died, when here was the evidence of his existence before their eyes?

Knowing my future was uncertain and I'd better mend bridges where I might, I arranged to take the boys to meet Delany in secret at a Portsmouth inn before returning the children to Seagrove. The bittersweet joy of that brief reunion touched even my barren heart.

Henry and Stephen grew up at Seagrove under the aegis of Richard's uncle – a pompous, pious man who refused to let their scandalous mother near them. It might not have been a loving upbringing but it was not the horror it might have been had Richard lived.

Henry died in a hunting accident at the age of seventeen without having sired an heir. Stephen, meanwhile, has a wife and a parcel of children. He and Delany have established a relationship of sorts, though I know the distance between them pains her. She attempted to write it all out, to give him the story of his birth and her disgrace – or as much as she knows of the matter. But from some cause or other, she never gave him the account. Perhaps she judged the truth too painful. A boy must respect his father's memory, after all.

Ever fearful of discovery and concerned for my part in her tale, I purloined the two volumes that most concerned me and hid them in the secret chamber through which I helped Scipio escape. The theft went unremarked. I do not think, once they were written, that Delany ever touched them or thought of them again.

I repent bitterly that I exchanged my child for Delany's that accursed night. Yet I do not regret the immorality of the action, merely the result.

Having extracted the location of William's shallow grave from Richard before his death, I found my child and carried him back to Seagrove. I buried his tiny body at the foot of the ruin on the northern Down so that I might see the tower wherever I am and remember him. The silver rattle . . . I do not know why I placed it in his grave. Perhaps to give my child one thing that should have been his birthright.

As for my other sins, they are too numerous to state. I *am* sorry for them but it is too late to repine. Had they served me as well as they might, I expect I should not write this confession.

Delany might have bested her husband eventually, who knows? But I am satisfied that my actions brought about her release. I do not like her. I never liked her. But I can respect her struggle and understand her pain.

For all I have done, Lord, I beg forgiveness.

I was ever a woman who asked for more than she deserved.

CHAPTER TWENTY-TWO

Liz

'So the nursemaid told the truth!' said Liz, floored by Margaret's story. Her fingers trembled with excitement as she slipped the confession back into the caddy.

'Yes,' said Theo, 'but Margaret had already switched her own child and the real Stephen, so it was the impostor who died. The real Stephen was brought back to Seagrove and eventually inherited.'

'Wow,' said Liz. Not even Delany's novels were this unbelievable. 'I wonder if Delany knew all this.'

Theo shrugged. 'Margaret predeceased her. Who else would have put the confession in Delany's tea caddy? Didn't you say that's where Delany kept her most prized possessions?'

Liz tilted her head. 'It's possible. I suppose we'll never know.' She shivered, thinking about those tiny bones buried at the folly. 'Poor little baby. And no wonder Margaret snapped. A person can only take so much before they break.'

'It's interesting, though, that it wasn't the baby's death that sent her over the edge,' said Theo. 'It was only when she realised she'd done it all for nothing, that he wouldn't marry her, that she killed him.'

People were unpredictable, that was certain. Liz stared into the distance, and felt a chill as the wind picked up. 'Do you know what would be nice? If we have some sort of memorial service for little William, up on the North Down. Perhaps we could put up a plaque, and then . . .'

She trailed off, cringing, heat rising to her cheeks. She'd said 'we', as if she still lived and worked here. As if she and Theo had a future.

Suddenly, she couldn't bear the thought of not being here with him. Even worse, of spending the coming days seeing him and talking to him while she negotiated the deal, yet knowing Theo didn't want her to be part of all this.

That he didn't want her.

'Sorry, I can't . . .' She pushed her chair away from the table and took off toward the terrace steps.

'Liz?' Theo called after her, but she hurried down the steps then broke into a run. She sprinted across the lawn and into the trees, stumbling over gnarled roots and stones, kicking up mud, feeling the damp from the ground seep through her shoes.

She heard the pounding of Theo's feet, his voice calling her, and she sped on, into a clearing full of tall grass. A cloud of butterflies, small and delicate, rose all around her, lifting and whirling above the grass, winging toward the sun.

Soft as petals, the wings brushed her cheek, her lips, settled in her hair, made their own tiny breezes that whispered over her skin. They were everywhere, gossamer-light wings of orange, primrose, brown, blue.

The butterfly meadow! She remembered a long-forgotten wish to come here. The mystery of Delany, Nick's demands, the cottage renovation and the Open Day had all crowded in, pushing it from her mind.

Typically, she'd blundered into the midst of these fine, bright creatures, making them panic and take flight, and quite possibly crushing a few of them underfoot. She needed to take more care with fragile things.

In seconds, they were gone and she stood by herself in the meadow, alone with her regrets.

A rustle sounded behind her. 'Liz.'

She felt Theo's presence but she didn't turn around. She wanted to tell him to go away, but it was his meadow, after all.

'I scared them off,' she said.

'They'll come back.' His hands rested lightly on her shoulders and she tensed, too bruised and sad to respond. She couldn't think what he meant by touching her like that, and struggled not to read anything into the gesture. He'd made it abundantly clear he didn't trust her, and without trust, there could be no love.

As if he read her thoughts, he let his hands fall from her shoulders. 'I wish this thing with McCann was over.'

That hurt. But she nodded and sighed. 'Me, too.' Then she could go back to her mundane life and stop dreaming of something more.

'I was serious about asking you to stay, Liz,' he said, confusing her further.

She swallowed hard. 'What's the point? I can't stay here, knowing you haven't forgiven me.'

Theo was silent for a moment. Then he said, 'I've made a lot of mistakes lately, trusting the wrong people. With you . . . well, Jesus, Liz, when you said you'd been lying to me all along, it was like I'd been sawn in two. I couldn't put myself back together. And I couldn't reconcile the Liz I thought I knew with the one who'd been sneaking around behind my back.'

She turned to face him, her lip quivering. 'I'm sorry —'

He held up a hand to stop her. 'No, you don't need to say it again. What I'm trying to tell you is, the reason it hurt was because of how much I cared about you. But I've been thinking about what you did when you were here. You were a friend to Gemma and to Maddie and the Jacksons. You worked your tail off on that Open Day. We couldn't have done it without you. Maybe it's just my old gullible self talking, but I can't believe all of that was fake. In life, you have to look at what people *do*, not necessarily what they say. Your actions show you're a good person, Liz. The way you're trying to get me and Nick together, even after all that's happened, shows guts and creativity. You're amazing. Liz, I want you to stay.'

Liz parted her lips to speak but she couldn't. Tears filled her eyes. 'Damn it!' She punched Theo on the arm, none too gently.

'Hey, what's that for?'

'You deserve it,' she said, pummelling him again. 'For making me cry.'

He caught her wrists and pulled her to him, and then they were falling into the soft grass, sending bright clouds of butterflies spiralling into the sky.

Sunlight speared through the grasses, glinting in his hair as Theo wrestled her squirming body beneath him. He raised his head to grin down at her and she laughed up at him, tears spilling from the corners of her eyes.

Then laughter fell away and his gaze grew intent. Liz's smile faltered and all at once her lungs seized and her mind blanked. Only her heart seemed to be working overtime. The damned thing was beating so hard he must feel it.

'I love you, Theo,' she whispered and finally, she knew that it was true.

'*Liz*,' he said softly, framing her face in his hands. Then he kissed her – not softly at all – but with the desperate hunger of a starving man. She speared her fingers through his short, un-Theo-like hair and squeezed her eyes shut as everything inside her caught fire.

Delany

Saltwater Cottage, 1811

Stephen's first visit to Delany in twenty years was a polite disaster. He was so stiff and coolly repelling that she took refuge in the trivial and the inane, desperate to establish her respectability so that Stephen might ignore her reputation and call on her again. Why she wished for a repeat performance of this tedious, stilted scene she hardly knew.

Writing those memoirs had been a terrible idea. She'd laboured over them for months in anticipation of laying the truth at his feet. Five minutes in her grown son's company had told her that giving a frank account of her past to someone so unsympathetic would be a terrible blunder.

After he left, she sat alone in her drawing room for a long time, hollowed out with renewed grief. She'd carried the hope of him for so long. During that interview, it seemed she'd lost him all over again.

Yet she was nothing if not tenacious. She would come about. She would forge a bond with her son, now that he was his own master and no father or guardian could stop her from seeing him. Inhaling a shaky breath, she resolved to let a little time pass, then ask him to call again. Step by step, she would win her way into his heart.

There came a subtle knocking from the fireplace behind her in a familiar rhythm. One knock. A long pause. Two short.

She wiped her eyes with care, then hurried to locate a small piece of frieze above the mantel. The panel beside her swung open.

Ducking his head, Julian stepped out of the darkness into the buttery sunlight of late afternoon. He scrutinised her face, black eyes soft with compassion.

'Was it very bad?' he murmured, and folded her in his arms.

'You warned me how it would be, did you not?' She rested her cheek against his chest, grateful for his solid warmth.

'Give him time,' said Julian. 'He might be a bit of a stickler – that's my uncle's influence – but he has a good heart.'

'I didn't hand him the memoirs,' she said after a pause. 'He seemed such a stranger to me that I could not.'

'An expurgated version might be better,' he said, a hint of laughter in his tone. 'You don't wish to shock the boy.'

'Perhaps.' But if she took out all the shocking parts, what would there be left to tell?

She let Julian take her hand and lead her to the couch. 'He is troubled over his legitimacy. That nursemaid from Lamerton Hall has been stirring up trouble.'

He shrugged. 'Who gives a fig for all that now?'

'I can see that Stephen does,' she said, settling on the couch beside Julian with a sigh. 'But what we suspect is too fantastical. He would never believe it. I'm not sure that I do.'

'Best not rake up the past.' Julian stretched his booted legs before him and crossed them at the ankles. 'He might as well resign himself to his position. I won't fight him for the privilege.'

She nodded. 'Yes, you're right. We should let it lie.' What proof did they have, after all?

After more conversation, Julian got a look about him that Delany recognised. 'Tell me, dear Rothwell . . .' he trailed a fingertip down her cheek, her throat, straying dangerously toward her décolletage, 'do we dine alone this evening?'

His lips curved into that devilish grin. She smiled back at him. How fortunate that her servants were discreet.

At various times over the years, she had tried to let Julian go. The two of them could never marry, so it was stolen, secret moments like this, or nothing. Living together openly was out of the question, even if she'd wished to tie Julian to her in that way. For her sons' sake, she'd remained outwardly respectable for the past twenty years.

Now, she was content. More than that, she was happy. Marriage, even to the best of men, became servitude of a sort. The thought of allowing another man – even Julian – dominion over her brought her a sense of creeping suffocation. She'd always craved independence. Like Lady Verena, she'd found it in her widowhood.

Following the success of *Widow's Peak*, she had become prolific. She had an occupation she loved, a roof over her head and sufficient income to keep her and her household in comfort. And of course, there was her widow's jointure and Saltwater Cottage, of which she had the use for the rest of her life.

Society's doors were still closed to her, and would be until her dying day. Lavinia continued to shun her, but Delany and Aunt Boddington carried on a desultory correspondence.

Selby had married a besotted heiress and would have run through her fortune in a month had not her wise papa tied it up so tight that Selby must go cap in hand for every penny. Stupid boy. He never would pay attention to settlements. Fearing he would vent his frustrations upon his wife, Delany had written her an earnest, interfering letter, offering her sanctuary if ever she should need it. She did not reply.

After a pleasant interlude with Julian, Delany rang for her maid to draw her a bath. While Jane suffered Julian's teasing – he could always glean a smile from the dour maid – Delany climbed the steps to the attic, where Margaret worked. A small pug, grandson of Lady Verena's pet, lay curled on a pink satin cushion by her feet.

A breeze carrying the scent of the sea swept through the dormer window, fluttering the curtains, rustling papers. Delany stood in the doorway, watching Margaret's sparrow-brown head bent over her books. She was here ostensibly to keep house and act as Delany's companion, but at Delany's urging, she continued Richard's history of the island. The two women took long, silent walks together along the cliffs, but otherwise, they let each other be.

If anyone had told Delany when she first married that this would be their future, she would have laughed in his face. Why should she choose to live with Margaret Smith?

She hardly knew the answer to that herself. They would never be friends. Moreover, she had several dark suspicions about Margaret that she had never voiced and never would. Like crimes of war, they were sealed in a brutal past.

She must have made a sound, for Margaret turned and gave Delany her usual wide-eyed stare.

'Julian is downstairs,' Delany said.

Hearing the name of his favourite, Pug sprang to life. He scrambled off his cushion and scampered past Delany and out the door, yapping an excited greeting.

Margaret inclined her head. 'I shall order a tray up here.'

'If you like. You are welcome to join us for dinner, though.'

But she had already taken up her pen. 'There is much to do,' she said, dipping the nib in a rather handsome inkwell Delany recognised as belonging at Seagrove. 'I cannot stop at this juncture.'

'As you wish.' Quietly, Delany closed the door.

Liz

Two years later

'Too good to be true, isn't it?' Nick said. With a satisfied sigh, he leaned back in his chair, drinking in the long summer twilight.

He and Liz sat on the terrace at Seagrove, replete after a dinner of mussels steamed with diced fresh tomatoes, garlic, parsley and white wine, mopped up with crusty bread. Proof that Theo could indeed make more than puttanesca.

Tuesday was their designated day of rest. Gemma had decreed they must have one twenty-four hour period to themselves after the hectic activity of the weekend weddings and parties and the Monday clean-up, before they began again.

'True all the same,' Liz said. Lately, she'd become so mellow, she didn't even try to sneak a peek at her mobile on a Tuesday. Not like Nick, who remained glued to his phone and was even now keeping half an eye on his messages while he enjoyed the day.

Liz let it all go, knowing that come tomorrow, they'd all throw every ounce of effort into their flourishing business. Spring and summer were the periods of most intense activity. Once the tourist trade tailed off and the cold set in, they had more time to themselves.

Liz and Nick watched as Maddie, Theo, Fergus and Gemma squabbled over a boisterous game of croquet on the lawn. You wouldn't think croquet could be boisterous, but the way the Nashes played, it was tantamount to a blood sport. Fergus's version seemed to involve tackling.

Liz now operated an events management business in partnership with Gemma, who had moved to Saltwater Cottage permanently with Fergus. The company's major client was Seagrove, of course, but they'd taken on enough outside work to build a solid reputation on the island. These days, the house occupied more and more of their time, so she and Gemma chose outside clients selectively and commanded high prices as a consequence.

While they focused on the events business, Theo had embarked on an ambitious project of his own. With Nick's financial backing and Fergus's expertise, he'd begun work restoring the park at Seagrove to its eighteenth-century heyday, adapting the original plans drawn up by Lancelot 'Capability' Brown.

'Looks like the honours go to Fergus and Maddie,' commented Nick.

Liz grinned. 'Judging by the victory dance, I'd say you're right.'

Still teasing and taunting one another, Gemma, Fergus and Maddie stomped up to the terrace and flopped down around the table.

'Rabble,' said Nick, but he was smiling as he turned off his phone and slipped it back into his pocket.

Theo stopped on the path below and called up to Liz. 'Come down. I want to show you something.'

She felt like Juliet, leaning over the balcony to kiss him, her hair swinging forward to curtain their faces. 'What?' she said, her forehead against his. At her insistence, he'd let his hair grow back to the way it was when she'd met him after he'd handed in his notice at the stock-broking firm.

He grinned. 'Come on. You'll see.'

It was quite a trek to the abandoned butterfly house. She remembered his mentioning it before but she'd never seen it properly. The structure was hidden away behind a screen of trees beyond a field to the east of the house.

When she saw it, Liz gasped. 'Oh, my God.'

Theo had turned the butterfly house into something extraordinary: a wisteria bower, dripping with blossom in alternating streamers of purple and white.

'This is amazing,' Liz said, staring at him in wonder. 'When did you get time to do this? Why didn't you tell me?'

He shrugged. People like Theo didn't need to talk about their plans; they simply got things done.

She walked around, gauging the space. 'This will be the most brilliant setting for weddings. Even a small reception . . .'

Liz turned in a slow circle. The beauty of it, the soft cloud of scent drifting down to her – not overpowering but faintly sweet – made tears gather in her eyes. How could such a gruff, practical man even think of creating this wonderland?

He came up behind her and put his hands on her waist, his chin on her shoulder. 'I was thinking . . .'

When he didn't continue, she twisted to look into his smiling green eyes. Then she turned in his arms to face him. 'Were you? What about?'

He traced a long strand of her hair, tucked it behind her ear. 'I was thinking . . . Maybe we should be the ones to get married here first. Christen the place.'

'Crikey,' said Liz, a little breathless. 'Was that a proposal?'

He laughed, eyes crinkling at the corners, and she thought, *God, how lucky am I?*

'If you like,' he said. He slanted a doubtful glance at the grubby floor. 'Do you want me to get down on one knee?'

'Well, it's just not the same if you have to ask,' Liz said, sliding her arms around his neck.

'Liz . . .'

'Yes,' she said, spearing her fingers into his thick, wild hair, pulling him down to her. 'The answer's yes.'

But he wasn't finished yet. 'Hold on.' He pulled away from her, digging in his pockets for something.

The box was an old one, pink with faded gold lettering on it. Not eighteenth century, perhaps, but old. Was this another treasure from the curiosity cabinet?

He opened it. 'I didn't buy this especially. I mean, it was my great-grandmother's. I hope you don't mind. I can get you something new, but I . . . Somehow this reminded me of you.'

If Theo was stumbling over his words, Liz herself was speechless. A rush of pure covetousness came over her when she saw that blaze of scintillating light.

She thought it must have been an Art Deco piece, because it was made along the geometric lines so popular in that era. A rectangular shape with a large rose-cut diamond in the centre with channels of smaller diamonds surrounding it, set in platinum, or maybe white gold.

'I love it,' she said. 'I cannot describe how much I love it. If you don't put it on my finger this minute, I'll explode.'

He no longer eyed her with bafflement when she said things like that, but accepted them as a matter of course. He took her hand and slid the ring onto her finger. In an awkward but endearing gesture, he raised her hand to his lips and kissed it.

Then he pulled her hard against him and took her mouth, and any thought of jewellery flew out of her head.

'I have a room,' said Theo, all husky in her ear.

'About thirty of them, by my count,' she murmured. 'Yes, let's adjourn. Besides, it's getting too dark to admire my bling.'

Liz was too excited not to share the news. They found the others up in the Gallery, admiring a new portrait that now took pride of place at the end of the long room. Or at least, an old portrait, newly restored to its proper milieu.

Delany, Lady Nash, magnificent in her red gown, smiled down upon them with that mixture of arrogance and tenacity that Liz had come to know and admire.

She glanced at Nick, who was busy popping champagne to celebrate Delany's arrival and filling glasses. Perhaps only she knew what it meant that he'd returned Delany's portrait to Seagrove. It was a testament to the measure of acceptance he'd found here in this house, with these people, that he'd shared this prized possession with them.

Gemma's eagle eye spotted Liz's new sparkle and suddenly she squealed her delight. Maddie whooped and clapped her hands and hugged Liz tightly.

'About bloody time, brother!' Gemma kissed Theo, then Liz. The men exchanged handshakes and shoulder slaps.

Nick, faintly smiling, leaned in and kissed Liz's cheek. 'Well, Jones. I trust you'll make me godfather to your children. After all, you'd never have done it without me.'

Mr and Mrs Jackson welcomed the news with joy and hearty embraces.

'To the future Lady Nash!' said Fergus, holding his glass aloft.

Liz nearly choked on her champagne.

AUTHOR'S NOTE

When an author creates a fictional estate on the Isle of Wight, she must either alter the geography or take over land that is already occupied. For Seagrove, I did a little of each, shamelessly appropriating the historic house Appuldurcombe on the Isle of Wight. I re-imagined Appuldurcombe, not as the hauntingly beautiful shell of a great house that was bombed during the Second World War, but as a going concern with some architectural modifications, and somewhat closer to the Undercliff than it is.

Similarly, Lord Nash's seaside property, Marine Cottage, was inspired by a retreat owned by Sir Richard Worsley of Appuldurcombe.

For Saltwater Cottage, I used the location of a delightful bed and breakfast called Lisle Combe, but Saltwater Cottage is far less beautiful than that lovely house.

The unusual microclimate of the Undercliff on the south coast of the Isle of Wight means it is possible to grow plants suited to subtropical regions there. I must apologise to Ventnor Botanic Gardens for stealing their marvellous multinational gardens for the Seagrove estate.

Sometimes an author's imagination reflects reality. When I catered for the Seagrove Open Day, I had no clue whether there was a tapas bar in Ventnor. However, in my fictional version of the Isle of Wight the author was Supreme Being, so the author would have a tapas bar in Ventnor.

If you have been to Ventnor, you will know how unlikely it is that there would be an authentic Spanish restaurant in this Victorian seaside town. But there it is, in brick and mortar, El Toro Contento. While visiting the Isle of Wight to finalise my research, I drank Spanish cider and ate razor clams, delighted that I had put this place in a book without knowing it was there. The waiter said that his boss had, indeed, cooked paella at the Botanic Gardens for a special event and showed me the evidence: a newspaper cutting that was pinned to the wall. Such moments of serendipity are a highlight of the writing process.

While the eighteenth-century events in this novel were inspired principally by my reading of Hallie Rubenhold's *The Lady in Red*, (retitled *The Scandalous Lady W*) and *The Criminal Conversation of Mrs Norton* by Diane Atkinson, in order to construct my court scenes I studied many reports and transcripts of actions for criminal conversation as well as legal texts and biographies of judges and barristers.

In this novel, I have used real barristers and a real judge of the period and attempted to strike a balance between what I know people expect from an English courtroom scene and the way it was actually done in the late eighteenth century. The language is modernised to some degree because this is fiction, but many expressions, principles and lines of argument are taken directly from speeches of the judge and advocates themselves in comparable cases.

One final note: the barrister Thomas Erskine was indeed a keen animal lover and did have a newfoundland dog called Phoss who presided over meetings in a wig and advocate's bands. Apparently, Erskine also consulted a couple of tame leeches about legal matters but, as they say, truth is stranger than fiction. Whether Phoss was alive at the time my book is set, I have not been able to discover, but I couldn't resist featuring him in *The Wife's Tale*.

ACKNOWLEDGEMENTS

When the kernel of this story first came to me over lunch with my editor, I had little idea of what a rewarding and challenging experience writing it would turn out to be. My heartfelt thanks go to Sarah Fairhall for her enthusiasm, dedication and editorial brilliance, and to everyone at Penguin Random House Australia for their hard work in bringing this novel to the bookshelves.

Thanks also to my agent, Helen Breitwieser, for her wise counsel. To Anna Campbell and Cheryl Leigh, your comments on early drafts were invaluable. To Denise Rossetti, thank you for all the brainstorming sessions and support along the way.

I am also grateful to several people and organisations who have assisted me with research for this novel, including Ian Diehm, Lorna McRobie, Dr Vicky Basford, Steffie Shields, the Isle of Wight Gardens Trust, Robert and Ruth Noyes, the Ventnor Heritage Museum and the Ventnor & District Local History Society. Of course, any mistakes are my own.

To Jamie, Allister and Adrian, Cheryl, Ian, Michael, Robin and George, thank you for your understanding, love and support.

AUTHOR BIOGRAPHY

Christine Wells worked as a corporate lawyer in a city firm before exchanging contracts and prospectuses for a different kind of fiction. In her novels, she draws on a lifelong love of British history and an abiding fascination for the way laws shape and reflect society. Christine is devoted to big dogs, good coffee, beachside holidays and the *Antiques Roadshow*, but above all to her husband and two sons, who live with her in Brisbane.

christine-wells.com